Motor City Witches 3

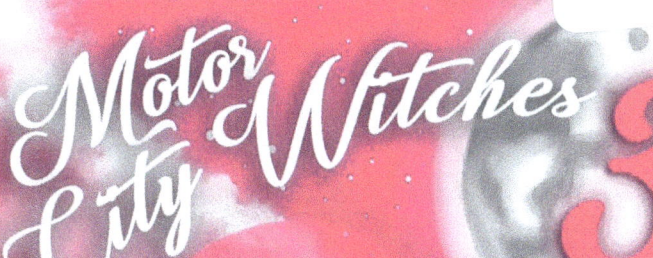

Goddess Rising

The Third Installment in the MCW Universe by

JADE AURORA

Motor City Witches
3

Goddess Rising

written and illustrated by

Jade Aurora

with art additions by some talented friends.

**Published by BlackGold Publishing, LLC in partnership with
The BlackGold Book League of Hampton Roads.**

1706 Todds Lane, Suite 258
Hampton, VA 23666

Edited by: Jamel
Designed by: John H.

Reviews For
Motor City Witches 2: Goddess Awakened

"My favorite part is the **growth of the characters**. Everyone seems to be on their own paths, but in a way that everyone is still connected and have that sisterhood family bond. The laughs and magic are great, but I love how the girls are always there for each other, and truly promote healthy friendship!"

"Are you a Black girl? Are you a witchy girl? Are you a queer girl? This is the book for you!"

""This is one of the best follow ups to a series I've read in ages! It's a great return of previous characters, as well as introducing new ones. What made the first story great is **DOUBLED** in the sequel!"

Acknowledgement

*A*s always, I want to thank **Tahara Saron**, and those at **BlackGold Publishing** for bringing this story to life. I am eternally grateful for the overwhelming support. Without your help, "Motor City Witches" would not have been possible.

I want to thank my **family and friends** for all the love and support you have shown me over the years. You continue to push me to be the best version of myself, and I am forever grateful.

A HUGE Thank you to **Khalil Toney-Brown, Andrea Conner, and Quanna McCree** for the STUNNING illustrations you have contributed to "Motor City Witches II". You have brought the characters to life in such a beautiful and magical way. Then again, we ARE Black Girl Magic.

I would like to thank my **readers and supporters**. Your overwhelming support and praise is what keeps me going, and I could not have made it this far without you.

I would also like to thank the following people for their donations to my Doctors Without Borders fundraiser: **Jessica Valentine and Ali H.**

Lastly, **I thank my Ancestors**. Without your strength, perseverance, and sacrifice, I would not exist. Thank you

Dedication

This book is dedicated to the **Beautiful, Ethereal, and DIVINE** Black mages who have to live in a world that wants to stifle their magic. A world that tells you that you are too loud, that you should be seen and not heard. NEVER feel you have to cut yourself down to make yourself more digestible to others, and never dim your light for others. Blind their asses and make them choke. Our very existence is an act of resistance.

A Divine Being does not concern themselves with the opinions of mortals.

Additionally, I dedicate this book in loving memory of two very important people in my life; To my beloved great grandmother, my Queen, **Rose Golson**. It is because of you, my grandmother, my mother, and my aunts that I am the woman I am today. While your departure has left a huge hole in my heart, you have shown me enough unwavering love, guidance, and support to last me over a thousand lifetimes. Rest in Power, my Silver Fox...

& to my uncle, **Marcus Golson, Sr.** I will always remember and miss your laughter, jokes, and hugs. You were the life of the party, and your presence will always be felt. You may be gone, but you will never be forgotten. Give my Grandma a kiss for me.

"Being a witch means living in this world consciously, powerfully, and unapologetically." — **Gabriela Herstik**

CONTENT WARNING

This book is for mature readers only, and contains the following:

Strong language, violence, sexual situations, mentions of depression and suicide, mention of child loss, bullying, homophobia, transphobia, racism, and nudity.

Reader discretion is advised.

Previously on Motor City Witches 2

*I*n Motor City Witches II: Goddess Awakened, we follow Detroit friends **Rachelle, Sarai, and Louise** as they continue their spiritual journey. They have come a long way, growing significantly stronger after a long road of trauma, self-doubt, and insecurity. Their transformation is thanks to embracing their ancestral power and recognizing themselves as the divine, magical beings they truly are.

Rachelle is in a happy, healthy relationship with her boyfriend, **Nick Ramirez**. Together, they work to expand her career as a model and content creator. Sarai enjoys newfound success as a published horror author with the release of her debut novel, Bloodlust. However, she is still haunted by past events and seeks closure. Louise continues to mentor her friends in their spiritual growth and soon takes another woman under her wing: **Trina Michaels**.

Trina, a young trans woman and aspiring fashion model, is forced to live on the streets after her bigoted mother kicks her out. One night, she is viciously attacked by a group of transphobic men and is saved from certain death by Louise, who happens upon the scene while at a gas station. Louise and her husband, Wilfred, offer their home to Trina and give her a job at Louise's store, RoxyJo Creations. Trina soon meets Rachelle, Sarai, Nick, and **Kiana**, Sarai's girlfriend. She instantly feels welcomed and finally has a true family.

Meanwhile**, Alexis Lawson**, Rachelle's cousin, meets **Vincent Davis**, a wealthy nightclub owner ten years her senior. Alexis is instantly smitten as Vincent, who calls himself "King Midas," wines and dines her, spoiling her with expensive gifts. He even moves her and her son, **Bryson**, into his home. Unfortunately, Alexis soon learns that everything that glitters isn't gold. She develops an addiction to cocaine and is coerced into sex work by Vincent, who is revealed to be a pimp. This is exacerbated by the fact that young women and girls are disappearing in Detroit, and human trafficking is suspected. One unfortunate victim, fifteen-year-old **Jasmine Sanders**, is found murdered, and the police have no leads. Louise and the others learn that Vincent is behind the disappearances. They also discover that he has an accomplice: **Cassandra Vasquez**, a former member of Children of Moonlight, a coven led by Louise's mother, **Kristy**. Cassandra misuses her spiritual gifts to lure unsuspecting girls to Vincent, who sells them to wealthy and high-profile clients.

After serving a year in prison for the shooting death of **Pastor Williams**, Sarai's father **Vernon** is released. He reconciles with Sarai, and they both agree to heal from their trauma together and move forward. Rachelle learns that she is carrying Nick's child. While initially shocked and apprehensive, she decides to move forward with the pregnancy. Nick is overjoyed at the prospect of building a family with the woman he loves.

Louise learns that Vincent is throwing a lavish New Year's Eve party at a secret location and decides to infiltrate it by posing as live entertainment. She enlists the help of Rachelle, Sarai, Nick, Kiana, Trina, and **Wilfred**. Louise distracts the crowd with a burlesque performance while Rachelle and Nick search for Alexis. They find Alexis tied to a bed, drugged and barely conscious. As they help her and the other victims escape, a fight with Cassandra ensues. Louise and her friends gain the upper hand, and Vincent, furious, shoots Louise. On the brink of death, Louise is visited by her late grandmother, **Diana**, on the astral plane. Diana is accompanied by their other ancestors, including a woman Louise has never seen before. The woman reveals herself as **Kamaria**, a princess of the lost Zira tribe and a High Ancestor of Louise's maternal line. The

Zira tribe was once a powerful East African tribe with supernatural powers. Unfortunately, they were attacked by a rival tribe and almost wiped out. The surviving members were rounded up and shipped to the Americas and Europe, victims of the Transatlantic Slave Trade. Kamaria was one such survivor, her powers passing through several generations, including Louise. Rachelle, Sarai, Nick, and Trina are also descendants of the tribe's survivors.

Louise channels Kamaria through herself and heals her injuries. She then strips Cassandra and her family of their powers. Cassandra and Vincent are arrested for their crimes. Vincent, facing life imprisonment, hangs himself while awaiting trial. Cassandra is sentenced to fifteen years in prison after pleading guilty to sex trafficking charges. Barely two months into her sentence, she is beaten to death by an inmate, a relative of one of her and Vincent's victims.

Trina achieves her dream of becoming a model by walking the runway at a Detroit fashion show. She is also recruited by a modeling agency that caters specifically to the transgender community. She decides to take the opportunity and moves to New York.

Rachelle and Nick move in together and prepare for the arrival of their twin daughters, whom they decide to name **Selena Atiena and Solana Osumare.** Alexis, who has since overcome her addiction, visits Rachelle. They set aside their differences and resolve to rebuild their strained relationship, with Alexis asking Rachelle to teach her magic...

Three Years Later

Chapter 1

I am Divine Femininity in the flesh. My gaze sets people's hearts ablaze. My beauty leaves people speechless, and I'm the baddest bitch to ever walk into a room. Wherever I go, I command respect and admiration,"

Rachelle chanted as she applied her makeup in front of her large, antique vanity mirror. It was Valentine's Day and Rachelle's twenty-eighth birthday. To celebrate, her aunt Veronica was throwing a lavish party inspired by Rachelle's favorite show, *Bridgerton*. Rachelle was obsessed with period dramas, so when her aunt suggested the idea for the party, she excitedly agreed and even handpicked the decorations. Little did she know, however, there was a huge surprise in store for her.

"Babe, you ready?" Nick asked as he entered their master bedroom, carrying their twin daughters, Selena and Solana. Nick looked dashing in a cream-colored Regency style suit with gold braided trim, which was custom made. He wore cream dress shoes, and his dark hair was combed back into an elegant style.

"Just a few more minutes," Rachelle replied as she admired herself in the mirror. For the party, Veronica had commissioned one of her designer friends to create a dress fit for royalty. Rachelle's gown was inspired by Queen Charlotte and was pale pink with silk roses and pearls along the neckline, accentuating her bust. The gown's bodice was embroidered with gold thread and tiny pearls. Her afro curls were brushed into an elegant updo, and atop her head sat a gold and pearl tiara. Her look was complete with pink heels embroidered with pearls, a pearl choker, and matching earrings. Her makeup was natural yet elegant, with gold eyeshadow and glossy lips. Rachelle looked truly regal.

"How do I look?"

"You look radiant," Nick replied, clearly in awe. He and Rachelle had been together for almost five years, yet she never failed to take his breath away. He smiled down at their daughters. "Doesn't Mommy look pretty?" The twins nodded excitedly, making Rachelle giggle. They looked adorable in matching pink dresses with pearl trim. Their dark curls were brushed into ponytails with pink bows. "Look at my pretty little princesses," Rachelle cooed, kissing her daughters' faces. Selena and Solana were truly beautiful children. They were the perfect blend of their parents, with Rachelle's bronze skin and curly hair, and Nick's piercing green eyes and nose. Although Rachelle had a difficult pregnancy and birth, resulting in an emergency C-section, she had zero regrets. Her girls were her life, and she couldn't imagine a life without them or Nick. There were even times she was glad that Lamar was such an asshole because if she had never left him, she would have never met Nick.

"I'll go start the car," Nick said, giving Rachelle a peck on the cheek and taking the girls downstairs. After checking herself in the mirror one last time, Rachelle followed them. After a forty-five-minute drive, they arrived at Veronica's beautiful West Bloomfield home, which was in a gated community. Since the party was invitation-only, security was waiting at the entrance, checking the guest list. Recognizing Rachelle and Nick, the guard ushered them into the house.

"Here is our guest of honor!" a voice exclaimed. Rachelle and Nick looked up to see Veronica descending the grand staircase. At fifty-two years old, Veronica looked no older than thirty. She was dressed in a gorgeous gold Armani ball gown, which made her brown skin all the more striking. Around her neck, she wore a pearl and topaz choker and matching earrings. Her long, black lace front wig was styled to perfection into an elegant chignon. Her look was complete with gold flowers in her hair, and her makeup was flawless. "You look spectacular, sweetheart. Then again, you always do."

"So do you, Auntie," Rachelle replied as she and Veronica hugged and kissed each other on the cheek. Just then, Sharon, Rachelle's mother and Veronica's sister, came down the stairs, looking absolutely regal. She was dressed in an ice-blue embroidered gown, accessorized with a pearl necklace and earrings, and her hair was styled in a high bun.

"There's my girls," Sharon said as she gave her daughter and granddaughters a loving hug. "It's good to see you too, Nick," she added, giving him a hug.

"You can go ahead and take the girls to the playroom upstairs. I'm sure Bryson will be happy to see them," Veronica said.

"Lexi is here already?" Rachelle asked.

"Yep," replied Veronica.
"Your friends are here, too. They're in the ballroom."

"You two go ahead. I'll take my grandbabies upstairs," Sharon said, taking the girls into her arms. Veronica then led Rachelle and Nick to the large ballroom, elegantly decorated in pink and gold. A live orchestra was playing a rendition of "Viva la Vida" as guests partook in refreshments, chatting amongst themselves. Rachelle spotted Sarai, Kiana, Louise, and Wilfred by the punch bowl with Alexis and walked over. Nick followed close behind.

"Look who finally showed up," Sarai said jokingly. Rachelle replied by playfully flipping her off before embracing her in a hug. "Happy Birthday, girl."

"I love your dress!" Kiana exclaimed. "Where did you get it?"

"Auntie Ronnie had it made for me," Rachelle replied, twirling around to show off her look. "I love yours, too, by the way." Kiana was wearing a plum-colored Regency gown with a black lace overlay. Around her neck, she wore a black lace choker, and in her ears, she wore silver earrings. Her hair was styled in a curly updo with aqua streaks throughout. Her ensemble was complemented by a pair of black lace heels. Sarai looked just as elegant in a black gown embellished with black pearls. Like her wife, she wore a black choker with onyx earrings. Her hot pink hair was pinned back, with her curls falling past her shoulders. On her feet, she wore black heels, and her makeup featured her signature purple smokey eyes, black eyeliner, and dark lipstick.

"Damn, your auntie went all out," Louise said, looking around the ballroom. She looked ethereal in a silver gown embellished with crystals and matching shoes. Around her neck, she wore a crescent moon choker, and in her ears, a pair of crescent moon earrings with clear quartz crystals. Her amethyst-colored hair was styled in an elegant, curled updo, with ringlets brushing her collarbone. Her look was complete with a silver halo crown, worn as an homage to her ancestress, Princess Kamaria. Wilfred wore a simple yet elegant dark blue suit, his locs tied back into a neat ponytail. His face was also clean-shaven.

"I know," Rachelle replied. "She definitely came through with this party."

"By the way, where's Artemis?"

"She's upstairs in the playroom, probably playing *Smash Bros.*," Louise replied. "She's just like her daddy. Always playing the game." Rachelle and the others giggled.

"I've never seen a live orchestra at a party before. At least not in person," Kiana said, watching the musicians. "Your aunt must have spent some serious bread."

"Only the best for my baby," Veronica said, walking towards them. "By the way, I have someone who's been dying to see you."

"Who?" Rachelle asked. Smiling, Veronica stepped aside to reveal none other than Trina, who was beaming from ear to ear.

"Oh my god!" Rachelle exclaimed, embracing her in a tight hug. "When did you get here? I thought you were unable to make it!"

"I lied," Trina replied. "Your aunt wanted to surprise you, so I flew in a few days ago, and she let me stay here."

"Really?"

"Of course. I wasn't going to let my daughter spend money on a hotel when I have plenty of room here," Veronica replied. For the past three years, Veronica had become a mentor to Trina, investing in her modeling career like she had done with Rachelle's, and introducing her to professionals in the industry, being the owner of a prestigious fashion magazine. Over time, Veronica had become a surrogate mother to her, giving her the love and support that Trina's birth mother, Esther, deprived her of.

"Well, it's great to see you either way," Rachelle replied, giving Trina another hug. Trina then went to greet the rest of her friends.

"Oh my god, you look so pretty!" Louise squealed as she admired Trina's look. Trina wore a peach satin gown with gold trim and matching heels. Her gown was accessorized with a simple pair of diamond studs and a diamond choker, gifted to her by Veronica. Her dark, curly hair was elegantly coiffed into a bun, with some of her curls hanging down. Her makeup, as always, was exquisite, with gold eyeshadow, winged eyeliner, and dark pink lips. "Looks like the gang's all here."

"Well, not the whole gang," Trina said, her eyes scanning the ballroom. "Where's Mike and Jay? And Chris and Khalil? I can't imagine them missing a party like this."

"Chris and Khalil are getting their pictures taken over there," Louise pointed to a room adjacent to the ballroom, where guests were waiting to have their photos taken in front of an elegant backdrop. "Mike is coming, too, minus Jay, since they're not together anymore."

"Damn, they broke up?" Trina asked, astonished. "What happened?"

"Girl, a lot. It's a hot ass mess," Rachelle said as they made their way to a nearby table, so they would be out of earshot.

"So, what's the tea?" Trina inquired as she sat in a chair.

"So, a few weeks ago, we all went to Gigi's, right?"

"Uh huh."

"So, while we were there, Jay suddenly needed to go to the bathroom. The thing is, though, he was gone for damn near forty-five minutes."

5

"Damn," Trina said.

"So Mike went to the bathroom to see if Jay was okay. Turns out he was more than okay."

"What do you mean?"

"Mike walked in on Jay getting slurped up by some rando," Kiana replied.

"Are you fucking serious?" Trina exclaimed, her eyes wide.

"Yep, except the guy wasn't random, at least not to Jay. Turns out he had been talking to ol' dude on the sneak tip for months, and Mike had no idea. Jay actually told the guy to meet him at Gigi's since we were already going there," Kiana said.

"That was pretty fucking bold of him," Trina stated. She couldn't believe that Jay would actually be so disrespectful as to ask his side piece to meet him at the same place his boyfriend was present. "So, what happened next?"

"Girl, Mike went *off*!" Louise said. "It got so bad that it actually came to physical blows, and we were asked to leave. Mike then told Jay to pack his shit and get out when they got home because they were over. So, Jay ended up having to go back to his mom's house."

"Damn," was all Trina could say. She certainly had missed out on a lot of Detroit tea, living in New York.

"That's not all, though," Sarai said.

"There's more?"

"So, here is where shit gets really wild. Jay texted me last week, asking if I could cast a love spell to get Mike to come back," Louise replied.

"Are you serious?"

"As a fucking heart attack," replied Louise as she took a sip of her cocktail. "Of course, I told his ass no. If Mike wants to be back with him, then he will come back on his own accord. I'm not about to manipulate him into taking back a cheater, and I told him exactly that."

"So, what did he say after you refused?" asked Trina. Louise reached into her silver clutch and pulled out her phone. She then pulled up her text messages and showed them to Trina. To say that Trina was shocked would be an understatement:

Jay: *Who are you to judge me? Yeah, I cheated, but who on this planet hasn't? He wasn't giving me what I needed, so I found someone that did. I got sick of seeing him lay around the house all the time, talking about he's "depressed." He stopped wanting to go out. He stopped wanting to have sex with me. He basically became a robot. What about me? What about my needs? I want to have fun, and I want to feel desired. That's why I went to Andrew. Can you really blame me?*

Louise: *See, this is why I'm not helping you. You refuse to take accountability for your shit! The reason why Mike was depressed was because HE LOST HIS FUCKING DAD! Please tell me you're not that insensitive. And if you were feeling so neglected, why didn't you communicate that to him? You claim to love him, right? So why couldn't you tell him how you were feeling, and get him help?*

Jay: *I DID tell him how I felt! But nothing changed! I was more than supportive. I was there when he needed a shoulder to cry on, or when he needed to vent. But I can only take so much. Was I supposed to put my life on hold while he works through his grief?*

Louise: *Then you should have broken things off with him instead of cheating! You can make all the excuses in the world, but at the end of the day, Jay, this is on YOU! What did you expect Mike to do when he caught you? Just say "Ok" and let it go? You fucked up, so you have to deal with the consequences. Like I said, Mike doesn't want to be with you anymore, and I'm not going to waste MY energy, my ancestors' energy, and my supplies to coerce him into taking you back. So you can fuck him over again? Just take the L.*

Jay: *You know what, Louise? I'm sick of your self-righteous ass! You have your head so far up your ass that you don't even want to see where I'm coming from! You act like you're so perfect, and that your shit doesn't stink. Fuck you and your ancestors! You make me sick! Sarai and Rachelle, too! But let's start with you, shall we? You wanna talk about consequences? Maybe your baby dying was a consequence for that curse you did on Rachelle's ex! And for what? Because his baby mama got slapped around a bit after putting a love spell on him? A mother lost her son because of you. Maybe now you know how she feels. Karma's a bitch, isn't it?*

Louise's blood began to boil reading Jay's messages all over again, especially at the jab he made about her child. One-year prior, Louise had gone into labor at only six months pregnant. The labor had been triggered when she and Wilfred were rear-ended while on their way home from a romantic dinner. As a result, she had delivered a premature son, whom they named Apollo Wilfred Eason. Tragically, however, baby Apollo died shortly after his birth, sending Louise into a deep depression. Her depression was so severe that she was even hospitalized due to a suicide attempt. However, with extensive therapy and the support of her friends and family, Louise was able to overcome her intense grief and get somewhat back to normal. However, no one truly gets over the loss of a child.

"I can't believe he would say that about your baby, especially knowing how hard it was on you," Trina said, disgusted at how heartless Jay was being, all because he couldn't get his way. "And did he really imply that Lamar didn't deserve what he got? He tried to kill a pregnant woman! And maybe if his mom hadn't enabled his shit, and bailed him out, you wouldn't have had to curse him. What the fuck is Jay even on?"

"It gets **worse**. Keep reading," Louise said, and Trina continued to read the conversation:

And don't even get me started on Sarai, with her Woe Is Me ass! Boo hoo, her family didn't accept her. Boo hoo, her stepmother abused her. Who gives a fuck? She's not the first one to be abused, and she won't be the last. My dad was abusive, but you don't see me bitching about it! Maybe her mother shouldn't have been a homewrecking whore. I can see why her stepmom didn't like her and her sister's asses. I'd be pissed, too, if I had to look my man's bastard kids in the face every damn day. She's better than me, because I would have never let them in my house if it were me. And she ain't put a gun to Sarai's sister's head and make her kill herself. She was just a weak-minded bitch! And don't get me started on her daddy! He definitely should have gotten more time for killing that pastor. Who the fuck kills a man over something they read in a fucking journal? What if that girl was lying? Sarai had NO right to do what she did. She practically committed murder. Yeah, she was abused, but taking a life is a greater sin than abuse. And let's not talk about that bullshit book she wrote! How the fuck is it a bestseller? It wasn't even that good! She must have cast a spell or something.

"Damn, it's like he was waiting for a reason to say all this!" Trina exclaimed.

"Exactly," said Sarai. "Like if you felt this way, why are you even friends with me? And yeah, I did cast a spell to get my book published, and for it to get noticed. And? I still had to work to get where I am. It's clear he's ignorant about how magic works. And as far as my mother is concerned, how was she a homewrecker when she didn't know my dad was engaged? Like, does he even know what the word 'homewrecker' means?"

"This is some hater ass shit," Trina stated.
"It's clear he's jealous of you."

"Wait till you see what he said about Rachelle. It's laughable," Louise said.

...And fuck Rachelle's fake woke, bougie ass! I still don't appreciate how she called herself trying to check me on Facebook because I said I didn't have a problem with white people wearing braids and dreads, talking about some "cultural appropriation." If I wanted a history lesson, I would have read a book. And what the fuck does she know about the struggles of Black people when she never had to struggle a day in her fucking life? Like bitch, you are a trust fund baby! And she only got that money because of her daddy! And she thinks she's hot shit because she's a so-called "model," and she got her little beauty line coming out. Bitch, you show your ass online, and thirsty niggas pay to look at you. You are a dime a dozen. And she doesn't even need the money, so she probably does it for

*attention. I honestly feel bad for those babies she got because they have a whore as a role model. But her cousin was a hoe too, so maybe it's a family thing. The only difference is that her cousin was a coke whore. I feel sorry for Artemis, too. I'd be so embarrassed if I had a mother who shook her ass on stage wearing pasties and a G string! You are nothing but a stripper! - And another thing. The only reason why you bitches have "success" is because you did magic to get it. You took shortcuts instead of working for it like the rest of us. **Fuck ya'll!***

"Wooowwww," said Trina as she finished reading the last text.

"Hmph. I wasn't a 'trust fund baby' when I gave him and Mike money when they were behind on rent," Rachelle said, amused by Jay's audacity.

"You gave them money?" Trina asked.

"Yep. $1200 to be exact," Rachelle replied. "They were in danger of being evicted, so I wanted to help them out. I know the pandemic had been hard on them when Jay got laid off. I didn't even ask for it back. I just wanted to be a good friend. It wasn't like I would miss it."

"Yet he had the nerve to disrespect you like that," Alexis chimed in, incensed that Jay would throw her drug addiction and past as an escort in her face. "He really needs his shit rocked."

"I'm not gonna lie, I wanted to hex his ass when he said that bullshit about my babies, but my Ancestors told me to let them handle it."

"Mine said the same thing," Sarai said.

"Jay is going to get his, and I hope I get to be there to witness it," Louise said, taking a sip from her glass. "The best part? I don't have to do a damn thing. I'd hate to have to waste my good herbs, oils, and candles on his dusty ass."

"Amen," Sarai added.

"Hey, Mike just texted me," Kiana said. "He said he had a family emergency, so he won't be able to make it."

"Oh wow," Rachelle said. "I hope everything is okay. No worries. We'll catch up some other time."

"Anyway...." Louise said, getting up to stretch. "I've had enough drama for one night. Let's party. I didn't get dressed up for nothing." The others agreed, and they all made their way to the dance floor. Since the orchestra was taking a break, a DJ was in charge of the music for the next set. Veronica had hired the DJ for those guests who wanted to hear something more high energy. David Guetta blasted from the speakers as the partygoers danced, moving their bodies to the beat. The couples danced close to each other, while Trina danced with a random guest. However, while Nick was immersed in the atmosphere of the party and having a good time, deep down, he was extremely nervous. For the past month, he often wondered how Rachelle would feel about the question he wanted to ask her. He played out every possible scenario in his head. What if she said no? How would he react if she said no? Would they break up and settle for a co-parenting relationship? How would their families feel? On the other hand, he couldn't imagine any reason for her saying no. Nick and Rachelle loved each other completely, and he couldn't imagine his life with anyone else. Sometimes, he even wondered if they knew each other in a past life because they were so in sync with each other and because of how quickly they had fallen for each other.

"Babe?" Rachelle asked softly, snapping Nick out of his thoughts. "Are you okay? You're really quiet."

"Yeah, I'm fine," Nick replied with a smile. "Just thinking."

"About?"

"About how lucky I am to have you and our girls." Nick gave her a soft kiss on the lips as they continued to dance, making Rachelle feel warm inside. No matter how often they did it, Rachelle could never get enough of Nick kissing her. Whether they were soft and sweet, or long and passionate, they never ceased to set her heart and body on fire. Nick never hesitated to show her how much he loved, valued, and desired her, something that her late ex-boyfriend never did. The time she spent with Nick made her realize that while she may have loved Lamar, Lamar only felt lust for her. Unlike Lamar, Nick never disrespected her or invalidated her feelings. He not only supported her in her dreams but actively worked with her to make them a reality. They were a perfect team together, and they brought out the best in each other. In fact, the only disagreements they had were over what to eat for dinner or what to watch on Netflix or Hulu. Not only did they strive to be the best partners they could be to each other, but they also strived to be the best parents they could be to their children. When Rachelle had gotten pregnant, she and Nick were unsure if they would be good parents. While they were financially stable, they were unsure if they were mentally ready since they were young and unprepared. However, with the support of their parents, they stepped into parenthood with ease. The sleepless nights, the blowout diapers, and the colds were all worth it. Selena and Solana were happy and healthy, and their parents couldn't be more proud.

"In about an hour, everyone, we will bring out the cake and sing 'Happy Birthday,' as well as make a toast!" Veronica announced into the microphone before going back to a table to converse with Sharon, as well as Ernest and Corrine, Alexis' parents. Joanna, Rachelle's maternal grandmother, was also present at the table. Rachelle decided to go with Louise and Alexis to check on their children upstairs. Wilfred, Nick, and Chris headed over to the punchbowl, while Khalil, Sarai, and Kiana sat at their table.

"So, I heard you're popping the question tonight," Chris said as he poured some punch into his glass.

"How did you hear about that?" Nick asked.

"Lou told Khalil that she and Sarai helped you pick out the ring."

"Yeah, I am," Nick replied.
"I'm going to do it after we make the birthday toast."

"Nice," Khalil replied.

"Mind if we see the ring?" Wilfred asked. Smiling, Nick reached into his pocket and pulled out a small red, velvet box. He then opened the box to reveal a gorgeous ring with a rose quartz heart with pearls on each side.

"Damn, that's a nice one. Is that rose quartz?"

"Yep. Rachelle always said she didn't want a diamond engagement ring," Nick replied, closing the box. "She really likes rose quartz and pearls, so I went to Etsy and found a shop that makes custom jewelry. It was also Black-owned, so that was a plus."

"I did the same thing when I was planning to propose to Lou," Wilfred stated. "She said either aquamarine, since that was her birthstone, moonstone, or amethyst. She felt diamonds were boring and she wanted something that resonated with her. So, I got her a moonstone and aquamarine ring. She actually plans to make the ring an heirloom, so she can pass it on to Mimi."

"Nice," Nick said, putting the box back in his pocket. The last thing he wanted was for Rachelle to see the ring before he proposed or overhear his plan. A few moments later, Rachelle returned to the ballroom, followed by Alexis and Louise.

"What are you men chatting about?" she asked, getting a glass of punch.

"Nothing," Nick and Wilfred responded in unison. Rachelle raised an eyebrow but simply shrugged and walked back to the table. Nick grabbed some more punch before following behind her.

"So, what were you talking about?" Louise asked her husband.

"Nothing. Nick was just showing us the ring he got for Rachelle," Wilfred replied.

"Ah," Louise simply said before taking a sip of her husband's drink.

"Hey!" Wilfred exclaimed. Louise simply stuck her tongue out at him before joining their friends at the table. Trina, however, was still on the dance floor, shaking her ass to "Thong Song."

"Hey, did you all see Trina's latest shoot?" Louise asked as she pulled out her phone. "The photographer actually shoots for *Vanity Fair*." She pulled up Trina's page and showed everyone the photos. Trina was in what appeared to be a mythical garden, wearing a flowing, mint-green gown. A flower crown adorned her loose curls. Her makeup looked professionally done, with shimmery highlights on her cheeks and nose.

"She looks sooo good in these," Rachelle remarked. "I'm so proud of her."

"I am, too," Louise replied. "I bet her egg donor is kicking herself right now."

"Especially since I refuse to fuck with her at all," Trina cut in as she took a seat, slightly out of breath from dancing. "Remember when she messaged me last year to ask for money? Talking about her unemployment had run out, and she was behind on bills. She also claimed she couldn't find another job due to the pandemic."

"Did you give her the money?" Alexis asked.

"Hell no," Trina replied. "At first, I considered it because I don't like to see people struggling. But then I saw on her page how she was taking trips to Vegas and Miami with her girlfriends. Like, I thought you didn't have a job. Either your friends were paying your way, or you were bullshitting. I honestly think it was the latter. Plus, I never forgot how she threw me out on the street, not knowing or caring if I was alive or dead. That gave me the backbone I needed to tell her no. Of course, she didn't like that very much."

"Of course," Louise stated. "I remember how she tried to guilt trip you into giving her the money. Then, when that didn't work, she got one of her friends to inbox you."

"Ugh, don't remind me," Trina said, shaking her head. She never cared for Esther's friends, especially when they supported her decision to throw Trina out. "I told her ass off, too. Like, if you're so concerned, then why don't you help her out? She had the nerve to tell me I should let go of my hurt and forgive Esther because I only get one mother."

"I can't stand that shit," Khalil said disdainfully, checking her makeup in her *Sailor Moon* compact mirror. "No one is entitled to your forgiveness, family or not. Plus, did she even apologize for how she treated you?"

"Nope," Trina said. "She basically gave me a non-apology, saying 'Well, I'm sorry if you felt I harmed you,' basically giving me the same tired 'tough love' excuse. She's so full of shit."

"So, she's not even acknowledging that she did you wrong, so why does she feel entitled to your grace?"

"That part," Louise interjected. "Like I have always said, don't ever feel guilty about setting boundaries for yourself. Do what you feel you need to do in order to protect your peace. If that means cutting a bitch off, then cut that bitch off. I will cut a bitch off in a heartbeat and not lose a wink of sleep. You don't owe that woman shit, Trina. Just because she pushed you out her coochie doesn't mean she's entitled to a damn thing from you. Don't let anyone tell you otherwise."

"Trust me, I know," Trina said with a smile. "My life has been so much better without that woman."

"Here's to cutting toxicity from our lives," Rachelle said, raising her glass. The rest of her friends followed suit.

"Cheers," they said in unison, touching their glasses together. After about thirty minutes, Sharon approached the table.

"Nick, Ronnie said she needs your help setting up Rachelle's surprise," she said, giving Nick a knowing look. "She wants you to go get the girls from the playroom." Nick simply nodded and got up from the table.

"I'll be right back, baby," he said, giving Rachelle a peck on the cheek before walking out of the ballroom.

"I'll go get Mimi. You know she's gonna want some cake," Wilfred said, getting up and leaving to follow Nick. Ten minutes later, a large, three-tiered cake was rolled into the ballroom. The cake was pink, with gold fondant roses throughout. The cake was topped with a miniature of a dark-skinned Venus, standing on a gold clam shell. Shortly after, servers began passing around flutes of champagne to each table. After some time, Nick and Wilfred returned with the twins and Artemis, who was dressed in a silver dress like her mother's, with a matching halo crown. Sharon followed close behind, holding Bryson by the hand. After handing Bryson over to his mother, Sharon went to join her sister in the middle of the ballroom. Standing next to them were Domingo and Marisol, Nick's parents, having only arrived fifteen minutes prior. Sitting at a table nearby were Nick's older sisters, Carmen and Daniela. Rachelle was led to an elegant throne chair in the middle of the dance floor, with a red carpet in front of it. Once she was seated, Veronica took the microphone.

"Good evening, everyone!" she began. "I would like to take a moment to thank you all for coming to celebrate my beautiful niece. My beautiful, brilliant niece, who has never ceased to amaze me with how incredible she is." Rachelle blushed, and Veronica continued. "First, we are going to sing 'Happy Birthday,' after which this gorgeous cake will be cut and served. Then, we will make a toast with the champagne that has been provided to you all." She then gave a signal to the orchestra, who began to play a classical rendition of "Happy Birthday" while the guests sang along. When they finished, Rachelle made a wish and blew out her candles, as everyone cheered. Then, the servers began to cut the cake and serve it to the guests. Once everyone was served, the guests were instructed to raise their champagne flutes while Sharon took the microphone from her sister.

"I'd like us to make a toast to my wonderful daughter." She then turned to Rachelle. "Baby, I know I always say this to you, but I want you to know how incredibly proud I am of you. You have blossomed into a beautiful, confident, and strong young woman, and you have carved out your place in the world on your own terms. And to see you step into motherhood with such grace, strength, and poise has been nothing short of a gift. And I know your father would be so proud of how far you have become." Sharon wiped away a tear. "I love you, my baby girl."

"I love you, too, Mommy," Rachelle said as she embraced her mother in a warm hug, as everyone applauded. As Rachelle sat back on the throne, Nick came down the red carpet.

The twins waddled ahead of him, holding a pink satin pillow. Atop the pillow sat the red ring box. Nick then took Rachelle's left hand and got down on one knee. Rachelle covered her mouth with her free hand, tears threatening to fall from her eyes.

"Rachelle……. the four years I have spent with you have been the best years of my life. You are so beautiful, inside and out. You have the biggest heart of anyone I've ever known, and you have given me the most precious gift anyone could ask for: our girls. I love you more than anything in the world, and there is something I want to ask you…." Nick took the box from the pillow and opened it, revealing the beautiful rose quartz and pearl ring. "Rachelle Dominique Lawson…. will you do me the honor of becoming my wife?" Some of the guests gasped, while others cheered, the loudest being their friends. Some of the guests were shouting for Rachelle to accept. Rachelle stared at the ring in shock. She thought she was dreaming. Was her birthday wish really manifesting? Was Nick, the love of her life, really standing in front of her, asking her to spend the rest of her life with him?

"You really mean it?" she asked in disbelief.

"Of course I mean it. What do you say?" Rachelle said nothing. She jumped into Nick's arms, giving him a passionate kiss. "YES! A thousand times, yes!" The ballroom erupted in cheers and applause as Nick took the ring out of the box and slipped it onto Rachelle's finger.

"Finally!" Carmen shouted from the table, earning a

laugh from some of the guests. "I love you," Nick said softly, looking into Rachelle's eyes, gently wiping away her tears. "I love you more," replied Rachelle before Nick captured her lips in a loving kiss. Rachelle was on cloud nine. She was now engaged to her soulmate and was excited for what the future held for them. "Rachelle Lawson-Ramirez. Has a nice ring to it, don't you think?" Nick asked. "I think so," Rachelle said playfully, kissing him again. Their friends then approached them.

"Congrats, man," Wilfred said, giving Nick a fist bump.

"Thanks. I appreciate it."

"So, I'm gonna be the Maid of Honor, right?" Sarai asked.

"Girl, what kind of question is that? Of course you are!" Rachelle said, giving Sarai a tight hug. Nick's parents and sisters embraced Rachelle and Nick in a group hug, congratulating them, and welcoming Rachelle into the family. Rachelle's family did the same with Nick.

"So, how do you like the ring?" Louise asked.

"Wait, did ya'll know he was going to propose?" Rachelle asked.

"Me and Sarai helped him pick out the ring for you," Louise replied.

"I love it!" Rachelle gushed, admiring the ring.
"Ya'll have some good taste."

"It suits you," Sharon said, giving Rachelle another hug. The party continued for another two hours before everyone went their separate ways. When the happy couple arrived home, they tucked their little ones into bed. Then, they made their way to the master bedroom to celebrate in a more intimate way. It wasn't until daybreak that they finally slept.

Chapter 2

*I*t was a cold, rainy morning when Rachelle and Nick arrived at Oakland Mall for the grand opening of Rachelle's new store, Melanin Siren. They came early to set up before the mall opened. Rachelle had conceived the idea for Melanin Siren a year earlier when she started making handmade hair and skincare products for herself and gifting them to friends and family. Her loved ones, impressed by the effectiveness of her products, encouraged her to start her own beauty line. With support from her mother and Aunt Veronica, who even offered to invest, Rachelle finally decided to launch the business, despite her initial apprehension about the saturated market.

"Are you nervous?" Nick asked as they headed to the escalators.

"Only a little," Rachelle replied, Nick could see right through her though, which prompted her to confess, "Okay, a lot."

"Don't be," Nick said, taking her hand. "You got this. Your grand opening will be a success, and we'll all be here rooting for you." Rachelle smiled lovingly at her fiancé, who gave her a gentle kiss. On the second floor, they were greeted by Louise, whose shop was next door to Rachelle's, along with Sarai, Kiana, and Artemis.

"Hey, neighbor!" Louise exclaimed, hugging Rachelle and Nick. "Ready for your debut into entrepreneurship?"

"Ready as I'll ever be," Rachelle replied.

"You'll be fine, trust me," Louise said. "Running a business is not easy, but the rewards are worth it." She glanced at Artemis, engrossed in her Nintendo Switch. "You'll be leaving behind a legacy your children can be proud of. Generational wealth."

"Your mom told me something similar when I went to get a reading from her," Rachelle said. Before making her final decision, she had sought guidance from Kristy, who reassured her that her business would be successful as long as she put in the work and trusted in her ancestors.

"And has she ever been wrong?" Sarai added.

"Nope. She's never wrong," Rachelle replied.

"So, where are my nieces?" Sarai asked.

"They're with my mom," Rachelle said.
"She'll be here with the girls later."

"Awesome! You know, Chelly, I'm really proud of you," Sarai said, putting her arm around Rachelle's shoulder.

"Thanks. That means a lot," Rachelle said, touched by Sarai's words. "And I am proud of all of you," Louise added, embracing her friends and cousin. "We've all come a long way in the last five years."

"Tell me about it," Sarai said, reflecting on the trauma she endured and the loss of her sister, Faith. While successful despite it, she knew emotional scars remained. Though she and her father, Vernon, repaired their relationship through therapy, she still resented his lack of backbone regarding their abusive stepmother, Thelma. Without Thelma, Sarai and Vernon were much better off. "Babe, where do you want me to put these?" Nick asked, carrying a large box of body butters. "The butters go on the bottom shelf with the bath bombs," Rachelle replied, helping with the display. Sarai and Kiana joined in while Louise went to her own store.

"By the way, Chell, I'm gonna need some more of that turmeric butter," Kiana said. "It has really helped with my eczema and hyperpigmentation. It's better than the stuff my dermatologist prescribed."

"Girl, you know I got you," Rachelle said, arranging the display. She then turned to Sarai. "I got some more hair butter for you, too."

"Awesome Sauce," Sarai replied.

After an hour, they finished setting up and waited by the entrance for customers. Soon, Kristy arrived with her son, Dannell, her daughter, Mariah, and Mariah's one-year-old daughter, Dy'Anna.

"What's up, fam?" Dannell said, hugging everyone and admiring the store's layout. "This looks amazing."

"Thanks," Rachelle replied, smiling. "Feel free to let me know if you have any questions."

"Yes, ma'am," Kristy said as she and Mariah browsed the shelves.

"You got anything for acne?" Dannell asked. Rachelle enthusiastically led him to the facial care display. More people entered the store, overwhelming Rachelle initially, but she took a moment to calm herself. I can do this, she thought, greeting the newcomers and answering their questions. Nick, filled with pride, watched Rachelle in her element. He admired her determination and fell even more in love with her, glad she was his future wife. "Nick, can you ring these people up, please?" Rachelle requested, snapping Nick out of his trance. He headed to the register, while Rachelle continued interacting with the customers. Her glamour ritual from the previous new moon made her aura magnetic, and people were easily drawn to her.

"Look at all these people, Chelly," Sarai exclaimed as more people entered the store. "You're definitely about to clean up!"

"I hope so," Rachelle replied.

"Trust me, you're going to make a killing today, especially since you enchanted your products. You're gonna have folks addicted," Sarai said.

Meanwhile, RoxyJo Creations was equally busy. Louise rang up customers while her employees, Niecy and Mya, tended to those browsing the displays. Behind the counter, Artemis happily played *Animal Crossing*.

"I see you're a busy bee over here, too," Kristy quipped as she approached the counter.

"It's always busy here when I have a sale," Louise replied, bagging a customer's purchase. She then hugged her mother and siblings, giving her niece a few kisses on the cheek, making her giggle. Artemis hugged her grandmother, uncle, and aunt before returning to her game.

"I can't believe she's almost seven," Louise said, proud of her "Moonbeam."

     "I know," Kristy said with a smile.
     "Has she decided on a theme for her birthday party yet?"

     "She said she wants a princess party."

     "Do we have to dress up?" Dannell asked.

"You don't have to, but it would be fun if you did. Of course, you know she and I will," Louise replied. Kristy chuckled. "You and your cosplay. Well, talk to you later, dear." She hugged Louise again before leaving the store with Dannell, Mariah, and Dy'Anna. A few minutes later, an older woman entered the store, approaching the counter.

     "Excuse me," she began. "I'm trying to find a gift for my granddaughter, and I was wondering if you had anything appropriate for a six-year-old."

"Sure, do you know what your granddaughter lik—" Louise's heart stopped when she met the woman's eyes. "M-Mrs. Everett?" She never expected to see her former high school teacher in her store. The last time she saw her was at her high school graduation.

     "I'm sorry, but do I know you?" asked the woman.

"Did you teach at Detroit Arts and Sciences Preparatory Academy?"

"Yes, I did. I retired from teaching three years ago."

"Well, you were my homeroom teacher. I graduated in 2010, a year before the school closed down," Louise said. The woman studied Louise's face.

"Louise Reynolds?"

"Well, it's Louise Eason now," Louise replied, flashing her wedding ring.

"Congratulations," Mrs. Everett said.
"When did you get married?"

"In 2014."

"Oh, so it was a few years ago. I didn't recognize you with the hair. Unusual choice of color," Mrs. Everett said, eyeing Louise's purple curls.

"Purple is my favorite color," Louise replied.

"A bit unprofessional, don't you think? Your manager approves of this?" Louise resisted the urge to roll her eyes. She remembered how judgmental Mrs. Everett was.

"I would hope so, since I am the manager... In fact, I'm the owner."

"This is your shop?" Mrs. Everett sounded surprised.

"You sound surprised," Louise said.

Mrs. Everett looked around the store. Her eyes searching every inch as if looking for something. "Well... I guess I shouldn't be. You were always the artistic one in my class. You and... what was that girl's name?"

"Artemis Hamilton," Louise said, her annoyance bubbling to the surface.

"Oh, that's right," Mrs. Everett said.
"Such a shame. So sad what happened to that girl."

"It wouldn't have happened if you had done your damn job," Louise spat, her blood boiling. She remembered how Mrs. Everett contributed to her best friend Missy's death...

They were like two peas in a pod. They were both gifted artists, honor students, and were avid anime fans and bookworms. Like Louise, Missy also came from a magical bloodline. They were kindred spirits, and often dreamed of owning their own clothing and accessory line, becoming business partners. To Louise, Missy was her sister for life. However, during their final year of high school, those dreams would tragically be shattered.

Missy began dating a fellow classmate, Demetrius Cooper, in the middle of their senior year. Demetrius was handsome, charismatic, and popular. He was also a bit of a bad boy, a complete contrast to Missy's bookish, shy nature. However, they seemed to click, and Missy soon found herself falling hard for him. She was so enamored with Demetrius, that after three months of dating, she had given herself to him. Unbeknownst to Missy, however, Demetrius did not reciprocate her feelings. To him, Missy was simply just another notch on his bedpost. Having gotten what he wanted, Demetrius' demeanor towards Missy did a complete 180. He became cold, brushing her off when Missy showed him affection, or wanted to sit with him at lunch. He was even brazen enough to flirt with other girls in her presence. Soon, it became apparent to Missy that Demetrius never loved her. He had used her, and it devastated her. However, the worst was yet to come.

A video of Missy and Demetrius' tryst had begun to circulate throughout the school and on social media. Demetrius had secretly recorded what Missy had considered an act of love, and sent it to all of his friends. Missy couldn't even walk to the restroom without slurs such as "slut" or "hoe" being hurled at her. Some of the teachers viewed her with either contempt or pity. Mrs. Everett was one such teacher. Whenever Missy was taunted in her class, Mrs. Everett would not lift a finger to reprimand her students. However, Missy wasn't surprised. Whenever she or Louise would complain about the bullying, Mrs. Everett dismissed it as simply "kids being kids", and that it "builds character". However, after the video was spread around the school, the bullying grew worse. When Missy complained, Mrs. Everett scolded her. She told her, "Maybe if you had more respect for yourself, instead of giving yourself to the first boy to show you attention, then you wouldn't be in this situation. You brought this on yourself." When Missy's parents had gone to the principal to complain about Mrs. Everett's remarks, Mrs. Everett had denied that the exchange ever took place. Because it was her word against Missy's, the school did nothing. Missy's parents had even gone to the police, but nothing could be done, especially since the age of consent was sixteen, and Missy was seventeen. Demetrius was eighteen. Also, there were no laws against revenge porn in Michigan passed until 2016.

Due to the intense bullying, Missy had become increasingly depressed and withdrawn, a shell of her former self. Her grades had begun to drop, and she would spend all her time in her room. Gone were the sleepovers and weekend mall outings. Sadly, two months before graduation, Missy had decided that life was no longer bearable. Her lifeless form was found by her mother, who had gone to her room to wake her up for school. Next to her was a suicide note, and an empty bottle of sleeping pills. In her memory, Louise had founded RoxyJo Creations. RoxyJo was a combination of both of their middle names, Roxann and Josephine. She had also named her daughter, Artemis, after her.

"Are you still holding a grudge about that?" Mrs. Everett asked incredulously. "That was over ten years ago! Don't you think it's time to let it go? It was just kids being immature." Louise wanted to punch her former teacher but resisted. She took a deep breath and turned to her daughter.

"Artemis, sweetie, can you go into the back room for a minute? Mommy needs to have a talk with this lady here." Artemis obeyed, sensing something was wrong. Louise also instructed Niecy and Mya to take a break. Once they were out of earshot, Louise confronted Mrs. Everett.

"Listen here, you old, wretched bitch. My best friend is dead because of you! That's not something you can just 'let go' of. You allowed your students to bully others with impunity. Talking about 'Bullying builds character,' or that 'Kids will be kids.' It's because of people like you that children as young as ten are killing themselves. You humiliated us and blamed us for being different. You were supposed to protect us!"

"Look, I'm sorry if you felt I did something to hurt you, but that wasn't my intention. I was just trying to motivate you," Mrs. Everett said, her face burning. "I mean, it looks like you made something of yourself." Louise's anger flared.

"I am where I am today because of my hard work, my Ancestors, my family, and friends. I am successful *in spite* of you, not because of you. Missy could have been successful too if she hadn't been pushed to take her own life. She loved Demetrius, and he played with her feelings and shared an intimate moment with the whole school. But you blamed her! You knew she was being bullied and did nothing. Missy is dead because of you! On top of that, you have the gall to talk about me holding a grudge? Get the fuck out of my shop and go straight to Hell!"

"Fine," Mrs. Everett said, scoffing. "I feel sorry for your daughter. It's a shame she has a mother that's so hateful."

"My daughter is very happy and well adjusted, thank you. I feel bad for your granddaughter if she has you as a role model." Mrs. Everett stormed out. Louise sighed in relief, feeling lighter. She knew her friends and husband would have a field day when she told them about this encounter.

"Mommy?" Artemis peeked out from the back room.
"Are you okay?"

"Mommy's okay, baby," Louise said.
"Hey, you hungry? Why don't we get some pizza downstairs?"

"Yeah!" Artemis replied excitedly, and they headed to the food court. There, they joined their friends.

"You guys will never believe what just happened," Louise said.

"What?" Kiana asked. Louise recounted her encounter with Mrs. Everett.

"Are you serious?" Sarai asked, astonished.

"Yup," Louise replied, dipping her breadstick in marinara sauce. "What really pissed me off was her non-apology and trying to take credit for my accomplishments."

"Some people are just so full of themselves," Sarai said.

"I just don't understand people like her," Nick added.
"Why be a teacher if you're not going to protect your students?"

"For real," Kiana said.
"It's good she's retired. People like her shouldn't be around kids."

"If she had just bought something and left, I would have been fine. But she just had to bring up Missy," Louise said.

"If you don't mind me asking, what happened to the guy who made the video?" Rachelle asked, taking a bite of her eggroll.

"He only got suspended, but couldn't be charged with anything. However, let's just say he and his homies died in a 'freak accident,'" Louise replied.

"Damn," Rachelle said, understanding the implication. "Can't say they didn't deserve it."

"I just wish Missy was still here. You would have loved her," Louise said.
"If she was anything like you, I know we definitely would have," Sarai said, putting a comforting arm around her cousin, with the others agreeing. The rest of the day went on without a hitch. Rachelle's grand opening was a success, boosting her confidence in her ability to run a business. She

knew it wouldn't be easy, but with her family, friends, and ancestors by her side, she was ready for the journey ahead.

Life can only go up from here...

Chapter 3

*L*ouise was awakened from her astral journey by the sounds of her phone alarm. "WAP" by Megan Thee Stallion and Cardi B played as she sat up in the king-sized bed she shared with her husband, stretching her arms. She knew Wilfred was already up and about, since he was always an early bird, while she was a night owl. Putting on her robe, she made her way down the hall to her daughter's room to help her get ready for school. Before she arrived at Artemis' room, however, she stopped at the door of what was meant to be Apollo's nursery. She simply stared at the door, lamenting on what could have been. She often wondered what kind of person her son would have grown to be if her family had not been robbed of him. She often wondered what kind of magical and spiritual gifts he would have developed. In her mind, she didn't lose her son; he was stolen from her because of another person's irresponsibility and disregard for others. While therapy had helped Louise cope with her grief, she harbored an intense hatred for the woman who rear-ended them that night. The woman who thought it was a good idea to get behind the wheel while intoxicated. While she was in prison for her crimes, Louise felt the woman deserved far worse. Sighing sadly, she continued walking. She arrived at Artemis' bedroom door and gave a gentle knock.

"Mimi?" she said.
"It's Mommy. Can I come in?"

After her daughter answered affirmatively, Louise opened the door and walked inside. Artemis was already dressed in her school uniform and sitting on the edge of her bed.

"There's my birthday girl."

"Good morning, Mommy," Artemis said, beaming as Louise gave her a kiss on the cheek. Louise went into the bathroom closet and grabbed a container of barrettes, along with a comb, brush, and a container of Rachelle's hair butter. She returned to the room and began styling her daughter's hair. "Have you said your affirmations this morning?" she asked. Artemis nodded, and Louise smiled. "Are you excited for your party later? I know I am. My baby is seven now. You know, seven is considered a lucky number."

"I know. Bibi told me," Artemis said as Louise twisted her hair, adorning it with colorful baubles. As she twisted her daughter's sandy brown curls, she prayed for protection over her and prayed for her daughter to be surrounded with happiness and positivity for the day. After twenty minutes, she was finished.

"You're good to go, Moonbeam," Louise said, admiring her handiwork. "Go on to the kitchen. Your daddy made you your favorite." Artemis excitedly jumped from the bed and ran downstairs, while Louise went to the bathroom to shower. After getting ready for the day, she checked herself out in the mirror. She had turned thirty the day before, but she didn't feel any different. She certainly didn't look that different. When she started planning her thirtieth birthday party, some people thought she was lying. There were some people who thought she was still in her mid-twenties, due to her youthful appearance, courtesy of her foremothers' genetics. Before her transition into the Ancestral Realm, her maternal great-grandmother, Priscilla, was known as the "Silver Fox" due to her stylish way of dress and the fact that even well into her nineties, she looked almost twenty years younger. While her twenties were fun, Louise knew that her thirties were when she would really reach her prime, according to her mother.

> *"Thirty looks good on you,"* she heard her cousin, Ivy, say. *"Lookin' just like your mama."*

"Thanks, cuz," Louise said as she smirked at her reflection. She then made her way downstairs to the dining room, where her husband and daughter were already seated and enjoying breakfast.

"Hey, babe," Wilfred said, giving Louise a peck on the lips, while Artemis playfully gagged. He then gave Louise a plate of French toast, scrambled eggs, and bacon, which Artemis was also eating. "So, Chris inboxed me last night. Guess who he and Khalil saw at GameStop?"

"Who?" Louise asked as she was carefully pouring syrup onto her French toast. "Mike and Jay," Wilfred replied. "Apparently, they were holding hands and flirting with each other. It was as if they never broke up." Louise rolled her eyes, irritated that Mike would take Jay back so easily after he had cheated, and especially after she had shown Mike the disgusting texts Jay had sent her.

"Hmph. That was goofy of Mike," Louise said, taking a bite of her food. "But he's grown. If he wants to be with someone who cheated on him for being depressed, then that's on him. He just better not bring Jay into this house, after what he said."

"To be honest, I don't even want Mike in the house, either," Wilfred added. "He saw the messages. He saw what Jay said not only about our son, but Sarai's abuse. What kind of person would date someone like that?"

"I agree with you. After I take Mimi to school, I'm gonna shoot Mike a text to tell him to not even bother coming to the party." Wilfred simply nodded and continued eating. After breakfast, Louise took Artemis to their spiritual room for their morning meditation, which was routine for them. After they finished, they both left offerings on the ancestral altar and left the house for Artemis' school.

"Make sure you let your teacher know to pass out the cupcakes I got you," Louise said as she drove.

"Okay," Artemis said from the backseat, looking out of the car window. "But Mommy, do I have to give cupcakes to everyone in my class?"

"What do you mean?" Louise inquired. "Do you have someone at school that you have a problem with?"

"Well, there's this girl in class who's always mean to me," replied Artemis. "Her name is Naomi Brown. She's mean to everybody, and if it's your birthday, she'll throw a tantrum because she's not the center of attention."

"Why didn't you tell me or Daddy about it?

"I don't know," Artemis said, shrugging.

"Well, did you tell your teacher?"

"She doesn't really do anything. She says kids will be kids and that I'm being too sensitive." Although Louise's face was calm, she was livid. Not only was her baby being bullied, like she had been, but her teacher was dismissing Artemis as if she was the problem. She was reminded of Mrs. Everett all over again. *Yeah, fuck that*, she thought. I'm definitely going to have a talk with the school about this. She parked in front of the school and turned to her child.

"Sweetie, listen to me," she began. "You're not too sensitive. That little girl has no business messing with you, and your teacher isn't doing her job. The next time that girl messes with you, and the teacher doesn't help you, then come tell me or your daddy, so we can talk to your school, okay?"

"But what if they don't listen?"

"Oh, they will, if I can help it," Louise replied, smiling at her daughter. "Now, may I have a hug before you go?" Artemis leaned forward and gave Louise a warm hug. "You don't have to be scared to talk to us. We're here to help you."

"I know. Love you," replied Artemis.

"Love you too, sweetie. Have a good day, and remember, you're a goddess." Artemis let her mother go and got out of the car, making her way to the school's entrance. Once she was safely inside the building, Louise pulled away and drove home. Normally, she would go to her shop after dropping off her daughter, but she had closed the shop for the day to prepare for their party. When she arrived home, she was greeted by

Wilfred in the living room, watching coding videos on YouTube. Wilfred turned to Louise and noticed the troubled look on her face.

"Is everything okay?" he asked, sincerely concerned.

Louise sighed as she set her purse on the table. "So, Mimi has a bully at school," she replied.

"Really? Who?"

"Some girl named Naomi Brown."

"Has her teacher done anything about it?"

"According to Mimi, no," replied Louise. "The teacher told her she was being 'too sensitive.'"

"Excuse me?" Wilfred said, getting up from the couch. Like Louise, he also had his own experiences with bullying. "So the teacher saw bullying happening in her class, and did nothing?"

"Yep," Louise said. "I told Mimi that if that girl messes with her again, and the teacher does nothing, to come to us, so we can go up to the school."

"Good, because that bitch is out of order."

"Well, hopefully, Mimi has a good day today," Louise said, taking off her shoes. "Imma go back to bed. Wake me up in about two hours, so we can go to the store." She then headed upstairs to their bedroom, but not before shooting Mike a text.

A FEW HOURS LATER

"Damn, nigga, will you quit calling me?" Louise barked as she declined yet another call from Mike. Ever since she disinvited him from her birthday party, he had been blowing up her phone.

"He's calling you again?" Sarai asked incredulously. She, Kiana, Rachelle, and Nick had come over to help set up before Artemis came home from school. Louise's mother, brother, and sister were also there.

"Yes!" Louise replied, exasperated. "I told him in the text message why he was no longer invited. There's nothing more to discuss! Go be with Jay's heartless ass, and leave me alone."

"I don't know what he expected. Like, why would you want to be friends with Jay after what he said? And for Mike to take him back, knowing what he said makes him just as bad."

"Thank you!" Louise exclaimed. "If Jay had only cheated, that would have been one thing. But the stuff he said about not only me, but my child, is unforgivable. All because he couldn't get his way. If Mike thinks Jay is still a person worth dating after that, he can go."

"Not only that, he took him back knowing Jay wanted to use magic to manipulate him back into the relationship?" Trina added as she arranged the treats on the table.

"He conveniently forgot that part. But if he likes it, I love it," said Sarai, who was helping Wilfred hang the streamers.

"Hey, Will, it's almost three. Can you go grab Mimi?" Louise asked as she began putting together the party favors.

"On it," Wilfred replied, grabbing his keys and heading out the door.

"Why are your friends always in some drama?" Mariah asked as she was feeding Dy'Anna a bottle. "Hell if I know," Louise replied with a shrug. "But they're not my friends anymore, so they can have that drama all to themselves." Suddenly, her phone went off again. "If you don't......" Louise grabbed her phone and declined Mike's call. She then promptly blocked his number, then went to block him on all of her social media platforms. Rachelle and the others did the same.

"So, Trina, any new shoots coming up?" Dannell asked, changing the subject.

"I have a shoot with *Allure* next month," replied Trina. "I'll also be walking in Versace's summer show."

"Alright now, look at you!" Kristy exclaimed, smiling.
"Achieving all your dreams. I'm proud of you."

"Well, I couldn't have done it without your help," Trina replied. "Not to mention, Mama Ronnie putting me on to her fashion connections really got my foot in the door."

"What's it like living in New York?" Mariah asked.

"Expensive," Trina replied. "But Mama Ronnie lets me live in her penthouse rent-free, so at least I don't have to worry about housing. Plus, the ballroom scene is amazing!"

"Do you belong to a house?" asked Dannell.

"As a matter of fact, I do," Trina said proudly.
"I'm actually the house mother."

Everyone looked at her, stunned. "Are you serious?" Louise asked, sitting up in her chair now, dripping in excitement. "What's your house name?"

"House of Nyx."

"Like the Greek goddess of night? Nice," replied Louise, awestruck.

"I only established the house about six months ago, but I already have eight children. We also already won four trophies."

"Yass!" exclaimed Kiana.

"The best part? They're all witches."

"Fuck yes!" Louise added. "A magical ballroom house? Sign me up!" She and Dannell both gave Trina a high five. Soon, everyone finished decorating. Since Artemis had chosen a princess theme for her party, the living and dining rooms were decorated in aqua blue, Artemis' favorite color, and gold. On the table were gold crown goblets filled with various sweets, and the table was covered in gold crown confetti. The walls were decorated with gold balloon garlands and aqua-colored streamers. At the head of the dining room table were two throne chairs for Artemis and Louise. Since their birthdays were a day apart, they decided to have a party to celebrate both. However, the real fun for Louise and her friends will begin when Artemis is in bed. "Do you think Mimi will like this?" Louise asked. "I think she will," Kristy replied, smiling. Suddenly, everyone heard the locks turn. A few moments later, Artemis bolted into the house, with Wilfred close behind. Artemis stood in the middle of the living room, staring at the decorations in awe. "Hey, baby. Happy Birthday," Louise said, opening her arms to her. Artemis excitedly ran to her mother's embrace. She then went to hug everyone else.

"Where's Pop Pop?" she asked, referring to her grandfather, Xavier.

"He had to work a funeral today, but he'll be here soon," Kristy said. Louise's father worked as an undertaker and owned his own funeral home. "Your Great Grandpa will be here, too."

"Why don't we go upstairs, so we can get ready for the party?" Louise said, smiling. Returning her mother's smile, Artemis followed her upstairs. The two of them put on matching aqua blue dresses, with Artemis' dress being more poofy and princess-like. Louise then untwisted her daughter's hair and brushed it into a poofy ponytail. She then placed a gold tiara on her head. "Ready for your first gift?"

"Oooh, what did you get me?" Artemis asked excitedly. Smiling, Louise went to her bedroom. She returned with a small white box. She opened the box to reveal a pair of aquamarine stud earrings. She then took the earrings out of the box and helped Artemis put them on. "Do you like them?" she asked. Artemis nodded happily and hugged her mother. "Thank you, Mommy," she said. "I love you." Louise hugged her tighter.

"I love you more, my moonbeam." After the two of them finished getting ready, they returned to the dining room, where everyone was waiting. William and Barbara, Artemis' divorced paternal grandparents, had just arrived, along with Wilfred's younger brother, Wes. Artemis' friends from school and dance class, had also arrived with their mothers.

"There's my princesses!" Leroy, Louise's grandfather, exclaimed as he got up from his seat. Artemis happily ran to hug her great-grandfather, with Louise following behind her. "Happy Birthday, you two."

"Thanks, Grandpa."

"It seems like it was only yesterday that I changed your poopy diapers. Now, you're thirty."

"Grandpa!" Louise exclaimed, her face heating up with embarrassment as her friends and siblings laughed.

"Where do we put the gifts?" Barbara asked.

"You can put them in the corner over there," Louise replied, pointing to a corner near their couch. Once all the guests had arrived, the party went off without a hitch. Artemis and her friends occupied themselves with the games and treats that were planned for them. Artemis was happy, which was all that mattered to Louise. The pandemic had been especially hard on her because she had been unable to visit her friends or have them come over. The loss of Apollo was also very difficult since Artemis was looking forward to being a big sister. Thankfully, with therapy, Artemis proved resilient.

"So, did anything happen at school with Mimi?" Louise asked her husband.

"Nope. She said that girl that bullied her wasn't at school today," replied Wilfred.

"Okay, good," Louise said, relieved that their daughter's day wasn't ruined.

"What's going on with Mimi?" Sarai asked.

"There's a girl bullying her at school, and the teacher is letting it happen."

"Excuse me, what?" Sarai replied.

"Don't worry, we're taking care of it," said Wilfred. "We're going to talk to the school and the girl's parents if it continues." Sarai nodded in understanding. She was thankful that her little cousin had such protective parents. When she was bullied in her adolescence, Vernon would only tell her to just ignore it. Thelma, on the other hand, would often imply that there was something wrong with Sarai that made her classmates pick on her. She would often tell her to lose weight or stop partaking in her hobbies since her peers considered them "weird." Of course, Vernon has since apologized for not doing more to help.

"If you need me to come to the school, let me know. I'll throw hands if needed," Mariah added, making her sister and mother laugh. Soon, it was time to sing "Happy Birthday." Kristy and Wilfred went into the kitchen and returned with a large marble cake with aqua blue frosting and gold fondant roses. In the center of the cake were the words, "Happy 7th Birthday Mimi!" written in gold. Kristy then went back into the kitchen and returned with a chocolate cake with white frosting and silver fondant moons and stars. "Happy 30th Birthday, Lulu!" was written in the center in silver. After they sang "Happy Birthday," Louise and Artemis made a wish and blew out their candles, eliciting applause from their guests. After cutting and serving the cakes, it was now time to open gifts. Louise and Wilfred had gotten their daughter a PS5, complete with new games. Kristy and Xavier had gotten her a dollhouse with dolls that once belonged to her great-grandmother, Diana, who was an avid doll collector. Rachelle and Nick had gotten Artemis new games for her Nintendo Switch, while Sarai and Kiana had gotten her an art set since Louise had mentioned Artemis developing an interest in art. From Mariah and Dannell, and her paternal grandparents and uncle, Artemis received new clothes and shoes. From Leroy, Artemis received a silver charm bracelet. Kristy also had a special gift for her eldest daughter. She led Louise into another room, so they were out of earshot. Reaching into her bag, she pulled out an old-fashioned wooden box. She then opened it to reveal a beautiful, silver antique necklace with a crescent moon pendant and glowing moonstone in the center.

"This necklace once belonged to your Grandma Henny," she began. "The stone belonged to her mother and was enchanted to only be worn by those in our bloodline.

Your great-great-great-grandfather, who was a silversmith, made the necklace himself and gave it to her as a wedding gift. Unfortunately, after your Grandma Henny was murdered, the necklace was stolen by the killer." Louise stared at the necklace in awe. She was captivated by the beautiful moonstone and the incredible design of the necklace.

"So, how did you find it, and get it back?" she asked.

"Apparently, the necklace was sent to a paranormal museum. The person who stole it gifted it to his wife, who tried to pass it on as an heirloom. However, every woman who wore that necklace died either horrible deaths or suffered terrible misfortunes. One was even murdered by her husband on her wedding night. So, believing it to be 'cursed,' the family donated it to the museum."

"Was the thief white?" asked Louise, although, deep down, she already knew the answer.

HENRIETTA "HENNY" MCRAE
1858–1926

"Of course he was," Kristy said. "Anyway, I saw the necklace being featured on YouTube about cursed objects. I immediately recognized it from a portrait of Grandma Henrietta wearing it, and of course, I used divination to confirm my suspicions. I got the museum's info and drove to California."

"Was that the time when you said you had some business to take care of out of town last year?"

"Yep. Trust me, it wasn't easy to get the necklace back. But, I was persuasive."

"You used the Commanding powder, didn't you?"

"Sure did," Kristy replied with a sly smile. "But, what's important is that this necklace is back where it belongs—our family." Louise gave her mother a tight hug.

"I love you, Mom." Kristy smiled and hugged her tighter.

"I love you too." After putting the necklace in Louise's room, Louise retrieved a small keepsake box from her nightstand, and the two returned to the living room, where Artemis and her friends were playing with her new dolls, while Wilfred was setting up the PS5.

"Hey, Mimi, I have another gift for you," Louise said, hiding the box behind her back. Artemis turned her attention to her mother, excitedly wondering what Louise had gotten her. Louise revealed the box and opened it. She then pulled out a gold necklace with Artemis' name, with an aquamarine point dangling from it. "This necklace used to belong to a very close friend of mine." Louise fastened the necklace around her daughter's neck.

"Her name was Artemis, too?" Artemis asked.

"Yep," Louise replied. "I named you after her."

"So where is she?" Louise took a deep breath to calm herself and to hold back the tears that were threatening to fall. She had wanted to wait until her daughter was older to give her the necklace but felt that now was the right time, especially since Artemis was starting to go through what her best friend had gone through. Louise hoped that the necklace would give Artemis comfort and that Missy would be there in spirit.

"She's with her Ancestors," she replied. "But she's always watching over you. Think of her as a guardian angel. Whenever you are feeling sad or scared, she'll always be with you." Seeing the sadness in her mother's eyes, Artemis gave her a warm hug, touching everyone in the room.

"I promise I'll take good care of it," said Artemis as she let go. She then went back to playing with her friends. When it started to get dark outside, it was time for the children to go home and for Artemis to go to bed. Once Artemis' friends, their parents, and her grandparents had left, it was time for Louise and her friends to really celebrate. With Artemis happily sound asleep, they went into their den, which Louise and Wilfred had turned into their designated "smoke room." Wilfred brought out the cannabis and blunts and began to roll up. They had also bought edibles for those that didn't want to inhale smoke.

"Hey, Lexi, are you okay with being in here?" Louise asked. She knew that while Alexis had been clean for over three years, a recovering addict was always at risk of a relapse.

"It's fine," Alexis replied with a smile. "I still smoke and take edibles occasionally. I just don't do hard drugs." Louise nodded and offered an edible, which Alexis accepted.

"Hey, Sarai, aren't you releasing your memoirs this year?" Khalil asked.

"Yep, on May 18," replied Sarai. May 18 was a significant date for Sarai, as it would be the fifteenth anniversary of her sister's suicide. Since she would be detailing the trauma and abuse that she and Faith had endured, she felt that May 18 was a fitting release date for her book. She also chose a fitting title: *Memoirs of a Phoenix*. Sarai truly had to rise from the ashes of her trauma to get to where she wanted to be.

"How does your dad feel about it?" Nick asked.

"Meh, he wasn't too happy at first, since at the time, he still held on to the mindset that you shouldn't air out your family's laundry for the world to see," replied Sarai. "But after my therapist explained to him how writing this book could help in the healing process, he's supportive. Plus, I think he still feels guilty about not protecting us as much as he should have."

"I really want to see Tasha's reaction when it drops," Rachelle said.

"Honestly, I don't really give a shit how she will feel about it," Sarai said with a shrug. "If she didn't want to be called out, she shouldn't have been a piece of shit."

"Preach!" Louise added as she took a puff from the blunt. Suddenly, the doorbell rang. "Babe, can you get that?" Wilfred got up and went to check the doorbell camera.

"Are you serious?" he murmured.

"Who is it?"

"Come take a look." Louise walked over to the camera, and to her annoyance, Mike and Jay were at the door. Her high was instantly blown.

"Why the hell are they even here?" she seethed as she and Wilfred went to the door. Rachelle and the others followed behind them. She opened the door and was greeted by Mike holding a gift bag. Jay was standing off to the side. "You do know you're trespassing, right?"

"Can't we talk about this like adults?" Mike replied. "You blocked me without even hearing me out. It's messed up that you want to end a friendship over who I'm dating." Louise rolled her eyes. *Not you playing victim!* she thought.

"Nigga, I told you why we're not friends anymore!" she spat. "But, since you lack reading comprehension, let me break it down for you: Your boyfriend here, who cheated on you for being depressed over your dad's death, came to me for a damn love spell to win you back." She cut her eyes at Jay. "Like, legit wanted to use magic to force you back to him. I told his ass no, and told him to take accountability for his actions because he was blaming you for him cheating. Instead of, you know, acknowledging that maybe the approach he was taking to the situation was not the best, he acted like a petulant child, and made disgusting remarks about not only me, but my deceased child, who had absolutely nothing to do with the situation. He then proceeded to talk crap about Sarai and her trauma, her sister's trauma, and Lexi's addiction and trauma. You saw those messages, yet you still felt he was someone worth being in a relationship with. You are just as bad, and that is why we are no longer friends."

"Look, I know what he said was messed up," Mike began. "But he said those things out of hurt because of the breakup. He didn't mean it."

"Mike, why are you speaking for him?" Sarai cut in, glaring at the couple. "Jay is a grown man. He can speak for himself."

"And spare me that 'He didn't mean it' crap," Louise added. "He meant every word of what he said about us. He was waiting to unleash that vitriol onto us. If he didn't mean it like you say, then why hasn't he apologized? I wouldn't have forgiven him, but at least he would have tried to make amends." Mike said nothing. Jay looked away. "What? Got nothing to say?"

"I definitely didn't appreciate the stuff you said about me," Rachelle cut in, her arms folded. "First, of all, I am very well aware that I have privilege. That still doesn't take away from my Blackness. I also use my privilege to help those without it. What have you done since you're talking so much crap? Also, me being a 'trust fund baby' wasn't a problem when I helped you with your rent since you were on the verge of being evicted!"

"Mmph!" Louise said, looking her former friends up and down. "Just pitiful. The dick must be real good if you're willing to give up your friends for it. Is your self-esteem that low, Michael dear? I almost feel sorry for you." Mike looked away, avoiding Louise's intense glare. "I'll tell you one thing, though: when, not if, he messes you over again, don't come crawling back."

"Trust me, he won't be crawling back because I'm not going to mess him over," Jay spat.

"Yeah, keep telling yourself that," Louise retorted. "Get the fuck off my property." Jay sucked his teeth.

"Babe, let's go," he said to Mike.
"We don't need these bitches."

"We don't need your jealous, weak-minded asses, either! Get off my porch." Before Jay or Mike could respond, the door was slammed in their faces. Wilfred peeked through the blinds to make sure the couple was gone. Upon hearing Mike's car pull off, the friends went back to the den. "Gimme that," Louise said, taking the blunt from her brother and taking a pull.

"The nerve," Rachelle said scornfully.

"Here, take this, too," Dannell said, giving Louise a glass of wine.

"I don't know why they even brought their asses over here," Kiana said. "You made it clear that they weren't welcome."

"Forget them," Nick added. "They showed their true colors. Misery loves company." The others murmured in agreement.

"Anyway, enough about them. I'm not about to let them mess up my birthday," Louise replied. "It's my Dirty Thirty, and I want to turn up."

"Yasss!" Dannell exclaimed as he turned on some music. The rest of the night was filled with dancing, gaming, and smoking. Louise was content. While she was disappointed that her friendship with Mike had ended, she knew it was for the best. Growing up, her mother and grandmother would always tell her that life was too short for negativity, and she took those words to heart. Life was too short to keep toxic people in her life. The people who truly mattered were right in that house with her, and that was all she needed.

Chapter 4

*I*t was a cool, breezy Tuesday morning when Louise pulled up to her daughter's school. Artemis was anxious. While she had enjoyed her birthday without incident, she dreaded encountering her bully again. She couldn't understand why Naomi singled her out when she hadn't done anything to her at all.

"Have a good day, sweetie," Louise said, smiling at Artemis through the rearview mirror. "And remember, if that girl gives you any more trouble, you come tell me or your daddy. Okay?" Artemis simply nodded. "Can I get a hug before you go?" Smiling, Artemis gave her mother a hug and a kiss before exiting the vehicle. Once she was safely inside, Louise drove off, making her way to Oakland Mall to open her shop. When she arrived, she noticed that Rachelle was already there.

"Hey girl!" Rachelle called out as she watched Louise step off the escalator.

"Hey," Louise replied with a smile.
"Where's Nick?"

"He's at his studio today," Rachelle replied. "The girls are with Carmen."

"Cool," Louise said, nodding. "So, have you two set a date yet?"

"Not yet. We're thinking sometime next year, though."

"Well, keep me posted," Louise replied, walking into her shop, where Niecy and Mya were waiting.

"Hey Lou!" Mya exclaimed from the back. "How was the baby's birthday?"

"It was fun," Louise replied, smiling.
"She was happy, so I'm happy."

"That's good," Niecy said as she was putting some earrings on display. Louise made her way behind the counter and waited for the business day to begin. It was still mid-morning, and it usually didn't get busy until late in the afternoon. However, that was fine with Louise since it gave her some time to relax. She counted her blessings that she had a business where she didn't have to answer to anyone but herself and could come and go as she pleased. She knew she and her family were blessed to have businesses that were still thriving in spite of a global pandemic, whereas other small businesses were forced to close. Her father, unfortunately, had never-ending business due to the countless funerals he oversaw due to Covid-related deaths.

"Hey, Lou, you okay?" Niecy asked.
"You're awfully quiet."

"I'm fine, just a little worried." replied Louise.

"About?"

"Mimi. She's having trouble with a bully at school."

"Oh boy," replied Niecy. She knew all too well that kids could be cruel. Her entire childhood, she had to endure endless taunts because of her weight. Although it was well over a decade ago, it still left emotional scars. Her heart went out to Artemis. "Kids can be such assholes."

"Yeah, but adults make them that way," Mya added. "It starts at home."

"True," said Niecy. "But I'm sure she'll be okay, and her teacher will step in before things get out of hand." *If that teacher knows what's good for her, she will,* Louise thought.

Meanwhile, at Melanin Siren, Rachelle was completing a transaction with a customer when a familiar face strolled in. She was slim-thick, with brown skin and light brown eyes. She sported a chic, shoulder-

47

length bob with blond highlights and wore ornate acrylic nails. Next to her was an adorable little girl who appeared to be no older than four years old. Rachelle recognized the young woman immediately. Her name was Keisha Howard, one of Lamar's "other" women. She was also the former girlfriend of Lamar's murderer, Andre 'Dre' Moore.

"Um, can I help you?" Rachelle asked. Keisha's eyes met hers, and Keisha simply stared at her, as if trying to remember how they knew each other.

"You look real familiar," she said.
"Weren't you Lamar's girl?"

"I was," Rachelle replied. "I definitely remember you, considering how you and your homegirls jumped me and my friend a few years back." Keisha sighed and looked down. She was disgusted with her past behavior. Rachelle had never done anything to her, yet she felt the need to round up her friends to jump the girlfriend of the man she cheated on her man with. When Keisha learned she was pregnant with a daughter, she vowed to be a better woman, someone her child could be proud of.

"I owe you an apology for that," she said, looking up at Rachelle. "Lamar came crying to me about how you broke his heart, and I felt so bad for him. I didn't realize until too late what a liar he was."

"Trust me, I know firsthand how manipulative he was," replied Rachelle.

"It still doesn't excuse what I did, though."

"The important thing is that you acknowledged you were wrong, and you apologized for it. And I forgave you a long time ago," Rachelle said, giving Keisha a small smile.

"Thanks," replied Keisha, looking around.
"Looks like you've been doing well for yourself."

"I can say the same about you." Rachelle smiled down at the little girl. "She's so cute."

"Thank you. Her name is Diamond. Unfortunately, her father is not in the picture. He was murdered before she was born." Rachelle studied the little girl's face. Her complexion was light brown, and she had silky, black curls. When Diamond looked up, Rachelle noticed she had striking hazel eyes. She was the spitting image of her deceased ex-boyfriend.

"I'm sorry to hear that."

"Don't be. He wasn't living his life right, and it caught up with him. He wouldn't have been a good role model for her anyway." Rachelle couldn't argue with her there. Lamar Rollins was self-centered, egotistical, and misogynistic, with no sense of responsibility. If he had lived, he would have continued to bring misery and heartache to those around him. The children he left behind were better off without him. "Anyway, I came here to see if you had anything for psoriasis."

"Absolutely," Rachelle said, beaming. "Right this way." She then led Keisha to the skincare display. After helping her choose the best-suited products, she led her to the register to ring her up.

"By the way," Keisha began, "I can't help but notice your gorgeous ring. When did you get engaged?"

"Valentine's Day," Rachelle said proudly. "It was also my birthday."

"Your birthday's on Valentine's Day for real?" Keisha asked, astonished. "Damn, you lucky as hell. Do you and your fiancé have any kids?"

"Yep. We have twin girls. They turn three in October."

"Whew. I don't know how you do it. I have my hands full with just one." The two women laughed, and Rachelle handed Keisha her bag.

"By the way, I've included a coupon for you to get 40% off your next purchase."

"Good looking out. I'll definitely be back. You take care."

"You too." Keisha smiled and led her daughter out of the store. It warmed Rachelle's heart that she was able to forgive Keisha. Life was too short to hold petty grudges, especially when the common denominator was long dead. Keisha appeared to have matured and evolved into a better person, putting her childish behavior behind her.

Mercury Retrograde must be in full force, she thought. *Never thought I'd run into her again. But maybe I was meant to run into her because she needed to apologize. Either way, it was nice that she did. Plus, she spent money at my store, so that's a bonus.* Rachelle quickly put her encounter with Keisha out of her mind and went about business as usual.

"Ew, where did you get those ugly shoes from? The Lost and Found?" Naomi Brown sneered as she pointed at her classmate's feet. Tony Ellis' eyes burned with tears as the other students laughed at his expense.

"His shirt smells like cat pee, too!" Farrah, another student, shouted. The class continued to laugh, expressing their disgust at the smell. Tony tried to ignore his classmates' cruel insults, but they had cut him deeply. Ever since his father died of Covid, his mother had been struggling to support him and his younger sister, Tessa. Their mother could not afford new clothes, so they had to make do with what they found in thrift stores and garage sales. It also didn't help that Snowball, their elderly cat, had urinated on his shirt the other day. Despite repeated washings, his mother just couldn't get the smell out.

> "Why don't you leave him alone, Naomi?" Artemis demanded.
> "He ain't did nothing to you!"

"And whatchu gonna do if I don't? Cast a spell on me?" Naomi taunted. Artemis' magical abilities were no secret. While she would never admit it, Naomi was secretly jealous of Artemis. She hated how the young witch could make objects float or move without touching them, or form light in her hands, while she couldn't. So, being the seven-year-old she was, she did the only thing she felt she could to make herself feel better: make those around her miserable. She was also able to get away with it because the teacher, Ms. Harlowe, was a friend of the family, having gone to school with Naomi's mother.

"You need to leave him alone, Naomi. He's not even bothering nobody!" Sasha Rogers, Artemis' friend, said. Naomi ignored her, focusing her attention on Artemis.

"You think you're special, don't you?"

"Excuse me?"

"You're not special," Naomi spat. "You're a freak! You and your mommy are both freaks! My momma and grandma said so! Auntie Nina, too!"

"Shut up!" Artemis cried, her face heating up in anger, and her aura glowing a dark red. Her necklace also began to glow.

"See, you're doing it again!" Naomi exclaimed, eyeing Artemis' necklace. She then reached for it, snatching it from around Artemis' neck.

"Give it back!" Artemis shouted, charging towards Naomi, who kept the necklace out of arm's reach. "My mom gave me that for my birthday! It's mine!" The necklace glowed brighter.

"Come get it, then!" Naomi taunted, holding the necklace higher above her.

"I said give it back!" Artemis yelled. Suddenly, Naomi was blown backward, her head hitting the chalkboard.

"Oooohhh!" shouted the rest of the class, who were both shocked and amazed at what had happened. However, they immediately quieted down when Ms. Harlowe entered the classroom after taking a bathroom break.

"What are you all doing out of your seats?" she demanded.

"Auntie Nina, Artemis pushed me!" Naomi cried immediately, rubbing the back of her head.

51

"Artemis, is that true?"

"She took my necklace!" Artemis countered.
"She was also messing with Tony!"

"No, I wasn't!" Naomi protested with tears in her eyes. "I just wanted to look at the necklace. But she got mad and pushed me!" Naomi handed the necklace to Ms. Harlowe. As the teacher examined it, it began to glow.

"Artemis, I thought I told you not to bring things like this to school," she scolded. "It distracts the other students."

"That's not fair!" Artemis protested. "Naomi gets to wear her jewelry, so why can't I wear mine?"

"Well, Naomi is wearing a cross, a religious symbol. Plus, her jewelry doesn't glow like yours. However, that is beside the point. You know better than to hit another student. Tell Naomi you're sorry."

"But I didn't do anythi—"

"Now, young lady!" Artemis took a deep breath. She was sick and tired of Naomi picking on her all the time, and then playing victim when called on it. She was also tired of Ms. Harlowe allowing Naomi to practically get away with murder, never holding her accountable for her actions. Why should she be the one in trouble when all she was doing was standing up for herself?

"No."

"I beg your pardon?"

"I'm not telling her I'm sorry because I'm not," Artemis said defiantly. "She is the one who's always messing with people!"

"It's true, Ms. Harlowe," Sasha added.
"Naomi was messing with Tony first."

"I don't believe I was talking to you, Sasha," Ms. Harlowe said. She then turned to Artemis. "Either you apologize to Naomi, or I'm sending you to Mr. Jacobs' office and calling your parents." Artemis said nothing and simply stared at Ms. Harlowe, unfazed by her threat. "Have it your way." Ms. Harlowe then grabbed Artemis by the arm and marched her to the principal's office, incensed by her blatant defiance. Artemis looked over her shoulder to see Naomi smirking at her.

Later…

"Mimi, what happened?" Louise inquired as she and Wilfred entered the office. When she had received a call from her daughter's school, she had first thought that Artemis had gotten sick and needed to come home. But when she was told that Artemis was being reprimanded, she was shocked. Artemis had never been in trouble at school before.

"Mr. and Mrs. Eason," a man's voice called out. They looked up to see Mr. Jacobs, their daughter's principal. Mr. Jacobs was middle-aged and bald, with dark skin. He was sporting a dark gray fitted suit and glasses. After exchanging pleasantries, Louise and Wilfred took a seat next to Artemis. "As you already know, Artemis was sent to the office for insubordination."

"Yes, I'm aware, but I want to hear my daughter's side of the story." Just then, Ms. Harlowe entered the office. She shot a glare at Artemis before going to stand next to Mr. Jacobs. Artemis looked at her parents, her anxiety through the roof.

"It's okay, sweetie," Wilfred told her. "You don't have to be scared." Artemis took a deep breath and began detailing the day's events, as well as all of the instances she endured bullying at the hands of Naomi. The more Louise listened to her daughter, the angrier she became. However, when Artemis told them about what happened with the necklace, Louise was downright furious. She gave Ms. Harlowe a piercing glare. If looks could kill, the teacher would have been cremated on the spot.

"So let me get this straight," she began in an even tone. "This girl has been harassing my child this entire school year, while you do nothing, and you punish her for standing up for herself?"

"Oh, she's just being dramatic as usual," Ms. Harlowe said dismissively. "Kids tease each other all the time."

"That doesn't make it okay!" Louise countered, turning to Mr. Jacobs. "What kind of school are you running?"

"Mrs. Eason, I can assure you, bullying is not tolerated at our school," Mr. Jacobs replied. "However, this is the first time I am hearing about this."

"Of course it is, because Ms. Harlowe here refuses to report it!" Louise said. "Is there a reason why this girl is terrorizing other students with impunity, under your watch?"

"Because Ms. Harlowe is her auntie," Artemis interjected.

"You shut your mou—"

"Oh, so you're showing favoritism?" Louise asked rhetorically. Now she was pissed.

"Ms. Harlowe, is that true?"

"O-Of course not!" Ms. Harlowe stammered, flustered. "She's lying! Yes, I am close friends with Naomi's mother, but I treat all my students the same."

"Then why were you trying to shut my daughter up when she mentioned it?" *Oh, this bitch is good!* Ms. Harlowe thought, annoyed that she had been caught.

"My personal relationship to Naomi Brown is irrelevant," she said in a haughty tone. "We are here because your daughter attacked her and refused to apologize when asked."

"Did you actually see Mimi attack this girl?" Wilfred asked.

"W-Well, no, but—"

"So you just took the girl's word for it?"

"Sasha tried to tell Ms. Harlowe that I didn't do it, but she wouldn't listen."

"Oh really?" Wilfred turned to glare at Ms. Harlowe. *That little bitch!*, the teacher thought angrily.

"Well, that child of yours is always causing a commotion!"

"I beg your pardon?" said Louise.

"Your daughter is a distraction, Mrs. Eason!" Ms. Harlowe pulled Artemis' necklace out of her pocket. "I have told her repeatedly not to wear things like this to my class, but she refuses to listen." Mr. Jacobs took the necklace and looked at it. Then, he handed it to Louise.

"I don't see the problem, Ms. Harlowe," he said.
"It looks like a simple name pendant."

"It glows!" Ms. Harlowe countered. "She always comes in wearing these crystal necklaces that glow, too!"

"She thinks crystals are evil," Artemis said.

"So, you're targeting my child for her spiritual beliefs," Louise said. "Because last time I checked, necklaces aren't against the dress code, as long as they're not obscene or offensive. I have seen students wearing cross necklaces and crucifixes with no problem, yet somehow it's not okay for my daughter to wear crystals, which she wears for spiritual reasons?"

"It's not just the jewelry. She can make objects move without touching them! She can even make light with her hands! It's not normal! It's an abomination! She belongs in a lab."

"Excuse me?" Louise stood up from her seat. Her blood was boiling. "Artemis is just like any other child at this school! She's just gifted. Yes, my child can move objects with her mind and levitate them. And you know what? So can I!" Louise waved her hand to levitate a book on the principal's desk. Mr. Jacobs stared at her in shock and awe. "We can talk to spirits, too. These gifts have been passed down through my family for generations, and I have instilled in my daughter that her gifts are to be embraced, not something to feel shame for! Her gifts are as much a part of her as the curls of her hair and the color of her eyes. She is far from an 'abomination,' Ms. Harlowe. As a teacher, you should be teaching your students that they shouldn't be afraid of or ridicule those that are different. However, it's apparent that you could use that lesson yourself."

"I agree," Mr. Jacobs stated, giving Ms. Harlowe a stern look. He was disgusted by her behavior and the things she was saying about a child, over something she couldn't help. It reminded him of the days when he was bullied as a child for his glasses. He couldn't help that he had bad eyesight. "Ms. Harlowe, I'm afraid I'm going to have to let you go." Ms. Harlowe scoffed.

"You can't be serious," she protested. "You're firing me because they can't control their freak of a child?" Louise smirked. She knew it would be a matter of time before Ms. Harlowe showed her true colors. Like her grandmother used to always tell her, you give someone enough rope, they'll hang themselves.

"Ms. Harlowe, at Langston Hughes Charter Academy, we prioritize the safety and well-being of our students. It is very apparent that you don't, so your services are no longer needed. You can pack your things."

"You can't fire me!" Ms. Harlowe protested. "I have given six years of my life to this school! Don't I have tenure?"

"Not at a charter school," Louise replied. "You can be terminated at will, for any reason. So, why don't you do what Mr. Jacobs says and skedaddle? Hopefully, this can teach you a lesson in empathy." Ms. Harlowe scowled, storming out of the office. Artemis tried her hardest to suppress a smile. Shaking his head, Mr. Jacobs turned to her parents.

"My sincerest apologies," he said. "I can assure you that nothing like this will ever happen again. Artemis is one of our brightest students, and we want her to feel welcome and valued."

"We accept your apology," Wilfred said. "Now, will our daughter still be punished?"

"Of course not. We have never had any trouble out of your daughter, so I think we can let things slide just this once," Mr. Jacobs said with a wink.

"Thank you," Louise said, as she and Wilfred shook the principal's hand. Artemis happily waved goodbye as she followed her parents out of the office. As they made their way to the exit, a child's voice called out.

"There she is, Grandma!" The trio turned around to see Naomi standing next to an older woman. The woman was none other than Mrs. Everett, Louise's former high school teacher. She had come to pick up Naomi from school since the girl's mother was still at work.

"Hmph. Looks like the apple doesn't fall too far from the tree," Mrs. Everett quipped. "I told you that anger was going to rub off on your child."

"Funny. I can say the same about you," Louise retorted, looking her former teacher up and down.

"You better teach that little girl to keep her hands off my grandbaby."

"Maybe you should teach your grandbaby not to be a bully or touch things that don't belong to her."

"Your daughter is just being a sensitive drama queen, just like you," Mrs. Everett said dismissively. "Maybe she should leave that necklace at home if she don't want people touching it." *I'm just about sick of this old bitch!* Louise thought angrily.

"Babe, let's just go home," Wilfred said, pulling his wife towards the exit.

"Hmph. Freaks like you shouldn't exist among normal people," Ms. Harlowe seethed as she emerged from her former classroom. Louise stopped in her tracks, turning to glare at her. It was one thing to be called a 'freak' for her supernatural gifts by ignorant people. She was used to it. However, for this bitch to fix her crusty ass mouth to say that not only she, but her baby, shouldn't be alive ignited an intense fury. The fact that this ignorance is being passed down to other children infuriated her even more. *I got something for these bitches!* she thought as she followed her husband and child outside.

"Will, don't pull off yet," she said as they entered the vehicle.

"Huh? Why?" Wilfred asked, his eyebrow raised.

"Just wait," Louise said simply. With a shrug, Wilfred sat back in his seat, turning on Spotify. A few moments later, Mrs. Everett exited the school with Naomi and Ms. Harlowe, ranting about the events from earlier. As they approached Ms. Harlowe's car, the sky began to darken.

"Lou, what are you doing?"

"Shh!" A few minutes later, a murder of crows appeared, flying in circles above Ms. Harlowe and Mrs. Everett. "Mommy, those look like the crows from our house," Artemis said, looking towards the sky. She would often see crows gathered in her mother's garden. She would leave little shiny trinkets for them, as well as seeds and leftover fruit. What Artemis didn't realize was that by doing so, she gained lifelong protectors.

"Yep. Did you know that crows were Missy's favorite birds? She would feed them all the time," Louise replied.

"Grandma, where did those birds come from?" Naomi asked in a frightened voice.

"I don't know, baby. Get in the car," Mrs. Everett said, opening the passenger door. As soon as the little girl entered the vehicle, the birds descended on the two women while Naomi screamed in terror.

"Damn it! Get off me!" Ms. Harlowe yelled as the crows pecked and scratched her skin. Mrs. Everett swung her purse at them in an attempt to drive them away, but to no avail. Laughing, Louise turned to her husband.

"Okay, now you can pull off." Holding in his laughter, Wilfred turned on the engine and pulled off, as "Wu-Tang Clan Ain't Nuthing Ta F'Wit" blared from the speakers. As they drove past the distressed women in the parking lot, Louise slightly rolled down her window. "That was for Missy, bitch!" With a wave of her hand, Ms. Harlowe was blown backward, falling to the ground. The crows attacked the former teacher further, as she screamed and kicked at them. "And that's for my daughter!" As they drove away, Louise waved her hand again. The crows suddenly stopped attacking and flew away as if nothing had happened. Mrs. Everett frantically got into her car and peeled off. Dirty and bleeding, Ms. Harlowe scrambled to her vehicle, no doubt traumatized by her ordeal. However, she and Mrs. Everett learned a valuable lesson: Don't fuck with Louise Eason.

Chapter 5

*T*he young man made his way off the bus and headed down the street to his apartment complex. He had spent the day at his friend's house, passing the time with video games and the latest episodes of *Jujutsu Kaisen*. He was happy to have seen friends he hadn't seen in a while, as they had all been busy with work and other obligations. Now, it was almost 2 a.m., and he knew his mother would be worried if he didn't get home soon. Seeing his building up ahead, he continued walking. Unbeknownst to him, however, he was being followed. "Odin, Ancestors, please watch over me as I walk, so that I arrive home safely," he prayed to himself as he walked. A practicing Norse Pagan, he always prayed before venturing out and on his way home. It brought him a sense of calm and gave him strength. The world was a treacherous place, and it never hurt to keep one's guard up.

"How dare you use Lord Odin's name in vain?" a female voice said menacingly. Perplexed, the young man turned around and was greeted by three white women, all dressed in black. They stared at him with contempt and disgust.

"Excuse me?" he said.

"You have no right to wear that Valknut," seethed one of the women. She was short and plump, with a short blond haircut with red streaks. She eyed the young man's Valknut pendant, a symbol of Odin, the Norse god of wisdom, death, and magic. "Our gods are not to be perverted by the likes of you. So, why don't you take off that necklace and hand it over?"

"Yeah, how about no," the young man replied. Unfortunately, he was no stranger to racism in the Pagan community, especially when it came to the Norse pantheon. Every other day on TikTok, he was greeted with "Black people can't be Norse Pagan!" comments. Never mind the fact that

Black Vikings existed. Being a Viking was an occupation and had nothing to do with race.

"We're not asking you, boy. We're telling you," the taller woman said. The trio's auras began to glow a dark purple.

"Boy?"

"Just hand us the necklace, and we'll let you live."

"Man, what the fuck ever," the young man quipped. His aura began to glow a bright orange. He wasn't afraid of these women. If he wanted to, he could electrocute his would-be robbers. However, he knew it could end badly if he did. If the police showed up and saw him with three unconscious white women, he could very well end up the next poster child for Black Lives Matter. Never mind the fact that he would have been defending himself. He knew he had to play it smart. "Look, I don't know what your problem is, but I'm not giving you shit. I have every right to wear this Valknut. Odin chose me as one of his children. He is the All-father, not the Some-father. If you were a true follower of his, you would know that. Why don't you three just leave me alone and let me go home in peace? That way, no one has to get hurt." He turned away and continued on his journey home, while checking behind him to make sure he wasn't being followed. However, the last thing he saw was a blinding light.

Sarai shot up in bed in a cold sweat, breathing heavily. She reached over to her left and grabbed her phone off the nightstand. She looked at the screen and saw that it was 4 a.m. She then looked over to her right to see Kiana still sound asleep, snoring softly. What the hell was that all about? she thought to herself. The dream, or rather, the nightmare that she had awakened from, felt so real and was so vivid. But why was she dreaming of a group of racist Pagans? Then again, she was no stranger to weird dreams, especially after smoking weed. Could it be a vision? She made a mental note to bring it up to Louise or Kristy the next time she saw them. With a shrug, she plopped her head back down onto her pillow and drifted off to sleep.

It was packed and busy at Dom & Mari's Supermarket. It was late afternoon, and the aisles were filled with families seeking what they needed for their meals that day. Dom & Mari's was owned by Domingo and Marisol Ramirez, Nick's parents and Rachelle's future in-laws. What started as a small store in Mexican-town ten years ago had expanded into a now successful enterprise.

"Excuse me, I was wondering if you had any oat milk?" a young woman asked Marisol, whose back was to her. She was occupied with stocking the spice shelves. Once she finished, she turned around and was greeted by a familiar face. She was of average height and slender, with brown skin and deep brown eyes. She also wore a chic black pixie cut.

"Kendra?" she asked. The young woman beamed and nodded. "Goodness! I almost didn't recognize you with the short hair. It's so good to see you! It's been years!"

"It's good to see you too, Mrs. Ramirez." Kendra Baker, along with her younger sister Octavia and mother, Donna, were once neighbors of the Ramirezes. However, about fifteen years ago, they moved across the country after Donna had been offered a new job, and the families lost contact. "I'm actually surprised you remember me."

"I will never forget a face," replied Marisol, smiling. "So how have you been? How's your mom?"

"Well, I've been good, but Mom, she..." Kendra let out a sigh. "Mom died about a year ago. Heart attack."

"Oh, dear. Honey, I'm so sorry," Marisol said. "How are you and your sister holding up?"

"We're coping, but it's been hard, you know?"

"Trust me, I know." Marisol's heart broke for the young sisters. She had lost her own mother, Carmen Batista, when she was only twenty-one years old, and it had left a wound that would never fully heal. While the loss became easier to deal with, there were times when she felt intense sorrow, especially during the holidays, her mother's birthday, or when she watched her grandchildren play. She knew her mother would have doted on and spoiled her great-granddaughters.

"So how's your family?" Kendra asked, changing the subject.

"Oh, they're great. Carmen works as a software developer, and Daniela works as a nurse. Nick works as a professional photographer. He also got engaged about a month ago."

"Little Nicky's getting married?"

"Well, he's not so little anymore," Marisol said, smiling proudly. "He also has twin girls with his fiancée."

"Oh wow," Kendra replied. "It seems like yesterday, he and Octavia were running around, having pretend Pokémon battles. Now he's got kids."

"Time sure does fly by. Hey, why don't you and your sister come to Nick's engagement party? It's in two weeks."

"Are you sure he won't mind?"

"Of course not. He'll be so happy to see you two, and I'm sure Rachelle would love to meet you. She's such a sweetheart."

"Well, I'll ask Tay to see if she wants to come, and I'll let you know," Kendra said.

"Perfect!" replied Marisol, and the two women exchanged phone numbers. "By the way, to answer your question, the oat milk is in aisle 7."

"Thank you so much," Kendra said, hugging Marisol before making her way to the aisle. Marisol continued making her rounds in the store, tending to whoever needed her assistance.

"You're late, Miss Thing," Kristy said as she let Louise into the house, Cerberus barking behind her. It was the night of the full moon, and the members of the Children of Moonlight coven were gathering for their monthly meeting.

"My bad, Ma. I lost track of time," Louise replied as she removed her jacket. "Plus, traffic was a bitch." Her mother led her into the living room, where the other coven members were seated, including Sarai, Kiana, Rachelle, Nick, Chris, and Khalil. Louise noticed that Trina was also present, albeit via Zoom, since she was currently back home in New York City. "Now that everyone is here, I think we can begin," Kristy said as she took a seat on the couch. "As most of you have probably seen on the news, Anthony Wallace was attacked last night. He is currently in the hospital in critical condition."

"Do the police have an idea of who did it?" Violet, Sarai's aunt, asked.

"I don't think so, but according to Sheila, it was racially motivated. Hopefully, when the attackers are caught, they'll be charged with a hate crime," Kristy replied.

"Is there anything we can do to help? Does Anthony need help with medical expenses?" Rachelle asked.

"I think that would be a big help, Rachelle," Kristy said. "We will also be doing a healing ritual tonight to help speed up his recovery." The other members murmured in agreement. Sarai, however, felt uneasy. She hadn't been able to put the dream she had the night before out of her mind. After learning of Anthony's attack, she wondered if her dream was even a dream at all. Was it possible that she had a premonition?

"Is everything okay, babe?" Kiana asked.

"I think I might have seen what happened to Anthony last night."

"What do you mean?" Louise asked. Sarai then proceeded to tell the coven about the dream she had, mentioning the three women she saw.

"You mean to tell me that we could be dealing with Nazi witches?" Simone asked.

"Possibly," Louise replied. "Unfortunately, white supremacists have slithered their asses into the Pagan community. The Norse Pagan community, especially." Louise turned up her nose in disgust. "They make me fucking sick."

"To be quite honest, I don't trust the cops with this situation, considering that a lot of them are racist as hell," Rachelle added. "Remember the George Floyd protests we had downtown?" Her friends nodded in agreement. They remembered all too well. The tear gas. The rubber bullets. The Detroit police in riot gear. Louise had already disliked them because of how they handled the investigation of Jasmine Sanders' murder, but after 2020, it was "Fuck the police" forever.

"I don't trust them either," Trina said. "For all we know, there could be racist witches on the force."

"Which is why I want you to be especially careful, Trina," Kristy said. "If there is a white supremacist group behind this, there could be multiple chapters. Always be on your guard and keep your protections up."

"Yes, ma'am," Trina said, nodding.

"That goes for all of you," Kristy added. "I don't want to have to visit you in the hospital, or worse, see you lying in a casket." Louise knew that statement was mostly directed at her. She remembered how frantic her mother was when she learned that she had been shot by Vincent, Alexis' deceased lover and pimp, at his New Year's Eve party. While Louise had survived the murder attempt, albeit with the help of ancestral magic, it didn't stop her parents from fussing over her. Although it annoyed her, she understood that her parents were frightened at the prospect of losing their eldest child. She would have reacted the same way if something had happened to Artemis. "Is everyone ready?" Rose, Violet's sister, asked. After everyone responded affirmatively, the coven made their way to the basement, where all coven rituals were performed. After everyone had gathered around the large altar, Kristy took a blue candle and began to inscribe Anthony's full name and date of birth, along with sigils for healing. She then dressed the candle with Healing Oil and rolled it in a mixture of rosemary, lavender, sea salt, eucalyptus, and powdered apple skins. After dressing the candle, she set it in the center of the altar, placing pieces of obsidian, amethyst, ruby, bloodstone, and rose quartz. Underneath the candle holder was a photo of Anthony. As Kristy lit the candle, the coven joined hands, and Kristy said the following prayer:

"Beloved Ancestors, our fierce protectors, and healers...

We ask that you be with us now on the full moon and hear our prayers...

We ask that you surround Anthony Maurice Wallace in loving, healing vibrations...

We ask that you surround him with protection as he recovers from his horrific and traumatic ordeal...

Make him healthy and strong again so that he can continue to fulfill his purpose in this life...

And may justice be visited upon his attackers swiftly and mercilessly.

Asè."

"*Asè!*" the coven shouted in unison. The candle's flame began to glow higher and brighter as the energy in the room grew. The crystals surrounding the candle began to glow, and the room grew warmer. After the candle burned down completely, the circle was opened, and offerings were left on the community altar for the Ancestors. The coven then retreated to the living room for refreshments. "So, *mi hijo,*" Marisol began as she poured herself a cup of lemonade. "Kendra Baker came into the store today. You remember her, don't you?"

"Yeah, I remember her," Nick replied. "But what was she doing in the store? I thought the family moved to Washington."

"They did, but Donna passed away, so Kendra and Octavia came back."

"Who's Octavia?" Rachelle chimed in.

"She was an old friend from when I was a kid," Nick replied. "My folks were friends with her family. Kendra is her older sister."

"Oh." Nick then turned his attention back to his mother.

"So, how did Ms. Baker..."

"A heart attack," Marisol replied.

"Damn." Nick always liked Donna. Whenever he came over to play with Octavia and her sister, Donna would always have treats for them. His heart went out to the sisters. Although she never met them, Rachelle's heart broke for them. She knew all too well the pain of losing a parent.

"I invited them to the engagement dinner. I hope that's alright with you two."

"Of course it is," Rachelle said, smiling at her future mother-in-law. "Any friends of Nick's are friends of mine." Nick kissed her on the cheek, making her blush. They then noticed everyone getting ready to leave.

"We should head home," Nick said. After saying goodbye to Nick's mother and sisters, and the rest of the coven, the couple went to Sharon's house to pick up their daughters before heading home. During the ride home, Rachelle thought about the prospect of meeting Nick's childhood friend and what she would think of her. She loved Nick and was more than happy to forge friendships with those dear to him. But would Octavia like her? She would just have to wait until the party to find out.

Chapter 6

"**B**abe, you ready?" Nick asked as he stood in the hallway, with the twins standing on both sides of him, holding his hands.

"Just a minute," Rachelle replied from behind the bathroom door. After spritzing herself with her rose perfume and fluffing out her thick curls, she opened the door. "Okay, now I'm ready." Nick gave her a peck on the lips, and they made their way to their car with their daughters in tow. It was the evening of their engagement dinner, so everyone was gathering at Sharon's home in Sherwood Forest, an affluent and historic Detroit neighborhood. Parking in front of the large Victorian home, they approached the door and rang the bell. Moments later, they were greeted by the smiling face of Ana, Sharon's housekeeper. Ana had been employed by the Lawson family for seven years and was considered a part of the family. Ana was like another mother to Rachelle, and she spoiled Selena and Solana whenever they came over.

"There's my favorite couple!" she said as she gave Rachelle and Nick a loving hug. She then turned her attention to the girls, opening her arms to them. Giggling, the twins ran to her, and she scooped them up into her arms, peppering their faces with kisses. She carried them into the house, with their parents following behind. When they entered the large dining room, they were greeted by Veronica, who embraced the couple in a hug. They were also greeted by Nick's parents and sisters. Their friends were also present, with the exception of Trina, who was currently in Tokyo for a fashion show.

"¡Ahí están mis princesitas!" Domingo exclaimed as he took the twins from Ana's arms. They squealed and laughed as their grandfather covered their faces in kisses. Rachelle couldn't help but feel a sting in her heart as she watched the exchange. It was during moments like these that she missed her father, Robert, tremendously. She knew that he would have been a doting grandfather like Domingo and would have spoiled her girls rotten. It also hurt her that Robert would not be around to walk her down the aisle on her wedding day, which he often talked about when she was a young girl. "You okay?" Nick whispered, giving Rachelle's hand a gentle squeeze. It was as if he could read her thoughts and sense what she was feeling. It was one of the many things she loved about him. Rachelle simply nodded, and Nick pulled out a chair for her to sit down.

"By the way, Mom and Dad weren't able to make it," Alexis said. "He tested positive for Covid a few days ago, so he's in quarantine. And of course, Mom's looking after him."

"Damn, that sucks," Rachelle replied.
"I hope he gets better. Where's Bryson?"

"It's his dad's weekend to have him, so Bryson's at his place." Two years ago, Alexis had reconciled her differences with Bryce, her ex-boyfriend. After apologizing for not being in Bryson's life, and a paternity test, Bryce had become a hands-on father. The two had fostered a healthy co-parenting relationship. In fact, it was Bryce who had supported Alexis through her cocaine addiction and her trauma from her relationship with Vincent.

"So when will you guys get back together?" Rachelle asked musingly.

"Pfft, never," Alexis replied. "Like, don't get me wrong, Bryce isn't a bad guy, but we just don't mesh as a couple. We're better off as friends."

"That's valid," Rachelle said with a nod.

"It's the same with me and Dy'Anna's daddy," Mariah chimed in. "We're good as friends and co-parents, but not as a couple." While Alexis and Mariah talked about their relationships with their children's fathers, Rachelle looked over at Sarai, who was looking at her phone with an angry look on her face.

"Hey, what's up?" she asked.

"Look at this bullshit Jay posted," Sarai spat.

"I thought you had him blocked."

"I do, but Mika sent me a screenshot." Sarai handed Rachelle her phone. Rachelle began reading the screenshotted Facebook post:

I can't stand bitches who act like their shit don't stink. Just because you got a book, a little business, or doing some fashion shows, don't mean shit! That don't make you better than nobody. Bitches need to humble themselves. Anybody can write a fucking book or shake their ass. You ain't special!

"Is he talking about us?" Rachelle asked.

"Of course he is," Louise cut in. She had also received the screenshot in her inbox. "But I'm trying to figure out when we ever said we were better than anybody. As far as us thinking we're special, I mean... we are. We're literally magical."

"And of course Nikki and Monique's asses heart-reacted the post," said Rachelle.

"It's obvious that he's jealous, but that's not your problem. He's projecting," Nick said.

"Oh, we know that," said Louise. "But he's going to have more problems if he doesn't keep my or my family's name out of his mouth."

"Mmmhmm," Sarai added. "I say we do a Return to Sender on his ass."

"I second that," Louise said. "The dark moon is in a few days, too."

"Shouldn't we divine on it first?" Kiana asked.

"My ancestors are already giving me the green light," Louise replied.

"Mmmhmm. Sure is," Diana, Louise's grandmother, said. *"That's the only way his ass gonna learn."*

"Bet," Rachelle said. Before they could say anything else, the doorbell rang. Ana walked over to the front door and returned a few moments later with Kendra Baker and another young woman. She was petite with light skin, brown eyes, and curly auburn hair which fell to her shoulder. Her cheeks and nose were kissed by freckles. She was dressed in a simple, olive green dress with a black belt. On her feet, she wore simple, black pumps. Marisol got up from the table to greet the young women.

"I'm so glad you two could make it," she said. She then turned to Sharon. "These are the two lovely young ladies I was telling you about." Sharon approached the women, smiling.

"Hello, my name is Sharon Lawson. Welcome to my home."

"Your home is beautiful, Mrs. Lawson," Kendra said, admiring the decor.

"Thank you," Sharon replied as she led them to the table.

"*Mi hijo*, look who's come to see you," Marisol said, smiling.

"Nicky!" the young woman squealed as she went to hug Nick. Kendra also gave him a hug. "It's so good to see you!"

"It's good to see you, too!" Nick said, flashing a smile. He then turned to Rachelle. "Babe, this is Octavia Baker. She's the old friend I was telling you about." As Octavia stared at Nick, she felt her face flush. He was far from the scrawny boy she knew fifteen years ago. He was taller, and Octavia could tell that he had been hitting the gym. However, one thing that didn't change was his piercing green eyes, which Octavia always found beautiful. She was utterly captivated. However, she knew she had to keep her hormones in check since she and her sister were there to celebrate his engagement. Her attention turned to Rachelle, who stood next to him. She was dressed in a royal blue pencil dress, which hugged her hourglass frame, a matching beret, and royal blue pumps. Her hair hung past her shoulders in fluffy curls, and Octavia could tell it was all hers. Her makeup was natural and made her look radiant. Around her neck was a sapphire pendant. Octavia was in awe of how stunning Rachelle was. It was easy to see why Nick wanted to marry her.

71

"I'm Rachelle. It's great to meet you," Rachelle held out her hand.

"Likewise," Octavia replied, shaking Rachelle's hand. "Congratulations."

"Thanks, Octavia. That means a lot," Nick said.

"Please, just call me Tay."

"By the way, I'm really sorry about your mom."

"So am I," added Rachelle.
"I lost my dad when I was 18, so I definitely know how it feels."

"Thank you," Octavia said. "We're just taking things one day at a time."
Rachelle's heart went out to Octavia and her sister. The pain that came
with losing a parent could be downright unbearable at times, and it was
a pain that no one truly gets over.

"Why don't you all take a seat? Food's just about done," Marisol said,
gesturing to the table. Rachelle and Nick returned to their seats, while

Kendra and Octavia sat across from them. The couple introduced the sisters to their friends and made small talk as they waited on the food.

"So, you're a photographer now?" Kendra asked Nick.

"Yep," Nick said, smiling.
"Some of my photos have even been published in *Metro Times*."

"That's so cool," Octavia said. She then turned to Rachelle.
"So, what do you do?"

"I'm a model," Rachelle said proudly.

"You definitely have the looks for it," Kendra said. She then turned to Sarai and the others. "What about you? What do you all do?"

"Well, I'm also a model, as well as a burlesque performer," replied Louise. "I also paint and design my own jewelry and accessories."

"I'm a published author," Sarai added.

"A bestselling author," Kiana stated.
"She wrote the *Bloodlust* series."

"That was you?" Octavia asked, amazed. "I have all the books! You're such a good writer."

"Thank you," Sarai said with a smile. "I'm glad you enjoy my work." Octavia smiled back.

"So, what do you do?" Louise asked.

"Well, when I was in Washington, I worked as a paralegal, but I'm currently unemployed since Kenni and I only moved back here two months ago," Octavia replied.

"Wow, so you worked with lawyers?" Kiana asked.
"Sounds stressful."

"It really is," replied Octavia.

"Well, if you're still looking to work in that field, my cousin is an attorney with his own law firm. I can give you his card if you want," Louise said.

"That'll be great. Thank you so much." Just then, Sharon and Marisol, with the help of Ana, began bringing the food into the dining room. Everyone salivated at the sight of jerk chicken, cornbread, greens, macaroni and cheese, arroz con pollo, and tamales. For dessert was Marisol's signature pineapple cake and Sharon's pecan pie. After the food was blessed, everyone started to dig in.

"You have no idea how much I've missed your cooking, Mrs. Ramirez," Kendra said, taking a bite of a tamale.

"I bet you have," Marisol said as she put some greens on her plate. "I'm surprised Nicky hasn't gained weight since he's always eating us out of the house and home."

"¡Mamí!" Nick exclaimed as Rachelle giggled. The girls giggled as well.

"Your babies are so adorable, Nick," Octavia said as she looked over at the twins, who were in Marisol's lap, eating arroz con pollo. "How old are they?"

"Two. They'll be three in October."

"So when's the wedding?" Kendra asked.

"Well, we're planning on getting married next summer, but we haven't set an exact date," Rachelle said. Octavia nodded and continued eating. However, she would sneak glances at Nick and Rachelle. Whenever he held her hand or kissed her, Octavia felt a twinge of jealousy. Unbeknownst to everyone, including her sister, Octavia had harbored a crush on Nick. However, her family had packed up and moved before she could tell him how she felt. Now, fifteen years later, he had started a life and family with someone else.

"Well, whatever date you pick, we'll definitely be there," Kendra said.

"Right, Tay?"

"Yeah, of course," Octavia said, smiling sheepishly. "Wouldn't miss it for the world." She then continued eating, hoping no one would catch the blush in her cheeks. However, Louise did catch it but said nothing. Octavia wasn't the only woman who blushed around Nick. He was a very handsome and charming man. Besides, Octavia clearly knew he was off-limits since this was his engagement dinner. Also, she was his friend, so she wouldn't try anything shady... right?

"By the way, if you're ever at Oakland Mall, you should check out RoxyJo Creations. It's the shop Louise owns. She has really amazing stuff. It's where I got this from," Daniela said, flashing a rose quartz bracelet she wore on her wrist.

"Rachelle also has a shop there. It's called Melanin Siren," Carmen added. "It just opened in February. She makes her own skin and hair care products." *So she's a model and has her own business?* Octavia thought to herself. *Nick really found himself quite a catch. And it's clear she comes from money, judging by this house.*

"Awesome. I'll check those places out," Kendra said as she put a piece of Sharon's pie on her plate. Soon, it was time to make a toast to the happy couple. Once everyone had their glasses, Sharon, Marisol, and Domingo stood up from their seats.

"I would like to take a moment to make a toast to my lovely daughter and future son-in-law," Sharon began. "I am so overjoyed to know that my baby girl will be marrying the man of her dreams." She then looked over at Nick. "Nick, when I first met you, I knew you were perfect for my daughter. Over the past five years, you have shown Rachelle nothing but the utmost respect, love, and support. I am very proud of both of you." Now, it was Marisol's turn to speak.

"And while I have always considered you part of our family, *mi hija*, I am looking forward to the day that we make it official. You have been such a wonderful partner to my son and an amazing mother to my grandbabies. Dom and I are very excited to see the two of you continue to grow together."

"To the bride and groom," Domingo said, raising his glass.

"To the bride and groom!" everyone said in unison. The dinner continued for another two hours before it was time for everyone to go home. However, Rachelle and Nick stayed behind to help clean up, while the girls played in the living room with Ana.

"So, what do you think of Kendra and Tay?" Nick asked as they were washing dishes.

"I think they're pretty cool," replied Rachelle. "Maybe I could invite them to hang out sometime."

"I think they'll like that."

"Maybe the two of you can hang out together to catch up."

"Yeah, it's been years since we've done that," Nick said. "It would be nice to rekindle our friendship."

"Can I ask you something, though?"

"You know you can ask me anything, *muñeca*. You know that."

"Was there any... you know... history between you two? Romantic, I mean."

"Of course not," Nick replied, turning to Rachelle. "I mean, we were thirteen when she left, and I never thought of her as anything more than a friend. I don't even think she liked me that way, either. You know I would have told you if she and I had anything." Rachelle sighed. Nick tilted her head up so that their eyes met. "I promise you that you have nothing to worry about. You're the only one for me." Rachelle smiled.

"I know," she said. "I trust you."

A FEW DAYS LATER

DING DONG!

"Coming!" Louise shouted as she headed to the door. It was the night of the dark moon, and she had invited her friends over to perform a group ritual against their former friend, Jay. Despite cutting him off almost two months ago, he was still running his mouth about them on social media and to their mutual friends. The last straw was when Jay began targeting Louise and Rachelle's businesses, leaving bogus complaints and one-star reviews. He did the same to Sarai's books. Talking crap about them to their friends and the anime community was one thing. Targeting their livelihoods, however, was another thing entirely. Jay needed a harsh reminder of who he was dealing with. Upon opening the door, she was greeted by Rachelle, Sarai, Kiana, and Alexis. Looks like the gang's all here! she thought. "Did you all ride in the same car or something?"

"Well, you said to meet at your house at 8:30," replied Sarai.

"True," Louise said as she let everyone inside, hanging their jackets in the front closet. "Y'all ready?"

"Oh hell yeah," Rachelle said as she opened her bag and pulled out a packaged beef tongue, which she had gotten from Dom & Mari's for free. She set the package on the table, and Louise cut it open with a knife. Louise then set the tongue on a metal plate that sat in the middle of the table. Using the knife, she cut a slit down the center. Louise then took a picture of Jay that she had printed from Facebook and wrote his full name and date of birth on the back. Underneath his birthdate, she also wrote his birth time.

"How do you know his birth time?" Kiana asked.

"I did his natal chart about two years ago," Louise replied. "You would think he would watch what he says about me since I have all of this info, but I guess he thinks he's invincible." Louise took a bottle of her mother's Shut the Fuck Up oil and put a drop on each corner of Jay's photo and in the center. "He's about to learn the hard way that he isn't, especially since he has no spiritual protection or wards. Goofy ass. Rachelle, the mirror." Rachelle reached into her bag and pulled out a small mirror that she had purchased from a craft store. She then handed it to Louise, careful not to look in its reflection. Louise then taped the photo to the mirror face-down.

"What is the mirror for?" Alexis asked.

"To reflect any bullshit energy Jay tries to send our way back onto himself."

"So, he would basically be hexing himself," Kiana said.

"Bingo," Louise said in a sing-song voice. "That's actually why it's one of my favorite spells to cast."

"What about Mike?" Kiana asked.
"Won't it affect him?"

"It may since he's dating Jay. However, it's collateral damage." Louise picked up a black candle and cut off the top. She then flipped it over and began carving a new taper. Once she was finished, she dressed the candle with oil and rolled it away from her in a mixture of alum, slippery elm, poppy seeds, cayenne pepper, chia seeds, and black pepper. She took the mirror with Jay's photo on it and carefully placed it inside the slit she had cut into the tongue. After sprinkling some of the herbs inside, she sprinkled the rest counterclockwise around the plate. Sarai then pulled out her phone, turning on her Baneful Magic playlist. As "Press" by Cardi B played, Louise took a large needle with red thread and began sewing the tongue shut. She prayed the following while sewing:

"Jason Lee Thomas,

you will keep our names out your motherfucking mouth!

You will no longer slander nor defame us.

You will no longer attempt to sabotage us.

May your crusty ass lips and tongue burn every time you speak ill of us, our loved ones, or our Ancestors.

May your mouth pucker whenever our names are on your lips.

May the bile you spew burn your throat, and your words condemn you.

May your true self be revealed to those around you and close to you.

Any and all negativity you send our way will be sent back to you tenfold.

And may you be revealed to be the toxic, jealous-hearted bitch you are.

Fuck you!
Asè!"

"*Asè!*" the others shouted in unison. As the candle burned, they began to pray Psalms 36 and 52. As each of them focused their energies into the candle and the beef tongue, the room grew hotter. The candle's flame began to pop and sizzle, a sign that their spiritual teams were working the spell with them. The flame grew taller and brighter, and the beef tongue began to glow with a fiery red energy. Louise continued to curse out Jay as she raised her energy, pouring all her hurt and anger into the spell, fueling its power. Once enough energy was raised, they let go and allowed the candle to burn down completely. They then bundled the spell remains in black cloth and took it to a park several blocks away from the house. There, they buried the remains near a crossroads. After returning to the house, they thoroughly cleansed themselves and the space of the negative energy they had built up during the ritual. Now, all they needed to do was wait for the spell to do its work.

Chapter 7

*W*hen Sarai entered Diana's Garden, she felt an instant sense of tranquility as her nose was greeted by the sweet aroma of lavender and orange incense. After meeting her father for lunch, she decided to stop by to replenish her supply of herbs and candles, as well as visit her cousins. Sarai truly enjoyed shopping at Diana's Garden because it made her feel at home, like she belonged. It was a feeling that her former church, Mount Sinai Christian Fellowship, never gave her. Whenever she set foot in that church with her father and stepmother, she felt nothing but judgment and negativity. A majority of the congregation seemed to care more about the latest church gossip and being the best dressed than the word of God. She was certainly not sorry that she left that toxic environment, and neither was her father.

"Hey!" Sarai turned around to see the cheerful face of her friend, Simone Monroe. Like Sarai, Simone was a former member of Mount Sinai and a soloist in the church's youth choir. However, she left due to the predatory behavior of the church elders, specifically their pastor, Jacob Williams. Pastor Williams had violated countless young girls and boys in his congregation, a fact that was swept under the rug. Those who spoke out were shunned and ostracized. Simone was one such victim, having been assaulted by the pastor at the age of fourteen. She only found the courage to speak out after Pastor Williams' demise at the hands of Vernon Patterson, who learned that he had done the same to Faith. However, upon speaking out, she was branded a liar by those in the congregation, including her own mother. As a result, Simone disowned her mother and left the church. Soon after, she discovered that she had supernatural gifts that, like Sarai, she had suppressed out of fear and shame. She found her way into Diana's Garden, and after a year of study, made the decision to become a witch. One year later, she was invited to join Kristy's coven. Simone had finally found a community that was loving, supportive, and actually practiced what they preached.

"We missed you at the engagement dinner," Sarai said as she gave Simone a hug.

"I know. I had to work, so I couldn't make it," Simone replied. Just then, Kristy emerged from the back of the store with Dy'Anna in her arms.

"What's up, cuz," Sarai said as she hugged her cousin. She then took the toddler into her arms, kissing her face.

"What brings you here today?" Kristy asked with a smile.

"Just wanted to stop by and say hi. I also needed a few things," replied Sarai. "You got any more floor washes?"

"I sure do. I just restocked them yesterday." Kristy then led Sarai to a display. "So, how's your dad doing?"

"He's doing good. His business is really taking off."

"What kind of business does he have again?" Simone asked.

"A catering business," replied Sarai.
"He's always loved cooking."

"I didn't know Mr. Patterson could cook," Simone said.

"Dad did all the cooking in the house since Thelma couldn't cook for shit. She just took credit for all of Dad's hard work to look good in front of any guests we had over. She believed that cooking was a woman's job."

"Wait, so that bomb-ass mac 'n' cheese, chicken, and cornbread ya'll brought to the church picnics wasn't made by Mrs. Patterson?"

"Nope. It was all Dad."

"Damn," Simone said. "Well, I'm glad he's able to make a living doing what he loves. I never understood that gender role BS. Ain't nothing wrong with a man throwing down in the kitchen."

"Exactly," Kristy cut in. "In fact, my husband and I cook together. It's one of the ways we bond."

"I know Cousin Xavier be throwing down, with him being from New Orleans," Sarai turned to Simone. "He makes the best gumbo and crème brûlée."

"I haven't had gumbo in a hot minute," Simone replied, her mouth salivating at the thought of having a hot bowl of gumbo.

"The next time he makes some, I'll be sure to invite you over," Kristy said with a smile. She then picked up her granddaughter. "I should get back to work. Holler if you need me." With Dy'Anna in tow, she made her way to the back room to finish packing orders while Sarai and Simone continued to browse. Then, a familiar voice stopped the women in their tracks.

"Hmph. I guess everything I taught you and your brother went in one ear and out the other, huh? Now, you're a Devil worshipper." Sarai and Simone turned around and were greeted by the angry face of Debra Monroe, Simone's estranged mother. Standing with Debra were Ruth-Ann Williams, the widow of Pastor Williams, and Paula Roberts, the mother of Shawna Roberts, and the new First Lady of Mount Sinai.

"What the hell are ya'll doing in here?" Simone asked.

"I should be asking you that," Debra said, stepping forward. "This place is of the Devil. You know God don't abide by none of this. I'm not surprised she is in here." Debra eyed Sarai with a look of contempt. "She has always rebelled against the Lord's teachings. However, I expected better from you. If Sister Williams hadn't called me and told me she saw you walk in here a few weeks ago, I wouldn't have believed it."

"Lord help her," Paula said, as Simone rolled her eyes.

"First of all, I'm a grown-ass woman, so I can come in here if I damn well please. What I do is none of your damn business!" Simone said.

"You watch your tone with me, Simone Christina!" Debra said sternly. "I am your mother. As long as there is breath in my body, you will always be my business." Simone laughed sardonically.

"You may have given birth to me, *Debra*, but you don't deserve to be called my mother," she spat. "A mother would never put a rapist before her own child." She then turned to Ruth-Ann. "As for you, you're pathetic. What kind of woman stays married to a child molester?" A few of the customers gasped.

"Don't you stand there telling lies about my Jacob!" Ruth-Ann exclaimed in a southern drawl with a hand on her hip, staring daggers at Simone. "He was a good man of God!"

"God rest his soul," Paula said.

"Good man of God, my ass!" Sarai cut in. "He did the same thing to my sister. Are you gonna say she's lying, too?"

"Your fast-tailed sister was a liar!" Ruth-Ann spat. "She seduced my husband and cried rape when it was more than she bargained—" *SMACK!* Ruth-Ann held her cheek in shock as Sarai glared at her. If looks could kill, the former first lady of the church would have been completely obliterated.

"Let's get one thing straight," Sarai began. "Don't you **ever** in your fucking life accuse my sister of seducing your nasty ass husband. Faith was a child, and Pastor Williams was an adult. Not only did he take her innocence, he destroyed her spirit to the point where she felt life was unbearable!" Sarai had to take a deep breath to keep from crying. "He and my bitch of a stepmother both did. I'm glad the bastard is dead. My dad did the world a favor when he capped his ass." Ruth-Ann was speechless. She looked around the store, hoping for someone to speak up in her defense. No one was on her side. They were disgusted. Some of the patrons already knew the story of the events leading up to the pastor's murder and were enraged that an adult woman would blame a child for her own assault. Some were abuse survivors themselves.

"Simone, I'm so disappointed in you," Debra said. "I tried to teach you how to live righteously, yet you're willing to throw all of that away."

"Give me a fucking break!" Simone barked. Debra gasped and clasped her chest, shocked at her daughter's coarse language. "You threw me away the moment you sided with that son of a bitch." Suddenly, Kristy reemerged from the back room.

"What on earth is going on here?" she demanded, her eyes scanning the room. "We came here to save this poor child from this forsaken place!" Ruth-Ann said. "You are doing the Devil's work." Kristy stared at Mrs. Williams with a blank expression. A few moments later, she burst out laughing.

"You're joking, right?" she said.
"God, you people are such hypocrites!"

"Excuse me?" Mrs. Williams said.

"You're going to stand here in my store, calling what I do the 'Devil's work,' yet I recall you coming in this very same place months ago asking me for a spell to break up Mrs. Roberts' marriage because you wanted the good Pastor Roberts for yourself?" Kristy could only laugh at the hypocrisy of some "Christians." They'll condemn her and others like her in public, yet come to her in private when it was convenient for them. If they don't get their way, they go right back to condemning her. "It wasn't the Devil's work then. Are you only calling it 'the Devil's work' because I told you I wouldn't do it, no matter how much you paid me? I wonder how much of that money came from the collection plate."

"WHAT?!" Paula shrieked, staring at Ruth-Ann.
"Ruthie, is this true?"

"Oh shit!" Simone whispered, her fist to her mouth.

"That's a lie!" Ruth-Ann cried.
"Adultery is a sin! I-I would never do that!"

"I may be a lot of things, Ruth-Ann, but I am not a liar," Kristy replied with a smirk. "Furthermore, I will not allow you to harass my customers. I don't go into your church telling you that your beliefs are wrong. I expect that same respect to be reciprocated."

"Mmhmm," said one of the patrons.

"You've been sleeping with Edward?" Paula demanded, crossing her arms.

"Paula, I-I can explain. He came on to me. He told me that y'all were having problems," Ruth-Ann said as she backed away from Paula, but Paula was having none of it. Advancing towards her husband's mistress, she snatched her wig clean off her head. The store erupted into hollering and laughter as Ruth-Ann tried to retrieve her wig from her friend.

"If you are going to fight, I would appreciate it if you did it outside," Kristy said, holding the door open, trying to stifle her laughter. Paula stormed out of the shop, Ruth-Ann following, pleading her case to no avail. Once they were outside, Paula proceeded to slap her in the face with the wig repeatedly, cursing her to Hell. Debra, clearly embarrassed by her friends' behavior, turned to Simone, hoping to accomplish what she came in there to do.

"Are you really not coming back to God?"

"I never left God, Debra," Simone began. Debra felt a pain in her heart hearing her daughter continue to address her by her first name. "I left your church. There's a difference. I don't need the church to have a relationship with God. Since I left Mount Sinai, I've been so much happier. I have been able to embrace my true self and the gifts I have been blessed with. Gifts that you tried to make me feel ashamed of."

"I was trying to save you!" Debra exclaimed. "Those 'gifts,' as you call them, are of the Devil. You have to renounce them, or else you'll burn in hell." Simone cackled. "If anyone is going to burn in Hell, it'll be you. Your duty as a mother is to protect and love your children unconditionally. You failed miserably. After Pastor Williams violated me, I went to you for help. Do you remember what you said to me?" Debra shook her head. Simone sighed. "Of course you don't, so allow me to refresh your memory. You called me a lying whore and said I just wanted to ruin a good Black man's name. I was fourteen! Do you have any idea how bad it hurt to hear my own mother call me that?"

"I never said that!" Debra replied. "You must have misheard me." *Here we go again with the gaslighting*, Simone thought.

"You did, and you know you did. Keep pretending if you want to, but know this: until you acknowledge your wrongs towards me and give a genuine apology, I want nothing to do with you. Honestly, even if you do apologize, I still wouldn't want anything to do with you. As far as I'm concerned, you're dead to me." Debra stood speechless as her daughter's words cut through her. She had heard Simone tell her she was done with her before, but her ego refused to believe that her daughter would actually disown her, even though they had been no contact for three years.

"You don't mean that," Debra said.
"We're family. You can't turn your back on family."

"Says who?" Simone questioned. "Just because we share the same blood doesn't mean we're family. Love makes you family. Loyalty makes you family. You showed me neither. Did you know I had stopped wanting to sing after what happened to me because it reminded me of him?" Debra looked away, saying nothing. "It was only because of counseling that I was able to reclaim my passion for music. I'm done letting you and what that bastard did to me hold me back anymore. Honestly, my life is better off without you in it." Debra said nothing as her eyes filled with tears. She knew she had failed her daughter, yet she couldn't bring herself to admit it. Now her eldest child wanted nothing to do with her. Her heart shattered, she made her way towards the door. However, she had one last thing to say to her daughter.

"I'mma pray for you," she said. "When you're ready to come back to the Lord, we'll be waiting. Your family will be waiting."

"Pray for yourself. You need it more than me," Simone replied. Before Debra could say anything else, Simone, using her telekinetic power, shoved her out of the store.

"Are you okay?" Sarai asked, putting her hand on Simone's shoulder. Simone let out a deep sigh.

"I'm fine," she replied. "I just don't understand why she can't accept that I want nothing to do with her. Like, was blocking her phone number and her social media accounts not a big enough hint?"

"Toxic parents can't handle losing control over their victims," Kristy said. "They'll pull all the stops to try to lure you back in. Manipulation, guilt tripping, gaslighting, you name it. You absolutely don't have to have that in your life. Keep setting your boundaries."

"She's definitely an expert at gaslighting and guilt tripping," Simone said. "She loves playing the victim, too. I know she's going to cry to everyone about how I don't want to talk to her."

  "Let her," Sarai said.
  "She made her bed. Let her lie in it."

"I think I'm going to need a spiritual bath after dealing with her."

"Say no more," Kristy said, grabbing a bag of her famous cleansing bath off the shelf. She also gave Simone a healing bath. "These are on the house."

"Thanks, Ms. Kristy." After Kristy rang up Simone and Sarai, they bid each other farewell before leaving the shop. Kristy's heart went out to the young women. They had endured trauma that no one should have to endure, yet she was proud of them for how far they had come. They were truly their ancestors' wildest dreams.

"Get the fuck out of here!" Louise exclaimed, unable to believe her ears. "You're bullshitting, right?"

"I wish I was," Sarai replied. It had been a few days since her encounter with Simone's mother and the church elders, and she was still astonished at the tea her cousin, Kristy, had spilled about them.

"So, not only was Pastor Williams' widow going to my mom for spellwork, but she was also fucking the new pastor, who is Shawna's father? Does Shawna know?" Louise asked.

"I have no clue, but I'm sure she'll hear about it, since church gossip spreads like wildfire," Sarai said, hooking up her PS5. It was their monthly "Girls Night," and this time, Louise was hosting at her home.

"Hmph, and she had the nerve to condemn y'all just for being in there," Rachelle cut in. "I'm glad Ms. Kristy called her out."

"For real," Kiana added. "Isn't one of the Ten Commandments 'Thou Shalt Not Commit Adultery'?"

"Yep. She's also extra grimy for fucking her friend's husband. With friends like that, who the hell needs enemies?" Simone said, as the others murmured in agreement.

"By the way, Lou, thanks for inviting Octavia," Rachelle said.

"Of course," Louise replied with a smile. "The more, the merrier. I think it's cool that she wants to hang with us, especially since she's a friend of Nick's." Hearing the oven timer go off, she made her way to the kitchen. She then took out a tray of cookies from the oven and set them on the stove to cool. "Give these about 5 minutes, then help yourselves."

"So, how's Mimi doing in school now that her teacher's been fired?" Khalil asked.

"She's doing so much better," Louise replied with a smile. "She tells me her new teacher is a lot nicer and doesn't play favorites like that other bitch did. The little brat that's been bullying my baby is apparently having a hard time because she's actually being held accountable for her behavior."

"That's a damn shame," said Trina.

"I bet her mother thinks she can do no wrong."

"Of course she does. Her grandma, too. Her grandma was actually my high school teacher, and she was a bitch, too. It's clear where she gets it from." Louise felt her blood boil at the memory of her last encounter with Ms. Harlowe and Mrs. Everett. Hearing her daughter's former teacher refer to her as an abomination filled her with a rage she couldn't explain. While she was no stranger to prejudice due to her heritage, she tried her best to shield her daughter from such ignorant people.

"I still can't believe you sent crows after her, though," Rachelle added.

"It got the message across. Don't fuck with me or mine."

"Amen!" Sarai exclaimed as she high-fived her cousin. "By the way, has your mom found out anything else about who attacked Anthony?" Rachelle asked.

"Unfortunately, no," Louise replied. "The police don't know anything either since there were no fingerprints or anything at the scene. All we know is what Anthony and his mother told us. If there is another witch behind this, they covered their tracks very well."

"Hmm. Well, whoever, or whatever it is, I hope someone gets to the bottom of it soon," Rachelle replied. Suddenly, the doorbell rang. Louise went to answer the door and was greeted by Octavia. After exchanging pleasantries, Louise led her into the house.

"Look who's here!" she said. "So, you already met Rachelle, Kiana, and Sarai. But you haven't met our other friends. Khalil, Trina, Simone, Alexis, this is Octavia Baker." Octavia smiled and greeted the women, and they greeted her with a hug.

"Alexis is my cousin, by the way," Rachelle said with a smile. Octavia nodded and turned to Trina.

"Hey, I think I saw you on the cover of *Vogue*!" she exclaimed. Trina beamed.

"Yep, that was me," she said.

"That's so awesome. I can't believe Nick knows so many successful people," Octavia replied. She looked around Louise's spacious home, admiring the elegant vintage decor.

"Make yourself at home," Louise said, offering her new guest a cookie and a plate of pizza rolls. "I also have some jerk chicken on the stove if you want some."

"Shit, I'll have some," Kiana said, making her way to the kitchen to make herself and Sarai a plate.

"So, Octavia, do you watch anime?" Louise asked.

"Oh definitely," Octavia replied enthusiastically.

"Good, because we're about to watch some tonight," Louise said. "So, what genres do you like? Shoujo? Slice of Life? Comedy? Magical Girl?"

"All of the above," Octavia said, and the other women giggled. "I also like a bit of horror."

"I guess we can watch the *Junji Ito Collection*," Sarai said, and they all gathered on the couch as Louise turned on the Crunchyroll app on the television. The women spent the evening binge-watching anime while having their fill of pizza, cookies, and Khalil's delicious cupcakes. As she spent time with her new acquaintances, Octavia began to feel at ease. Normally, she would be anxious when meeting new people, but she felt like she knew these girls for years. They all seemed genuinely interested in getting to know her, and they had so much in common.

"So, Trina, what's New York like?" she asked as they were watching an episode of *Ouran High School Host Club*.

"Expensive," Trina replied, and they all laughed. "But seriously, though, I really like it. Before I started my modeling career, I had never been outside of Michigan. To be fair, though, traveling is the last thing on your mind when you're trying to survive on the streets."

"You lived on the streets?"

"Yep. When I started to transition, my so-called mother threw me out with nothing but the clothes on my back. She practically left me for dead. If it wasn't for Lou, I probably wouldn't be here." Trina then proceeded to tell Octavia how Louise saved her from certain death, opening her home to her. "Nick also helped me get started modeling. He did my very first shoot."

"Really?"

"Yep. He, as well as Louise, Sarai, and Rachelle all showed me the love that I should have been getting from my own family."

"W-Wow," Octavia said.
"I'm so sorry you went through that."

"Don't be," Trina said. "That's all behind me. I'm much happier now. I don't need Esther. Blood doesn't always make you family."

"That's what my mom always used to tell me," Octavia replied. "She adopted me when I was a baby, but she never made me feel like I wasn't her child."

"What happened to your birth parents, if you don't mind me asking?" Kiana asked.

"I don't know, unfortunately. It was a closed adoption. The only thing I know about them is that my birth mother was White, and my birth father was Black."

"Damn," Kiana said. "I'm sorry to hear that. I don't know who my dad is, either. He took off after he knocked up my mom, and she hadn't heard from him since."

"Do you have a good relationship with your mom?" Octavia asked.

"We don't have a relationship at all. When I came out as a lesbian, she went ballistic and kicked me out. We haven't spoken since I was fifteen. After she kicked me out, my aunt took me in and adopted me after my donor signed her rights away. Unfortunately, she died of a heart attack two years ago, so she didn't get to see me get married."

"I'm sorry."

"Don't be," Kiana said, taking Sarai's hand in hers. "My wife is my family, and that's all I need." Sarai smiled and gave her a peck on the lips.

"How long have you two been married?"

"It'll be a year on Halloween," Sarai said.

"You guys got married on Halloween?"

"Sure did," Kiana said. "It wasn't anything huge. We got married at the courthouse, with Rachelle, Nick, Louise, and Sarai's dad as witnesses. After the wedding, we celebrated at Youmacon."

"What's Youmacon?" Octavia asked. "Only one of the biggest anime and gaming conventions in Michigan," Rachelle said. "It's a lot of fun. I actually met Nick there."

"You should also cosplay if you go," Louise added.

"Sounds fun. I'll definitely check it out," Octavia said. "When is it?"

"It's in November," Sarai said. Octavia nodded, and the friends continued their anime binge. Their fun lasted well into the wee hours of the night, with them all falling asleep in the middle of the living room. However, Octavia had trouble sleeping. Her earlier conversation with Kiana brought up a lot of unanswered questions. While she loved her mother and was grateful to her for raising her, she still wanted to know where she came from. Like a lot of adoptees, she felt as if there was a missing piece to the puzzle of her identity. *Maybe I can take one of those DNA tests to trace my family tree,* she thought as she stared up at the ceiling. *What if my biological parents had other children? There's nothing wrong with wanting to know...right?*

Chapter 8

*I*t was three in the afternoon when Rachelle and Nick arrived at Veronica's home with their daughters. The purpose of their visit was to discuss plans for their upcoming wedding. Rachelle was nervous because she had never planned a wedding before and had no idea what to do. Her aunt had taken it upon herself to hire a wedding planner to make the experience as stress-free as possible, which Rachelle greatly appreciated. After announcing their arrival to Francis, Veronica's butler, the couple was led to the parlor where Veronica was seated with Sharon and Joanna. Also seated with them was a woman whom Rachelle assumed was the wedding planner.

"Hey, baby," Joanna said as she hugged and kissed her only grandchild. She then greeted Nick and the twins the same way. Selena and Solana were then taken to the playroom so the adults could talk without distractions. "Rachelle, this is Amina Agarwal-Russell," Veronica began, gesturing to the Indian woman, who smiled. "She planned my last two weddings, so I hired her to help you with yours."

"It's a pleasure to meet you, Rachelle," Amina said as she shook Rachelle's hand. "Your aunt has told me so much about you." She then shook Nick's hand. As they shook hands, Nick couldn't help but notice the tattoo on Amina's left wrist.

"Hey, is that the *Aum* symbol?" he asked.

"It sure is," Amina replied, smiling.
"I assume you know what it means?"

"Doesn't it represent the essence of supreme consciousness and the universe?"

"Exactly," Amina replied, happy to meet someone who actually knew the meaning of her tattoo. She would often encounter non-Hindus, especially white girls, with Hindu symbols tattooed on their bodies, particularly below the waist, which was considered very offensive in Hinduism. "I'm sorry if I sound excited. You have no idea how often my culture and religion are appropriated."

"Trust us, we know," Nick said as he and Rachelle sat down. "We have to deal with the same thing in our cultures."

"Do people call you 'sensitive' or accuse you of 'pulling the race card' when you call it out? Or get told, 'It's not that deep?'"

"Yep," Rachelle and Nick replied in unison.

"I have to deal with it all the time on TikTok. It's exhausting!" Amina replied.

"Who are you tellin'?" Rachelle added, and Amina shook her head.

"So, Veronica tells me that you two want to have your wedding next summer. Do you have a specific date?"

"We were thinking July or August," Nick said. Amina nodded and wrote his response in her notebook.

"Do you have a specific theme in mind?" asked Amina.

"Well, we were thinking of a vintage theme," Rachelle said. "We also want to combine both our families' cultures."

"Interesting," Amina replied, writing in her notebook. "If you don't mind me asking, what are your cultural backgrounds?"

"Well, Nick's family is Cuban and Puerto Rican. My mother's family is Black American, and my dad's side is of Jamaican and Black American descent."

"Hmm, I think we can definitely come up with something," Amina said. "Do you have a color scheme?"

"Pink and gold," Rachelle replied, and Nick nodded in agreement.

"Perfect. Now, how many are in your bridal party?" Rachelle and Nick thought for a moment.

"Well, I have about nine bridesmaids, and Nick has seven groomsmen. There were nine groomsmen, but we had a falling out with two friends of ours," Rachelle said. "Our daughters will be our flower girls, along with my friend's daughter. My little cousin will be our ring bearer."

"Sounds good," Amina said as she wrote everything down. She then pulled out a large black binder from her bag and set it on the coffee table, opening it. "So, here is a list of vendors I have compiled for you, according to your budget..." As Amina went over everything in her binder, Rachelle began to feel less overwhelmed about wedding planning. She knew her aunt had made the right call by hiring Amina, who was more than happy to assist the happy couple in making their wedding a day to remember. "There is one more thing: will your wedding be child-free or not?"

"Uh..." Rachelle and Nick replied in unison, looking at each other. While they wanted both their families there, they knew that small children could become restless and get into anything and everything. Rachelle's mind went back to the time she had attended the wedding of a college classmate a few years prior. She cringed at the memory of the bride's nephew knocking over the very elaborate, and very expensive, ice sculpture. She and Nick looked over at Veronica, unsure of what to say.

"It's completely up to you," Veronica said, smiling. "If it'll give you some peace of mind, I can hire babysitters. I don't mind."

"Then I guess we will have children there," Rachelle said.

"Excellent!" Amina replied, getting up from the sofa. "I'm going to call The Roostertail right away to see if they have any dates available for July or August. Once you two have decided on a date, I'll call the vendors."

"Thank you so much for your help," Rachelle said. After shaking hands once more, Amina left the house.

"By the way, sweetheart, I have something for you," Joanna said. "Nick, honey, can you give us a moment?" Nick nodded and went to the playroom to check on the twins. Veronica then stepped out of the room and returned a few minutes later with a large box. She set it on the table and opened it, pulling out a beautiful ivory silk gown. It appeared to have been made in the 1940s, with a fitted bodice and sweetheart neckline. The gown was accompanied by a delicate lace veil. Rachelle recognized the gown immediately, for it had belonged to Joanna, who received it from her mother, Phyllis, who had passed away when Rachelle was only three years old. She had seen photos of her great-grandparents' and Joanna's weddings, and would often comment on how Phyllis and Joanna looked like princesses in the gown.

"Grandma..." she began, staring at the dress in awe. "You're giving me your mother's gown?"

"That's right," Joanna said, smiling at her only grandchild. "I know how much you like vintage clothing, so I thought a vintage wedding dress would be perfect for you. The veil is yours, too. Consider them your 'Something Old.'"

"Also, since you mentioned that pink and gold are the colors for your wedding, we can have the dress and veil dyed pink," Sharon added. Rachelle looked at Joanna.

"Grandma, are you okay with me dyeing it?"

"The dress is yours now, honey. You can do whatever you want with it," Joanna replied.

"Grandma, I love it! Thank you." Rachelle and Joanna embraced each other in a big hug.

"You're going to be so beautiful, baby," Joanna said, her eyes brimming with tears. "And I am so happy that you found someone who loves you in the way that you deserve. I can be happy knowing that you will never have to suffer like I had." Rachelle looked at her grandmother and could see the sadness in her eyes. She knew that her grandmother's first marriage to her late grandfather, Theodore, had been unhappy, and that was putting it lightly.

When Joanna was nineteen years old and living in Tennessee, she met and fell in love with Theodore Williams, a man five years her senior. Theodore, known to his friends and family as "Teddy," said and did all the right things to woo the naive teenager. Within months of their courtship, Joanna became pregnant with their first child, Veronica. Against her parents' wishes, she married Teddy at City Hall when she was three months pregnant. However, after Veronica was born, Teddy's true colors began to show. While he was a hard worker and a good provider, he was a womanizer who was no stranger to the bars. Joanna, who was deeply in love with her husband, at first ignored the whispers and gossip about his dalliances with other women. However, once she caught him in the act, she could no longer turn a blind eye. Teddy, ever the charmer, begged and pleaded for Joanna's forgiveness, swearing to never cheat on her again. And Joanna forgave him, only for Teddy to go out and do it again. Even the birth of their second child, Sharon, was not enough to make Teddy settle down. Still, Joanna was determined to make it work. Not only did she want her daughters to have both parents in the home, she didn't want to hear her parents say, "I told you so." However, when Teddy started to become violent due to his drinking, Joanna decided that she had enough. In the dead of night, when Teddy was passed out drunk, Joanna packed whatever valuables she could find, and left the house with her young daughters, only wearing the clothes on their backs. She was able to purchase a bus ticket to Detroit, where her aunt, Bernice, lived. Once she was safely away from Teddy, she filed for divorce. However, the divorce was never finalized, due to Teddy's death in a drunken brawl at a pool hall. Finally, free, Joanna was able to build a new life for herself and her children. She was also able to find love again when she married her second husband, Jacob Bivens, five years later. Sadly, Jacob died ten years later from throat cancer.

"I promise I will cherish this dress as long as I live," Rachelle said.

"I know you will," Joanna said, hugging Rachelle once more. When they heard footsteps, Rachelle put the gown and veil back into the box. Nick entered the room with the twins in his arms.

"Hey, babe, you ready?" he asked. Rachelle nodded and got up from the couch. Nick set the girls down, and they ran to give hugs to Joanna, Veronica, and Sharon.

"Nick, you take care of my baby, ya hear?" Joanna said.

"Always," Nick replied, giving Joanna a hug. After giving her mother and aunt another hug, she and Nick left with their daughters.

"So, what did your grandma give you?" Nick asked as he drove.

"She gave me her old wedding dress."

"That was cool of her."

"Yeah. She even said I can dye it to match the theme of the wedding. You can't see it until the ceremony, though."

"Yeah, I know," Nick replied. "But I can't wait to see it on you... and off you." Rachelle playfully hit his arm. "Nasty ass."

"You know you like it," Nick said with a smirk. Rachelle stuck out her tongue at him and continued to look out the window. Sometimes, she wondered how she had become so lucky.

"So what time will you be back home?" Rachelle asked as she dressed the girls. She was taking them to join her mother for brunch, which was a monthly ritual for them. Nick was getting ready to meet up with Octavia, so they could catch up. "I should be back before 4," Nick replied as he kneeled down to his daughters' level. "Promise to be good girls for your *mamí* and *abuelita*?"

"Yeah," Selena and Solana answered in unison, giving their father a toothy grin.

"That's my girls," Nick replied, kissing their cheeks. He then stood up and gave Rachelle a peck on the lips. "Have fun at brunch."

"You have fun, too," Rachelle replied. She then took the girls to the car and strapped them into their car seats. Once they were securely fastened, she got into the vehicle and drove off. Nick then got into his car and drove to the coffee shop where Octavia was waiting.

"Nicky! You made it!" she exclaimed as Nick approached her table. Her red hair was styled in a messy bun, and she wore no makeup except for lip gloss. She was dressed in a simple pair of dark jeans and a Slipknot T-shirt. After giving her a hug, he sat down across from her. "It's great seeing you again."

"It's great seeing you, too," Nick replied with a smile, which made Octavia's heart skip a beat.

"How's Rachelle?"

"She's great. She took the girls to meet her mom for brunch."

"Sounds nice," Octavia replied, and Nick could detect a hint of sadness in her voice. "I'm sorry. I didn't mean to be insensitive." Before Octavia could respond, her name was called by the barista. She got up to go to the counter and returned with two mocha frappes.

"I hope you didn't mind me ordering for you," she said as she handed

Nick a frappe.

"No, not at all," Nick replied.
"Again, I'm sorry."

"You don't have to apologize. While I do still get sad about Mom at times, you don't have to walk on eggshells around me." Nick nodded in understanding, taking a sip of his frappe.

"So, how did you enjoy Louise's sleepover? Rachelle told me she invited you."

"I had fun," Octavia replied.

"So what did you guys do?" Nick asked.

"We sat around eating pizza and watching anime." Nick chuckled.
"Yeah, that sounds about right."

"I did feel a bit intimidated, though," Octavia said.

"Intimidated? Why?"

"I don't know if 'intimidated' is the right word, but you are engaged to, and are friends with, successful women. Rachelle and Louise have their own businesses, and they have a friend who's a runway model. Not to mention that Rachelle's best friend is my favorite author. And Louise being a burlesque performer? I don't have even half the confidence to do what she does. I guess I'm... in awe of them?"

"That makes sense," Nick replied, taking another sip. He understood where Octavia was coming from. Rachelle and her friends were powerful in every sense of the word, and that could be intimidating for some people. In fact, he was intimidated when he first met Louise and shot with her for the first time. She gave off such a powerful aura, and her energy was intoxicating. He also had the same feeling when he laid eyes on Rachelle. "They are pretty amazing. I'm glad you're getting along with them."

"They also mentioned something called Youmacon and said I should go," Octavia said.

"Oh yeah, Youmacon is pretty fun. There's also a cosplay beach party in August."

"There's nerdy beach parties, too?" Octavia asked, astonished. "Where was all this stuff when we were kids?"

"I know, right?" Nick took another sip. "So, what was Washington like?"

"It was nice, I guess. I didn't have a lot of friends while I was there, but I didn't mind since I had Kendra and Mom."

"Did you date at all?"

"Meh, not really," Octavia replied with a shrug. "I've been on dates and had casual hookups, but nothing serious. I guess I'm still looking for the right person."

"That's understandable," Nick said, nodding. "I was the same way before I met Rachelle. Now, I can't see myself with anyone else." Octavia felt a sting in her heart when he said that. No matter how hard she tried, she could never shake the feelings she had for Nick, which had developed over the course of their friendship. However, she didn't want to scare him off by professing her love for him. *I'll tell him when the time is right*, she thought.

"It sounds like you're really happy together," she said, forcing a smile.

"We are," Nick replied.
"I'm sure you'll find someone who makes you just as happy."

"Maybe," Octavia said. The two friends continued to chat, making up for lost time. Octavia stared at Nick in awe as he spoke. She admired how mature he had become, not just in looks, but in mindset as well. He was ambitious, creative, and insightful, while still taking joy in his nerdy hobbies and interests. She loved the way his eyes lit up when he talked about his family, especially his daughters. If it were possible, Octavia fell even more in love with Nick.

"We should definitely hang out again," Nick said as they walked out of the coffee shop. They had been there for almost three hours, and it was time for them to part ways.

"Definitely," Octavia said.

"I'm sure Rachelle wouldn't mind inviting you over for dinner." Octavia gave a small smile, masking her annoyance at the mention of Rachelle's name.

"That sounds great. Just let me know when," she said as they gave each other a hug and went to their separate vehicles. As Octavia was driving home, all she could think about was Nick and the time they spent together. Her heart was full knowing that her childhood friend was back in her life, and she had no intention of leaving him again. She found herself wondering what it would be like to be with Nick. She knew that she shouldn't have these thoughts because Nick was taken, but the heart wants what the heart wants. And her heart wanted Nick.

Chapter 9

"You don't think we'll run into Mike and Jay here, do you?" Kiana asked as she and the others stepped off the SMART Shuttle. They had arrived in downtown Ferndale, which was celebrating its annual Pride event. "I don't know, and even if we do, who gives a fuck?" Louise replied as they made their way through the crowd. "If our spell hit its target, and I'm confident it did, Jay probably won't even look in our direction."

"Exactly," Sarai added. "Besides, I'm here to have fun, not worry about a couple of fake-ass losers."

"Amen," Rachelle said, and the group made their way to the Otaku Detroit booth, which was run by their friends, Terry and Angelo. Otaku Detroit was a small shop in Madison Heights that sold various anime merchandise, as well as items from local artists. As the gang approached the booth, they were greeted with cheerful waves.

"Hey, what's up?" Terry said.

"Nothing much. We just got here," Louise replied as she began browsing the displays of anime figures. "How have you been?"

"We've been pretty good," Angelo replied. "We've been pretty busy, though."

"I hear that," Louise said.

"Mommy, can I have that one?" Artemis asked, pointing to a Todoroki figure. Louise picked up the box and handed it to Artemis. "Go take it to the counter so Terry can ring you up," Louise replied with a smile, handing Artemis a fifty-dollar bill. After happily thanking her mother, Artemis skipped to the counter with the box.

"So, Sarai, are you going to write another *Bloodlust* book?" Angelo asked, taking a bite of a Pocky stick. Before Sarai could respond, they were interrupted by a loud snort.

"You actually want to read more of that woke garbage?" a wheezy voice sneered. Sarai and her friends turned around and were greeted by the sight of a portly white male, who appeared to be in his late thirties. He was red due to the heat, and the front of his dirty, wrinkled *DragonBall* t-shirt was drenched with sweat. The front of his jeans was stained with a dried-up white substance that looked suspiciously like semen. His greasy, mousy brown hair was matted and adorned by a black trilby hat, and he sported a patchy beard that was stained with Cheeto dust. The stench of body odor, stale Cheetos, and old cheese invaded the nostrils of those in his proximity. The gang realized, to their horror and annoyance, that they were face to face with a neckbeard.

"Woke garbage?" Sarai repeated. "What exactly about my books is 'woke'?" Sarai knew that the term 'woke' was code for anything centering marginalized groups, but she wanted to see how deep a hole this neckbeard would dig for himself. "I mean, everything," Neckbeard replied. "Black vampires? Everyone knows that vampires can't be Black."

"Says who? You?" Louise said. Neckbeard scoffed.

"It's scientifically impossible. Vampires have pale skin because they lose their melanin when they turn," he countered. "Of course, I don't expect a *female* like you to understand. I'm sick of the media pushing their liberal agenda on us." Sarai suddenly burst out laughing. *Not this troglodyte using science to justify his racism!* she thought. She was no stranger to people like this. She encountered them online regularly in nerd spaces. She had received racist comments on her cosplays, in addition to the fatphobic remarks. However, to see someone use a scientific argument in reference to mythological beings was downright comical! She laughed for a good few minutes before stopping to catch her breath.

"Do you know how fucking goofy you sound right now?" she said.

"Why? Because I'm right?" the neckbeard replied smugly. "This is why *females* shouldn't write books. They have no substance. I mean, look at your trash series. You made the main character a Black *female*. A Black main character isn't relatable. It's clear you wrote your books to pander to liberal snowflakes. And you made her the leader of her clan? That's not attractive. *Females* don't belong in leadership roles. Their duties are to cook, clean, bear children to continue the bloodline, and submit to their men." *Oh my fucking god*, Sarai thought. It was obvious that Neckbeard failed history class. She could only stare at him with a deadpan expression.

"Is this nigga for real?" Ivy, Sarai's mother, asked.

"He is, Mom. He's deadass serious," Sarai replied in her head.

"That's a damn shame. He needs to wash his behind instead of worrying about what he thinks women should be doing," Faith cut in.

"Mmmhmm," Ivy said.

"The characters aren't relatable to you because you're not even the target audience," Rachelle cut in. "The books weren't made for you, and frankly, nobody asked for your input. It's her story, her universe, her rules. Don't like it? Write your own damn book."

"Furthermore, stories about Black vampires have been written before," Louise added. "*The Black Vampyre: A Legend of St. Domingo? The Blood of the Vampire?* Both of those stories were written in the nineteenth century. If you actually did your research, you would have known that. Also, the fact that you're getting so bent out of shape over fictional beings is frankly pathetic. About as pathetic as that raggedy-ass beard." Neckbeard shot Louise a death glare, clearly incensed that a woman dared to call him pathetic and insult his precious beard.

"For real," Terry said.

"If you have such a problem with the 'liberal agenda,' why are you at a Pride event?"

"Thank you!" Angelo exclaimed, throwing his hands up.

"I came here to show the *females* the errors of their ways," Neckbeard said with a wheezy chuckle.

"Excuse me?" Louise replied.

"The only reason that these *females* think they're 'gay' is because they haven't been with a real alpha male."

"What the fuck," Wilfred and Nick muttered under their breaths, pinching the bridges of their noses in annoyance. They had encountered their fair share of men with this mindset at various points in their lives. Nick actually had to cut off a friend he had known since high school because he refused to evolve from this way of thinking, as well as for making disgusting remarks about Rachelle's line of work and their daughters.

"I mean, think about it. When these *females* get together, they're denying men their right to companionship and intimacy."

"Be fucking for real," Kiana said. "Women owe you jack shit, you degenerate! You're not entitled to us just because you're a man."

"You *females* are so emotional," Neckbeard replied with a smug look. "I never said you owe me anything. I'm just saying you never even bother to give us a chance. Maybe if you weren't messing with these Chads and beta males, you wouldn't be gay."

"First of all, I'm not gay because of a so-called 'beta male,'" Kiana said, eyeing Neckbeard with contempt and disgust. "I'm gay because I've always preferred women."

"Ha! You just never met a guy like me yet, m'lady," Neckbeard said, tipping his hat. "I usually wouldn't consider Black girls as a first choice, but I'm willing to give it a try." He then winked at Kiana.

"Sir, if any woman, gay or straight, met you, they would run in the other direction," Rachelle cut in, looking him up and down, holding her hand over her nose. His repulsive odor was making her nauseous. "Please go away."

"You should also take a bath," Artemis added, and the others had to keep from laughing.

"Well, fuck you!" Neckbeard spat.
"I wasn't going to buy anything from you anyway!"

"Then get the fuck on," Louise shot back. The neckbeard shot her a death glare before stomping away from the booth. Giggling, Artemis waved her hand, causing Neckbeard to trip, which resulted in him falling into a nearby booth. He was then escorted from the event, to the applause of the attendees.

"I can't stand fucking neckbeards," Rachelle said, uncovering her nose. "They're so smug for no damn reason."

"They also don't know how to read the room," Sarai added.

"And they stink," Artemis said, making everyone laugh.

"I'm sure he's going to complain on social media about how 'females can't handle his superior pheromones and would rather bang Chads,'" Kiana added. The others murmured in agreement.

"Anyway, let's go check out the other booths," Louise said. They bid Terry and Angelo goodbye and went to check out the other vendors. Putting their encounter with Neckbeard behind them, they continued to enjoy themselves. The energy was lively and positive, and everyone seemed to enjoy the vibe. Also, there was no chance of the attendees encountering any religious protesters, since Ferndale was practically the capital for Michigan's queer community.

"I'm kinda hungry. Y'all want some pizza?" Trina asked. The others answered in the affirmative, and the group made their way to Hungry Howie's. After getting their food, they sat at a nearby table. Suddenly, they were approached by two young women, who were accompanied by a young man. One woman was of slim build, with light brown skin and curly hair dyed electric blue. She was dressed in a black maxi dress with silver sandals and silver hoop earrings. She also wore glasses embellished with tiny pieces of rose quartz on the rims. The young woman next to her was a head shorter and thick, with dark brown skin and long green locs. She wore black shorts, a red crop top, and gold sandals. She also wore gold hoop earrings. The young man with them was of average height and slender, with fair skin and short brown hair. He wore a blue t-shirt and jeans and had the transgender flag draped over his shoulder.

"Hey, are you Trina Michaels?" the blue-haired woman asked. Trina turned to her and smiled.

"Yes, I am," she replied. The others squealed with excitement.

"I absolutely love your photos!" the blue-haired woman exclaimed. "I follow you on social media, and you are one of the prettiest models I've ever seen."

"Aww, thank you," Trina said, blushing.

"I've also read the interview you did with *Out Magazine*, where you talked about your journey with transitioning," the young man cut in. "You're an inspiration to a lot of us in the trans community." Trina was touched by the young man's words. No one had ever called her an inspiration before.

"W-Well, thank you for that. It really means a lot." The blue-haired woman then turned to Sarai.

"I also want you to know that I really love your books," she said. "I also bought a copy of your memoir. I am so sorry you and your sister had to go through that. I'm glad your stepmom got what she deserved, though."

"Thank you," Sarai replied.
"That means a lot, truly."

"Wait," the green-haired woman said, staring at Louise. "I remember you. You were at that New Year's party a few years back. The one that got raided?"

"Yeah, I remember," Louise said. The woman stepped closer to the table so they were out of earshot. "You more than likely don't know me, but I was one of the girls you saved that night. I just want to thank you."

"What's your name, hun?" Louise asked.

"Marni," the woman replied. She then gestured to her friends. "This is my girlfriend, Alia, and our friend, Rae."

"Well, nice to meet you three," Louise said, smiling. "And Marni, I'm so sorry you had to go through that. I'm glad to see that you're out of that situation."

"Trust me, I am, too," Marni said.
"If it wasn't for you, I don't know if I would even be here."

"The important thing is that you're safe," Louise said. Marni smiled at her.

"I know. I'm also glad that I have my partner and friends' support." Alia kissed her cheek. "Um, is it okay if I hug you?"

"Of course," Louise replied as she stood up. She then embraced Marni in a warm hug. Her heart broke for the young woman, and her insides bubbled with anger at Vincent and Cassandra for the trauma they had inflicted on so many vulnerable people. A young girl had lost her life at the tender age of fifteen because of them. She sincerely hoped that their rotten spirits knew no peace. "Anyway, we just wanted to say hi," Marni said, pulling away. "I hope we didn't disturb you."

"Not at all," Louise said, smiling. The trio said goodbye and disappeared into the crowd.

"They seemed nice," Rachelle said as she took a bite of her pizza.

"Yeah," Sarai said.
"I'm glad that we're inspiring people."

"Hey, look who's here," Kiana said in a low voice. The group turned to see Mike at a booth with Jay, browsing sex toys. However, the couple was not alone. Next to them was none other than Nikki Jacobs, a former friend of

Rachelle, Sarai, and Louise. Their friendship had deteriorated due to Nikki's treacherous nature. Nikki was envious of Rachelle and Louise's success as models and the fact that they came from privileged families. She had also slept with Lamar behind Rachelle's back and dated him until his brutal murder.

"Hmph. Three snake-ass bitches together," Louise said disdainfully. "Not surprised."

"I just find it funny how they're hanging with each other when Mike and Jay used to talk mad shit about her," Sarai said.

"Well, what they eat doesn't make me shit," Louise replied. "They can have each other." After they had their fill of pizza, they made their way back into the crowd, passing their ex-friends.

"Bitch," Nikki muttered under her breath. Louise immediately stopped and turned to face her nemesis.

"Excuse me?" she demanded, staring Nikki down.

"You heard me," Nikki spat back, putting her hand on her hip. *See, this bitch still hasn't learned not to fuck with me*, Louise thought.

"Well, it takes one to know one," Rachelle quipped.

"That's real mature," Nikki retorted, rolling her eyes. Then, Mike stepped forward. Jay said nothing, glaring at the group.

"Hey, I don't know what you did to Jay, but I really don't appreciate it," Mike said.

"Whatever do you mean?" Louise replied, resisting the urge to smirk.

"Don't play innocent, Louise!" Mike countered. "You hexed him, didn't you? He lost his job and totaled his car because of you!"

"What makes you think I had anything to do with that? Because I'm a witch, you assume that anything bad that happens in your life is my fault?" Louise knew that her spell had worked because she had done divination a month after casting it. However, she didn't anticipate it working this well.

"Jay lost his job literally a week after he made that post, and he crashed his car a few days after that! Admit it! You put a hex on him!"

"I didn't hex Jason. We simply returned the same energy your man sent to us. If anything, he hexed himself," Louise replied in a snide tone.

"We?"

"Yes, we," Sarai said. "Maybe his mouth shouldn't be writing checks that his ass can't cash."

"You realize this affects me, too, right?" Mike countered, hurt that his former friends would do this. "Since he no longer has a job, I've been picking up the slack and paying all the bills. That's really fucked up."

"No, what's fucked up is how you practically spit in our faces for your piece-of-shit boyfriend!" Louise spat. "You were our friends, and we confided in you about the traumas we went through. We trusted you. How do you repay us? By throwing it in our faces! You threw away a seven-year friendship for dick! You don't get to play victim in this, because both of you were wrong as hell! Jason got what he deserved. You were just collateral damage." Nikki sucked her teeth.

"You must think you're hot shit, don't you?" she spat. "You think that because you got magical powers, that you're all that." Louise rolled her eyes. *I see you're still a hating-ass bitch*, she thought.

"I don't have to think I'm anything, sweetheart. I know I'm the shit."

"Don't be mad at us just because you hate yourself," Trina added. Nikki looked her up and down.

"I do love myself, actually, unlike some people," she said. "At least I'm not out here cosplaying as a woman." Louise and Sarai advanced towards Nikki but were held back by Wilfred and Kiana.

113

"So, y'all are gay, but are okay with hanging with a transphobe?" Rachelle asked incredulously, as she looked at Mike and Jay with contempt.

"Well, she shouldn't have come for Nikki," Jay replied.

"God, y'all are so fucking weak," Louise said.

"I'm more of a woman than you'll ever be, honey," Trina retorted, flipping her long, curly hair. Three years ago, transphobic remarks like Nikki's would have cut her deep. Now, she was strong and confident within herself, so Nikki's bullshit didn't affect her. Women like Nikki were a dime a dozen: insecure, jealous, and spiteful. "If you loved yourself like you claim you do, then you wouldn't feel the need to put down other people. A blind man can see how unhappy you are with yourself. It's actually quite sad." *Yasss, girl! Read her ass for filth!* Louise thought to herself.

"Please, ain't nobody jealous of y'all," Nikki said, waving Trina off. Louise smirked as she watched Nikki's aura turn a sickly green.

"Whatever helps you sleep at night, sweetheart," Rachelle said as the group turned to leave.

"So, you're not gonna take off this bullshit spell you put on me?" Jay demanded. Louise scoffed.

"Nope," she said. "If you want to get rid of it so damn badly, then maybe try actually being a good person. The reason why your life has gone to shit is because of your actions." She then took Artemis' hand and began walking away. However, Nikki was not done.

"Hey, Nick, when you get tired of Rachelle's stuck-up ass, feel free to hit me up," she said, giving Nick a flirtatious look, making his skin crawl. "I know her pussy must be shot out after having two kids." Rachelle nearly lunged at Nikki but Nick held Rachelle back, giving Nikki a look of disgust. "I wouldn't fuck you if you were the last *puta* on Earth," he spat. "Keep my fiancée's name out of your mouth."

"And for your information, my pussy isn't 'shot out' from having kids. Pick up a biology book sometime, you goofy-ass bitch," Rachelle added as she and Nick began to walk away. Incensed, Nikki hurled her tropical smoothie at Rachelle's head. However, before the drink could hit its intended target, Rachelle, without turning around, stopped the cup in its tracks and hurled it back at Nikki. The cup hit Nikki square in the face, drenching her and the front of her halter top with pineapple, banana, and mango. Then, with a wave of Rachelle's hand, Nikki was blown backward, crashing into the display of various sex toys, to the astonishment of Mike and Jay, as well as the other attendees. After being chewed out by the vendor, which led to Nikki growing belligerent, the trio was asked to leave. Amused by this turn of events, Rachelle and her friends went about their business. The rest of the day was uneventful. Aside from their encounters with Neckbeard and their former friends, they ultimately had a good time and even made some new friends in the process while catching up with old ones. Soon, it was nightfall, and the group took a shuttle back to the middle school, where their vehicles were parked.

"Man, I'm beat," Kiana said, yawning.
"I had fun, though."

"Same," Rachelle replied as she and Nick made their way to their car. "By the way, my store is having a sale next weekend."

"Bet," Sarai said.
"I need some new stuff for my hair."

"Y'all, don't forget about my Glamour Magic workshop next month!" Louise shouted from her car. "We'll be there," Rachelle replied from her window. After bidding each other farewell, the friends went their separate ways.

"Do you think we should tell Tay about the workshop?" Nick asked. "She did mention being interested in magic when we talked on Messenger today."

"I think it'll be a good idea," Rachelle replied.

"Cool. I'll tell her about it when we get home." On the drive home, Nick's mind went back to their encounter with Nikki and her attempts to make a pass at him. "I still can't believe she said that bullshit."

"I'm not surprised, honestly," Rachelle said, looking out the window. "She's a trifling-ass bitch and hates to see other people happy. She's gonna end up messing with the wrong one, and she's gonna get fucked up."

"She's a sad and pathetic person," Nick said. "Don't even sweat her. She only wants to get under your skin because she wishes she was half the woman you are." Rachelle smiled at him.

"I'm not worried about her, or Mike and Jay, for that matter," she replied. "They can rot together for all I care." Nick simply nodded in agreement and continued to drive. Since the twins were spending the weekend with Nick's parents, the couple went straight home and retired to bed.

Chapter 10

*I*t was a hot, humid afternoon when Sarai pulled up in front of her aunts' home. It was the week of her twenty-eighth birthday, and she had decided to visit her aunts and grandmother before spending the weekend with Kiana and their friends. Although Sarai had only become acquainted with her maternal relatives five years ago, they had developed a strong, loving bond, and she visited them as often as she could. "Is that my baby?" Rose exclaimed as she stepped onto the porch while Sarai approached.

"Hey, Auntie!" Sarai replied as they hugged.
"How are you?"

"I can't complain. Come on, let's get out of this heat," Rose replied, leading Sarai into the house. She felt instant relief as the coolness of the air conditioning hit her face. "Look who's here, Mama." They entered the living room, where Natalie sat in her wheelchair, watching *Days of Our Lives*. "Hey, Grandma," Sarai said as she placed her purse on the coffee table and gave Natalie a hug and a kiss on the cheek.

"How's my grandbaby?" Natalie asked, letting go of Sarai.

"I'm good," Sarai replied, smiling.
"What about you?"

"I'm hanging in there, baby," Natalie replied.
"Haven't been feeling too good, though."

"Is everything okay?"

"I'm sure it's nothing. Just feeling under the weather. So, how's that wife of yours?"

"She's good," Sarai replied. "She had to catch up on some work today, though. That's why she didn't come with me." Rose and Violet took their seats on the couch, on opposite sides of Sarai.

"So, we read your new book," Rose said.
"We are so proud of you, honey."

"We really are," Violet added, kissing Sarai on the cheek. "You followed your dream and achieved it, even with so many obstacles stacked against you. Your mama would be so proud of you."

"I know she is," Sarai said, smiling as the spirits of Ivy and Faith appeared in the living room, smiling back at her.

"How did your daddy like the book?" Natalie asked.

"He liked it, too," Sarai replied. "At first, he didn't like the idea of me airing out our family's laundry, but he understands this is a way for me to heal. He still feels kind of guilty about not protecting me and Faith more."

"Hmm," Rose said. "I hope he's still not beating himself up over that. Dwelling on 'Coulda, Woulda, Shoulda' does nobody any good. Ivy and Faith wouldn't want that for him."

"I know. I tell him that all the time. Therapy has been helping him cope better, though."

"I'm glad," Natalie said.
"How's his catering business going?"

"It's going really well. He catered six events last month. He's also going to be catering Rachelle's wedding."

"How is Rachelle doing, by the way?" Violet asked. "I know she's got her hands full with those babies." Sarai laughed.

"She's doing great, and so are my nieces. They're talking in almost full sentences now. Rachelle's business is also going pretty well."

"How's Lulu?"

"She's good. She and Will adopted a cat a couple of weeks ago."

"Really?" Rose asked.

"Yep. She got it for Mimi since she got straight A's on her report card."

"That baby is going places," Rose said as she went into the kitchen. She returned to the living room a few minutes later with a tray carrying four glasses of lavender lemonade. "She has always been so bright, just like her mama." The others murmured in agreement as they each took a glass off the tray. They continued to chat about their family and friends and the new developments in their lives. Whenever Sarai was around her aunts and grandmother, she never felt like she had to hide parts of herself. She could freely talk to them about her hobbies and interests without fear of ridicule or judgment. She could express her feelings without being dismissed as 'dramatic,' and they always gave her sound advice. Through Natalie, Rose, and Violet, Sarai was able to receive the maternal love and guidance that she had craved throughout her adolescence and early adulthood.

"So, Dad is having his folks over for dinner next month for his birthday," Sarai said.

"How do you feel about that?" Violet asked, taking a sip of her lemonade. Sarai let out a sigh.

"I don't know, to be honest," she replied. "On one hand, I feel Dad should have told them to kick rocks because they abandoned him when he needed them. On the other hand, I know it is ultimately up to him if he decides to have them in his life." Sarai felt nothing but contempt and disgust when she thought about the paternal side of her family. Like Thelma's family, they were judgmental, hypocritical, and ignorant. When Sarai had exposed Thelma for abusing her and Faith, as well as Pastor Williams for violating Faith, she was shamed by her paternal relatives for "putting family business on the internet" and "lying on a man of God." When Vernon was imprisoned for the pastor's murder, no one in his family came to visit him. They would write to him, but only to admonish him for his actions. In Sarai's eyes, they had chosen abusers over their own flesh and blood. That was unforgivable to her. However, Vernon's mother was suffering from various health issues, and he did not want her to die without attempting to repair their relationship.

"Have you talked to your daddy about it?" Rose asked.

"I have, but he thinks things will be different," Sarai replied. "I'll believe it when I see it, and even so, I'm keeping them at a distance."

"And you have every right to," Natalie said. "Just be there for your daddy in case things don't work out." Sarai simply nodded and drank from her glass.

"So, Lulu told me y'all ran into those old friends of yours at Pride," Violet said. "What were their names again?"

"Mike and Jay," Sarai said with a sigh. She hated how their friendship had ended, but she knew it would do her no good to keep toxic people in her life. "Yeah, we ran into them. Apparently, Jay lost his job and totaled his car after that Return to Sender spell we did. They had the nerve to ask us to remove it."

"Did they apologize for what they said about y'all?" Rose asked.

"Nope," Sarai replied, taking another sip.

"Hmph," Violet said. "Well, you don't need friends like that, and I am using the term 'friend' loosely here. A real friend would lift you up and bring positivity to your life, not drag you down."

"Amen," Rose added.

"I just hate that it ended so badly," Sarai said. Natalie wheeled herself closer to Sarai and took her hands in hers.

"Honey, let me tell you something that your great-grandma used to tell me: Friends come into your life for a reason, a season, or a lifetime. Look at Lulu. She came into your life to show you who you truly are, and to bring you back to us. She came into your life for a reason. Rachelle came into your life when you needed a friend, and she has been there ever since. She is a lifetime friend, and you don't get a friend like that very often. You're lucky if you get one. You have *six*. Those boys Mike and Jay? Those were seasonal friends. Fairweather friends. They have run their course. Sometimes, friendships aren't meant to last forever, and that's okay." Sarai allowed her grandmother's words to sink in. She knew that Natalie was right. Rachelle had come into her life when they were seven years old, and their bond had only grown stronger. Rachelle had been Sarai's shoulder to cry on, and had proven her loyalty time and time again. To her, Rachelle was more of a sister. She had only met Louise seven years ago, yet if it weren't for her, Sarai would have never learned of her true heritage. Kiana showed her what it felt like to be in love, and had been her rock through some of her darkest moments. In fact, Kiana was there when Sarai confronted her stepmother about what had happened to her sister. Trina had been Sarai's friend for three years, and had always been nothing short of supportive. The same was true for Nick and Wilfred. Mike and Jay were fun to hang around, yet they never really offered much in terms of emotional support. However, whenever Mike or Jay experienced hardship, she was always there. Sarai realized that her friendship with them was truly one-sided, and that hurt the most.

"Your grandma is right, baby," Violet added. "Those that are truly down for you will show you that they are down for you. They will be there for you during your sorrows, as well as your triumphs. Lulu, Rachelle, Trina, and Kiana? Those are your Ride-or-Die friends. You hold onto them, ya hear?"

"Yes, ma'am," Sarai said, and Violet smiled. The four women continued talking well into the night, looking at old photo albums and reminiscing about their younger years and the moments they shared with Sarai's mother, Ivy. It wasn't Sarai's first time hearing these stories, but she never got tired of them. It was through them that she truly got to know her mother and the kind of woman she was.

"Grandma?"

"Yes, baby?"

"Does it bother you that I don't want to have children?" Natalie looked at Sarai, bewildered.

"Of course it doesn't bother me, sweetheart," she said. "What on Earth gave you that idea?"

"I know how important it is for our family to honor our Ancestors. Isn't continuing our bloodline a part of that?"

"Sarai, listen to me," Natalie began. "Honoring those that came before us is more than continuing our lineage. It's also about being the best that you can be in this life."

"The Ancestors aren't going to abandon you for not having babies," Rose cut in. "You know why?"

"Why?"

"Because you have something that those before us didn't, and that's freedom," Rose continued. "Back in the day, women didn't have a lot of choices, especially Black women. But for you, the sky's the limit. Our Ancestors weren't even allowed to read and write, and here you are, a published, bestselling author. Your very existence is an act of resistance."

"Your auntie's right, baby," Ivy said. "Your life is yours to live, and you have to live it for you. What anyone else has to say is irrelevant."

"Besides, our bloodline is doing just fine," Violet added, making Sarai smile.

"Baby, all I want for you to do is to be happy, and you are doing a fine job at that," Natalie said, kissing Sarai on the cheek. "I love you, Sarai, and I am so proud of you."

"I love you, too, Grandma," Sarai replied, and the two embraced in a warm hug. Soon, it was late, and at her aunts' insistence, Sarai decided to stay the night. She retired to the guest room while Rose and Violet went to give Natalie a bath and prepare her for bed.

"Goodnight, Mama," Violet said, after making sure Natalie was comfortable.

"Goodnight, baby," Natalie replied, giving her daughters a sleepy smile. "Y'all sleep tight." Giving their mother one last hug, they retired to their respective bedrooms. With a smile, Natalie drifted off to sleep.

Several Hours Later

Natalie awoke to find herself in the astral plane. She was surrounded by a beautiful, lush garden, her nostrils greeted by the sweet scents of rose, lavender, and honeysuckle. Mockingbirds and sparrows sang in the distance, and above her, the moon shone brightly in the night sky. In the middle of the garden sat a beautiful stone fountain, overgrown with white roses. To Natalie's surprise, she noticed that she was standing.

"Welcome home, Natalie," a woman's voice called out. Natalie looked up to see Princess Kamaria standing near the fountain, smiling sweetly.

"What do you mean by 'Welcome home'?" Natalie asked. "And why am I standing?" Kamaria walked over to her, taking Natalie's hands in hers.

"You have lived a long life, Natalie," she said, her silver eyes sparkling. "You have served your community well, and have used the gifts I bestowed upon you to better the lives of others. You have done our sacred

123

bloodline very proud. Now, it is time for you to take your place among the Ancestors." Realization suddenly dawned on Natalie.

"I've passed on, haven't I?"

"On the physical plane, yes," Kamaria replied. "However, death is never truly the end of the journey." She then led Natalie to a large mirror. Natalie stared in amazement at her reflection. She looked fifty years younger, with not a single wrinkle in sight. Her silver hair had returned to its jet black color, elegantly styled. Instead of a nightgown, she was wearing an olive green, 1960s pencil dress, with a white fur stole draped over her shoulder. Around her neck was a simple pearl necklace, complete with matching earrings. On her feet were a pair of olive green pumps. Natalie also noticed that her aura was now a bright white, giving her an ethereal glow.

"Took you long enough, Sis." Natalie turned around to see her older sister, Diana, smiling at her. Diana looked just as elegant, in a royal blue A-line dress and matching pumps. Standing with her was their mother, Priscilla, Ivy, and Faith. "Didi!" Natalie exclaimed, hugging her. "It's so good to see you again."
"Hey, Mama," Ivy said, stepping forward. Mother and daughter embraced, crying. "Welcome home." Ivy then turned to Faith, smiling. "Aren't you gonna greet your grandma?"

"Hi, baby," Natalie said, opening her arms wide. Giggling, Faith ran to her grandmother, who embraced her in a bear hug.

"There's someone else who's been waiting to see you," Diana said. Natalie looked up to see a handsome man walking towards them. He was dressed in a gray two-piece suit with a matching fedora. He had dark brown skin and bright, piercing hazel eyes. When he smiled, tiny dimples appeared at the corners of his mouth.

"Ricky?" Natalie said. Grinning, Natalie's husband Richard stepped closer.

"Welcome home, Baby Doll," he replied, and the two embraced, sharing a loving kiss. "I've missed you."

"I've missed you more," Natalie said, with tears in her eyes.

"Now, you won't have to miss me anymore," Richard replied, kissing her again. "We're together now." With a content sigh, Natalie snuggled into his chest, inhaling his cologne. While it hurt to leave her daughters and grandchild behind, she was now at peace. She was reunited with her baby girl, her sister, and the love of her life. She was now truly home.

Sarai was awakened by the light of the sun hitting her face. After taking a moment to stretch, she made her way to the bathroom to shower. Once she was freshened up and dressed, she headed to her grandmother's bedroom to wish her a good morning. "Grandma?" she called through the crack of the door. However, she received no response. She entered the room to find Natalie lying in her bed. This struck Sarai as odd, as her grandmother would usually be wide awake, watching television in her bed. However, she chalked it up to her just being tired. *She did say she hadn't been feeling well lately*, she thought. Sarai approached the bed and gently shook Natalie. Still no response. Sarai then grabbed Natalie's hand, and to her horror, it was ice cold. She laid her head on Natalie's chest and found no heartbeat.

"Grandma!? Grandma, wake up!" Sarai cried frantically, shaking Natalie again, but to no avail. Natalie remained motionless, her face serene. Her eyes burning with tears, Sarai continued to shake her grandmother, desperation in her voice as she begged her to open her eyes. *"She's gone, baby,"* Ivy said gently, placing a hand on her daughter's shoulder. *"Your grandma is with the Ancestors now."* Tears flowing down her face, Sarai laid her head on Natalie's chest, and let out an earth-shattering scream, weeping.

Chapter 11

TWO WEEKS LATER

*I*t was a somber day in the Reynolds household. It was the morning of Natalie's funeral, and everyone had gathered at Kristy's home to wait for the limousine that would transport them to the funeral home. Sarai was numb. It had been two weeks since she had found her grandmother lifeless in her bed, yet she couldn't fully bring herself to accept that Natalie was gone. She kept telling herself that it was just a bad dream, that she would wake up soon to the soothing, loving voice of her grandmother and receive a big, warm hug. Louise's heart broke for her cousin. She knew exactly how Sarai was feeling because she experienced the same emotions when her own grandmother, Diana, had lost her battle with cancer. It was only when she saw her grandmother lying in a casket that she accepted the reality that she was gone. Her only comfort was that Diana and Natalie were together again, at peace, free from any earthly pain and suffering.

"Poor Sarai," Rachelle said in a low voice, as she and Nick sat on a couch across from her. The twins slept in their laps. "She was only given five years to build a relationship with Ms. Natalie, and now she's gone. It's cruel."

"I know," Nick said.
"I can only imagine what she's going through right now."

Just then, the doorbell rang. Kristy opened the door, allowing her husband, Xavier, to enter the home with another man. He had brown skin, was bald, and was dressed in a dark suit.

"Good morning, everyone," the man greeted. "My name is Victor, and I will be driving you to the funeral service. I will also be driving you to the cemetery for the burial and then to the repast. Before we leave, Brother Xavier would like to lead the family in prayer."

"Of course," Kristy said, joining hands with her husband and children. After everyone had joined hands, Xavier led them in prayer:

"Heavenly Father,
We ask that you be with our family during this difficult time.
We ask that you and the Ancestors take Natalie into your arms and
surround her with peace and love.
We ask that you wipe away every tear and comfort our hearts.
And may we all know that by your divine mercy, death will never have
the last word.
Amen."

"Amen," replied the others in unison.

Xavier and Victor then led Rose and Violet to the limousine, followed by Sarai and Kiana, Amir, Marcus, Kristy, Dannell, Leroy, and Mariah. Louise, Wilfred, and Artemis also joined their family, while Rachelle, Nick, and Vernon opted to follow in their own vehicles. Once everyone arrived at Reynolds Funeral Home, they were led inside for Family Hour. Rachelle, Nick, and their daughters waited in the lobby with Vernon and friends of the family. Sarai felt her heart race as she walked down the aisle towards the casket. Kiana gently squeezed her hand in an attempt to calm her. However, when she heard her aunts weeping, her own tears began to flow. When she approached Natalie's casket, reality hit her like a ton of bricks. Before her was her beloved grandmother, clad in a crimson silk gown, wearing a simple opal pendant. Her long, silver hair was elegantly styled, and her expression was serene, as if she was simply asleep. To Sarai, she looked like a queen. Seeing Natalie in her casket confirmed what Sarai could no longer deny: she was truly gone. She reached out her shaking hand, gently caressing Natalie's face, and broke down sobbing. Kiana gently rubbed her wife's back, wishing she could take her pain away, but she found herself unable to stop her own tears.

When she had first met Natalie, the elderly woman never judged her or made her feel unwelcome, like Thelma had. Natalie immediately opened her home and heart to the young woman who loved her granddaughter completely and treated her like a second grandchild. Kiana had expected Natalie to condemn her, like other older women had.

127

However, that was never Natalie's nature. All she wanted was for Sarai to be happy. Kiana made her happy, and that was enough for her.

"You okay?" Wilfred whispered as he and Louise descended the aisle with their daughter. Louise simply nodded as they approached the casket. Tears flowed freely down her face as she touched her great aunt's hand. Unlike Sarai, Louise had known Natalie her entire life. In fact, it was Natalie who was present at her birth, since Diana was working at the time. Natalie was like a second grandmother who helped mold Louise into the woman she was today.

"Just try to think of the happy times you shared with her," Kristy whispered, putting her hand on Louise's shoulder. Louise looked at her mother, who was also crying. "I know it hurts, but your Auntie Natalie lived a full life. She loved you, and was very proud of you, just like your Grandma. She was just ready to go."

"I know," Louise said, wiping her eyes.
"Now she's with Grandma."

"Exactly," Kristy said, hugging her daughter. "And they'll both watch after Apollo for you." Kristy rubbed Louise's back as she sobbed. Louise was then led to her seat by her mother and husband, with her daughter following behind.

After Family Hour was over, friends and acquaintances of Natalie were let in to view the body, including Rachelle, Nick, and Vernon. After everyone had paid their respects, they were seated. Sarai was amazed to see how full the funeral home was, but she was not surprised. Natalie Hesper-Turner was a beam of light to everyone who knew her and was beloved by the community she served.

"I'd like to thank everyone for coming today, as we pay our respects to Natalie," Xavier said, trying his hardest to hold back his tears. While he was no stranger to death and grief, Natalie was family, which made him preparing her send-off all the more personal. After another prayer, he called Kristy to the podium for the reading of the obituary. After the reading, it was time for friends and family to come up to give their remarks. The first to speak was Rose.

"Good day, everyone," she began. "My name is Rose Carter, and I am Natalie's eldest daughter. Natalie came into my life shortly after the death of my biological mother, and after she married my father, she adopted Violet and me as her own. I owe a lot to my mother because she molded me into who I am today." Rose took a deep breath as Violet rubbed her back. "Mama was the type of person who would give her last if you needed it, and she always did it with a smile. She could brighten the darkest day just by saying hello and knew just the right thing to say when you were feeling down." A few people murmured in agreement, and Rose continued. "She was the sweetest woman I had ever known, but she was also not one to play around with. I actually debated telling this story, but I feel it should be told, in order to show just how strong our mother and aunt were." Kristy smiled, knowing what Rose was referring to. "After Daddy died, Mama used the money from his life insurance to move us here from Cincinnati. Ivy was still a baby at the time. We moved into the same neighborhood as our aunt Diana, which used to be an all-White neighborhood. It was about three years after the riot, so White folks didn't take too kindly to us being in their neighborhoods, so we had to deal with a lot of prejudice."

"Ain't that the truth," said an older woman, as a few others chuckled.

"Vi and I used to play with these girls next door, and they were a White family. One day, we got into it because one of the girls had lost at Double Dutch and accused us of cheating. She hit me, so I hit her back. Her sister ran into the house to get their mama and lied and said we jumped on her sister."

"Typical White tears," Rachelle whispered.

"Their mama came out of the house, screaming at us and throwing Coke bottles. Mind you, this was the early 1970s, so Coke was sold in glass bottles. Vi and I ran into the house and told Aunt Diana what happened. Mama was still at work, so our aunt would watch us until she came home. Auntie told us to stay in the house, and we waited for Mama to come back. Remember, Ivy and Kristy were small, so they couldn't be left in the house by themselves. Mama came home around 5:30. I still remember how she looked that day. She drove a Cadillac, and because she worked at a bank, she was wearing a suit, and her hair was always nicely done. Mama always had this rule that we were not to bother her for at least an hour so she could have a Pepsi and a cigarette. Once the hour was up, Aunt Diana brought me to her, and I told her what happened with the lady next door. I have never seen Mama get so angry." Rose chuckled at the memory. "She and Auntie went into the garage, and they grabbed aluminum bats. They marched next door, and that White lady was talking to somebody in the driveway. Mama tapped her on the shoulder and asked her, 'Did you throw glass at my children?' That woman went on a tirade, calling us all types of niggas. Next thing we knew, Mama cracked her upside the head with the bat." Everyone in the funeral home erupted in laughter. Louise and Sarai simply smirked. They had heard this story many times, and it never got old. "Mama and Aunt Diana beat her up and down the street, and she was screaming for help. But no one came to her aid, probably because they knew how insufferable she was. Her own kids locked her out of the house, and everyone else locked their doors. Mama even used her magic to lift that woman into mid-air, which made her more hysterical. Her friend drove to the police station, and when the cops came to the neighborhood, the woman started screaming that Mama and Auntie were witches and how they lifted her in the air. However, no one in the neighborhood saw anything, and the police thought she had taken drugs, so they had taken her in for disturbing the peace. She and her kids ended up moving a few months later. But that incident taught me three things: always be about your business, take care of your family, and don't let anyone mess with your family."

"Amen!" a woman shouted, and a few others applauded.

"Vi and I take comfort in knowing that Mama lived a long life, and a fulfilling life. She is surrounded by the love of our Ancestors, and is at peace. Today, we do not mourn her death but celebrate the life she lived." The room erupted in applause as more people got up to speak. Soon, it was Sarai's turn to speak. Her stomach was in knots as she stared into the crowd, unsure of what to say. Kiana squeezed her hand to reassure her, and in the corner of her eye, Sarai could see the spirits of her mother, sister, grandparents, great-grandparents, and great aunt.

"It's okay, baby," a woman said from the crowd. Sarai took a deep breath and addressed the crowd.

"For those that don't know me, my name is Sarai Patterson, and I am Natalie's granddaughter. To be honest, there is really nothing I can say about Grandma that hasn't already been said. However, it touches my heart to know how loved she was. Unfortunately, due to circumstances out of my control, I didn't know my grandmother until five years ago." Sarai glanced at her father, who looked down in shame. "But through those five years, I received enough love and wisdom from her to last me over a hundred lifetimes." Sarai stopped to wipe away her tears. "Despite everything that I've been through, I am grateful to my grandmother. With her, I was able to be myself without judgment, and she had always been in my corner. It was because of the love of my grandmother, aunts, my wife, my best friend, and my cousins that I was able to become the woman that I was meant to be. For that, I will always be grateful. Thank you." The crowd applauded as Sarai stepped down from the podium and made her way back to her seat.

After the funeral, Louise, Kristy, Mariah, Sarai, and her aunts carried the flowers to the hearse, while Xavier, Dannell, Marcus, and Amir helped carry the casket. After Natalie's casket was loaded into the hearse, they drove to Mount Elliott Cemetery, where Ivy, Faith, and Priscilla, Sarai and Louise's great-grandmother, were buried. After everyone had gathered under the tent, Xavier said another prayer:

"Heavenly Father,
We have gathered here to commit our dearly beloved Natalie to the
ground.
Earth to earth,
Ashes to ashes,
Dust to dust.
In sure and certain hope that she finds peace and love among the
Ancestors.
Amen."

After the prayer, everyone took a rose off the casket to take with them. The family then got back into the limousine, while the others got into their respective vehicles, and drove to the repast. On the way to the venue, Sarai was silent the entire time, her emotions in a whirlwind. She was saddened by the loss of her grandmother and at the same time relieved that Natalie was free of illness and suffering. However, the funeral brought up feelings of resentment towards her father. She still felt anger that she only got five years with Natalie, while Louise had her throughout her entire life. While she had long forgiven Vernon for his deception, understanding that he was also a victim of her stepmother's abuse and his family's toxicity, she couldn't forget. She was robbed of a loving family, all because of religion and Thelma's jealousy.

"You okay, cuz?" Marcus asked. Sarai simply nodded and stared out the window. Louise knew her emotions had to be all over the place since she had been in Sarai's shoes. Grief was a complex thing, and it manifested itself in different ways.

"Just know that we're here for you when you need us," Amir added. About twenty minutes later, they arrived at the Venetian Hall. When she entered the building, Sarai was greeted with the aroma of her father's signature fried chicken, collard greens, and mac-n-cheese, and she sighed in satisfaction. However, the smell had the opposite effect on Louise, who immediately ran to the restroom. Concerned, Kristy and Mariah followed her, along with Rachelle, Sarai, and Kiana. When they entered the restroom, they could hear Louise retching in one of the stalls. Kristy went into the stall and held her daughter's hair as she vomited.

"Lou? Is everything okay?" Rachelle asked. "You don't have a virus, do you?" Louise flushed the toilet and exited the stall. Mariah left the restroom and returned with a bottle of water. Louise took it and rinsed out her mouth.

"You good?" Mariah asked.

"I think it was the smell of the chicken that made me nauseous," Louise replied.

"But you like fried chicken. How are you nau-" Kristy said, but then it hit her. "Louise...are you pregnant?" Louise simply nodded. "How far along are you?"

"Only thirteen weeks," Louise replied. "I was going to tell you and Mariah when we went to brunch, but then we got the call about Auntie Natalie."

"Oh, sweetie," Kristy said, hugging Louise.

"I'm so happy for you."

"So, you were the fish in Dannell's dream," Mariah cut in.

"Dannell had a fish dream?" Louise asked.

"Yep, about a month ago," Kristy replied. "I was just waiting to see who it was." Just then, Artemis walked into the restroom.

"Mommy?" she asked. "Are you okay? Did you eat something bad?" Louise smiled down at her daughter.

"I'm okay, Moonbeam, but I have a surprise for you."

"What is it?"

"You're gonna be a big sister," Kristy said, smiling. Squealing excitedly, Artemis ran to her mother, hugging her.

"Congrats, Lou," Kiana said. Everyone embraced Louise in a group hug before returning to the dinner. Louise and Wilfred quietly informed the rest of the family of the pregnancy and were met with excitement. They knew how the loss of Apollo had affected the couple and were elated that they were blessed with another pregnancy. This news was the silver lining to the sorrow they were experiencing. The rest of the evening was spent in celebration, with music, dancing, and family, the way Natalie would have wanted. When Sarai returned home, her heart felt fuller. While she knew it would take time for her to fully heal from her grief, she knew that her grandmother would always be with her.

"Mommy, are we there yet? It's hot," Artemis complained as they walked through the cemetery, the afternoon sun beating down on them.

"Just a few more steps, baby," Louise replied, carrying a large wreath. It was June 24th, which would have been Missy's thirtieth birthday. Ever since her tragic suicide, Louise would visit her grave every year on her birthday to leave flowers and to talk to her. When Artemis was five years old, Louise started bringing her along. After all, she was Missy's namesake and would-be godchild.

"Finally!" Artemis exclaimed as they reached their destination. In front of them was a large, heart-shaped headstone, with a stone angel embracing it:

Artemis Roxann Beatriz Hamilton
"Missy"
Beloved Daughter, Sister, & Friend
June 24, 1992 - April 17, 2010

"Hey, Missy," Louise began. "Well, Happy Dirty Thirty. I'm sure you're getting lit with your ancestors right now. It's just so unfair that you're not here on Earth. You and I should be out celebrating. But I know you're in a better place, and at peace." She set down the wreath, which was made of pink roses and sunflowers, Missy's favorite flowers. "By the way, I brought your godbaby with me."

"Hey, Auntie Missy," Artemis said cheerfully. "I made a present for you." Artemis reached into her pocket and pulled out a handmade bracelet with pink and gold beads.

"Your baby has gotten so big." Louise looked up to see an apparition of Missy standing near her grave. She looked radiant in a pink, flowing dress and wore a sunflower crown atop her curly hair. *"Aww, and she made me a present! Thank you, sweetie."* Artemis smiled at her. Missy turned her attention back to Louise. *"So, I heard you're pregnant again."*

"Yep," Louise replied as she buried the bracelet in the dirt, along with a pack of Lemonheads.

"You know just what I like," Missy mused. Louise chuckled.

"You would eat a pack of Lemonheads every day at school. Of course, I know what you like."

"I also saw what you did with Mrs. Everett. She had it coming."

"She hadn't changed one bit," Louise said. "Still a bitter, miserable, old

hag. Unfortunately, the apple didn't fall far from the tree."

"Yeah, I know," Missy replied. *"Hopefully, that girl grows out of her bullying behavior." Louise snorted.*

"I doubt it, especially given who's raising her."

"People can change, though," Missy said. *"I mean look at my brother. He grew up and stopped being annoying."* Louise and Missy laughed. When they were in school, Julius, Missy's younger brother, used to constantly pester and tease them. *"Can you believe he has kids now? Speaking of which, I see them coming this way."* Louise turned around to see Julius walking towards her, carrying a bouquet of sunflowers and balloons. He was tall, with a muscular build, and clean-cut, a far cry from the whiny, scrawny boy she knew growing up. Running behind him were two boys, who looked to be at least four and six years old. Next to Julius was Pandora Hamilton, Julius and Missy's mother. She looked as beautiful as Louise remembered, a Guyanese-American woman with smooth, dark brown skin, brown eyes, and beautiful black curls. Upon seeing Louise, Pandora smiled.

"I thought I was looking at your mama," she said, greeting Louise with a hug. She then turned to Artemis. "Is this your baby? She was an itty-bitty thing the last time I saw her."

"Yep, this is Artemis. She's seven now," Louise said proudly. "Sweetie, this is Missy's mommy, Ms. Dora."

"Hi," Artemis said with a smile.

"Julius, how have you been? It's been ages," Louise said, giving the young man a hug.

"I know, right?" Julius replied with a grin. "Kids, say hi to Ms. Louise. She was a friend of your auntie."

"Hi," the boys said in unison.

"Their names are Julius, Jr., and Nathan."

"They're adorable," Louise said. She then let out a sigh. "I can't believe it's been twelve years."

"I know," Pandora said. "I think about that every day." She wiped away a tear. "But I know she would have been so proud of how far you've come."

"She's right, you know," Missy said, leaning against her headstone.

"It's just so unfair, though," Louise thought. Every day without Missy was a reminder of how cruel life was. She was supposed to be at a bar or club with Missy, celebrating. She wasn't supposed to be in a cemetery, putting flowers on a grave.

"So, how's your folks?"

"Busy as always with the store," Louise replied.
"Dad, of course, is busy with the funeral home."

"I need to stop by and see them," Pandora replied.

"I know they'll be happy to see you," Louise said.
"Mama definitely will."

"By the way, congratulations. I saw on your page that you're pregnant."

"Thank you," Louise replied, beaming. "You know Mama's gonna have her hands full with three grandkids." Pandora sighed. She always wondered what Missy's children would have looked like if she had lived long enough to marry and have a family. "I know," Louise said, as if reading Pandora's mind. "I think about it, too."

"Thank you for always being a good friend to her," Pandora said, giving Louise a hug.

"Of course," Louise replied. After chatting some more, she bid the family farewell, and she made her way back to the car with Artemis. When they approached the vehicle, they saw that there were several monarch butterflies on the hood and windshield. A crow was perched on the rearview mirror. Louise looked back at the gravesite and smiled.

"Mommy, what does this mean?" Artemis asked.

"It means everything is going to be okay, sweetie," Louise said. "It means our loved ones are watching over us." She then looked up at the sky and smiled.

"Happy Birthday, girl. I love you."

Chapter 12

"*M*ommy, why can't I go to your class?" Artemis asked, looking up from her game. "I could help you teach."

"If this were any other class, I'd love to have you there, but this class is for adults, sweetie," Louise replied. "We'll be discussing things that aren't for little girls."

"Aww," Artemis said, pouting.

"When I'm done, I'll take you out for ice cream. How does that sound?" Artemis' eyes immediately lit up at the mention of her favorite treat. The sight of her daughter's smile made Louise's heart melt.

"Okay!" Artemis chirped. After checking to ensure she had everything, Louise was ready.

"Don't forget to give Comet her food," she said as she petted the feline's head, earning a purr of satisfaction. She then gave Wilfred and Artemis a kiss and went on her way. Once she arrived at Diana's Garden, she saw that Rachelle, Sarai, and Kiana were already there, along with her mother and sister.

"Took you long enough," Mariah teased as Louise entered the store.

"Whatever," Louise said as she began to set up.
"Class doesn't even start for another ten minutes."

"It sucks that you don't teach classes at the Pagan Pathways Temple anymore," Rachelle lamented.

"Yeah, but what can you do?" Louise said with a shrug. Two years prior, the Pagan Pathways Temple closed due to toxic behavior within the board and allegations of abuse and predatory behavior. "Besides, Mom's store is bigger and can hold more people."

"True," Rachelle said as she sat in one of the chairs.

"So, how's the wedding planning coming, Rachelle?" Kristy asked.

"It's going pretty good," Rachelle replied.
"Although, we ran into an issue with Nick's side of the family."

"What do you mean?" Louise asked.

"His cousin Rafael wanted to propose to his girlfriend at the wedding, and he and his mama are throwing a hissy fit because we told him no," Rachelle said, frowning at the memory. She already didn't like Inez, Nick's aunt, because of how judgmental she was and her colorist remarks. However, when she had become pregnant with the twins, Inez had toned it down when Nick threatened to cut her off if she made any remarks about their daughters' complexions or disrespected Rachelle any further. To be honest, the family only tolerated Inez because she was the caregiver of Nick's grandmother, Magdalena, since they both lived in Puerto Rico. Despite her toxicity, Inez did take good care of her mother, so to keep a close relationship with Magdalena, they tolerated Inez, albeit in very small doses.

"Well, it's your wedding, so you and Nick aren't in the wrong," Louise said. "Besides, hijacking someone else's big day to propose is just tacky and lazy."

"For real," Mariah interjected.

"The good thing is that Nick's parents are 100% on our side. Nick also said that if Inez and Rafael don't drop it, they'll be uninvited from the wedding. So far, they haven't said anything else, especially since Inez doesn't want to be cut off from her only nephew."

"Good," Sarai said. "But know that if they try any shit, I got you. That's my job as your Maid of Honor."

"I got you, too," Louise added.

"I know, and I appreciate ya'll, but don't worry. Nick and I are hiring security in case anyone decides to cut up," Rachelle said. After a few more minutes, people started pouring into the store for Louise's glamour magic class. Once everyone was seated and ready, Louise walked up to the front.

"Welcome, everyone," she began cheerfully. "Most of you already know me, but for those that don't, my name is Louise. I am Kristy's daughter, and today, I will be teaching you all about glamour magic. Does anyone here have an idea as to what glamour magic is?" A few people raised their hands. Louise pointed to a young woman with short locs, since she was the first to raise her hand.

"Beauty magic?" she responded.

"That's part of it, but it's a lot deeper than that," Louise said. "While glamour magic can be used to enhance beauty, it's more about changing how people perceive you energetically."

"What does that mean?" the young woman asked.

"It means you can change how your energy comes off to others," Kristy interjected. "For example, if you want to appear more confident and assertive, glamour magic can be utilized to accomplish that."

"Oh, I get it now," the young woman said, nodding.

"Unfortunately, glamour magic doesn't necessarily get the respect it deserves because it's seen as 'frivolous'," Louise continued. "I, however, beg to differ. I see glamour magic as a form of healing."

"How?" asked another woman with long, dark hair.

"If you are confident within yourself, or feel beautiful, your mental health benefits," Louise replied. "Your mental health is just as important as your physical health. The two go hand in hand."

"Period!" Sarai exclaimed, and the other students murmured in agreement, catching on to what Louise was saying. "Now, we are going to discuss herbs and plants that can be used in glamo-" Louise was interrupted by the opening of the door. Octavia entered the shop, looking around awkwardly.

"Sorry I'm late," she said.
"I got stuck in traffic."

"No worries. Have a seat. We were just getting started," Louise said, giving Octavia a reassuring smile. Octavia quietly took a seat next to Kiana, who happily greeted her. "Now, as I was saying before, here are some common herbs used in glamour spells..." Everyone hung on Louise's every word as she went in depth about the herbs and their associations, such as catnip, rose petals, and hibiscus.

"Does it matter what color roses you use?" another person asked.

"Every color has its own association," Louise explained. "For beauty and love, you would use red and pink roses. For friendship, yellow would be used. You can also use white roses if that's all you have. Now, on to crystals. My favorite crystals to use in glamour magic are rose quartz, carnelian, and moonstone. rose quartz is used for self-love. However, if you combine it with carnelian, it can boost not only your confidence but also sexual energy and creativity. moonstone can be carried or worn to connect with your divine feminine energy." Louise held up her left wrist to show the rose quartz and carnelian bracelets she was wearing. She also showed the class a moonstone ring she was wearing. Octavia looked around to see everyone taking notes. She, too, was soaking in the information Louise was giving her, hoping to one day have use for it.

"Are there any oils we can use in a glamour spell?"

"I'm so glad you asked that," Louise said, smiling. "Simple olive oil can be used, as well as rose essential oil. However, if you want to kick things up a notch, I have samples of my Venus and Bad Bitch oils." She then handed the box of oil samples to her sister, who began passing them around to everyone in the room. "These oils can be used to dress candles, and they

141

can also be worn as perfume. Also, for my exotic dancers, escorts, and OnlyFans girls, I have Jezebel oil." Louise then held up a small bottle for everyone to see.

"I highly recommend her Jezebel oil," Rachelle said. "It also contains real Jezebel root, not that tree mulch shit people sell."

"You also don't have to be a sex worker to use it," Louise continued. "If you work in a restaurant, you can use it to get bigger tips. You can also use it to get a promotion. It can also be used to dominate a man, or attract a wealthy one." Louise began handing out samples of Jezebel oil to those who wanted it. After handing out her oil samples, she began to delve into different spells and rituals, including rituals involving sex and bodily fluids. "So, for those who have a uterus, the most powerful bodily fluid we have is our menstrual blood," she continued. "It's so potent because it is our literal life force. It's a liquid version of ourselves. Because of this, it is also extremely dangerous if used irresponsibly."

"How so?" the young woman with dark hair asked.

"Menstrual blood, or blood in general, is binding. When used in spellwork, it can tether you to that spell, which is why you should never use it in baneful work, at least not your own blood. It is especially dangerous if used in a love binding. If there is anyone here from the South, or have family in the South, I'm sure you've heard of the spaghetti trick."

"Mmmhmm," replied an older Black woman.

"Using your blood in someone's food or drink is not only a biohazard, but a surefire way to end up with a stalker or on *The First 48*," Louise said. "It can make your partner obsessive and possessive."

"What if that's what I want, though?" a blond woman asked. Louise had to resist the urge to facepalm.

"Trust me, you don't," she replied. "I actually know a woman who not only nearly lost her life but the life of her unborn child because she tried to bind someone to her that did not want to settle down." Louise then gave Rachelle and Sarai a knowing glance. They knew Louise was referring to Shawna and Lamar. "Thankfully, she got away, and her child is doing well. However, not everyone is that lucky." Louise paused for a moment to allow her words to sink in. "Besides, do you honestly want someone who is only with you because you manipulated them with magic?"

"No," the others answered in unison.

"Now, this isn't to say that love magic as a whole is bad," Kristy added. "Love magic is an umbrella. In fact, our people used love bindings for survival, especially during slavery when families were torn apart. In the early 20th century, Black women used love bindings to keep their men with them because they didn't have a lot of options. If their men had left them and their children, they would have been destitute. However, love binding is no longer necessary since women have more options than they ever did before. If you want to use magic on yourself to get a specific person's attention or use magic to strengthen a connection that is already there, then that is perfectly fine. However, you don't want to bind someone who doesn't want you."

"Or a man who ain't shit," Louise cut in.

"Facts," Sarai added. Louise continued on with the workshop, giving tips on enchanting jewelry, cosmetics, and even clothing. She also shared some of her glamour sigils and affirmations with them and gave information on love and beauty deities they could work with. At least, deities that were not part of closed practices. After an hour had passed, the class was over. Some of the students left, while others decided to stay and shop. Louise's friends also chose to stay behind.

"Awesome class, Lou," Sarai said.

"Thanks, cuz," Louise replied as she was putting her materials away. She then turned to Octavia. "So, what did you think of my workshop? Was it helpful?"

"It definitely was," Octavia said.
"I didn't realize there was so much information, though."

"Yeah, it can be a bit overwhelming, but you don't have to immediately jump into it. Take it one step at a time."

"Hey, how much is this Oshun statue?" Louise looked up to see a young woman walking up to them. She was white and petite, with blond 'locs' that resembled The Grinch's fingers and forest green eyes. On her upper left arm was a tattoo of a veve, a religious symbol in Haitian Vodou. In her hand, she held a small bronze statue of Oshun, the Orisha of beauty, love, rivers, and fertility. "Uh, that statue is $45, but I don't think it will be a good idea for you to buy that," Louise replied.

"Why not?"

"Well, Oshun is an Orisha. The Orisha are a closed practice." The young lady scoffed and rolled her eyes.

"How can it be closed if Oshun chose me?" she countered. "She came to me in a dream and said she wanted to work with me." It took everything in Louise to not roll her eyes. Her mother would get people like Grinch Fingers in her shop every blue moon. People who think they can collect spiritual practices like Infinity Stones, even when they don't even belong to the cultures the practices originated. "Ma'am, I don't know what kind of spirit reached out to you, but I can assure you that it was definitely not Oshun," she said. "In order to work with the Orisha, you have to be initiated. To be initiated, you need to go to a Babalawo for a divination to see if an Orisha even rules your head. Furthermore, Ifa is a Yoruba religion. Yoruba is West African."

"Spirit doesn't see color, and spirituality has no rules," Grinch Fingers countered smugly. "If you think that I can't worship Oshun because I'm White, then you're racist. During your workshop, you said you work with Aphrodite. How would you feel if I said you can't work with her because you're Black?"

*This bitch...*Louise thought to herself. She figured that Grinch Fingers was going to pull that card. "First of all, Hellenic Paganism is an open practice, so your point is moot. Secondly, African spiritual practices have rules and protocols that are in place for a reason. Ancestor reverence is a huge part of those practices. Do you honestly think that the spirits of those that were enslaved, colonized, and oppressed actually want to work with someone that looks like their oppressor?"

"You better listen to her," Rachelle interjected. "She knows what she's talking about, and she's trying to keep you from getting hurt. It would be in your best interest to heed her advice." Grinch Fingers scoffed again.

"I'm not going to get hurt. I'm divinely protected," she said. "As I said before, Oshun chose me. Papa Legba did, too." She then turned to show Louise the veve tattoo. "So, are you gonna sell me the statue or not?"

This bitch is goofy! Louise thought, fully irritated. *That's Baron Samedi's veve, not Papa Legba's! You're not even supposed to be getting veves tattooed on you in the first place!* "Ma'am, my daughter has very clearly explained to you why you should not buy that statue. We do not cosign cultural appropriation here. If you are unable or unwilling to understand and respect that, perhaps it's best that you leave." Kristy interjected calmly but firmly. Grinch Fingers shot her a death glare.

"Fine!" she spat, slamming the statue on the counter.
"You've just lost yourself a customer!"

"Trust me, it's no loss for us," Louise replied coolly. "Also, just an FYI: That's not Papa Legba's veve you got tattooed on you. You should look into getting that removed." Grinch Fingers flipped Louise off before storming out of the shop. The other shoppers simply shook their heads at the woman's entitled behavior.

"What a Karen," Kiana said.

"Really," Sarai added.
"You were just trying to educate her."

"Unfortunately, not everyone wants to be educated or helped," Kristy replied, lighting some Dragon's Blood incense. "She'll just have to learn the hard way." The others murmured in agreement.

"Excuse me, what kind of stone is this?" Octavia inquired, holding up a bracelet with milky white beads with hints of blue and pink.

"That's opalite," Louise said. "It's good for soothing the heart and mind. It's a really good stone to have if you have depression and anxiety."

"Good to know," Octavia said as she placed the bracelet on the counter. Louise happily rang her up and handed the bracelet to Octavia in a silk organza pouch.

"Enjoy," she said with a smile.

"Thanks," Octavia said softly.
"I should get going."

"It was good seeing you again," Rachelle said.

"Um, you, too. Tell Nick I said hi." Octavia then exited the store.

"I should get going, too," Louise stated. "I promised my baby an ice cream date."

"Give my grandbaby a kiss for me," Kristy said as she gave Louise a hug.

"Will do," Louise replied. She also hugged her sister and friends before departing to head home.

It was 5:30 pm when Sarai arrived at Vernon's townhome on Warrington Drive with Kiana and Rachelle. It was Vernon's fifty-third birthday, so he decided to have his family and a few friends over for dinner. While Sarai was annoyed at the prospect of interacting with her paternal relatives, she wanted to support her father. However, she vowed to herself that if any of them acted out of pocket, she would have no qualms about putting them in their place. It also helped that she would have Kiana and Rachelle there to back her up and give her moral support.

"Hope we're not too early," she said as she rang the doorbell. A few minutes later, the door opened, and the trio was greeted with Vernon's smiling face.

"Hey, baby!" he said. "Come on in." Vernon stepped aside to allow the women into his home. The townhome was not as big as the home Sarai had grown up in, but it was cozy and well-furnished. Plus, it made sense for Vernon to downsize since he was the only one living there.

"Happy Birthday, old man," Sarai teased as the two hugged. Kiana and Rachelle also hugged him, wishing him a happy birthday.

"So, how have you all been?" Vernon asked.

"We've been good," Sarai replied.
"Busy, though."

"I bet, with all those interviews you've been doing," Vernon said. "I saw that podcast you did last week."

"Really?"

"Of course. I've watched and read every interview you did," Vernon replied as he went into the kitchen to check the oven. He soon emerged with a dish of freshly baked macaroni and cheese. "I'm really proud of you. My baby, a famous author."

"Thanks, Dad," Sarai said, smiling. Although this was not the first time she had heard her father say that he was proud of her, she never got tired of hearing it.

"So, Rachelle, how's your mama?"

"She's doing good," Rachelle replied. "She said she'll be here in a half hour, actually." Vernon nodded, smiling.

"What about your fiancé? How come you didn't bring him with you?"

"He's catching up on some photo editing for some clients, so he's at his studio. The girls are with his sister." Vernon nodded and went back into the kitchen. Sarai, Kiana, and Rachelle assisted Vernon with setting the table since it would be twenty minutes before the rest of his guests arrived. Teddy Pendergrass' smooth, soulful voice flowed from the speakers as Vernon put the finishing touches on the food. The home was soon filled with the delicious aromas of macaroni and cheese, cornbread, collard greens, and glazed ham. Rachelle had also brought some homemade tamales, while Sarai and Kiana brought a birthday cake and key lime pie. It was 6:15 pm when the doorbell rang again. Vernon went to answer the door and was greeted by his sister-in-law, Geraldine, the widow of his older brother, Simon. Behind her were her daughter Lola and her son Gerald. After exchanging pleasantries, Vernon led his relatives to the dining room.

"Why you sitting there acting like you don't know nobody?" Geraldine teased in her Mississippi accent. She was plump, with rich, brown skin, and dark, brown eyes. Her black hair was relaxed and styled into a simple bob and was dressed in a simple blue blouse and jeans. Around her neck was a simple gold cross necklace. Sarai got up and gave her a half-hearted hug. "I see your fashion sense hasn't changed," she said, eyeing Sarai's look. She was wearing a black Pierce the Veil t-shirt with dark jeans and black combat boots. Her hair was in a ponytail, and she wore a pair of obsidian point earrings. Around her neck was an obsidian pendant. For makeup, she wore black eyeshadow, black eyeliner, and black lipstick.

"Geri, don't start," Vernon warned.

"What? I'm just messing with her," Geraldine said defensively. Sarai said nothing. Her cousins simply acknowledged her with a nod. Lola was twenty-five and average height, with a thick build. Her skin was a toffee brown, and she had brown eyes. She wore her hair in black Passion Twists, which fell to her back. Her makeup was natural and flawless. She wore an orange sundress that clung to her figure, with gold sandals, bangles, and gold hoop earrings. Gerald was thirty, with dark, brown skin and brown eyes. He was a head taller than his sister, with an average build. His hair was styled in locs that he kept in a ponytail. He wore dark, baggy jeans with a simple white t-shirt and white Jordans on his feet.

"By the way, Mama sends her love," Geraldine said as she sat down. "She's not feeling well, so she wasn't able to make the trip."

"I figured," Vernon said. His mother's health issues had been getting worse, so he didn't expect her to come. At least they were able to talk on the phone earlier that day.

"And who is this?" Geraldine inquired, gesturing to Rachelle.

"This is Rachelle. She's Sarai's best friend. I've known her and her mama since Sarai was little."

"Pleased to meet you," Rachelle said politely, offering her hand, which Geraldine shook. She already had a negative perception of Vernon's family because of everything Sarai had told her. However, she decided to remain cordial for her best friend's sake.

"So, you must be the 'model' I've heard so much about," Geraldine said. Rachelle didn't care for the tone that Geraldine used when referring to her profession, but she brushed it off. She figured Thelma and Tasha must've run their mouths to the family about her. Lola looked Rachelle up and down, eyeing her ensemble and accessories. As always, Rachelle was sharp. She wore a burgundy pencil skirt with a white vintage halter top. Around her neck was a simple pearl necklace, and she wore matching pearl earrings. Her natural hair was pulled back into a simple ponytail, and her makeup was natural, save for her favorite dark red lipstick. Her look was complete with burgundy pumps.

She must be one of those bougie bitches, Lola thought disdainfully. However, Gerald was staring at Rachelle, mentally undressing her.

"This is Kiana, Sarai's wife," Vernon said. Kiana held out her hand for Geraldine to shake. Geraldine, however, stared at Kiana's hand as if it were a foreign object.

"Auntie, aren't you gonna shake her hand?" Sarai said.

"Right...." she said as she begrudgingly shook Kiana's hand. As she went back to her seat, however, she wiped her hand on her pants. Kiana's feelings were hurt by this, but she didn't let it show, not wanting to give Geraldine the satisfaction of knowing she got to her. Sarai squeezed her hand reassuringly, and the two sat at the table next to Rachelle. A few minutes later, Sharon arrived.

"Mommy!" Rachelle exclaimed as she went over to her mother, who embraced her in a warm hug."

"Hey, baby," Sharon said, kissing her daughter on the cheek. Vernon then led her to the dinner table and introduced her to his family. After the rest of Vernon's guests had arrived, it was time for the food to be blessed. After grace was said, everyone dug in. Sarai piled a helping of ham, cornbread, greens, macaroni and cheese, and a tamale on her plate, as Geraldine looked on disapprovingly. However, Sarai paid her no mind. She loved herself the way she was and was not going to allow anyone to make her feel bad about it anymore.

"So Rachelle, how's business going?" Vernon asked, taking a bite of his cornbread.

"It's going really well," Rachelle replied, smiling.

"You own a business?" Stephen, one of Vernon's friends, asked. "What kind of business is it?"

"I make my own skin and hair care products," Rachelle answered. "It's called Melanin Siren, at Oakland Mall."

"My daughter uses those products," Stephen said, impressed. "That's really cool. We need more Black-owned businesses." The others answered in agreement as they ate. Rachelle could feel Lola's gaze burning into her, and so could Sarai. However, Sarai brushed it off. She always knew her cousin to be bitter and envious of other people. Lola was a fuck-up. At her young age, she already had four children under the age of five, all by different fathers. Lola's story was a dime a dozen. She thought that she could keep a man by having his child, and it always blew up in her face. Her brother was no better. Gerald was an aspiring rapper that was content with living off his mother. He also had five children by five different women and was a typical deadbeat father. He was basically Lamar 2.0, and like Lamar, Gerald's mother coddled him.

"So, Rachelle, um, you got a man?" Gerald asked, giving Rachelle a lecherous look, making her skin crawl.

"Yes, I do. In fact, we're engaged," Rachelle said, showing her ring.

"So, he won't let you have friends?"

"She's not interested, Gerald," Sarai cut in.
"Learn to take a hint."

"Hey, no need to get all sensitive," Gerald said, putting his hands up defensively. "I was just playing." *Whatever, nigga!* Sarai thought to herself as she ate her food. She knew Gerald wasn't joking. He was thirsty over anyone who had a big ass and a smile. However, she was not going to allow him to creep on her friends, especially her taken friends.

"What are these?" Lola asked, eyeing the plate of tamales.

"Those are tamales," Rachelle explained.

"Why is there Mexican food here? We ain't Mexican," Lola said. *Oh, you're one of those bitches*, Rachelle thought.

"You know tamales are not exclusively Mexican, right?" Rachelle countered. "I got the recipe from my fiancé's mother, who's Cuban."

"Whatever," Lola said, rolling her eyes. Aside from Gerald and Lola's comments, dinner was otherwise uneventful. Vernon was discussing sports and business with his friends, while Sarai, Kiana, and Rachelle chatted among themselves. Sharon made small talk with Geraldine, while Lola and Gerald ate in silence, Lola throwing dirty looks at the trio every so often. The atmosphere was positive and fun, and everyone was enjoying themselves. Then, the topic of Sarai's book came up.

"I don't understand why you young people feel the need to air out your family's business nowadays," Geraldine commented. "First that little white girl who was glad her mama died, and now you." She shot a look at Sarai. "In my day, whatever happened in the family stayed in the family."

"Yes, and that's why our community is so messed up now," Rachelle said. "Ya'll would rather sweep issues under the rug, instead of facing them head-on and holding folks accountable."

"I believe I was talking to my niece and not you, Miss Thang," Geraldine spat.

"Well, your niece agrees with everything her best friend said," Sarai cut in. "Don't get mad at her for telling the truth. Besides, the names in the book were changed, so no one knows who you are outside of us." Geraldine turned to Vernon, hoping for backup. There was none.

"Don't look at me," he said, shrugging.

"So, you're okay with your daughter bashing you and your wife for the whole world to see?" Geraldine asked.

"She didn't bash me, Geri," Vernon countered, annoyed. "She was holding me accountable. I wasn't the best parent to Sarai and her sister. Thelma was abusing my girls under my nose, and I didn't put my foot down until it was too late. I have to live with that. I shouldn't have married that woman in the first place."

"And you think that devil-worshipping harlot was a better choice?" Geraldine asked incredulously. Sarai jumped up from her seat, ready to fight, but Vernon stopped her.

"Ivy wasn't a harlot, Geri," he argued. "She was the mother of my children, and the love of my life. She didn't know I was engaged to Thelma when I started dating her. I was two-timing them, which was wrong."

"Be that as it may, Thelma was a good woman to take care of those girls like she did after you cheated on her. Sarai should be a little more grateful."

"Grateful?" Sarai repeated. "Grateful for what? Trauma? Low self-esteem? The fact that I no longer have my sister? What exactly should I be grateful for?"

"There you go being dramatic again," Geraldine said as she rolled her eyes. "Look, what happened to Faith was unfortunate, but that was not your mama's fault. She didn't make her kill herself. That woman fed you, clothed you, and kept a roof over your head. And how do you repay her? By painting her as some kind of monster?"

"First of all, do not call that woman my mama!" Sarai barked. "A mother is supposed to love, nurture, and protect her children. Thelma did neither of those things. I'm not gonna give her brownie points for shit Faith and I didn't even ask for! We didn't ask to be here! Thelma was nothing but a bitter-ass, jealous-ass, evil-ass woman who allowed a child molester around us! If you call that being a good woman, you are just as sick as she was!" She then shot a glare at Lola and Gerald. "No wonder your kids are losers!"

"Bitch! Who the fuck are you calling losers!" Lola raged as she charged at Sarai. However, before she could reach her intended target, she was blown backward over the table, knocking over the bowl of collard greens. She looked up to see Sarai, Kiana, and Rachelle standing over her, their auras glowing. After Gerald helped her up, she quickly backed away. The other guests stared in stunned silence. Sharon, however, had a proud smirk on her face.

"Yo, what kind of voodoo shit did you do to my sister?" Gerald demanded.

"I haven't done anything to her... yet," Sarai replied.
"If she knows what's good for her, she'll watch her mouth."

"Fuck you, bitch!" Lola seethed. "I ain't watching shit! I ain't no loser! You think you're hot shit just because you got them wack-ass books! Then, you got your friend over there who thinks she's too good for the brothers! Don't even get me started on that dyke you're with!"

"Lola!" Geraldine scolded.

"Mama, don't act like you haven't been saying the same thing!" Lola countered. "You were just saying the other day how Sarai is now all stuck up, and thinks she's too good for the family."

153

"I mean, you did say that, Ma," Gerald added.

"Why would I want to be around people who bring nothing but negativity?" Sarai countered.

"That's enough, you two," Geraldine warned, ignoring Sarai. "We're here to celebrate your uncle's birthday. This is not the ti-"

"Nah, fuck that!" Lola spat, cutting her mother off. "I'm not about to bite my tongue for no damn body!" She then turned to Sarai. "You ain't better than nobody, Sarai. You're a lame. A nobody. Look at you. You're damn near thirty, and you still dress like it's Halloween, and you still read comic books and watch cartoons like a damn kid. Grow up. And you got that damn ring in your nose, looking like a damn cow."

"She still looks better than your dusty ass," Kiana cut in, looking Lola up and down. "I guess Rachelle and I are lames, too, since we engage in the same hobbies she does."

"I know your lesbo ass ain't talking!" Lola spat, stepping closer. "You probably only date girls because no nigga would want your ass."

"And I know you're not talking, with all them baby daddies you got," Sarai countered. "Wasn't one of them a married man? Maybe you should look at yourself before trying to come for somebody else." Lola advanced towards her, but Vernon stepped in to block her path.

"Lola, go sit your ass down somewhere!" he said sternly.
"Acting like you have no damn sense."

"Don't talk to my child like that!" Geraldine cut in. "You need to be checking your daughter and her little friends."

"I have no reason to check them," Vernon said. "You came at my daughter, and now ya'll mad that she told ya'll about yourselves."

"She called my children losers, and you think that's okay?"

"Look, Sarai may have been harsh, but honestly, Geri, is she wrong?" Vernon gestured to Lola and Gerald. "Your son is a grown-ass man with no job and no intentions of getting one, yet you let him mooch off you. He's out here making babies with all these girls, and he's not taking care of them. Does he even know their names or their birthdays?" Gerald looked away, and Vernon continued. "Not to mention he's been 'rapping' for ten years and has nothing to show for it. I'm all for having a dream, but at some point, you gotta hang it up, especially when you can't rap for shit." Sarai, Kiana, and Rachelle nearly choked on their drinks as they tried to stifle their laughter.

"Hey, lay off my brother!" Lola exclaimed. Vernon then rounded on her. "Don't even get me started on you, Lola!" he began. "You had every opportunity handed to you, and you threw them away for some no-good ass niggas. You dropped out of college because you banked on some knucklehead getting a record deal, only to find out he was lying. On top of that, you let him knock you up." Lola opened her mouth to protest, but Vernon shot her a glare that shut her up. "It would have been one thing if you had learned your lesson after that, but you didn't. You kept ripping and running the streets. Yet, you have the nerve to judge my child? Sarai has achieved success that most of us in this family could only dream of. She chased her dreams and found her place in the world on her own terms. So did her friends and her wife. Sarai stands in who she is, regardless of what anyone says or thinks, and I couldn't be more proud. Can you say the same for yourselves?" Lola looked away, seething. She was enraged that her uncle would throw her failures in her face, as well as her brother's. While Vernon was right, her ego would not let her accept criticism. In her mind, Vernon was putting his daughter on a pedestal and rubbing her success in their faces.

"Your daughter is a sinner!" Geraldine spat. "The only reason why she has the good fortune that she has is because she sold her soul to the Devil. On top of that, she is living in sin with a woman and making a mockery of marriage by referring to that woman as her wife! Ever since she found those heathens, she has turned her back on everything she was taught."

"If you're referring to my mother's family, they're not 'heathens'. They're witches and rootworkers," Sarai said. "It is because of them, that I am able to be who I truly am. They showed me more love than this so-called family ever did."

"Witchcraft is an abomination," Geraldine countered. "What you and those people are doing goes against God. And we do love you. That's why we're trying to steer you back in the right direction."

"Well, it sounds like your love is conditional, so you can keep that," Sarai said. "I'm a witch, and I'm married to a woman. Deal with it. I'm not going to change who I am just because you don't like it. Also, maybe you should actually read your bible, because there's magic all up and through that book. Whenever you pray, you're also doing magic because you're calling on a higher power to manifest what you want. You're just too brainwashed to see that."

"Should we go?" Stephen whispered to Sharon.

"Ya'll don't have to leave," Vernon said. He then turned to Geraldine, Lola, and Gerald. "You three, however, can go."

"You're not serious," Geraldine replied. "You would really kick us out after your daughter disrespected us?"

"Sarai was standing up for herself and her friends. That's not disrespect," Vernon said. "However, you and your daughter have disrespected her, as well as my guests, so you need to leave." Geraldine scoffed.

"Fine," she spat, grabbing her purse. "Mama's gonna hear about this." Vernon waved her off as she stormed out of the house, her children following behind her. He let out a long, deep sigh.

"I'm so sorry about that, y'all," he said, sitting back down. "I shouldn't have let that go on the way it did."

"Don't worry about it, man," Stephen said, helping himself to another tamale.

"Yeah, you're not the only one who had a fight at the dinner table," Larry, another one of Vernon's friends, added. "You should have seen my house at Christmas last year." Everyone laughed as they helped themselves to more food.

"Anyway, I think it's time for cake," Sarai called out as she and Kiana brought the birthday cake into the dining room. After lighting the candles, Sarai pulled out her phone and turned on Spotify. "Happy Birthday" by Stevie Wonder played, and everyone sang along. After Vernon blew out his candles, the guests applauded, and the tension seemed to evaporate. Everyone went back to having a good time. Vernon and his buddies played cards as the women chatted among themselves, still shocked at what had unfolded earlier.

"Do you think I went too far?" Sarai asked, taking a bite of her cake.

"Hell no," Kiana said. "Your aunt and cousin were way out of pocket. Your aunt started it when she brought up your stepmom."

"Exactly," Rachelle added. "You had every right to write that book, and you had every right to call out the people that hurt you. If you don't want to be exposed for being a terrible person, then don't be a terrible person."

"That part," Kiana cosigned.

"I guess you're right," Sarai said. "No, I know you're right. I'm just sick of people trying to shame me for speaking out."

"That's their problem, not yours, sweetheart," Sharon said, putting a hand on Sarai's shoulder. "You took your pain and turned it into something positive. That's a powerful thing, and don't let anyone try to take that away from you. I, for one, am very proud of you." Sarai smiled at Sharon.

"Thanks, Ms. Sharon," she said. "I've never said this before, but you have been more of a mother to me than Thelma ever was."

"Oh, honey," Sharon said, giving Sarai a warm hug. "I'm touched that you think of me that way."

"Group hug!" Kiana exclaimed, and the four women joined in a long hug, giggling. Vernon looked over at his daughter and couldn't help but smile. While he couldn't change the past, he vowed to support his daughter no matter what. He knew that the sky was the limit for her, and his heart soared thinking about the endless blessings the universe had in store for her. He was one proud father.

Chapter 13

"**G**irl! You will not believe the day I've had!" Alexis fumed as Rachelle let her into her luxurious Georgian-style home. Her face was red, and her ears were hot. Rachelle could practically see steam coming out of them.

"Everything okay?" she asked, leading Alexis to the couch. She then went to the kitchen and returned with a glass of water. After taking a few sips, Alexis began to calm down. She then started to tell her cousin what had gotten her so riled up.

An Hour Earlier

After paying for gas and snacks at the counter, Alexis made her way outside to fill up her tank. As she approached her vehicle, a small group of men began to catcall her, which she brushed off. However, one of the men had other plans. "Hey, shorty, lemme holla at you for a minute!" he called out, approaching her. He was short, with an average build, dark brown skin, and short locs. Rolling her eyes, Alexis turned to face him.

"My name isn't 'Shorty'," she said, with her hand on her hip, looking him up and down.

> *"Damn, why you gotta say it like that?" the man said defensively. "Well, what's your name then?"*

"Why do you need to know?" Alexis demanded. She didn't have time for lame attempts at flirtation. "I'm just trying to get to know you, baby," the man replied. "You know what, you look kinda familiar." He looked Alexis up and down, eyeing her curvy frame. "Did you use to dance at the King Midas club?" Alexis cursed inwardly. While she knew it was a possibility that she would run into patrons from her former stomping grounds, it didn't make it less annoying.

"Who wants to know?"

"I know who she is!" another man exclaimed.
"That's Queen! She was Midas' girl!"

"Oh, shit, it is Queen!" the short man said. "Damn, you're still bad as fuck. What club you strip at now?"

"I don't strip anymore," Alexis replied.

"Damn, for real? That's a shame. My brother is having a party this weekend to celebrate him getting out. Maybe we can hire you for a private dance?" The other men looked Alexis up and down, undressing her with their eyes. It made Alexis' skin crawl.

"What part of 'I don't strip anymore' do you not understand?" Alexis replied, irritation evident in her voice.

"Oh, so you're too good for me and my boys now?" the short one said with a sneer. "You weren't this stuck up when you were sucking and fucking my boys in the VIP room." The other men laughed and gave each other a high five. Alexis was incensed.

"Yeah, and if I recall, your bum ass tried to pay for a dance with your mama's bridge card!" she spat venomously. "Even if I was still stripping, your ass couldn't afford me."

"Dayum!" an onlooker shouted as the others clowned the young man, wounding his inflated ego.

"Oh, I see you got jokes," he said with a chuckle. "Well, laugh at this, bitch!" He then slammed Alexis onto the hood of her car and pulled out a switchblade. Seeing the fear in Alexis' eyes made him feel powerful. "What, you ain't got nothing to say now? You had a smart-ass mouth a minute ago!"

"Yo, Ray, chill out!" a tall, light-skinned young man said. "We're in broad daylight."

"Fuck that shit, T!" Ray spat, his blade still at Alexis' throat. "I'm not about to let a bitch disrespect me! Especially not a stripper bitch!" He then turned his attention back to Alexis. "See, Midas ain't here to protect your ass. I can slit your throat right now, and nobody will give a fuck. You're a hoe, and that's all you'll ever be." Alexis said nothing. All she could think about was how she might never see her son again, all because some lowlife couldn't handle rejection. Tears stinging her eyes, she silently prayed that her ancestors would get her home in one piece.

"Hey! Break that shit up, before I call the police!" Omar, the gas station's owner, shouted. The small crowd quickly dispersed, and Ray immediately withdrew his blade. The last thing he needed was a probation violation. "Man, let's go," he said. He then spat on the ground near Alexis' feet. "Fuck this coked-out hoe." He got into his friend's vehicle, and the group drove off. Full of adrenaline, Alexis immediately got into her vehicle and drove away.

"Lexi, why didn't you use your powers?" Rachelle asked.

Like Rachelle, Alexis also possessed telekinesis, having discovered it two years ago.

"I was scared, Rachelle!" Alexis exclaimed. "He had a fucking knife to my throat! My power requires focus. I was too scared to focus in that moment. I'm sure that if I so much as blinked wrong, that nigga would have killed me."

"Good point," Rachelle replied.
"Damn. I'm just glad you got away."

"Yeah, me too," Alexis said.
"But that wasn't the worst part."

"What do you mean?"

"On the way here, I called Mama to tell her what happened. You wanna know what she said?"

"What?"

"She was like, 'Well, Alexis, what did you expect? You sold your body and degraded yourself. Of course men aren't going to respect you.' I am so sick of her throwing my past in my face!" Alexis then broke down in sobs. Rachelle held her cousin close to her and allowed her to cry on her shoulder. "I'm sick of it! I've been clean for three years, and I'm not in that lifestyle anymore, but it's like she can't let the shit go." Rachelle's heart broke for Alexis. While she had made some bad decisions, she learned from them. After completing rehab, she went back to school to complete her journalism degree. After interning at a prestigious Detroit lifestyle magazine, she was hired as an editor, thanks to Veronica, who was once married to the magazine's owner. However, it seemed as if this was not enough for Corrine Lawson. While their relationship was already somewhat strained before Alexis' relationship with Vincent, the events of three years' prior have made things worse.

"I'm so sorry, Lexi," Rachelle said, rubbing her cousin's back. "Aunt Corrine was wrong as hell for that. What you did in your past doesn't give anyone the right to disrespect you. Also, you were coerced into doing all that shit! Vincent was a predator."

"It seems that no matter what I do, I'll always be a fuck-up in her eyes," Alexis said with a sniffle. "She was always comparing me to you and criticizing me. It's like she wanted you to be her daughter."

"That's fucking weird," Rachelle said, handing Alexis a tissue. "She needs to appreciate what the fuck is in front of her. Lexi, you haven't touched anything stronger than weed in three years. Do you know how much strength it takes to beat a cocaine addiction? You went back to school and got your degree, and you're an editor for one of the biggest magazines in Detroit. Any mother would be bursting with pride. Hell, I'm proud of you, and so is Uncle Ernie and Bryson. Don't worry about what Aunt Corrine thinks. You are more than enough. If she can't see that, then that's on her, not you." Alexis gave Rachelle a small smile.

"Thanks, cuz," she said as the two shared a hug.
"Thanks for always having my back."

"That's what family is for," Rachelle replied. "Even though we had our differences, I've always had love for you."

"I know," Alexis said as she got up. "I should get going, so I can pick up Bryson. I just needed a listening ear."

"You know I'm always here if you need me."

"Tell Nick I said hi," Alexis said as she and Rachelle hugged again. Rachelle then led her to the door, and they bid each other goodbye. After Alexis had left, Rachelle went upstairs to the nursery. She walked in to see her daughters wide awake. When the twins saw their mother, they smiled and reached for her. Scooping the girls into her arms, Rachelle went back downstairs to the living room. After setting the girls in their playpen, she turned on *Gracie's Corner* and went into the kitchen. Later that evening, Octavia would be coming over for dinner, so Rachelle began to prepare the evening's meal. About an hour after Alexis left, Nick had returned home.

"Daddy!" the twins cried happily. Nick picked up his girls and kissed their faces. He then set them back down and went into the kitchen.

"Hey, baby," he said, kissing Rachelle on the lips. "How was your day?"

"It was pretty good," Rachelle replied as she was placing chicken wings in Caribbean jerk marinade. "Alexis came over earlier."

"Really?" Nick asked. "How's she doing?"

"Well, she was a bit shaken up."

"What? Why?" Rachelle then told Nick about Alexis' encounter with her former clients at the gas station, and what Corrine had told her.

"Are you serious? What kind of mother says something like that?"

"The kind of mother who cares more about what people think than her child," Rachelle replied. "You know, I love Aunt Corrine, but I have always side-eyed her for the way she always compared me and Lexi to each other, and pushed her into activities that she didn't want to do, just because I was doing them. However, I held my tongue out of respect. I'll give Uncle Ernie credit, though. He did put his foot down when it was needed. I think Aunt Corrine resents him for that."

"That's messed up," Nick replied as he helped Rachelle cook. "It explains a lot, though."

"Yeah," Rachelle said. "If Aunt Corrine hadn't been projecting her insecurities onto Lexi, she and I wouldn't have fallen out."

"Well, it's a good thing you two were able to repair your relationship." Rachelle smiled, and the couple continued to cook while their daughters played in the living room. It was around 6 pm when Octavia arrived, carrying a plate of freshly baked brownies.

"I hope you didn't mind me bringing brownies," she said as Nick took the plate from her. "I didn't want to come empty-handed."

"It's not a problem at all," Rachelle said with a smile. "The girls love sweets." Octavia set her purse on the marble coffee table. The twins looked up from their building blocks and smiled at her.

"Hey, cuties," she cooed. She then turned to Nick. "I still can't get over how adorable they are."

"I know, right?" Nick said, as Rachelle picked the twins up and carried them to the kitchen. She then gave them each a plate of Spanish rice and Caribbean jerk chicken. After making Octavia, Nick, and herself a plate, they all sat down and dug in.

"So, how are things at the law firm?" Nick asked as he took a bite of his Spanish rice. "You've been working there for about two months, right?"

"Yeah, and I really like it so far. I'm really grateful to Louise for putting in a good word for me," Octavia replied as she savored her food. "How have things been with you two?"

"Things have been pretty good," Nick replied. "I've been busy with the studio, and Rachelle's been busy with her store. We've also got our hands full with the girls and the wedding." Octavia felt her heart sink at the mention of Nick and Rachelle's upcoming wedding. However, she hid her feelings behind a smile.

"That's cool," she said. "I'm really happy for you two. Other than work, nothing much has been going on with me. However, me and Kendra had a bit of a falling out."

"Really? Why?" Nick asked.

"Well, I told her that I wanted to order one of those ancestry DNA tests, and she thought it was unnecessary. She doesn't think any good could come from it."

"Hmm. I don't see it as unnecessary," Nick replied. "There's nothing wrong with wanting to know where you come from."

"That's what I said," Octavia said. "But she doesn't agree. She said, 'Even if you get results and find relatives, they're strangers to you. They haven't been in your life for this long. What makes you think anything would change now?' I don't expect her to get it. Don't get me wrong, I love Mom, and I am grateful to her, but I don't want to spend the rest of my life wondering about my heritage."

"That's completely valid," Nick said. "If you want to get the test done, then do it. Don't worry about what other people think."

"Exactly," Rachelle added. "Nick and I have an account on 23 & Me, and so does my cousin. Who knows, we might be related." The three of them laughed.

"I doubt it, but it would be interesting," Octavia said as she continued to eat. "So, I saw on Facebook that Louise is pregnant."

"Yep," Rachelle said. "I'm really happy for her. She had a really rough time last year after losing her son."

"Wow," Octavia said.
"I hope she has a healthy pregnancy."

"We all do," Nick replied.

"So, have you and Rachelle thought about having more children?" Rachelle nearly choked on her food, and Nick chuckled.

"Well, I think we're good with our two princesses, but I'm not opposed to more kids in the future," he said. He looked over to see Selena yawning and smiled.

"Somebody's sleepy," Rachelle cooed as she took Selena into her arms.

"No sleepy," Selena mumbled, rubbing her eyes and yawning again.

"Yeah, I've heard that before," Rachelle said as she carried the toddler to the bathroom to give her a bath.

"We're gonna be up there for a while, so make yourself at home," Nick said as he picked up Solana and followed his fiancée upstairs. After finishing her food, Octavia went into the living room to watch television. While Nick and Rachelle were preoccupied with their children, she took a moment to admire their beautiful home. The spacious living room was adorned with elegant vintage furniture that reminded her of the old Hollywood films she would watch with Donna growing up. The entertainment system was state-of-the-art, complete with all the latest game consoles. The walls were adorned with elegant artwork, all done by Rachelle. There were also portraits of Rachelle in vintage attire, shot by Nick and other photographers, framed shots from her maternity shoot, and photos of the twins. However, one portrait that really got Octavia's attention was the one above the sofa. It was a large portrait of Nick, Rachelle, and their twins as newborns. The couple was beaming with joy and cuddled together, while the twins slept serenely in Rachelle's arms, both swaddled in pink. Octavia felt a twinge of envy at the happy family. She never really had much luck in love, but she one day hoped to marry and have children of her own. Seeing Nick with his own family made her regret leaving, although it was not by choice. In her mind, if she had never left, she would be in the portrait instead of Rachelle.

If only I had come back sooner... she thought wistfully. Her thoughts were interrupted by the sounds of thunder and lightning, and strong winds. Well, the news did say it would storm tonight. An hour had passed before Nick and Rachelle returned downstairs, having gotten their daughters to sleep.

"I hope you weren't too bored down here," Nick said as he and Rachelle cleared the table. "Those girls are always fighting sleep." Octavia giggled.

"It's not a problem, Nicky," she said.
"That food really hit the spot, though. Especially that chicken."

"I know, right?" Nick said. "My baby can definitely throw down in the kitchen." Octavia had to resist the urge to roll her eyes.

"Hey, you helped," Rachelle replied as she peeked through the window. "Damn, it's really pouring out there." Nick walked over and peeked outside as well.

"Damn, it is," he said. He then turned to Octavia. "Tay, why don't you sleep in one of the guest rooms tonight?"

"I don't want to impose," Octavia said.

"Nonsense! It's no trouble at all," Rachelle said. "It's storming really bad out, so the roads are slick. We wouldn't feel comfortable with you driving in that. You can leave in the morning when the weather isn't so bad."

"We insist," Nick added, smiling at Octavia, making her blush.

"Well, if you insist," Octavia replied.
"I don't have anything to sleep in, though."

"No worries, girl. I got you," Rachelle said as she led Octavia to the guest room. The room was spacious and elegantly decorated, complete with a beautiful queen-sized bed. Octavia sat on the edge of the bed while Rachelle went to the master bedroom. Five minutes later, she returned with a pair of black pajama shorts and a blue tank top. "These may be a bit big for you, but they should do."

"These are perfect. Thank you," Octavia said, taking the clothes from Rachelle.

"The bathroom's down the hall to the left. Towels and washcloths are in the closet next to it. Have a good night," Rachelle said as she went back to the bedroom, where Nick was waiting for her, shirtless and sitting up in their king-sized bed. Smirking, Rachelle closed the door behind her, locking it. Nick, with a sly smile, got up and walked over to Rachelle, kissing her passionately. Rachelle put her arms around his neck as Nick pulled her top over her head. He then began to kiss her neck, whispering sweet nothings to her in Spanish, something he knew was a major turn-on for Rachelle. Rachelle reached between them and began to palm Nick through his pajama pants, making him moan into the kiss. She smirked when she felt that he was already rock hard. He rubbed his hands all over her body, earning a soft, breathy moan from her.

"Damn," Nick whispered, still kissing her neck. "You're sexy as hell." Rachelle giggled as Nick picked her up and carried her to the bed.

"*Te amo*," Rachelle whispered. Nick looked into her eyes, seeing nothing but pure love. "*Te amo también*," he whispered back, kissing her again. After taking a long, hot shower, Octavia exited the bathroom. As she made her way down the hall, she heard passionate moans coming from the master bedroom. Against her better judgment, she put her ear to the door. She could hear the bed creaking, the sound of skin slapping, and Rachelle's wanton moans.

"Oh fuck… oh fuck…" Rachelle moaned breathlessly as Nick thrust deep inside her, kissing and nibbling her neck. The way her fiancé moved within her felt like pure heaven. His powerful thrusts, combined with his sweet kisses and the sound of his husky voice talking dirty to her in Spanish, made her dizzy with pleasure.

"Eres tan hermosa," he moaned in her ear as he thrusted deeper. "Fuck…" Octavia's heart was pounding as she listened to the couple's passionate lovemaking. She found herself imagining that she was in Rachelle's position, and she couldn't help but feel aroused. She wished she was the one Nick was pleasuring, the one he was marrying. When she heard Nick and Rachelle climax, she almost came on the spot.

"You don't think we woke the babies up, do you?" Nick asked as he pulled Rachelle close to him.

"I wasn't that loud, Nick," Rachelle replied, playfully hitting his arm.

"I'm just kidding, babe," Nick said, giving Rachelle a deep kiss. "I really needed that, though."

"God, same," Rachelle said, yawning. "I'm about to head to the bathroom." Nick playfully slapped Rachelle on the ass as she got up. When Octavia heard Rachelle approaching the bedroom door, she immediately went back to the guest room. Soon after Rachelle was finished, Nick stepped out of the bedroom. Octavia peeked out of the guest room to get a look at Nick's body, and she was not disappointed. His strong biceps and toned chest made her heart race, and she saw that he was definitely blessed below the waist. She envied Rachelle for how lucky she was. She was more determined than ever to win Nick's heart, and Rachelle had better watch herself.

"I wonder what this meeting is about," Carmen said as she and Daniela approached Kristy's home. Rachelle, Nick, and Alexis followed behind

169

them. It was a new moon, which meant it was time for the members of Children of Moonlight to meet.

"When I talked to Lou, she said that Ms. Kristy had some new info about what happened to Anthony," Rachelle said as she rang the doorbell.

"Do you think she knows anything about the attack on the Affirmations building last week?" Daniela asked.

"I guess we'll find out at the meeting," Rachelle replied. A few minutes later, the door opened, and the group was greeted by Kristy, who was dressed in all black, complete with a black head wrap atop her black curls. She led them into the living room, where Louise, Dannell, Mariah, Sarai, and Kiana were waiting. Rose and Violet were seated on the couch across from them with their sons, Amir and Marcus. Trina was overseas for a fashion show, so she was not present. Also present was a woman that Rachelle and her friends had never seen before. She was average height and curvy, with bronze skin. She had dark curly hair with silver streaks throughout. Her eyes were a deep brown and piercing.

"Before we get started, I'd first like to introduce you to Bernadette Devereaux. We often call her Bernie. She is the priestess of our New Orleans chapter," Kristy said.

"I'm pleased to meet all of you," Bernadette said, giving a small smile. Rachelle and the others returned her greeting.

"Where's Simone?" Rachelle asked. Kristy sighed deeply.

"What? Is she okay?"

"Simone was in a car accident a few nights ago," Louise replied.

"What?" Rachelle cried.
"Is she okay?"

"She has a broken leg and a fractured rib, but she'll pull through," Kristy said as she sat on the couch. "However, that's not why I called you all here. I called this meeting because I received a breakthrough regarding these random attacks on us. You were right. Witches are behind this."

"Why, though?" Carmen asked.
"What are they gaining from this?"

"Control," Louise said. "That's what it's all about. Bigots are panicking because they are becoming the minority, so they want to maintain the status quo by any means necessary.

"Is this a small group, or a coven like us?" Nick asked.

"There is a group called The Daughters of Odin," Kristy replied. "They are a female-centered coven. However, they use this coven as a cover for their White supremacist ideals."

"How did you even find this information?" Rachelle asked. Kristy chuckled as she opened her laptop. "You underestimate me, Rachelle," she said with a smirk. "Well, for starters, they had left pamphlets near my shop, so I was able to find their website." She then pulled up the webpage and turned the laptop around for everyone to see. "The Daughters of Odin was established in 2010 and currently has chapters in Michigan, New York, Utah, and Louisiana. They have a total of 6,000 members."

"Damn..." Carmen said.
"Who's their high priestess?"

"Their main high priestess is a woman by the name of Queen Nanna. Her true name is unknown," Kristy replied. "They are one of only a few female-only White supremacist groups and are known to collaborate with other supremacist organizations as well, such as The Aryan Alliance."

"The Aryan Alliance?" Sarai repeated.
"They were at Motor City Pride four years ago!"

"Oh yeah!" Kiana said. "Lou had set their flag on fire."

"I think a few of their members had stormed the Capitol, too," Rachelle added. "They have also been behind terrorist attacks as well," Kristy stated. "That is why Bernie is here. Just recently, a Baptist church in New Orleans had been firebombed. Just like the fire set to the Affirmations building, there was no sign of evidence linking anyone to the attacks."

"So the coven could be helping to cover their tracks," Daniela concluded.

"Exactly," Bernadette said.
"A women's clinic was also firebombed in New York."

"Trina was telling me about that the other day," Louise said. "This is getting out of hand."

"Wait, so this coven is anti-abortion, too?" Kiana asked.

"Yep," Kristy replied.
"They believe abortion is 'White genocide'."

"Why am I not surprised?" Louise said.

"They also support the Blue Lives Matter movement," Sarai said as she read from the coven's website.

"I wouldn't be surprised if some of their members are cops," Kiana added.

"So, now that we have this information, what do we do now?" Carmen asked. "We can't just let them keep doing this."

"We also can't just jump in blindly, *mi hija*," Marisol interjected. "We need to be vigilant and strengthen our defenses."

"Exactly," Kristy said. "Which is why we made these for you." Rose handed Kristy a wooden box engraved with the coven's emblem. Kristy opened the box to reveal various trinkets and pieces of jewelry. "I and the elders of the coven have been working on these for three moon cycles, and they are now ready. Each of these items has been enchanted to not only protect you but to amplify your power." Kristy pulled out an exquisite, antique sun brooch. In the sun's center sat a polished sunstone crystal, and tiny pearls embellished the brooch's edge. It began to glow with a bright light and floated out of the box. To the astonishment of everyone in the room, it gravitated towards Rachelle, who took it into her hands.

"Is this mine?" Rachelle asked.

"It is," Kristy replied with a smile.
"It seems to resonate with your energy the best."

"Kind of similar to how the jewelry chooses the characters in the *MagnifiqueNOIR* books," Sarai said in amazement. Kristy chuckled.

"I guess you can look at it like that," she said. Rachelle continued to admire the brooch's beauty. "Also, if you are ever in distress, the brooch will send a signal to the coven to come to your aid." Kristy then pulled out a gothic-style locket with a skull engraved into it. She opened it to reveal a glowing onyx stone. The locket then floated towards Sarai, who happily took it. She could feel the energy vibrating from the locket, traveling throughout her body. Kiana received an onyx ring, while Nick received a pendant of lightning-struck quartz, a stone that is only found in the Serra de Epinacho, a mountain range in Brazil that is known to be frequently hit with thunderstorms and lightning.

"How were you able to even get this?" Nick asked as he admired the pendant.

"I actually have a friend in Brazil who owns a metaphysical shop," Kristy explained. She then pulled out a gold seashell hair clip embellished with clear quartz and aquamarine. Its aura glowing a bright aqua color, it chose Carmen to be its owner. Daniela received a silver deer pendant with an amethyst crystal hanging from it. She had connected with it immediately, the deer being one of the many symbols of her Orisha, Oya. For Louise, Kristy had taken the moonstone necklace she had given her for her birthday and enchanted it. Dannell had received a clear quartz and obsidian bracelet, and Mariah had received an opal brooch. Alexis had received a set of handcrafted hairpins with amethyst points on the ends.

"I wonder what Trina and Simone will get," Sarai said.

173

"Trina came to pick out hers before she had left for her show," Kristy said. "I'll have Simone choose hers when she has recovered."

"What did Trina get?"

"A jeweled comb," Kristy replied with a smile.

"Of course, it should go without saying that you should not let anyone touch the items you received, and please don't lose them," Rose said. "Enchanting these items drained a lot of energy from us."

"We understand," Nick said as he put the pendant around his neck.

"Also, we have created portals in various places in the city, specifically Downtown, Midtown, Brightmoor, and Southwest Detroit, so that coven members outside of Michigan have a way to get to us when needed. I will send each of you a text with their specific locations," Kristy said. "Only we know where those portals are, and they are not to be shared with anyone outside of our coven. Understood?"

"We understand," they all answered.

"Since Simone has listed me as her emergency contact, I will keep you all updated," Kristy said. "Now, does anyone have any questions?"

"Not really," Louise said.
"Especially now that we know what we're up against."

"Still, I want you all to be careful," Kristy replied. "Bernie and I will remain in communication. I will also remain in communication with Angela from our Harlem chapter. It is now more important than ever that we stick together."

"Kristy is right," Bernadette added. "If this coven is as dangerous as we think they are, they will not rest until they wipe us out. We can't let that happen."

"We won't let that happen," Louise said. "Our ancestors won't let it happen, either. They couldn't wipe us out four hundred years ago. They're not gonna do it now."

Chapter 14

"Look who's here!" Sarai exclaimed as Rachelle pulled into the parking lot of Reneé's Bridal. It was five minutes until noon, and Rachelle and her bridal party had an appointment for their dress fittings. When Rachelle exited the vehicle with her daughters, she saw Sarai, Louise, Artemis, Kiana, Alexis, Khalil, Mariah, Carmen, and Daniela waiting outside the shop. Sharon, Veronica, Joanna, Marisol, Inez, and Magdalena were also present.

"Sorry," Rachelle said.
"There was a traffic jam."

"No worries, honey," Veronica replied.
"Some of us just arrived ourselves."

"Aww, why the long faces?" Sharon cooed, picking up her granddaughters and carrying them inside. "Girl, what did you do to my grandbabies?"

"I didn't do anything," Rachelle replied. "They're just pouting because I told them they couldn't have ice cream for breakfast."

Louise laughed. "I remember those days. When Mimi was that age, she threw a fit because I didn't want to play 'Let It Go' in the car for the billionth time in a row."

"Girl, not 'Let It Go'," Rachelle replied.
"But at least it wasn't 'Baby Shark.'"

"Right?"

"Don't worry, Grandma will get you some ice cream when we leave today," Sharon said, and the girls smiled. "Good afternoon, ladies," a woman called out. Everyone turned to see an attractive, slender, brown-skinned woman walking in. Her brown curls were styled in an updo, and she was dressed in a chic gray suit. "Everyone, this is Reneé Milano. She's a designer and a very good friend of mine," Veronica said.

"Isn't she the one who made Rachelle's birthday gown?" Carmen asked.

"The very one," Veronica said with a smile. "She will also be designing your gowns for Rachelle's big day. Also, don't worry about costs, because I will be taking care of everything."

"It won't be any trouble, will it?" Marisol asked.
"I have no problem paying for my gown."

"Of course not," Veronica replied. "Nothing is too much when it comes to my niece. I assure you, it's not trouble at all."

"That's very generous of you. Thank you," Marisol said.

"Thank you, Ms. Ronnie," Sarai said, and everyone else followed suit. Everyone except Inez, who kept mumbling remarks accusing Veronica of "showing off" and calling Rachelle "spoiled." Rachelle brushed her off, familiar with comments regarding her privilege. This was not the first time Inez had something snide to say. When Rachelle and Nick threw their twins a lavish party for their first birthday, Inez had remarked that the girls would grow up to be "entitled brats" if their parents continued to spoil them. Nick immediately shut his aunt down. Their wedding would be no different. If Veronica wanted to plan a lavish wedding for her only niece, Rachelle was not going to complain. She knew her aunt was doing this out of love, and she was not going to let anyone diminish that, especially Inez Cruz.

"So, Veronica told me your colors are pink and gold, and that you already have a wedding gown that you wanted to dye pink," Reneé said.

"Yes, that's correct," Rachelle said.

"So, I have some fabric samples for you to look over, as well as some design sketches. Also, do you have the gown with you?"

"As a matter of fact, I do," Rachelle said as she handed Reneé a garment bag. They unzipped it and pulled out Joanna's old wedding gown.

"Oh my, this is exquisite," Reneé gushed, staring at the gown in awe. "Where did you find this?"

"It was my mother's," Veronica stated, gesturing to Joanna, who was sitting next to Sharon.

"It's beautiful," Marisol added.

"It really is, and it suits Rachelle so much," Daniela added.

"I agree," Reneé said. "Rachelle, why don't you go into the fitting room to put on this beautiful gown?" Smiling, Rachelle took the gown and headed to the fitting room, while Sharon, Veronica, and Joanna followed behind her. Reneé then began to take the measurements of everyone in the bridal party, while also showing them the designs she had sketched.

"I absolutely love your figure," she said as she was measuring Sarai. "I think this mermaid gown would be perfect for you. The gold would bring out your beautiful complexion and eyes."

"I totally agree," Kiana cosigned. "Especially about her figure." Sarai blushed, and Kiana kissed her on the cheek. Inez stared at them, shocked and appalled at the display of affection.

"Also, since you are the Maid of Honor, I think your gown should be beaded to stand out."

"Sounds good," Sarai said, admiring the design sketch. Reneé then left the room to check on Rachelle.

"So, what are you going to do with your hair?" Inez asked, eyeing Sarai's pink curls.

"What do you mean?" Sarai asked, raising an eyebrow.

"I hope you plan on changing your hair color. Pink hair is very tacky for a wedding. You should also cover those tattoos."

"Inez!" Magdalena cut in sharply, hitting Inez on the arm. *"Eso no es necesario."*

"Yeah, that was very uncalled for," Carmen said, glaring at Inez.

"If Sarai's hair color was an issue, I'm sure Rachelle would have said something by now," Louise added. "Also, Rachelle is the bride, so it's her opinion that matters," Trina chimed in.

"Exactly," Sarai said.

"I would expect someone like you to agree," Inez said under her breath. However, Trina heard her loud and clear.

"Excuse me?" she said.

"I know all about you," Inez said. "I see your face on all those fashion magazines, with everyone praising you for being 'brave,' when all you are is confused."

"¡Inez, cierra tu maldita boca!" Marisol barked, getting up from her seat. "Say one more thing, and it's gonna be me and you."

"You're okay with this?" Inez countered.
"You're okay with a man being a bridesmaid? It's a mockery!"

"You got one more time to disrespect our friend," Louise warned. However, before things could escalate, Reneé came running into the room, with Rachelle, Sharon, Joanna, and Veronica coming behind her, having heard the commotion.

"What's going on here?" she demanded.

"That's what I wanna know," Rachelle added.

"Miss Inez over here called Trina a man, and said having her as a bridesmaid would be a mockery at your wedding," Louise said, shooting Inez a death glare. "She also said that me having pink hair and tattoos would be too 'tacky.'"

"Oh, is that right?" Rachelle said, walking towards Inez, taking care to not step on her gown. "Well, if that's how you feel, then you don't have to come to our wedding."

"What are you saying?" Inez demanded.

"What I'm saying is, *tu invitación ha sido rescindida*."

"You can't uninvite me!" Inez yelled.
"Nick won't allow it! I'm his *familia*!"

"Actually, Nick is 100% behind me on this. We are a united front when it comes to you, and he told me that if you did or said anything out of line, you would not be welcome at our wedding. See, not only did you insult my friends, but his friends, too." Inez looked at Marisol, Magdalena, and her nieces, hoping for someone to defend her. However, she had no takers. "What about *Mamá*?" she countered. "Who's going to look after her if I'm not at the wedding?"

"Don't worry, we will look after her," Carmen said.

"Ma'am, I think I speak for everyone when I say, please leave," Reneé said, gesturing towards the door. Inez scowled and grabbed her purse, storming to the door in a huff. "Byeee!" Solana exclaimed as Inez stormed past her. The adults tried their hardest to stifle their laughter.

"My sincerest apologies, ladies," Reneé said. "That kind of behavior is not accepted at this establishment."

"You don't need to apologize," Sarai said. "You can't control a grown adult's behavior. She's too damn old to be so disrespectful and rude."

"For real," Daniela cosigned.
"Anyway, we're not here for her. We're here for Rachelle."

"Exactly," Reneé said as she led Rachelle to the platform and helped her step up. Everyone stared at her in awe. She looked radiant and regal, and the gown fit her like a glove.

"Oh, Chelly, you look gorgeous," Sarai said, awestruck.

"You look like a princess," Marisol said. She then turned to the twins. "Doesn't your mommy look bonita?"

"*Sí*," the twins said in unison, giving their mother a toothy grin.

"So, I'm thinking we can dye this gown and the veil a dusty rose color," Reneé began, as she circled around Rachelle. "I can also add pearl and crystal beading to the bodice and add a train to the back. Your flower girls can wear dusty rose dresses, and for the reception, I can design a pink evening gown. What do you think?"

"That sounds perfect," Rachelle replied as she looked in the mirror, beaming. As she stared at her reflection, she couldn't help but get emotional. As a little girl, she always imagined her dream wedding. Now, it was actually becoming a reality. If only her father could see her.

"Honey, are you okay?" Sharon asked.

"I'm fine," Rachelle said, wiping a tear from her eye.
"I just can't believe this is actually happening."

"I can," Sharon said as she put her arm around her daughter's shoulder. "I've been dreaming of this from the moment you were born. You are a beautiful, strong, and intelligent woman. Any man would be lucky to have you as a wife."

"Thanks, Mommy," Rachelle said, as she and Sharon shared a hug.

"You should see the designs Reneé came up with for the bridesmaids' dresses," Sarai cut in. Rachelle stepped down from the platform and walked over to the table with Reneé's design book and fabric samples.

"Oh, these are nice," she said. "I love these."

"I'm so glad you like them," Reneé said, smiling proudly. "I promise you will all look positively divine."

"I have no doubt about that," Rachelle replied. "The gown you made for my birthday party was proof enough."

"So, now that I have all of your measurements, I will place the fabric orders as soon as you leave. I should have the shipment in about three weeks. After that, I will get to work. I should have all of your gowns done within about six months. However, I will call you in for final fittings, in case I need to make any adjustments."

"Sounds good," Rachelle said.

"Thank you again, Reneé," Veronica added.

"Of course. Anything for my most loyal client," Reneé replied, and the two women gave each other a kiss on the cheek. After paying the deposit on the gowns, Veronica took the women out to lunch as a treat, with Sharon treating her granddaughters to ice cream as promised. After lunch, everyone went their separate ways, and Rachelle took her girls home. When they arrived, Nick was in the living room, watching anime.

"Hey, you," she said, giving Nick a quick peck. Their daughters made a beeline to their toys, while Rachelle took a seat next to Nick on the couch.

"How was the fitting?" Nick asked.

"It was nice," Rachelle replied. "Your auntie just couldn't help herself with her bullshit comments, though."

"Yeah, *Mamá* called and told me about that," Nick said. "I don't know what *tía* expected, though. She was out of line, and I don't want that kind of negativity on our big day."

"Thankfully, your mom will look after your grandma when she comes here for the wedding,"

"Yeah," Nick said, as he pulled Rachelle close to him, and the two of them snuggled while watching *Jojo's Bizarre Adventure*. The twins waddled over to the couch and climbed up, to the amusement of their parents. It was moments like these that reminded them how blessed they were. No matter what life threw at them, seeing the happy faces of their children made everything worth it.

"It sucks that we won't be able to get in the water this year," Kiana stated as she and Sarai exited their vehicle. They had just arrived at Kensington Metropark, where the annual Cosplay Beach Party was being held. However, the actual beach was closed off due to a chemical spill.

"Yeah, but that doesn't mean we still can't have fun," Sarai said as they walked towards the party. As they were walking, they were spotted by Rachelle and Nick, who called them over. They noticed that Octavia was also with them.

"Hey, you made it!" Rachelle exclaimed.

"Of course we did," Sarai replied. She then turned to Octavia.

"Hey, it's good to see you again."

"Likewise," Octavia said, giving a small smile.

"Your cosplay is so hot," Kiana said, admiring Rachelle's look. She was dressed as Princess Kitana from *Mortal Kombat 3*, wearing her signature blue bodysuit with the plunging neckline. Her hair was brushed into a puff ponytail, and in her hand were two large fans. Nick opted not to wear a cosplay, and was dressed in a pair of shorts and a blue t-shirt. Octavia wore a simple yellow two-piece swimsuit, which showed off her slender frame, and her red curls were styled in a ponytail.

"Thanks," Rachelle replied. "You two look adorable." Sarai was cosplaying as a swimsuit version of Princess Bubblegum from *Adventure Time*, complete with a pink one-piece swimsuit and a gold crown atop her hot pink hair. Kiana was dressed as Misa Amane from *Death Note*, with a black gothic swimsuit and a honey blonde wig.

"Where's Lou and Will?" Sarai asked.

"Lou is at her booth," Rachelle replied, pointing towards the vendor area. "Will took Mimi to get some food." Rachelle gestured towards the shelter, where people were working the grill. "

Cool," Sarai said as she unfolded her chair and sat down. "Damn, it's hot as shit."

"For real," Rachelle cosigned, as she used one of her fans to cool herself. "Good thing we didn't bring the girls. They would have been miserable."

"Where are my nieces, anyway?" Sarai asked.

"They're with my parents this weekend," Nick answered.

"By the way, guess who called me this morning before we got here?" Sarai said.

"Who?" Rachelle asked.

"My nana," Sarai replied.
"She didn't like how I spoke to Aunt Geraldine and my cousins."

"They deserved it, though!" Rachelle said.

"That's what I told her, but she said that it didn't matter what Aunt Geraldine said to me, I should respect my elders." Rachelle sucked her teeth.

"Typical," she said. "Old folks think they can talk to us any kind of way, but if we return their energy, we're the disrespectful ones."

"Word," Kiana chimed in.

"She also said I should forgive Thelma and let go of the past." Sarai then let out a loud cackle. "First of all, how can I forgive someone who's already dead, and who also never acknowledged that she did anything wrong? She stood ten toes down in her bullshit! I don't have to forgive anything!"

"What did you say to your grandma after that?" Nick asked.

"I told her I don't owe anyone forgiveness, and that if she wants to continue to dismiss my trauma, then it's best that we don't talk for a while. I hung up and blocked her number after that. I'm sick of her making excuses for our family's toxicity."

"I don't blame you," Rachelle said.

"Man, I'm glad Lou has her booth in the shade," Kiana said. "I can't imagine dealing with this heat while being pregnant."

"Speaking of Lou, let's go check on her," Sarai said as she got up. She and Kiana made their way to Louise's booth, and Rachelle followed behind them. When they approached the booth, Louise was preoccupied with a customer, so they waited until she finished her transaction.

"Hey, ya'll," Louise said, taking a sip of water. She was dressed as a human Luna from *Sailor Moon*, wearing a bright yellow one-piece swimsuit with ruching in the front. Her hair was styled in two buns on the top, with the rest of her curls hanging down. "Having fun?"

"Not yet, since we just got here," Sarai replied, browsing her cousin's merchandise. She picked up a resin rolling tray that said "Witch Bitch." "Ooh, I really like this."

"You can have it for $20," Louise said.

"Bet," Sarai said, taking a twenty-dollar bill from her purse. After receiving the money, Louise wrapped up the tray and handed it to her cousin in a gift bag.

"Thank you, cuz," Sarai said.

"Hey, babe. Sorry it took so long. It was a long line," Wilfred said as he approached the booth with Artemis, who was happily savoring a hot dog. Wilfred handed his wife a double cheeseburger and a can of red Faygo.

"I'm not surprised," Louise said as she bit into her burger. "There's a lot of people here."

"Mimi, your swimsuit is so cute," Kiana cooed. Artemis was dressed in a *Sailor Moon* inspired swimsuit, and her sandy brown hair was styled in two puff ponytails, complete with red hair balls.

"Thank you," Artemis replied, smiling at Kiana.

"This party has a huge turnout so far," Rachelle remarked, observing the large crowd gathering near the DJ booth. "A lot more since the last party."

"Yeah," Louise said as she finished off her burger.

"Do you think we'll run into You-Know-Who here?" Kiana asked. Louise sucked her teeth.

"Considering how damn near everyone in the Michigan anime community is here, I wouldn't be surprised if we did," she said. "Even if we do, who cares? They're not gonna stop me from having fun or getting my bag."

"I know that's right!" Rachelle said, giving Louise a high five.

"Hey, why don't we check out the watermelon smashing contest?" Sarai suggested.

"Sounds good to me," Wilfred said. He then turned to Artemis. "Hey, Princess, wanna go smash some melons?"

"Yeah!" Artemis said excitedly, and father and daughter walked off together. Sarai and Kiana trailed behind them.

"Yeah, they can have fun with that. I'm not messing up my cosplay," Rachelle said, and Louise laughed.

"For real," she said. "Well, I'm gonna be here for about another half hour, and then I'm gonna take a break."

"Alrighty then," Rachelle said, and she left Louise's booth and went back to where Nick and Octavia were sitting. The two of them were chatting with Chris and Khalil, who had just arrived.

"Hey, girlie!" Khalil chirped, giving Rachelle a hug. Rachelle then walked over to Nick and gave him a kiss.

"So, what are ya'll talking about?" she asked.

"We were talking about *My Hero Academia*," Nick replied, as Rachelle sat on his lap. Octavia burned with envy as she watched Nick and Rachelle flirt with each other, and seeing how lovey-dovey they were made her nauseous. However, she knew she had to hide her irritation. She didn't want to be seen as the jealous female friend.

"So, Octavia, how are you enjoying the party so far?" Rachelle asked.

I would enjoy it a lot more if I didn't have to see you all over Nicky! Octavia thought to herself. However, she knew that being hostile to Rachelle would make her look bad in Nick's eyes. "It's pretty fun," she said, forcing a smile. "I wish we had something like this when I was in Washington."

"It's really muggy out here, though," Khalil said.
"It's a good thing we're out of the sun."

"Right?" Rachelle cosigned as she fanned herself. Suddenly, a young brunette dressed as Pikachu came over. "Hey. I just wanted to say that I really love your cosplay," she said.

"Aww, thank you," Rachelle replied, and Octavia couldn't help but roll her eyes. Thankfully, no one noticed. "My boyfriend is making a cosplay music video, and I was wondering if you'd like to be in it."

"Sure!" Rachelle said as she got off Nick's lap.

"Have fun, babe," he said, giving Rachelle a peck on the cheek. Giggling, Rachelle walked away with the cosplayer towards the DJ booth. Octavia watched the two women as they walked away, her envy festering. *She thinks she's such hot shit*, she seethed to herself. The only reason they want her in that video is so guys can ogle her.

"Hey, is everything okay?" Nick asked, abruptly interrupting Octavia's thoughts. "You're awfully quiet."

"Yeah, I'm fine," Octavia replied as she sipped from her water bottle. It's now or never, she thought. "Hey, Nicky, do you think we can go someplace and talk? Alone?" Nick raised an eyebrow.

"Uh, sure thing," he said, getting up. He turned to Chris and Khalil and said, "If Rachelle comes back and I'm not here, just tell her that Octavia needed to talk to me about something." The couple nodded, and Nick walked off with Octavia, looking for a place to talk out of earshot. They eventually settled on a tree that was not too far away from the party. "So... what's on your mind?" Octavia's heart was beating a mile a minute. Over the past few months since returning to Michigan, she and Nick have been able to rekindle their friendship. However, her feelings towards him were no longer platonic. She thought of Nick constantly and even dreamt of him. While she knew Nick was engaged to and created a family with someone else, she had to tell him how she felt. Otherwise, she would regret it for the rest of her life. Also, what if there was a chance that Nick shared her feelings? She wouldn't know unless she told him.

"I've been wanting to talk to you about this for a while, but I don't know how you would take it," she began.

"Tay, you're my friend. You can talk to me about anything. So, what's up?" Nick replied.

"Well, we've been friends for a long time, and I'm very grateful we found each other again. When I was in Washington, it was really lonely, and the only people I knew there were Mom and Kendra. Then, I lost Mom, and I was in a really dark place."

"I can only imagine how hard that was for you," Nick said.

"When you came back into my life, it was like a breath of fresh air. It was like I never left," Octavia continued. "When I was gone, Nick, I never stopped thinking about you, and..." Octavia slightly hesitated.

"And?" Nick repeated. Octavia took a deep breath and continued.

"What I'm trying to say is... I'm in love with you, Nicky. I love you so much." Nick was speechless. The last thing he expected from Octavia was a love confession. While Octavia was attractive, kind, intelligent, and shared the same hobbies and interests as him, he never thought of her as more than a good friend. His heart belonged to Rachelle Lawson, the mother of his children. He knew he had to let Octavia down gently, so as not to hurt her or jeopardize their friendship. While he did not have romantic feelings for her, he did care about her well-being. Octavia stared at Nick, growing more anxious at his silence. *Damn it!* she thought. *Now our friendship is over.*

"I see..." Nick began, reeling from Octavia's confession. "I wasn't expecting that. Um, but you do know I'm with Rachelle, right?"

"I know," Octavia said. "I'm not asking you to dump her or anything. I just wanted you to know how I felt." Nick let out a sigh and ran his hand through his hair.

"Well... I appreciate you telling me," he said. "Tay, you're an awesome person, and any man will be lucky to have you as a partner. Unfortunately, that man can never be me. I love Rachelle, and we have a family together. I plan on spending the rest of my life with her. You and I can never be more than friends. If that is something you can't accept, I understand, and I wish you the best." Octavia felt her heart shatter into a million pieces at that very moment. While she knew it was unlikely that Nick would return her romantic feelings, she still held out a glimmer of hope that he loved her, too. However, hearing Nick say that he only saw her as a friend crushed her. Hearing him say that he loved Rachelle made Octavia resent her even more.

"I-I understand," she said, letting out a sigh. "I just want you to be happy. I hope this doesn't ruin our friendship. I don't want to lose you again."

"We'll always be friends," Nick said, and the two shared a brief hug before heading back to their spot, where Rachelle was waiting. Sarai, Kiana, Louise, Wilfred, and Artemis were also with her.

"Everything good?" Rachelle asked.

"Yeah, everything's fine," Nick said. He then leaned closer to her, so they were out of earshot, and whispered, "I'll tell you about it later." Rachelle simply nodded.

"So, Lou, how has business been?" she asked.

"Pretty good. I'm almost sold out," Louise replied.
"Khalil told me you were invited to dance for a music video."

"Yep. I can't wait to see how it turns out," Rachelle replied.
"Also, guess who I ran into?"

"Who?"

"Ashley."

"Ain't that Nick's ex?" Louise asked.

"Yep," Rachelle said. "She avoided me though, so there were no issues, other than her little friends talking shit about my cosplay under their breaths. I did catch her staring at my ring, though. I know she was mad."

"That's what she gets for being a racist piece of shit," Sarai said.

"Anyway, who wants to go back out and dance?" Rachelle asked, changing the subject. "The party ends in about three hours."

"I'm down," Kiana said, and she headed to the DJ area with Sarai, while Louise followed with Artemis. Wilfred followed them to watch.

"You wanna dance, too?" Rachelle asked, looking at Nick.

"Sure," Nick replied, and the two walked off, hand in hand. Octavia watched bitterly as the couples danced, fighting back her tears. Seeing Nick hold Rachelle close to him and kissing her tore at her heart. Seeing them so happy and in love filled her with a jealousy so intense that she couldn't describe it. While she knew it was wrong for her to feel this way, her heart and her ego wouldn't allow her to see reason. *What does she have that I don't?* she asked herself. Another reason why she resented Rachelle was not only because she had Nick, but because she reminded Octavia of the type of girls that tormented her in school: pretty, popular, and privileged. While she knew Rachelle was not like those girls, and was nothing short of kind to her, Octavia's resentment only grew. *What did she do to deserve him? I knew him longer. I bet she used magic to seduce him*, she seethed to herself. It wasn't fair that Rachelle was the mother of Nick's children, that she was living with Nick, and got to fuck Nick on a regular basis. *It should be me, not her! One way or another, I'm going to make Nick see that I'm the one for him.*

Chapter 15

"Hey, Tay!" Kendra called from the kitchen as Octavia entered their home, exhausted from a long day at the law firm. "How was work?"

"Meh. Same as always. Tiring," Octavia replied as she set her purse on the coffee table. She then kicked off her low-heel pumps and sat on the couch.

"I feel you. Work tired me out, too," Kendra said as she came into the living room with two glasses of ginger ale and sat on the couch next to her sister. While Octavia worked as a paralegal, Kendra worked as a dental assistant. "So, how was that beach party you went to? You never told me how it went."

"There really wasn't much to tell," Octavia said with a shrug. "I mean, it was fun, but that's about it." Octavia then continued to scroll through Facebook, not really interested in conversation. This was odd to Kendra. Octavia would usually talk her ear off about her workday, celebrity gossip, or something she saw online. Yet this past week, she had been quiet and distant.

"Is everything okay, Tay?" she asked.
"You know you can talk to me if there's anything wrong."

"I'm fine," Octavia said flatly. "I just had a long day at work, that's all." She then got up from the couch. "I'll be in my room. Yell if you need me."

"But you didn't finish your pop."

"I'm not thirsty." Before Kendra could say anything further, Octavia went upstairs to her bedroom and closed the door. Kendra knew her sister had something on her mind other than her workload, but the last thing she wanted to do was pry and risk pushing Octavia away.

She'll talk whenever she's ready, she thought as she continued to watch television. Meanwhile, Octavia lay in bed, staring up at the ceiling. She had logged off Facebook due to her feed being bombarded with photos from the beach party. Seeing Nick and Rachelle dancing together and kissing cut her deeply, and seeing people comment about what a cute couple they were made her feel even worse. It had been a week since she had confessed her feelings to Nick, and the pain of his rejection was still fresh. *"You and I can never be more than friends."* Those words echoed in Octavia's mind, replaying over and over like a broken record. She could hardly sleep because every time she closed her eyes, she saw Nick's face. Thankfully, her work performance hadn't suffered. She knew Kendra would never let her hear the end of it if she lost her job because she let her emotions distract her. She let out a deep sigh. *Maybe I should give dating another try*, she thought. *It might take my mind off him*. Octavia was snapped out of her melancholy when she received a notification on her phone. With an annoyed sigh, she reached over to the left of her and grabbed it. Her mood was instantly lifted when she saw that she had an email from 23 & Me.

My test results! she thought to herself as she clicked the link in the email. After logging in, she was taken to a page summarizing her DNA test results. No longer able to contain her excitement, she began to read the breakdown of her genetic makeup.

"Hmm, so I'm 28% Norwegian, 25% Nigerian, and 12% Irish..." she read. The breakdown also showed that she had ancestry from Uganda, France, Wales, Germany, and Ghana, as well as Spain and Scotland. Octavia was elated. Her entire life, she had questioned who she was, where she came from. Now, she had answers. *Maybe now I'll be able to find my birth parents*, she thought hopefully. She checked to see if there was anyone on the site that shared her DNA, and to her surprise, there were over a hundred matches. However, a majority of the family trees the matches were linked to were private. But there was one that was public, and to her shock, it was none other than Alexis Lawson.

"Rachelle's cousin?" she whispered to herself. However, what was even more shocking was that Alexis was shown to be a potential sibling. *There's no fucking way!* she thought in disbelief. She clicked on Alexis' tree, and her parents were listed as Ernest and Corrine Lawson.

193

Their photos were also shown. *Well, my birth mother is white, so Alexis and I don't have the same mother, so that must mean Ernest is my father!*

Octavia's head was spinning. Her sister is the cousin of the woman who she believed stole Nick from her! Also, since Ernest was the twin brother of Rachelle's father, that made Rachelle her cousin, too! This infuriated Octavia. "So, not only did that spoiled little bitch steal Nicky from me, I share DNA with her!" she fumed to herself. This revelation was too much for her. To be connected by blood to the woman who bore Nick's children, and whom Nick was planning to spend the rest of his life with, made Octavia sick with envy. In her mind, Nick was bewitched by Rachelle. If Rachelle wasn't in the picture, then maybe Nick would have chosen her instead. *Since she used magic to get him, maybe I can use magic to break them up!* she thought. *All's fair in love and war, right?* She grabbed her phone and went to TikTok. She typed in "Break Up Spells" in the search section and began to watch video after video on how to break up relationships using magic. She was eventually led to a page that had their shop listed in their bio. After placing her order, she decided to go to sleep, feeling like a weight was lifted from her shoulders.

Two Weeks Later

"Hey, I'm gonna go meet Nikita downtown for drinks. I probably won't be back until late, so don't wait up," Kendra said as she walked into the living room. Octavia was sitting on the couch, watching YouTube videos on the television.

"Have fun," Octavia said. She was glad she was going to be alone in the house. She didn't want any distractions while she did what she planned to do that night. After checking herself out in the hallway mirror, Kendra left the house. Octavia then went upstairs into her bedroom and grabbed the package she had ordered from the occult shop, which was delivered to her two days ago. It was now a waning moon, the perfect time to do a break-up spell. She had decided to perform the ritual because she felt that if Nick and Rachelle's engagement was broken, then the road would be clear for her to have Nick for herself. However, she knew she couldn't go into Diana's Garden for the materials she needed, or any local metaphysical shops, for fear that word would get back to Nick. So, she went online for the supplies.

"Here goes nothing," she said as she opened the package, which contained a black prayer candle, a bottle of Break Up oil, and a packet of Break Up Spell herbs. After laying out the materials, she grabbed the tin pan she had purchased from the dollar store and set it in the middle of the table. She then took a photo of Rachelle and Nick from their engagement shoot, which she had printed from Facebook, and wrote their names and birthdates on the back. She took the bottle of oil and put a drop on each of the four corners of the photo and in the center. She then sprinkled some of the herbs onto the photo and folded it away from her. After dressing the candle, she set it in the pan on top of the photo and sprinkled the remaining herbs counterclockwise around the candle. Admiring her setup, she pulled up a break-up playlist on Spotify that she had created and lit the candle. She closed her eyes and visualized Nick and Rachelle arguing, fighting, and hurling insults at each other. She even imagined Rachelle taking off her engagement ring and throwing it at Nick, which made her smile. She opened her eyes, and to her disappointment, the candle's flame was burning low. However, she did not let that discourage her. Taking a deep breath, she began to recite the incantation on the card that came with the spell kit:

"Nick and Rachelle,
Your love is no more
Like oil and vinegar, you shall become,
Your relationship will sour
Your love will turn to hate
May you fight
May you argue
May you be utterly repulsed by the sight of each other,
And never speak again
By the power of three times three
As I will it,
So mote it be."

Octavia continued to visualize her desired outcome as the candle burned. After about an hour, she snuffed out the candle. She then cleaned up the space and burned incense to cleanse the energy. Afterwards, she put the items under the bathroom sink. The next day, she lit the candle again and repeated the incantation and visualization. She continued the ritual for seven more days. On the ninth night, she burned the photo and blew the ashes into the wind away from her home. She then went home and cleansed herself after throwing away the empty glass. Her sister was none the wiser. Octavia made sure to do the ritual while Kendra was either asleep or out of the house. It was a good thing that Kendra was a heavy sleeper. Octavia knew that if her sister knew what she was up to, she would not approve and would try to stop her. She knew she couldn't tell anyone what she was doing because she would be labeled as "crazy" or a "weirdo" for using magic to break up her friend's relationship. If she told Kendra how much she resented Rachelle, she knew her sister would tell her to move on. "It just wasn't meant to be." "If you really care about Nick, you would let him be happy," was what she imagined Kendra would say. However, that was not what she needed. She needed Rachelle out of the way so that Nick would be hers. Now that she had cast the spell, she was confident that she would have what she wanted. All she needed to do was be patient and have faith in the Universe.

Chapter 16

One Month Later

"*L*ena! Lana! Stay out of Mommy's purse," Rachelle gently scolded as she pushed the shopping cart down the aisle. It was the day of the twins' third birthday party, and Rachelle and Nick needed to get some last-minute items.

"So, what's next on the list?" Nick asked. Rachelle reached into her purse and pulled out a small piece of paper.

"Hmm, looks like we need candy for the party favors," she said, and they headed towards the candy aisle. The shelves were nearly empty due to the Halloween season. "At least they didn't take all the chocolate." Rachelle took a few bags of mixed chocolates and put them in the cart. She then looked at the list again.

"Is that it?" Nick asked.

"Looks like all we need to get are the balloons, and we're all set," Rachelle replied, and the couple made their way to the party section, which was on the other side of the store.

"Hey, babe?"

"Yeah?"

"Are you sure you don't mind Tay being at the party?" Nick asked. "The last thing I want is for you to be uncomfortable."

"Nick, it's fine," Rachelle replied. "While I know Octavia has feelings for you, she did agree to the two of you being just friends, and so far, she hasn't crossed any boundaries. I have no reason to be uncomfortable." Nick smiled and gave Rachelle a quick peck on the lips. "I love you."

"I love you more."

"Wuv you," Selena said, smiling up at her parents.

"We love you, too," Rachelle said as she and Nick kissed their daughters' faces, making them squeal and laugh.

"Rachelle? Is that you?" a familiar voice called. Rachelle turned around and saw none other than Shawna Roberts, her former romantic rival. However, she looked completely different. Her fiery red hair was covered with a dark gray hijab, and she had also grown a bit thicker. When she came face-to-face with Rachelle, she smiled.

"Shawna? Oh my god, how have you been? It's been ages!"

"It has," Shawna said. "Last time we saw each other was at Sarai's first book signing. I see that you two have been doing really well for yourselves."

"We have," Rachelle said with a smile.
"So, how's your son?"

"He's been well, although he's sick with a cold right now," Shawna replied. "He's at home with his father."

"His father?" Rachelle asked, confused. "I thought that—"

"My husband's not Emmanuel's biological father. He adopted him after we married," Shawna clarified.

"When did you get married?"

"Last year," Shawna said, flashing her wedding ring. "Don't worry, I didn't use any magic to get him. I definitely learned my lesson."

"Congratulations," Rachelle said. "I'm happy for you."

"Thank you," Shawna replied.
"You're one of the few people that actually are."

"What do you mean?"

"My parents weren't too happy about me marrying a Muslim and converting," Shawna replied.

"But Muslims believe in God, too," Rachelle said.
"Allah simply means 'God' in Arabic."

"Exactly, but you know how the folks in that church are. To them, anything that's not strictly Jesus is wrong. However, I could care less what they think. I love Ahmad, and he makes me happy. He's also an excellent father to Emmanuel."

"Well, you deserve to be happy after what you went through."

"So do you," Shawna said with a smile.
"Sarai told me you got engaged. Congratulations."

"Thank you," Rachelle said, beaming.

"Well, I should get going. I came here to get some medicine for my son. It was good to see you. Y'all take care."

"Same to you. I hope Emmanuel gets better," Rachelle said. Shawna smiled and walked away to complete her errands. "I'm glad she's doing well."

"Same here," Nick said as they headed to the checkout line. "By the way, did you peep that amethyst bracelet she was wearing?"

"Well, Lou did say Shawna had been messaging her and Ms. Kristy about spirituality," Rachelle replied. After paying for their items, they headed home to get the place ready for the party. Sarai, Kiana, Sharon, and Trina came over to help decorate.

"I'm glad Shawna's doing well," Sarai said as she and Kiana were putting up streamers. Rachelle had just told her about their encounter in the grocery store. "To think that you two couldn't stand each other."

"That's all in the past," Rachelle said as she was filling up balloons with a helium machine. "Besides, Lamar was the problem."

"True," Sarai said.
"I'm also glad she got away from that church."

"For real," Rachelle said.
"It would be pretty interesting if she has powers like us, though."

"I'd pay to see the look on her daddy's face if that's the case," Sarai said, and the others laughed. "By the way, have you talked to Simone?"

"Yeah, I talked to her yesterday," Rachelle said. "She's still a bit shaken up about what happened to her, but she said she'll try to make it. I don't blame her if she's not up for it, though."

"Yeah," Sarai said. After about two hours, the home was completely decorated with silver and gold, with suns, moons, and rainbows. Satisfied with the decor, Rachelle took the girls upstairs to bathe them and get them dressed. The twins looked like little princesses, with Solana in a rainbow-colored dress with a gold tiara, and Selena in a dark blue dress with silver moons and stars, and a silver tiara. Once the girls were ready, Rachelle brought them back downstairs, where the guests were waiting. Alexis had just arrived with Bryson and her parents, and Louise and Wilfred had arrived with Artemis. Soon after, Dannell had arrived with Mariah and Dy'Anna.

"Aww, you two look so pretty," Louise cooed as the twins twirled around, showing off their dresses.

"What do you say?" Nick asked.

"Tank you," the twins replied in unison. The children were left to play in the den area, as the adults chatted among themselves in the dining room.

"So, have you heard from Octavia?" Rachelle asked.

"She just texted me. She and Kendra are on their way," Nick replied. Rachelle simply nodded as she put a tray of brownies on the table.

"So, Trina, how have things been going? You've been on the move lately," she said. Trina giggled.

"Things are good. I'm currently seeing someone."

"Okay, we want details," Sarai chimed in, leaning forward. "Don't you dare leave anything out!"

"Well, his name is Pierre. He's a fashion model, and we met at London Fashion Week," Trina replied. "We've been dating for almost six months now."

"Yasss, bitch!" Kiana exclaimed, giving Trina a high five. "So, do you have a picture?" Smirking, Trina pulled out her phone and went into her photo gallery. She showed the group a photo of herself with a tall, handsome man with light bronze skin, hazel eyes, and soft, dark curls.

"Okay, he's fine as fuck," Louise remarked. "Does he treat you right?"

"Oh, definitely," Trina said.

"Good, because I don't want to have to hex a nigga," Louise replied.

"Trust me, I got that covered if he steps out of line."

"Period!" Mariah chimed in.

"So, Sarai, how have things been going with your books?" Nick asked.

"Things are pretty good," Sarai replied. "My memoir has been on the bestseller list for two months now."

"That's what I'm talking about!" Rachelle exclaimed.

"I'm so happy for you." Sarai beamed at her.

"How are things at the studio?" Kiana asked.

"Things have been pretty busy," Nick replied. "I had to do a lot of baby portraits this month, plus a shoot with the twins. You know I can't get those girls to sit still for anything." Rachelle and Sarai laughed.

"You're right about that," Rachelle said.

"You better chill on my grandbabies," Marisol said, playfully hitting Nick on the arm. Suddenly, the doorbell rang.

"I'll get it," Rachelle announced as she went to the door. When she opened it, she was greeted with the smiling faces of Octavia and Kendra.

"Hey!" Kendra exclaimed.
"Sorry we're late."

"Oh, it's no problem at all," Rachelle said as she stepped aside to let them in. She then took the gift bags they brought and set them on the table with the other birthday gifts and cards.

"Hey, you made it!" Nick said as he gave the sisters a hug.

"Of course," Octavia said with a smile. Nick led her and Kendra to the table and offered them pizza and brownies, which they happily accepted.

"Your girls look so adorable," Kendra remarked as she took a bite of her pepperoni pizza. "
Don't they?" Rachelle said as she watched the children play. She then let out a wistful sigh. "Sometimes, I wish they could stay little forever."

"All parents have that feeling," Sharon said, putting her hand on Rachelle's shoulder. "However, the true gift is watching them grow into their best selves. With you as a mother, I'm sure they will grow into wonderful, strong women."

"Thanks, Mom," Rachelle said, smiling at Sharon.

"Mommy?" Bryson asked, walking over to the table.
"Can we have some cake now?"

"I don't know, baby," Alexis said. She turned to Rachelle.
"What do you say, cuz?"

"It's about time to bring out the cake, anyway," Rachelle stated as she went into the kitchen, with Sharon following her. A few minutes later, they returned to the dining room with a large marble cake. Half the cake was gold with a rainbow topper, and the other half was dark blue with a silver moon topper. In the center, "Happy 3rd Birthday Lena and Lana!" was written in white icing. Nick brought the twins to the table, sitting them in front of the cake. Once everyone had gathered around them, they all sang "Happy Birthday." With their parents' assistance, the twins blew out the candle, earning applause from the other guests. Afterwards, Rachelle cut the cake and began serving slices to everyone. Happy that they got their dessert, the children ran back to the den, where Encanto was playing on the large television.

"So, Louise, how's the pregnancy coming along?" Trina asked. Louise smiled.

"It's coming along nicely," she replied. "I don't get morning sickness as much anymore, so that's a bonus."

"Have you gotten any weird cravings?" Kendra asked.

"No, but she likes coming into my dreams to ask me if I could drive to 7-Eleven to get her some ice cream. I'm fighting a dragon, and she pops in like, 'Hey, I know this seems like a bad time to ask, but I need you to go to the store.'" Rachelle, Sarai, and Kiana burst out laughing.

"What?" Sarai exclaimed, turning to Louise.
"You actually astral project into his dreams to ask for food?"

"Yep, sure do," Louise said, shoving a forkful of cake into her mouth. "He knows not to say no, either."

"Astral project? What's that?" Kendra asked.

"Astral projection is basically an out-of-body experience," Rachelle explained. "We do this all the time when we dream, but we're asleep when it happens. Astral projection is consciously traveling the astral realm."

"Interesting," Kendra remarked. "Octavia did mention something like that. She's been doing a lot of research on magic. She also told me she took a class on beauty magic."

"That was my class," Louise said.

"Cool," Kendra said. "So, you're a witch?"

"Yep," Louise said with a smirk.
"Everyone on my mother's side is."

"That's dope," Kendra said, continuing to eat her cake. Octavia, however, was in her own world. Her attention was turned to Nick and Rachelle. She watched their interactions, hoping to see some kind of tension between them, a sign of her spell working. However, to her chagrin, they were more lovey-dovey than ever. *It has been a whole fucking month!* she cursed to herself. While she had read that spells can sometimes take up to three moon cycles to fully manifest, she hoped to see some signs after a month. She wondered if the spell kit she purchased was a dud. Her eyes then landed on Alexis, who was singing along to the movie with her son, with Ernest and Corrine looking on. She studied Alexis' face, looking for signs of a family resemblance. While she was a spitting image of her mother, Corrine, Octavia noticed that she and Alexis had similar noses, and their lips were also similar. Octavia glanced at Ernest, who was playing with his grandson. Anger began to bubble inside her. How could he allow her to be given away, yet build a family with someone else? *I wonder if his wife knows about me,* she thought. Octavia debated whether or not she should reveal what she learned to Alexis. If she had a sibling out in the world, she would want someone to tell her. However, she knew she needed to be tactful. She couldn't just drop a bomb like this in front of a house full of party guests. Maybe I can get her alone and tell her then.

"Hey, Tay," Kendra said, snapping her sister out of her thoughts. "You good? You're kind of zoned out."

"Y-Yeah, I'm fine," Octavia replied, finishing the last of her cake. Kendra simply shrugged and grabbed another slice of pizza. Taking a deep breath, Octavia got up and walked over to Alexis. Upon seeing Octavia, she smiled.

"Hey, what's up?" she said.

"Hey, um, I was wondering if you and I can go somewhere and talk? It's kind of important," Octavia said. Alexis raised an eyebrow.

"Sure," she said. "Why don't we go outside?" Nodding, Octavia followed Alexis out the door, and the two of them walked over to Alexis' car. "So, what's up? What did you need to talk to me about?" Octavia was trembling. She knew the bomb she was going to drop on Alexis had the potential to cause chaos in her family. However, she knew Alexis had the right to know. It's better that she finds out from me than someone else, she reasoned. She let out a sigh.

"Look, I know you don't know me all that well, and I know you probably won't believe me if I told you this, but…"

"But what?" Alexis cut in, urging Octavia to go on.

"A while ago, I took an ancestry DNA test, and I got the results about a month ago."

"Okay…" Alexis said, wondering what this had to do with her.

"The results listed you as a match," Octavia replied. Alexis was silent, no doubt stunned by what Alexis had just told her.

"So, what you're saying is that we're related."

"Not just that, it listed you as a potential sibling," Octavia said. Alexis burst out laughing.

"You're joking, right?"

"I wish I was," Octavia said, reaching into her purse and pulling out her phone. She pulled up the 23 & Me website and showed Alexis the page with her DNA matches. She handed her phone to Alexis, who began reading the page. "I know it's hard for you to believe, but DNA doesn't lie."

"But how?" Alexis said. "Mom and Dad had been dating since college. If you're my sister, that would mean my dad cheated."

"I'm sorry," Octavia said. "I didn't know if I should tell you, but I know that if I had a sibling out there, I would want to know." Alexis said nothing. Her head was spinning. How could her father have another child and not tell her? What else could he be hiding?

"Excuse me," she said, and before Octavia could say anything else, Alexis stormed back into the house, with Octavia's phone in hand, as Octavia ran after her. She located her parents and stomped over to them.

"Lexi?" Ernest asked.
"Everything okay, baby?"

"You tell me!" Alexis spat as she held up the phone.

"What am I supposed to be looking at?"

"Octavia here had a DNA test done, and the results say that we're siblings!" Alexis said, her voice raised. Everyone stopped what they were doing and turned their attention to Alexis and her parents. Octavia stood by the table, looking down at the floor.

"Lexi, what's going on?" Rachelle asked.

"Ask Daddy!" Alexis cried, pointing at Ernest. "Apparently, he cheated with Octavia's mother and never told anyone!"

"What?" Kendra exclaimed, turning to Octavia.

"Tay, what is she talking about?"

"I took the DNA tests, and the results say that me and Alexis are related," Octavia said, still looking at the floor.

"You took the test, after I told you it wasn't a good idea?" Kendra asked incredulously.

"Uncle Ernie… you had a kid before Lexi and never told us?"

"No!" Ernest cried, looking from Rachelle to Alexis.
"Lexi, baby, you're my only child! I promise you that!"

"Then explain this, then!" Alexis shouted.

"I don't think we should discuss this in front of the guests," Sharon said.

"I agree," Rachelle said, and she led her aunt, uncle, and cousin to her home office. "Don't worry, we'll keep the babies occupied," Sarai said, as Nick followed Rachelle, along with Sharon.

"Damn. I hope everything's okay," Kiana said.

"I hope so, too," Louise added. Once Rachelle and her family were in the office, she locked the door so there would be no interruptions. Once they were out of earshot, Alexis rounded on her father.

"Well?" she demanded, folding her arms, staring daggers at Ernest. "Explain how I have another sibling!"

"Lexi, I don't know what you saw on there, but I can assure you that I never cheated on your mother. I don't have any children other than you."

"DNA doesn't lie, Dad!" Alexis shouted with tears in her eyes. "It says right there that Octavia and I are related! It lists you as my father. If me and Octavia are siblings, it either means that A. you cheated, or B. Mom had a kid that she gave up and never told us. Which one is it? Honestly, I highly doubt that it's the latter!"

"I promise you, I never cheated on your mom, baby," Ernest protested. He seemed genuinely confused. However, Corrine's face was as white as a sheet, and she was unusually quiet. Rachelle realized that her uncle was telling the truth.

"Aunt Corrine, you're awfully pale," she said.
"Is everything alright?"

"You've also been really quiet. That's not like you," Sharon added. Corrine could feel everyone's eyes boring into her, and she felt sick to her stomach. However, she knew she had to come clean. She let out a deep sigh.

"I'm sorry," she said softly.

"Sorry? For what?" Alexis questioned.

"Ernest isn't your real father, Alexis," Corrine said, her eyes brimming with tears.

"What?!" Alexis and Ernest cried in unison.

"What do you mean, he's not my father?" Alexis demanded. Corrine held her head in her hands. She dreaded that this day would come. However, the truth was out in the open, and she could no longer run from it.

"Well, when I was in my senior year in college, your father and I were having issues in our relationship, so we went on a break. At the time, I wasn't ready to fully commit, and I wasn't sure of what I wanted. While we were on our break, I started seeing Kevin Simmons. He was the star quarterback of my university's football team."

"And?" Alexis said. "What happened?"

"Kevin and I fooled around for a few weeks before he got bored and moved on to someone else. Afterwards, I found out I was pregnant."

"Did Dad know there was a possibility another man could be my father? How were you so sure it was Kevin's?"

"No, he didn't know," Corrine said. "He didn't go to my school and would only visit on weekends, so it was easy to date Kevin without him knowing."

"Did Kevin know you were pregnant?"

"No," Corrine said, shaking her head. "He wouldn't have stuck around even if he did. He was a player who slept with half the girls on campus and in my sorority. Besides, things worked out in the end. When I told Ernest I was pregnant, he never questioned being the father because we did sleep together before our break. I knew he would be a stable presence in my life and yours."

"So, I was the safe option," Ernest concluded as he stared at Corrine coldly. "No!" Corrine cried, reaching for Ernest's hand. However, Ernest snatched his hand away, making her flinch. "I loved you, and I still do. I just didn't want to lose you. That's why I didn't tell you."

"So, you were only thinking about yourself!" Alexis spat. "What if I needed a kidney, or a blood transfusion, Mom? What were you gonna do if the doctors said Dad wasn't a match?" Corrine scoffed.

"Oh, don't be so dramatic, Alexis," she said.

"You always do this shit!" Alexis shrieked. "Every time I try to talk to you and tell you that something you did or said hurt me, you always say I'm being dramatic! I'm sick of it!"

"You better watch your tone with me, girl!" Corrine spat.

"No, she's right!" Ernest interjected. "Not only did you lie to me, but you lied to her! She has every right to be upset right now!"

"I agree," Sharon added, glaring at Corrine. "Corrine, when you first told me you were pregnant, I asked you if Kevin was the father. You swore up and down that Ernest was the dad, and I believed you."

"Well, if I told you the truth, you would have gone and told Robert!" Corrine countered. Alexis laughed bitterly. Tears were flowing down her face, and her insides were burning with rage. All the years of resentment she felt towards her mother were bubbling to the surface. The years of being compared to Rachelle and other girls, her mother pushing her dreams onto her, her judgment, all came rushing back.

"All this time, you've always made me feel like I wasn't good enough because I didn't want to fit into the box you wanted to force me into. You didn't like that I didn't want to do pageants. You didn't like that I didn't want to be a debutante. You didn't like that I pursued journalism instead of teaching. You didn't like that I didn't want to join a sorority. And ever since I got pregnant with Bryson, you never let me forget how much I disappointed you. Don't even get me started on everything that happened with Vincent. And when I called you to talk to you about how I almost had my throat slit, you defended those men! All these years, you've made me feel like shit when you're nothing but a lying, selfish bitch." *SLAP!* Alexis held her face, which stung from her mother's slap. Enraged, she slapped Corrine back.

"Lexi!" Ernest shouted.

"You can slap me as much as you want, it doesn't change the fact that you're a liar," Alexis said, glaring at Corrine. Her hazel eyes were cold and piercing. "You're a liar and a hypocrite, and right now, I don't want anything to do with you." Alexis then unlocked the door and stormed out of the office, with Rachelle running after her.

"Alexis!" Corrine shouted as she attempted to follow her daughter. However, Sharon blocked the doorway.

"Let her go, Corrine," she said. "She needs space to process what she just learned." Corrine turned to her husband. Hurt and anger were etched on his face.

"Ernie, I'm sor—" she began, but Ernest held up his hand, cutting her off.

"Save it," he said, not looking at her. "I'm going to stay at a hotel while I figure out what I want to do. I think it's best that you don't call me. I'll call you when I'm ready to talk." Corrine broke down in sobs as Ernest left the office. He walked towards the front door and saw that Alexis and Rachelle were outside, with Rachelle consoling her.

"Lexi, no matter what that test says, you're still my cousin," she said, rubbing her back.

"I hate her!" Alexis sobbed into Rachelle's shoulder.

"You don't mean that. I know you don't. You're just upset," Rachelle said.

"How could she keep this from me?"

"I don't know. I really don't know."

"What if Dad doesn't want anything to do with me anymore?"

"That will never happen." Alexis turned around to see that Ernest had come outside. With tears in his eyes, he held out his arms. Alexis allowed him to pull her into his arms, rubbing her back as she cried. This gave Alexis a bit of comfort, as Ernest would often do this when she was a child. "I don't care what that damn test says. You'll always be my little girl."

"So, what's going to happen now?" Alexis asked. "Are you and Mom getting a divorce?" Ernest sighed deeply.

"I don't know," he replied. "We're going to live apart for a while. I'm going to go home and pack a few things, and I'll be staying at a hotel."

"You don't have to do that," Alexis said with a sniffle. "You can stay with me and Bryson. We have plenty of room, and I'm sure Bryson will be happy."

"Are you sure?"

"Of course. You're always welcome. You know that." Ernest hugged Alexis again.

"I love you, Lexi."

"I love you, too, Dad." Alexis then let go and went inside to get Bryson. She noticed Octavia and Kendra were preparing to leave as well.

"Alexis, I'm so sorry," Octavia said softly. "The last thing I wanted to do was cause trouble for your family."

"It's not your fault," Alexis said as she helped Bryson into his jacket. "It was bound to come out sooner or later." She turned to Bryson. "Say 'Bye.'"

"Bye," Bryson said, smiling, and the two left the house. Rachelle came back inside and began to clean up. Nick and their friends pitched in to help. A while later, Sharon came out of the office with a sobbing Corrine.

"Rachelle, I'm going to take your aunt home," she said as she led Corrine to the door.

"Drive safe," Rachelle said as she and Sharon gave each other a hug and a kiss on the cheek. Seeing the exchange between mother and daughter made Corrine sob louder. Rolling her eyes, Sharon led her outside to her car. Octavia and Kendra left shortly after. Rachelle let out a long sigh.

"Is Lexi okay?" Sarai asked as she put the frosting-stained plates in the trash. "Nick told us what happened."

"Honestly, no," Rachelle replied.
"I just can't believe Aunt Corrine's been lying all these years."

"Yeah, that's messed up," Sarai said. She knew all too well how it felt to learn a family secret. She knew that Alexis was going through a whirlwind of emotions. Meanwhile, on the drive home, Kendra was giving her sister an earful.

"What the hell were you thinking, Tay?" she cried. "What were you thinking, dropping a bomb like that, and at a birthday party, no less!"

"She had a right to know!" Octavia argued. "Besides, I didn't think she was going to confront her parents the way she did! I told her in private."

"Why did you even have to take that test in the first place? I told you that no good would come from it!"

"You just don't get it!" Octavia countered. "You don't know what it's like to not know who you are."

"But you do know who you are, Tay!" Kendra said. "You are Octavia Baker. A kind, intelligent, and beautiful person."

"You know what I mean." Kendra let out a deep sigh.

"Look, I know I don't understand everything that you've been feeling," she said. "I'm not adopted, so I don't know what it's like to not know where you come from, but Mom and Dad had always made you feel like you were loved, and so did I. I just don't know why you're so obsessed with this ancestry thing. Suppose you do find your birth parents. What are you expecting from them? What if you reach out to them, and they decide that they want nothing to do with you? What then?"

"I don't know!" Octavia said, staring out the window. While she was sorry that Alexis' world had been turned upside down, she was relieved that she now knew who her father was, even though it was not Ernest Lawson. *My father's name is Kevin Simmons, she thought. Now, all I have to do is find where he is. Then, I can find out who my birth mother is. Once I have that information, I'll finally have the answers I've been looking for.*

Chapter 17

"*H*ave a good day, babe," Wilfred said as he pulled into the Oakland Mall parking lot. It was 2 PM, and Louise was opening her shop late due to a prenatal appointment earlier that day. Throughout her first and second trimesters, Louise's anxiety was at an all-time high. She feared complications or another premature birth, like with Apollo. Thankfully, everything pointed to a healthy pregnancy, and the couple eagerly awaited their little girl's arrival. "You too," Louise said, giving her husband a sweet kiss. After exiting the vehicle, she made her way into the mall. Instead of taking the stairs, she took the elevator to the second floor. As she approached her shop, she saw Rachelle standing outside Melanin Siren.

"Hey, girlie!" Rachelle said.
"How was your appointment?"

"It was good," Louise replied, smiling.
"I just can't wait for her to get here."

"I bet Mimi is excited about getting a sister," Rachelle said, beaming at her friend.

"Oh, she definitely is," Louise said. "She also acts as my nurse at home. She'll help Will make food for me or rub my back if it hurts."

"That's so sweet," Rachelle replied. Louise's thoughts then turned to Alexis.

"How's your cousin holding up?" Louise asked.

"She's going through it," Rachelle said with a sigh. "Uncle Ernie filed for divorce, and she's taking it pretty hard, even though she supports his decision. At that Halloween party, I had to stop her from getting wasted. I'm really worried she's going to relapse."

"Geez…" Louise remarked.
"I'm really sorry, Chell."

"I am too," Rachelle said.
"I can't even begin to imagine what she's going through."

"We just need to continue being there to support her," Louise said, and Rachelle nodded. "I'll whip up some healing baths for her."

"Thanks, Lou. That means a lot," Rachelle replied, and the two hugged.

"Let me hurry up and open," Louise said, letting go.
"Time to get this money."

"You ain't never lied," Rachelle remarked, and the two friends went into their respective places of business. For Louise, the day was uneventful. It was simply another business day. Thankfully, she didn't have to be on her feet all day and spent most of her time behind the counter. As she rubbed her growing belly, she imagined what her child would be like. Would she take after her or Will, or both? What kind of spiritual gifts would she have? Would she be as gifted, bright, and kind-hearted as her older sister? *Soleil Céleste…* she thought as she stared into space. *We can't wait for you to get here*. Louise was snapped out of her thoughts as the door to her shop opened. Putting on her best customer service voice, she said,

"Hey, welcome to RoxyJo's. How may I hel-" She was stunned to see Mike standing before her. Seeing him was like seeing a ghost, although seeing ghosts was nothing new to her.

"Hey," Mike mumbled, giving a weak wave.

"What are you doing here?" Louise demanded coldly, making Mike wince. He let out a sigh. "I deserve that," he uttered. "I'm pretty sure I'm the last person you want to see in here." Louise said nothing and continued to stare at him coldly. Mike felt like he was an inch tall as her gaze bore into him. His eyes landed on Louise's stomach. "Congratulations, by the way. When are you du-"

"What are you doing here?" Louise repeated, cutting him off.

"I came to... I came to apologize," Mike replied.
"You were right about Jay."

"Was I now?" Louise asked rhetorically. She knew it would be a matter of time before Jay proved her words right: *"I'll tell you one thing, though: when, not if, he fucks you over again, don't come crawling back."* She didn't need cards or the spirits to tell her that Jay was still on his selfish bullshit. However, her curiosity was piqued. "What did he do?"

Mike looked down at the floor, his eyes burning with tears. Jay's betrayal was still fresh, although he should have seen it coming. "Well, shortly after you ran into us at Ferndale Pride, Jay and Nikki started getting super friendly with each other, and they would often hang out when I'm at work," he began. "He then started being distant again, but whenever I brought it up, he would gaslight me and say that it's all in my head. Then he started being really secretive with his phone." Mike wiped a tear from his eye. "Last week, I came home from work...and found Jay in bed with Andrew and Nikki. They were having a damn threesome!" Louise was speechless. While she knew Jay was bisexual, she never thought he would go for Nikki's trifling ass, as often as he talked shit about her. *This is fucking wild!* she thought.

"Damn," she muttered after a few minutes of silence. She felt a slight twinge of pity for her former friend. "I'm sorry. What did he do when you caught them?"

"He tried to pull the 'It's not what it looks like!' card, like I'm fucking blind. When he realized that I wasn't buying what he was selling, he tried to shift blame to me."

"Just like the last time you caught him," Louise said matter-of-factly.

"I know," Mike said with a sigh. "I know. I should've listened to you. I should have never given him another chance, especially after what he said to you. I know I don't deserve your forgiveness, but I truly am sorry. If you never want to see my face again after this, I understand." Louise let out a deep sigh and took a moment to let Mike's words sink in. She believed that his apology was genuine, and she truly felt bad that he was betrayed the way he was, in his own home no less. However, her view of Mike had been forever changed. Even if she decided to be his friend again, would she ever be able to trust him?

"Well, Mike, I appreciate your apology, but you really have some issues you need to work through," she said. "Right now, I'm not sure that I can trust you. However, that doesn't mean I'm not open to being friends again. I just need time."

"That's fair," Mike said. "I know I have self-esteem issues, and I'll have to deal with those problems on my own. I'll give you all the space you need."

"I'm also not the only one you need to apologize to."

"I apologized to Rachelle before I came here," Mike said.
"I know I still need to apologize to Sarai."

"I know you're going through a lot right now, but trust me, you'll get through it. You just have to do the inner work," Louise replied. Mike nodded and handed her a gift bag.

"I know you and Mimi's birthdays were eight months ago, but...well, you know what happened." Louise opened the bag and saw a *Sailor Moon*-themed pendant and hair accessories for Artemis, and a *Sailor Moon* makeup brush set for herself.

"Thank you," Louise said, giving Mike a small smile.
"I appreciate this. Mimi will too."

"No problem," Mike said.
"Well, I should get going."

"I wish you the best, Mike."

"You too," Mike replied as he headed to the door. "Tell Will I said hello." He then left the store and descended down the escalator. Louise went back behind the counter. As she waited for more customers, she tried to process what had transpired. Louise felt sorry for Mike. After his father had died, he had fallen into a deep depression and was a shell of his former self. Then, if that wasn't bad enough, he was betrayed by the one person who was supposed to be there for him in his time of need. Anyone's self-esteem would take a hit after that. Louise's heart became hot with hatred towards Jay and Nikki. However, Nikki's actions did not surprise her. She was two-faced, conniving, and self-absorbed. She had zero qualms about screwing other people's partners, even if those other people were her friends. In her mind, if your man came to her, you weren't doing a good job pleasing him. Your loss, her gain. Jay, however, shocked Louise. On the surface, he always seemed like a supportive, caring friend. Louise learned the hard way that the support was one-sided. Jay was the kind of person who used people as his emotional dumping ground, yet couldn't be bothered when asked to reciprocate the support he was given. When Louise came to this realization, she knew that her life was better off without Jay in it, the vile text messages he sent being the last straw. Because who needs trash in their lives? she thought to herself as she continued sitting behind the counter. Suddenly, Rachelle entered the shop.

"Girl! Tell me why Mike came into my shop!" she said as she sauntered to the counter.

"I know," Louise said. "He told me."

"He apologized to you, too?"

"Yep."

"What did you say?" asked Rachelle.

"I told him that I appreciated the apology, but he really needed to work on himself. However, I'm not opposed to being friends again," Louise replied. "

I pretty much said the same thing," Rachelle said. "I really hope he learns from his bad decisions and heals."

"You and I both."

"I'm going to head to the food court," Rachelle said. "Want me to get you anything? It's my treat." Louise pondered for a moment, then gave her friend a wide smile.

"A pepperoni slice with breadsticks and marinara would be nice if it isn't too much trouble." Rachelle let out a chuckle.

"I got you," she said as she turned to leave.
"You want a Pepsi with that, right?"

"Yes, ma'am. You're the best!"

Louise found herself standing in the parlor of a large manor. The room was dark, decorated with Norse runes and Viking imagery. In front of Louise was a large altar with a statue of Odin. The altar was adorned with black candles, a Smoky Quartz point, and a small painting of a raven. In front of the statue sat a plate of beef and fish. Sandalwood incense wafted into the air. Where am I? Louise thought as she continued to survey her surroundings. In front of the large Viking tapestry sat an iron, throne-like chair with deep red cushions. Before she could approach the chair to get a closer look, she heard voices and footsteps. She immediately hid behind a column. She didn't know who or what she was up against, so she felt it best to stay out of sight. She silently watched as a group of women entered the room one by one. They were all dressed in long black dresses and wore black cloaks. As they entered the room, they split into two lines, ten women on the left and ten women on the right. A few moments later, an elegantly dressed woman entered the room. She was middle-aged, with a slender build, and golden hair that fell to her waist. Her eyes were ice blue and seemed to glow in the dimly lit room. Louise watched curiously as the woman descended down the aisle towards her throne. Once she was seated, she addressed the other women. "I'm sure you are all wondering why I have called you here at such an ungodly hour." The other women remained silent, and she continued. "It has been brought to my attention that there is a traitor within our ranks." The room erupted in gasps of shock and whispers of disbelief. I wonder if this is the Daughters of Odin coven Mom was talking about, Louise thought to herself. This must be Queen Nanna. The women continued to speculate amongst themselves as to who the traitor could be until Nanna demanded silence. Once their attention returned to her, she spoke again.

"Astrid, dear, can you step forward, please?" The crowd turned to a young, petite woman with chestnut hair and forest green eyes. She appeared nervous but did as she was asked. Nanna stood up from her throne and approached her. Her expression was cold, yet her eyes were alight with fury.

"You know why I called you here, don't you, Astrid?"

"I-I don't know what you mean, My Lady."

"Come now, why are you so nervous?" Nanna asked in an amused tone, tracing along Astrid's face with her slender finger. "We're all sisters here, are we not?"

"O-Of course we are."

"Then there's no need to be nervous, Astrid... or shall I call you... Michelle?" Astrid's blood immediately ran cold. "That is your real name, right?" Astrid's heart was beating a mile a minute. When she joined Daughters of Odin, Astrid was the only name she had given. Before she could say anything in her defense, Nanna grabbed her by the throat and lifted her into the air. Astrid clawed at Nanna's hands, gasping for air as she attempted to break free. Nanna then turned to the stunned crowd while still maintaining her grip on her victim. "This lovely lady here is Michelle Robinson," she announced, squeezing the woman's neck tighter. "Michelle here is an informant and has been reporting our movements to the FBI." The crowd began to jeer and shout obscenities at the unfortunate young woman.

"How do we deal with traitors, ladies?"

"We eliminate them!" several women shouted.

"Precisely," Nanna said, grinning evilly. Her aura began to glow a bright, fiery red. Glowing, red vines grew from her aura, wrapping themselves around Michelle's limbs, torso, and neck. The vines began to drain

Michelle of her life force and power. Louise watched in horror as Michelle's body began to shrivel. The grotesque sight reminded her of an episode of Dragonball Z, where Cell completely drained a man of all his organs. However, she never imagined she would witness that kind of horror in real life. When Michelle's life was completely drained from her, Nanna threw her to the ground as if she were a rag doll. She then turned to the horrified coven members. "Let this be a lesson to you all," she began. "The price you pay for disloyalty is your life. Do I make myself clear?" After the coven answered in the affirmative, she went back to her throne. She stared down at Michelle's shriveled remains in disgust. "Now, clean this mess up."

Louise immediately shot up in bed, her skin covered in a cold sweat. She was hyperventilating, her mind reeling from what she had just witnessed. Was it all a dream or a vision like Sarai had? No, it felt too real for it to be a dream. It was like she was in the room with them. She knew she needed to tell her mother what she had seen and divine on the situation.

"Babe, you okay?" Wilfred asked groggily. He sat up in bed with a concerned look on his face. "What's wrong?"

"I-I think I just had a premonition," Louise said.

"A premonition?" Wilfred repeated, rubbing his wife's back. "About what?" Louise began to recollect what she had witnessed. "Damn... yeah, you really gotta tell your mom."

"I know," Louise said.

"For now, though, you should go back to sleep. We have a long day ahead of us." Louise let out a sigh. It was 3 AM, and their baby shower was later that afternoon.

"You're right," she said as she laid back down. Wilfred gave her a peck on the cheek and snuggled close to her, rubbing her belly. With a smile, Louise drifted off to sleep, hoping for more peaceful dreams.

A few hours later, "Ooh, don't you look cute!" Kristy remarked as Louise and Wilfred entered the banquet hall, with Artemis following behind them. Louise was dressed to the nines in a yellow maternity gown, with gold sun earrings, a matching necklace, and gold ballet flats. Her hair was pin-curled, adorned with a gold sun hair clip. Wilfred was dressed in a yellow plaid button-up shirt, tan slacks, and brown leather shoes. Artemis looked adorable in a bright yellow dress, white tights, and gold Mary Jane shoes. Her hair was styled in ringlets and adorned with gold ribbons.

"You know it," Louise said as she hugged her mother. "Where's Mariah and Dannell?"

"Your sister went to get Dy'Anna from her daddy's, and your brother is on his way," Kristy answered as she took a bag of ice from Xavier and emptied it into the large cooler. "Now, you go have a seat while we finish setting up. You're the guest of honor, remember?" Wilfred led Louise to

two large throne chairs, which were surrounded by white and gold balloons, and the couple took their seats, while Artemis assisted her grandparents. Shortly after their arrival, their friends arrived.

"There's the mommy-to-be!" Sarai exclaimed as the cousins shared a hug. "Girl, you are glowing!" Louise beamed as she rubbed her belly.

"I'm really digging the sun theme," Kiana remarked as she looked around. In honor of the baby's name, Soleil, the hall was decorated in white and gold, with bouquets of sunflowers as table centerpieces. On the dessert table were trays of sun-shaped cookies and a three-tiered gold cake with a gold 'S' on top, all made by Khalil.

"How are you feeling?" Rachelle asked.

"Pretty good, although I had a rough night," Louise replied.

"What do you mean?" Sarai asked. Louise then explained the premonition she had about the Daughters of Odin coven and the murder she witnessed.

"Holy shit," Kiana remarked.

"Well, if it's true, we'll definitely be hearing about it, especially if it was an FBI informant that was killed," Nick added. "Have you told your mom?"

"Not yet," Louise said. "I'll tell her after the shower, though. I wouldn't be surprised if she had premonitions too." The others murmured in agreement.

"Hey, look who's here!" Kiana said as she gestured towards the entrance. Trina, smiling ear to ear, headed towards them and embraced Louise and Wilfred in a bear hug.

"Oh my god, you look so pretty!" she gushed, admiring Louise's look.

"Girl, so do you!" Louise said. "I'm loving the hair." Trina was wearing a golden brown, lace-front wig that fell to the middle of her back. "So, how are things with your model boo?"

"Things are great," Trina replied, blushing.
"Things are definitely getting more serious."

"So, we'll be getting wedding invites, right?" Sarai asked.

"It's a little soon for that, but I'll let you know in about a year," Trina said with a giggle.

"Oh, Lexi just texted. She's on her way," Rachelle cut in.

"By the way, how is she?" Trina asked.

"She's doing okay, but still having a hard time," Rachelle replied. "She still refuses to talk to her mom, though."

"I don't really blame her, to be honest," Trina said.

"Yeah," Louise added.

"Mommy, Mommy!" Artemis exclaimed as she ran towards them. "Grandma and Grandpa are here!" Louise looked up to see that her in-laws had just arrived. She also noticed that some of her other relatives had arrived, including those from New Orleans. Smiling, she got up from her chair, and she and Wilfred made their rounds greeting the guests. Rachelle and the others then took their gifts to the designated table. About twenty minutes later, Octavia arrived.

"Hey, you made it!" Nick said as he gave her a hug, making her heart flutter. Octavia then gave Rachelle a small smile, which Rachelle returned.

"So, where do I put this?" Octavia asked, holding up a large gift bag. Nick directed her to the gift table. Octavia took the gift to the table and returned a few moments later.

"So, when did you guys get here?" she asked.

"About twenty or thirty minutes ago," Nick replied.

"This place looks really nice," Octavia said as she admired the decor.

"Doesn't it?" Rachelle said.
"It's fitting, given the name they picked for the baby."

"Sol something, right?" Octavia asked.

"Soleil," Nick said.

"It's French for 'sun'."

"Louise is French?"

"Creole," Nick replied.
"She was born in New Orleans."

"Wow," Octavia remarked. "Interesting." They all made their way to a table and took their seats.

"So, where's your sister?" Sarai asked.

"She wasn't feeling well, so she's at home," Octavia replied.

"Oh wow, I'm sorry to hear that," Nick said. "By the way, how are you holding up? I know what happened at the twins' party wasn't easy for you." *Oh Nicky, you're so sweet to be worried about me*, Octavia thought.

"I'm fine," she said.
"How is Alexis doing, though?"

"She's fine," Rachelle interjected. "Speaking of which, she just walked in." Octavia turned around to see Alexis looking around. Rachelle got her attention and waved her over. Alexis made her way to the table and took a seat next to Rachelle. "Hey, y'all," she said, giving everyone a small smile. She then turned to Octavia. "Hey."

"Hey," Octavia said.
"How's it going?"

"It's going," Alexis replied. "Just been busy with work and Bryson." Octavia nodded in understanding.

"How is my nephew?" she asked.

"He's well," Alexis said in a curt tone. "I'm going to head to the bathroom." Before Octavia could say anything else, Alexis got up and made her way towards the restroom.

"Did I say something wrong?" Octavia asked, confused.

"Just give her time," Rachelle said.
"She's still processing everything."

"I understand," Octavia replied as she looked around. *Damn, how much processing do you need to do? It's been over a month*, she thought. Once all the guests were seated, Xavier got up to bless the food. After the prayer, each table was called, and the guests stood in line to receive their helpings of gumbo, jambalaya, jerk chicken, macaroni and cheese, cornbread, and spaghetti, all provided by Vernon's Catering.

"Girl, your daddy's food is bomb!" Mariah exclaimed as she dug into her jambalaya. "This jambalaya is almost as good as Dad's." Sarai giggled.

"Thanks, cuz," she replied as she ate. After everyone had finished eating, it was time for the games. One such game was a Celebrity Baby Name Match, which Trina won hands down, which wasn't a surprise to anyone, given her fame. They also played the Safety Pin Challenge, where the players were blindfolded and had to pick out as many safety pins as they could out of a plate of rice before time ran out. Magic was not allowed to be used at these games, of course. Sarai won the Safety Pin Challenge. After the games, everyone gathered around the thrones as Louise and Wilfred opened gifts. Joy radiated from the couple as they showed their gifts to the crowd and posed for pictures. Artemis even talked to her mother's belly, which made Louise's heart soar. As Octavia watched the festivities, she grew envious. She found herself imagining that this was her baby shower and that she and Nick were the parents-to-be. She grew even more incensed as she watched Nick and Rachelle. It had been two months since the breakup spell was cast, yet the couple was still going strong. Octavia mentally kicked herself for wasting money on what she felt was a useless ritual. Thankfully, she had a plan B. When Nick and Rachelle had taken the twins to their car to get them cleaned up, Octavia saw her chance. She reached into her purse and pulled out a small glass vial, which contained her menstrual blood. She had remembered Louise mentioning the use of blood in love bindings during her glamour magic class. Although Louise had warned against it, Octavia was desperate. *Here goes nothing*, she thought to herself as she looked around to see if anyone was watching. Thankfully, Nick and Rachelle were still tending to their twins, and their friends had gone off to the restroom. Louise and Wilfred were also busy with their families. Confident that the coast was clear, she made her way to the table and removed the cork from the vial. She then held the open vial over Nick's cup and began to carefully pour the blood. However, before she could fully empty the contents of the vial, someone grabbed her wrist.

"What the hell do you think you're doing?" Octavia slowly turned around and was met with a very angry Carmen. Her heart was pounding against her chest. She knew she had been busted.

"C-Carmen!" she stuttered. "How have you bee–"

"Cut the shit, Octavia!" Carmen spat, her green eyes ablaze. "What the hell did you put in my brother's drink?"

"N-Nothing!" Octavia cried.

"Oh really?" Carmen replied as she bent down to pick up the vial, which was sitting in the now spilled blood. She took a sniff of the inside, and the pungent odor was undeniable. "Oh, you nasty bitch!" Before Octavia could respond, she was met with a resounding slap.

"Hey! What's going on here?" Louise demanded as she waddled over. Staring daggers at Octavia, Carmen handed Louise the vial, who also sniffed it. Octavia held her stinging cheek, her eyes burning with tears. "I know this is not what the fuck I think it is!" She and Carmen stormed outside, while Octavia ran behind them, trying to plead her case. Sarai, Kiana, Trina, Alexis, and Wilfred gathered outside near the door to see what the commotion was about.

"Hey, what's going on?" Rachelle asked.

"Your little friend here thought it was a good idea to try to slip period blood into Nick's drink!" Carmen replied.

"What?" Nick exclaimed, looking from his sister to Octavia. "Tay wouldn't do that!"

227

"It's true, Nick," Louise said, handing Rachelle the vial.

"They're lying, Nicky!" Octavia cried. Rachelle and Nick both sniffed the vial, the metallic stench of blood filling their nostrils. Nick was dumbfounded. Would Octavia really go as far as to cast a blood binding on him? He looked at Octavia with an expression that was a mixture of hurt and disgust. "Nicky, I can explain," Octavia cried, tears rolling down her face.

"Un-fucking-believable," Rachelle remarked. She was livid. She knew Octavia had feelings for Nick, but she never imagined she would do this!

"I can't believe you, Tay!" Nick exclaimed.

"I'm sorry!" Octavia sobbed.
"I just wanted you to love me!"

"You thought putting this shit in my drink would make me love you?" Nick was disgusted and enraged. "I thought we had an understanding! I love Rachelle, not you! I told you that I will never see you as more than a friend. You told me that you understood! Now, I can't even see you as a friend anymore."

"You don't mean that!" Octavia protested.
"We've known each other for too long!"

"No, I thought I knew you," Nick said. His gaze held so much contempt, and it broke Octavia's heart. "The Octavia I knew wouldn't be so fucking selfish! The Octavia I knew would have been happy for me, no matter who I chose to be with. Rachelle has been nothing but kind and welcoming to you, and this is what you do?!"

"Nicky, I'm sor-" Octavia began, but Nick held up his hand.

"I think it's best that you leave," he said. He couldn't even look at her.

"Nicky!"

"Leave. Now," Louise said. Octavia looked at the others, hoping for someone to defend her. However, they remained silent. "Alexis!" she cried. "You're not going to let them kick me out, are you, sis?"

"Look, Octavia, we may share DNA, but we barely know each other," Alexis said. "My loyalty is to my cousin."

"Nicky, pleas-"

"Just go, Octavia!" Nick shouted.

"Now!" Louise added. Octavia was shattered. Not only had she lost her childhood friend, her only friend, but she was also being ousted out of his friend circle. Realizing there was nothing she could do or say in her defense, she got into her car and drove away. Nick then let out a long, deep sigh.

"You okay?" Rachelle asked.

"Yeah," Nick replied as he put his arm around her. "Let's... let's just go back inside." Rachelle nodded, and the two of them went back into the banquet hall with their girls in tow. Louise and the others followed behind them. While Nick was devastated that he lost a fifteen-year friendship, he knew it was for the best. The rest of the baby shower went off without a hitch. In spite of everything that happened with Octavia, Louise and Wilfred were surrounded with nothing but love and joy. Little Soleil was being welcomed with open arms and was going to enter the world covered in love. Life could only go up from here.

Chapter 18

*W*hen Rachelle and Nick entered Diana's Garden, they were greeted by the scents of lavender and frankincense incense. "I Put a Spell on You" by Nina Simone played from the speakers as shoppers browsed the shelves of home-grown herbs and crystals. The couple made their way to the counter, where Kristy and Dannell were finishing a transaction.

"Hey, you two!" Dannell said with a smile. "What can we do for you?"

"We came here for a reading," Nick replied. It had been two weeks since the baby shower, and his confrontation with Octavia still weighed heavily on his mind. He needed answers, and he knew that Kristy and her family were the right people to get them from. "Certainly," Kristy said as she stepped from behind the counter and led the couple to the blue curtain. She peeked behind the curtain, where Louise was cleansing the divination room with frankincense.

"You got clients, Miss Thang," she said.

"Send them in," Louise said. Kristy nodded and stepped aside for Rachelle and Nick to enter.

"Hey, y'all! What's popping?" Nick let out a sigh as he and Rachelle sat across from their friend.

"Well, you already know what happened at the baby shower," Nick began. Louise nodded, and Nick continued, "For the past month, though, I've been having these weird dreams."

"Really? What kind of dreams?" Louise asked.

"Dreams where I'm surrounded by snakes," Nick replied. "I keep seeing black snakes in my bed, the shower... everywhere."

"Interesting," Louise said as she began shuffling the cards. "Sounds like you have unknown enemies."

"I've been having those same dreams," Rachelle interjected. "We've also been having these really bad headaches and have been feeling really fatigued. We've been to the doctor, and we've had MRIs done, but they couldn't find anything. We think someone cast a spell on us, but we want to make sure."

"Say no more," Louise said as she finished shuffling. She handed the cards to Nick and Rachelle, who also shuffled them. Louise then pulled a card from the deck, laid it on the table face down, and turned it over, revealing The Lovers card in reverse. She also pulled the Five of Wands, The Devil, the Five of Cups, and the Three of Swords.

"God damn!" Rachelle said, astonished. She knew this was a bad sign. Everyone's ears began to ring, a telltale sign that ancestral spirits were near and wanted to talk.

"What is it?" Rachelle asked.

"Sounds like that redbone done put a break-up spell on y'all!" Lula, Rachelle's paternal grandmother, said.

"What?!" Rachelle and Nick shouted in unison.

"A break-up spell?" Nick repeated.
"Are you sure?"

"Son, I may tell you a joke, but I'll never tell you a lie!" Lula said.

"When was this?" Rachelle asked.

"Two months ago," Diana, Louise's grandmother, said.

"That girl is not right." It was Carmen, Nick's maternal grandmother. *"¡Ella está mal de la cabeza!"*

"Your grandma ain't lying," Louise remarked. Suddenly, she heard a woman shouting in Jamaican Patois.

"She's a badmind pussyhole!" the woman exclaimed. It was Loretta, Rachelle's paternal great-grandmother. "Um, what does that mean?" Nick asked.

"She's saying Octavia is an envious motherfucker," Rachelle replied.

"Well, she definitely got that right," Nick said. He turned to Louise. "So, she actually cast a spell on us?"

"Yep," Louise said as she put her cards to the side. "All the signs add up. The dreams, the unexplained headaches and fatigue. They're all classic signs of baneful magic."

"So what do we do?" Rachelle asked.

"Well, the good news is that your Ancestors were able to stop the spell from fully manifesting, so don't worry about your relationship suffering," Louise began. "However, I still recommend that the two of you take an Uncrossing and Protection bath."

"Damn," Nick said as he put his head in his hands. His heart sank to the pits of his stomach. He trusted Octavia, and she betrayed him in the worst way. There was no coming back from this. *"You also need to go to your mother for a limpia,"* Carmen said, and Nick simply nodded.

"I'm really sorry," Louise said. Her heart went out to Nick. Like him, she was also disappointed in Octavia. She seemed sweet, genuine, and fun. However, Louise knew better than anyone that people were not always who they presented themselves to be.

"I'm sorry, too..." Nick said as he and Rachelle got up from their seats. Louise led the couple to the display of spiritual bath kits and selected both an Uncrossing and Protection bath kit for them.

"Since her spell didn't really hit, you only need to do these baths for seven days," she said. "That's enough to remove all the funky-ass energy she sent your way. Do the Uncrossing bath for seven days first, then do the Protection bath for another seven days. Y'all should be good after that."

"Thanks again, Lou," Rachelle said.

"Girl, bye!" Louise said as she hugged Rachelle and Nick. "We're family. I'm always gonna have your back." Louise took the bath kits and went behind the counter to ring them up. "By the way, make sure you keep some obsidian and selenite on you, too. black tourmaline also works."

"Trust me, we're way ahead of you on that," Nick said as Louise handed him the bag with their merchandise.

"Give those babies a kiss for me," Louise said, hugging them again.

"Will do. Thanks again," Rachelle said as she and Nick left the shop. "Hey, why don't we go to the Riverwalk? It might do us some good, and I'm sure Mommy won't mind keeping the girls for a bit longer." Nick smiled at her.

"Your call, Baby Doll," he said as they got in the car, and the two headed downtown. The couple took a romantic stroll, hands intertwined as they admired the Detroit River.

"It's so beautiful out here," Rachelle said, staring up at the starlit sky.

"Yeah, it is," Nick said as the two stood near the railing, with him embracing Rachelle from behind. "Though, you are more beautiful." Rachelle giggled as Nick kissed her cheek.

"You're so corny," she teased.

"You like it, though," Nick said.

"You're right, I do," Rachelle replied as Nick turned her around, pulling her closer. However, before their lips met, Nick's phone went off. With an annoyed sigh, he pulled out his phone and answered. To his chagrin, the caller was his former childhood friend.

"N-Nicky!" Octavia cried. "Look, I-I know I messed up, but-"

"Why are you calling me, Octavia?" Nick demanded.
"I have nothing to say to you!"

"Nicky, I'm sorry!"

"Octavia, stop!" Nick spat. "You can say you're sorry until you're blue in the face. It doesn't change what you did!" Octavia began to sob on the other line. "What does she have that I don't?" Octavia asked. "Why are you tossing me aside for her?"

"Octavia, do you hear yourself?" Nick countered. "You sound like a jealous girlfriend, and we've never even been in a fucking relationship! We were just friends, Octavia, and you were gone for fifteen fucking years! What did you think was going to happen in all that time? Look, I'm sorry you're hurting, but that doesn't excuse what you did! Don't call me anymore!" Before Octavia could protest, Nick hung up.

"What did she want?" Rachelle asked.

"She's still trying to apologize," Nick said, running a hand through his hair. "She was also on some jealous shit, talking about how I'm 'tossing her aside' for you. She's acting like I fucking dumped her!"

"Wow," was all Rachelle could say.
"That's wild."

"Tell me about it," Nick said. Rachelle took his hand and kissed the back of it, which put Nick at ease. They began to walk again, just enjoying the atmosphere and each other's company.

"I still can't believe she did that, though," Rachelle said.

"I can't believe it either, but it is what it is," Nick replied.

"Yeah," Rachelle said. Nick's phone went off again. Nick, clearly irritated now, grabbed his phone to see that Octavia had texted him. However, as he read her message, he grew angry. "What is it?" Nick handed the phone to Rachelle, and she began to read:

I can't believe you're letting that stuck-up bitch come between us, Nicky! I've known you for far longer than she has, and we have so much more in common! I only did what I did because I love you. You left me no choice! You really prefer that slut over me?? You really want to marry a bitch who posts half-naked pictures of herself? You want to be with a bitch that has that little self-respect? Really, Nick? That's really what you want?? I feel sorry for you.

"This bitch has really lost her mind!" Rachelle seethed. She had been nothing but kind to Octavia, yet Octavia was disparaging her in a text message! She had welcomed Octavia into her home, yet she was plotting on Nick the whole time! The whole time, Octavia was a fucking snake! "I don't have self-respect because I'm a boudoir model, even though my fiancé was the one who took the photos?" After she had said that, Nick received another text notification. Rachelle looked down at the phone, and what she saw had her wanting to drive to Octavia's place and knock her teeth down her throat. "Oh, hell no!"

"Babe, what is it?" Nick asked. Rachelle shoved the phone into Nick's hand. Nick looked at the screen, and to his shock and disgust, was met with a fully nude Octavia, who was posing seductively with her ass towards the camera, looking coyly over her shoulder. The photo was accompanied by a message:

Just wanted to send you this, since this is clearly the type of woman you want. I bet she can't fuck you like I could.

"Unbelievable," Nick remarked as he closed out of the message. What the hell is her problem? he thought as he blocked Octavia's number, all while Octavia was typing another message. Rachelle let out a sigh. "I don't think we have to worry about her anymore."

"I hope so," Rachelle said.

"Now, why don't we go get the girls from your mom's, and after we put them to bed, we can really relieve some stress?" Nick gave Rachelle a suggestive smirk, which made her blush, and her center throb with desire. "Lead the way, *papi,*" she said, and the two made their way back to the parking structure. Once they were home, and the twins were sound asleep, the happy couple spent the rest of the night unwinding after a stressful day. Little did they know, however, they had not heard the last of Octavia Baker.

CLICK! CLICK! "Perfect! Now, can you tilt your head a bit towards me?" Nick said as he snapped away at his camera. The model did as she was told, and Nick snapped a few more shots. "Now, you said you had another outfit you wanted to shoot with, right?"

"Yep," the attractive redhead replied as she relaxed.
"Can I change into it, now?"

"Sure, go ahead," Nick said with a smile, and the model went into the dressing room. Suddenly, Traci, Nick's receptionist, entered the studio area.

"Hey, Nick?" she began. "There's a woman at the front who says she needs to see you."

"Did she say who she was?" Nick asked as he was adjusting the lighting.

"No, but she says it's urgent," Traci said. Nick sighed.

"Alright," he said. "Give me a sec." Traci nodded and returned to the lobby. After adjusting his lighting, Nick made his way to the lobby area, wondering what was so urgent. *I wonder if it's Ms. Kristy. Maybe she has an update about that coven she told us about. It can't be my family, or Sarai, or else Traci would have told me that,* he thought to himself as he reached the lobby. However, it wasn't Kristy that was waiting for him, but Octavia, and she was a mess. She looked like she hadn't slept in days, and her eyes were puffy and red. Her red curls were tangled, as if she had just gotten out of bed. Seeing Octavia in this state broke Nick's heart. This wasn't the bubbly, sweet girl he knew. However, when he remembered everything she had done, his sympathy for her began to wane. Upon seeing Nick, Octavia's eyes lit up.

"Nicky," she began. "I'm so glad to see yo-"

"What are you doing here, Octavia?" Nick demanded.

"I tried to call and message you, but you blocked me."

"That should tell you something!" Nick snapped.

"You're still mad at me," Octavia said, her voice barely above a whisper.

"You think?" Nick replied. "Why would I want to talk to you after all the bullshit you pulled? A breakup spell, Octavia? Really?" Octavia's eyes widened. *How did he know about that?* She thought. "I-I don't know what you're talking about, Nicky," she said. "I nev-"

"Cut the shit, alright?" Nick spat, cutting her off. "For the past two months, Rachelle and I had been getting these weird-ass dreams, and we both were getting these unexplained headaches. We went to Louise for a reading. Come to find out, you had been doing magic on us! You thought I wasn't going to figure it out, when you know we both practice?" *Damn it!* Octavia cursed to herself. *That bitch ratted me out!* "I can't believe you would go that far to sabotage my relationship!" Nick continued. "How could you be so fucking grimy?"

"I-I didn't mean it!" Octavia protested.
"It was just a joke."

"Magic isn't a fucking joke, Octavia!" Nick shouted, making both Octavia and Traci wince. They had never heard Nick raise his voice. "Spells have real consequences, especially when you don't know what the hell you're doing! People can get hurt!"

"I wasn't trying to hurt you!" Octavia cried.
"I just wanted you to-"

"You wanted me to love you. Yeah, I know," Nick said. "If you truly loved me, you would want me to be happy, no matter who I choose to share that happiness with. The shit you're doing, Octavia? That isn't love. That's limerence." Octavia stared at the floor, unable to look Nick in the eyes. "Then, you disrespected the mother of my kids with those bullshit texts you sent when she was nothing but nice to you!"

"I didn't mean what I said in those messages. I swear!" Octavia said, wiping tears from her eyes. Nick was having none of it.

"Yes, you did, Octavia," he countered. "If you didn't, you wouldn't have sent that naked picture of yourself." Octavia looked down at the floor again, completely embarrassed. She knew she had crossed a major boundary when she sent that photo. She had hoped it would entice Nick into desiring her. Unfortunately, it had the opposite effect.

"I know I crossed the line with that," she conceded, slowly lifting her head to meet Nick's gaze. "You have every right to be angry. I just... I just don't want to lose you."

"Well, it's too late for that," Nick said.

"What does she have that I don't, Nick?"

"What?"

"What does Rachelle have that is making you so quick to throw away a fifteen-year friendship? Is the sex that good?"

"Nobody threw away a damn thing but you, Octavia!" Nick spat. "You! Nobody else! You want to know what Rachelle has that you don't? Integrity. Maturity. Rachelle doesn't throw a damn tantrum like a child when she doesn't get her way. She doesn't stab her friends in the back. She's strong, she's selfless, and she cares about the happiness and well-being of those close to her. To answer your question, yes, the sex is good. The sex is amazing, actually. However, that's not why I'm with her! I love her for who she is on the inside!" Octavia's eyes again burned with tears. Nick knew his delivery was harsh, but he was done handling Octavia with kid gloves. She had crossed the line far too many times, and she wasn't even remorseful. She was only sorry she had been caught. Nick couldn't have someone like that in his life, as much as it pained him. With a sigh, he said, "Just go, Octavia, and don't come back here."

"Nick!"

"Get the fuck out, Octavia, or I'll call the police!" Nick warned. Octavia was speechless. She couldn't believe that Nick, her best friend, and the man she had loved for fifteen years, would actually call the cops on her. While tempted to call his bluff, she couldn't risk losing her job by getting arrested, since she worked at a law firm. With a heavy heart, she left Nick's place of business without another word. After Octavia had left, Nick breathed a sigh of relief.

"Um, Nick?" Nick turned around to see the red-haired model standing in the doorway. "I'm ready when you are."

"Awesome, I'll be right there. Sorry to keep you waiting," Nick said as he made his way to the back. Putting Octavia out of his mind, he continued his shoot without further interruptions. He sincerely hoped that his former friend would get professional help and get herself together. However, he knew she would have to do that on her own. He couldn't do it for her.

Chapter 19

*R*achelle was awakened from her tranquil slumber by the sound of "Barbie Girl" playing as her phone alarm. After stretching her arms, she got out of bed and headed to the twins' room to get them ready for the day. Once the twins had their cereal and were happily watching Pocoyó, Rachelle went to take a shower and get dressed. Afterwards, she prepared breakfast for herself and Nick.

"Hey, babe," Nick said with a yawn as he entered the dining room. Rachelle greeted her fiancé with a sweet kiss as he took his seat at the table. She then gave him a plate of waffles, scrambled eggs, and bacon.

"Sleep well?" she asked as she sat across from him, pouring syrup over her own waffles.

"I slept okay, I guess," Nick replied.

"You're still thinking about Octavia, aren't you?" Rachelle asked. Nick let out a sigh. "Yeah," he said. "I just don't understand. Like, I get she had feelings for me, but for her to go as far as she did?"

"I know," Rachelle said, taking Nick's hand in hers.
"I know it hurt to cut her off."

"I guess it's true what they say: friendship breakups can be just as painful as romantic ones, if not more."

"You're right," Rachelle remarked. "But you did what you had to do to protect yourself and our family." Nick gave a small smile and kissed the back of Rachelle's hand.

"I'd do anything to protect you three," he said, looking back at the twins, whose eyes were glued to the screen. He then sighed sadly. "I just hope she gets professional help."

"I hope so, too," Rachelle said, and the two continued eating. After they finished, Rachelle gave Nick and the girls a kiss before leaving for Oakland Mall to open up her shop. Nick took the girls with him to the studio. When she arrived at her shop, she saw that Melanie, her new personal assistant, was waiting for her at the entrance. "Good morning, Miss Lawson," Melanie said cheerfully as Rachelle unlocked the doors.

"Melanie, you don't have to be so formal with me," Rachelle said as they entered the shop. "Just call me Rachelle." Melanie simply nodded and handed Rachelle a cold bottle of water.

"Is there anything else you need?"

"Not at the moment," Rachelle said.
"Now, we just wait for customers."

"Hey, girlie!" Louise exclaimed from the store entrance, and Rachelle waved her inside.

"Hey!" Rachelle said. Melanie went to retrieve another bottle of water for Louise. "How's it going?"

"It's going," Louise said, rubbing her belly.
"I just can't wait to drop this baby."

"I feel you," Rachelle said.
"When I was in my eighth month with the girls, I was over it."

"How's Nick doing?" Rachelle sighed.

"He's doing okay," she said.
"He's still bummed about Octavia, though."

"It's a damn shame," Louise said, shaking her head. "I really thought she would have been a good friend. Something's not right with her."

"Who are you telling?" Rachelle remarked. "I let this woman into my house and around my kids. The whole time, she wanted to take my place in Nick's life. Thankfully, she's out of our lives."

"Yeah," Louise said, taking a sip of water. "Well, I'm gonna head back to my place of business. Let me know when you're ready to go get lunch."

"Bet," Rachelle replied as the two women hugged. Louise then waddled out of the store. By noon, Melanin Siren had grown quite busy, but Rachelle handled her customers with ease. It brought her immense joy to see that so many people enjoyed her products. There were even requests for her to expand into creating makeup products! When Rachelle had opened her store, she never imagined it would grow this much, and it hadn't even been a year. She was thankful she made the decision to hire a personal assistant. It made processing orders and managing her inventory ten times easier. Around 3 pm, Rachelle and Louise both closed up shop for lunch, and they made their way to the food court, with Melanie joining them.

"Girl, did you hear Simone's song on Spotify?" Louise asked.

"You mean 'Bad Witch Bitch'?" Rachelle replied.
"That song is fire."

"For real," Louise said.
"She said she's doing a music video for it soon."

"Get out! Really?"

"Yep," Louise said. "She said it's going to be occult-themed, and she wants us to be in it."

"Say less," Rachelle said as they headed over to Panda Express. "I would pay to see her mom's face when the video comes out."

"Girl, who are you telling?" Louise replied. "I still remember how she brought her judgmental, Bible-thumping self into Mom's shop, calling herself trying to chastise us."

"I'm so glad Simone broke away from that toxicity," Rachelle said. "Her mother would have only held her back from her dreams. Also, only a trash person would take a predator's side over their own child."

"That part," Louise said.
"By the way, have you seen Trina's latest photos?"

"Girl, yes!" Rachelle said as they received their food and went to a nearby table. "She killed it, as always. I'm so proud of her."

"I am, too," Louise said. "I'm so glad she didn't let that egg donor of hers keep her down." Rachelle nodded in agreement, and the two began to savor their food while taking in their surroundings. The mall was alive with the laughter of small children and the chatter of shoppers buying gifts for the holiday season. However, there was one face that neither Louise nor Rachelle was happy to see.

"This woman," Rachelle cursed under her breath. Standing near the trash cans was none other than Octavia...

"I know," Louise whispered. "Let's just ignore her. If we don't give her any attention, she'll most likely go away. Hopefully." Rachelle nodded and continued eating, acting as if Octavia was not even there. However, Octavia had other plans for her perceived rival. She calmly walked past the two friends, went over to Subway to order a soda, and after receiving her beverage, made her way back to where Rachelle and Louise were sitting. She then dumped her drink on Rachelle's head. With a shriek, Rachelle jumped up from her seat.

"What the fuck is your problem!?" she demanded.

"You ruined everything!" Octavia seethed.
"You ruined everything!"

"What exactly did I ruin?" Rachelle said, folding her arms.

"Nicky's not talking to me anymore!" Octavia cried, her eyes burning with tears. "He wants nothing to do with me, and it's all your fault!"

"Hold up!" Louise interjected, rising from her seat. "Nick not talking to you is your own fault. Did you forget how I caught you trying to slip your period blood in Nick's drink at my baby shower?"

"That's just trifling," one of the onlookers said in disgust, and her friends agreed.

"Not only that, you sent him nude photos after he told you not to contact him anymore," Rachelle added. Octavia glared at her, shaking with anger. However, Rachelle was unfazed. "I'm sorry you got your feelings hurt, but get over it. Nick fell in love with me, not you. He proposed to me, not you." Rachelle held up her left hand, flashing her engagement ring. "I gave Nick two beautiful babies, not you. You're acting like a bitter ex-girlfriend when Nick never even dated you! He never even slept with you! You're delusional and need to grow up."

"For real," Louise added.
"Now, you got five seconds to get out of our faces."

"I honestly should beat your ass for that stunt you pulled with the soda, but since you're not worth me catching an assault charge, I'll let you walk away." Octavia and Rachelle stared each other down. Rachelle's aura began to glow a dark red, which scared Octavia. She looked around to see that everyone who witnessed the exchange was staring at her with a mixture of contempt, disgust, and confusion. However, she didn't care. It was Rachelle's fault that she lost the love of her life. She was in the way of her happiness, or so she told herself. Octavia also blamed Louise for her current predicament. If Louise and her nosy spirits hadn't told Nick about the separation spell, she might have had a chance at repairing her friendship with Nick. For some reason, Octavia just couldn't look inward. If she had, she would have known that it was her fault that Nick cut her out of his life. Yet, her ego wouldn't allow her to admit that. So, she did the only thing she felt she could to save face.

"Fuck you!" she spat venomously, while simultaneously punching Rachelle in the face. Before Rachelle could react, Octavia lunged at her, slapping, punching, and scratching. Rachelle swung back, her fist colliding with Octavia's nose, busting it wide open. Enraged, Octavia tackled Rachelle to the ground, and the two women tussled. The food court erupted in pandemonium, with some of the onlookers recording the altercation with their phones. Melanie immediately ran to get security, while Louise tried in vain to pull Octavia off Rachelle. While she didn't want to use her powers in full view of a large crowd, she knew it was the only option. With a wave of her hand, Octavia was thrown off Rachelle, colliding with a nearby table. Rachelle grabbed Louise's hand, allowing her to pull her to her feet. She was full of adrenaline, her chest heaving, and her face covered in scratches. While she was tempted to use her healing powers on her wounds, she knew she needed evidence for the authorities.

"What the hell happened here?" Rachelle turned to see a security guard approaching her and Louise, with Melanie close behind him. Melanie took a napkin and handed it to Rachelle, who used it to wipe the blood from her face.

"She attacked me!" Octavia shrieked hysterically, pointing at Rachelle. "She attacked me out of nowhere and broke my nose!" Louise glared at her, resisting the urge to incinerate her on the spot. *This lying heifer!* she thought. Of course, she's playing the victim.

"You hit her first!" a blond teenage girl shouted.

"Shut up!" Octavia barked. The security guard approached the girl. "Is that true?" he asked, gesturing towards Octavia. "Did she instigate the fight?"

"Yep," the blond said as she pulled out her phone, pulling up her videos. She held up the phone to the security guard, showing him a recording of the fight. The video clearly showed Octavia as the aggressor.

"I think I've seen enough," the guard said, glaring at Octavia, who was shaking. He then turned to Rachelle. "Ma'am, would you like for me to contact the police so you can press charges?"

"Yes, sir," Rachelle said forcefully, shooting Octavia a death glare. Octavia cried and pleaded as she was placed under citizen's arrest. The police were called, and she was formally arrested and charged with assault and battery. After making a formal police report, Rachelle decided to close shop early, having had enough excitement for one day. On the way home, she called Nick to tell him what had transpired.

"Are you serious?" he exclaimed on the other end of the phone. "She actually attacked you in the food court!?"

"She sure did," Rachelle replied as she drove. "The bitch scratched up my face, too."

Nick's blood began to boil. A part of him wanted to pull up to Octavia's place to beat her ass, but he knew his mother would not approve of him hitting a woman. So, he decided to let the police handle it. However, whatever sympathy he had for Octavia was now completely gone. "I'm glad you pressed charges," he remarked. "Hopefully, we can get a restraining order."

"I hope so," Rachelle said.
"I never want to see that woman's face again."

Nick sighed. "Rachelle... I'm sorry."

"Sorry?" Rachelle repeated. "Sorry for what?"

Nick let out a tired yet remorseful sigh. "None of this would have happened if I hadn't allowed her back into my life."

"Baby, stop it," Rachelle said. "None of this is your fault, you hear me? You thought you were rekindling an old friendship, and she genuinely seemed like a good person. You didn't know she was going to do this. Octavia is a grown woman. She knows right from wrong, yet she has continuously chosen to do wrong. That's not on you."

"I know," Nick replied.
"I know you're right. I just can't help but feel guilty."

"Well, don't. You have nothing to feel guilty about," Rachelle said. Nick took a deep breath.

"I'm gonna go ahead and get dinner ready. When you get home, I want you to relax. I'll also run a bubble bath for you. Sound good?"

"That sounds perfect," Rachelle said, beaming.
"I love you."

"I love you more," Nick said before hanging up. Rachelle felt a hundred times lighter. Talking to Nick always seemed to have that effect on her. While she had a chaotic day, she knew that with Nick, she had peace and serenity. She couldn't wait to get home to him and their girls. Rachelle sighed contently as she continued to drive, the soulful voice of Phyllis Hyman serenading her. "Everything's going to be just fine."

Chapter 20

Two Days Before Christmas

"So, what should we bring to Rachelle's party?" Kiana asked as they strolled around the store with their buggy. "I know Rachelle and Nick asked for people to bring dessert since they're doing the main meal."

"Hmm," Sarai said as she looked around.
"We can make a couple of key lime pies."

"Sounds good," Kiana remarked, and the couple made their way to the baking aisle to get the necessary ingredients. While they were in the aisle, Sarai noticed an older woman struggling to get some cans off a shelf, dropping a few of them. Feeling pity for the woman, Sarai walked over to her.

"Here you go, ma'am," she said, picking up the can and handing it to the woman with a smile.

"Thank you, honey," the older woman said as she took the can and put it in her cart. She then looked up, her heart nearly stopping, her eyes widening in shock. "S-Sarai?"

Sarai's eyes met the woman's, and she was equally as shocked. Standing in front of her was none other than Tasha Rollins, the sister of her deceased stepmother. However, this was not the Tasha that Sarai knew. She had lost a significant amount of weight, and her skin looked ashen. Her brown eyes, which were always full of life, were now dull. Although she was wearing a winter coat, it appeared that Tasha had lost all of her beautiful, thick hair.

"Tasha?" Sarai asked.

"Yeah, it's me," Tasha said.
"I see you still got that pink hair."

"Yep, sure do," Sarai said, resisting the urge to roll her eyes.
"You look... different."

"Please, I look like shit. You ain't got to sugarcoat it," Tasha said with a bitter laugh.

"...What happened?" Sarai inquired.

"I have stage three ovarian cancer," Tasha answered, and Sarai felt her heart drop to her feet. *That's why she lost so much weight!* she thought to herself. Seeing her "aunt" brought so many conflicting emotions. While she felt pity for Tasha, she still held some resentment and anger towards her. For twenty-three years of her life, she had to listen to Thelma and Tasha ridicule and demean her for everything from her skin tone to her hobbies. For twenty-three years, she was told by these women that she would never amount to anything, that she was "ungodly." No matter what Sarai did, it was never good enough for them. She wasn't worthy of their praise or love. Now, Sarai is thriving, with a successful career as an author, great friends who support and encourage her, a loving family, and an amazing wife. Meanwhile, Thelma and Lamar were worm food, destroyed by their own evil, and here was Tasha, alone and wasting away from the cancer that was wreaking havoc on her body. While she ceased all contact with Tasha after not only learning of her true heritage but also the events that lead to the tragic suicide of Faith, she was dumbfounded. She never thought she would run into Tasha again. However, she shouldn't be surprised, since Detroit was a large city. You're bound to run into old friends, family, and acquaintances at some point. However, she was conflicted. What does she say to her? Would Tasha acknowledge the harm she had caused, or stand ten toes down like her sister had?

"C-Cancer?" she repeated.
"When did you-"

"I was diagnosed about a year ago," Tasha replied. "On my baby's birthday, no less! Ironic, isn't it?" Tasha then coughed into her arm.

"W-Wow," Sarai said. "I'm sorry...."

"Don't be," Tasha said. "I'm sure this is my 'karma,' right?" " God is punishing me for my sins."

"I wouldn't say that."

"I wouldn't blame you if that's what you think," Tasha said. "I read your memoir, by the way."

"Really?" Sarai asked, and Tasha nodded. She then let out a sigh.

"I did. You're a very talented writer, Sarai. God has truly blessed you with a gift." Sarai could have sworn she was living in an alternate timeline. Never, in a million years, did she ever think she would receive a compliment from Tasha. The older woman chuckled at the younger's shocked expression, as if reading her mind. "I know. I know this is the first time I've ever said anything nice to you, and for that, I'm sorry."

"Come again?"

"I'm sorry," Tasha repeated, her eyes wet with tears. "I know that I'm years too late, and I have no right to ask for your forgiveness, but I truly am sorry. There is no excuse for the way you and Faith were treated."

"Are you sorry because you truly feel remorse, or because you're sick?" Sarai asked. Tasha sighed and looked down.

"You have every right to ask that question," she said. "To be honest, it's both. I am disgusted with myself for how I treated you girls, especially Faith. She was so sweet, beautiful, and full of life. I'm sure she would have grown to be successful, too."

"Did you know? About Pastor Williams, I mean."

"I had no idea," Tasha answered. "That night on Thanksgiving, I was just as shocked as your daddy. Thelma never told me what Faith had told her." Sarai was speechless. *So Thelma was lying to her own sister, too? She truly had no shame!* she thought.

"*None!*" Ivy said.

"I see," Sarai said. She was still in shock. The Tasha standing before her was not the Tasha she had grown up with. The Tasha Rollins she knew never apologized for anything, unless it had to do with her precious baby boy. *I have to be living in a different timeline! This is fucking unreal!* "So, why did you treat us the way you did?" Tasha let out a long sigh.

"There really isn't a good reason I can give for that, other than I felt some kind of twisted loyalty to my only sibling. Growing up, we were taught that blood was thicker than water, no matter what."

"You know that quote is wrong, right?" Sarai said. "It's 'The blood of the covenant is thicker than the water of the womb.' It means that family is not about blood, but those who love and support you." Tasha cackled.

"You always were a smart one," she said. "Anyway, contrary to what you think, Thelma did try to love you girls. She really did, but it was too much, because ya'll looked too much like ya'll mama."

"So, why didn't she just leave?" Sarai countered.

"She did... once," Tasha replied. "You were too young to remember, but when you and Faith were two years old, Thelma had a miscarriage. After that, no matter how hard she and your daddy tried, she could never get pregnant again. I think that, combined with the fact that another woman had given Vernon something that she couldn't, it really messed with her. So, she packed her bags while he was at work and left to stay with our parents. She was preparing to divorce your daddy."

"So, what happened?" Sarai asked.
"What made her change her mind?"

251

"Our parents had something to do with that, more specifically, our mother," Tasha replied. "See, Mama was really obsessed with appearances, especially in the church. Every woman's goal was to find a man and get married. Thelma really wanted Pastor Williams, but he was already married, so she settled for your daddy."

"I told you!" Ivy exclaimed. "What did I tell you?"

"Vernon really did try to love Thelma, but she was cold towards him. So, I honestly can't blame him for being with your mama. Anyway, when you girls were born, we told the church that Vernon and Thelma adopted you, after your mother died in childbirth. They didn't know that Vernon was your biological father. Thelma definitely didn't want the congregation to know. Your daddy's relationship with your mama made her feel undesirable, like there was something wrong with her. When she found out about your mama, she talked so much shit about her. She called her a Black bitch, a gorilla, a nappy-headed whore, all types of messed up shit. She was jealous and felt threatened."

"Hmph," Sarai said.

"So, she went to Mama and told her she wanted to get a divorce. Mama was having none of it. She told Thelma that divorce was a sin and that she didn't want to have to deal with church gossip. So, Thelma decided to stay. However, she became bitter and angry..."

"Then she started taking that anger and bitterness out on us," Sarai concluded.

"Yes," Tasha said. "Thelma was simply a broken woman. Now, that absolutely does not excuse her mistreatment of you. At all. You and Faith didn't ask to be here. We were both wrong." Tasha took a deep breath as a tear rolled down her face. "I was also wrong in how I raised Lamar. I spoiled him to make up for his father not being there, but I ended up creating an entitled, immature man. Rachelle was such a sweet, beautiful, and smart girl, and I truly thought she would have been a positive influence on him. But you know Lamar was stubborn and spoiled as hell. That girl didn't deserve any of the disrespect we showed her. You're lucky to have a friend like her."

"I know I am," Sarai said with a small smile.

"You've done really well for yourself, Sarai," Tasha said. "I know it doesn't mean anything to you, but I am truly proud of who you've become. Don't ever let anyone else tell you that you can't do something."

"I won't. Never again."

"Now, while I don't understand the gay and witch thing, I was wrong for calling you an abomination. I was ignorant."

"I appreciate your apology," Sarai replied.

"Can you also tell Rachelle that I'm sorry?"

"I'll be sure to tell her."

"How has she been, anyway?" Tasha inquired.

"She's been great," Sarai said with a smile. "She's still modeling. She has twin girls, and she's also currently planning her wedding." Sarai then reached into her purse and pulled out a Melanin Siren business card, showing it to Tasha. "She also has her own beauty line." Tasha stared at the card in awe.

"Wow," she said. "Well, she always had a good head on her shoulders. I was just too petty and jealous to truly appreciate it." Tasha sighed sadly. "I'm disgusted with myself for what I said about her father. He raised a fine young woman. God has truly blessed her."

"I'll be sure to tell Rachelle that," Sarai said. "Kiana and I should get going, though. We need to get these pies ready for Rachelle's Christmas party tomorrow."

"Well, it was good to see you again," Tasha said, giving a feeble smile. "I wish you all continued success and happiness."

"Thank you. If you want, I can pray for your healing," Sarai said.

"I don't know what good it'll do, but if you want, I appreciate it. You take care," Tasha said as she turned to walk away. Sarai's heart broke for Tasha. Whatever anger she held towards seemed to just evaporate. All she felt at that moment was compassion. Tasha was no longer the loud, boisterous woman she once was. She was frail and alone, her entire family gone. Sarai wasn't even sure if Shawna allowed Tasha to see her grandson. Had she even met Lamar's daughter? In an instant, the lifelong hatred she had felt towards her former adoptive family went up in smoke. She felt that the universe had punished Tasha enough. She could only imagine how lonely Tasha must have been, especially during the holidays.

"Hey, Tasha!" she called out before Tasha was out of sight. The sickly woman turned around.

"Yes?"
"Would you like to come to the Christmas party? I'll call Rachelle to make sure it's okay, but I'm sure after I explain, she wouldn't mind having you," Sarai said. Tasha gave her a warm smile.

"I'd like that very much."

Christmas Eve

"Thanks for allowing Tasha to come to the party, Chelly," Sarai said as she helped decorate the large Christmas tree.

"No problem," Rachelle replied with a smile. "I stopped hating her a long time ago. It takes too much energy. It's really sad that she has cancer, though."

"Yeah," Kiana added. "Not only that, she doesn't have any real support while she's fighting it." The others murmured in agreement as they continued to decorate, with "The Christmas Song" by Nat King Cole playing from the speakers. The twins happily played with Dy'Anna, while Artemis and Bryson watched How the Grinch Stole Christmas from the couch. "You know, I don't blame The Grinch for being the way he is," "I'd be mean, too, if every five minutes, someone sang about what a piece of crap I was." Rachelle, Sarai, and Louise laughed.

"For real," Rachelle said as she hung an ornament on the tree. She and Nick were glad they were hosting the holiday festivities this year. It was a welcome distraction from all the drama they were going through with Octavia. After being arrested for attacking Rachelle at Oakland Mall, she was fired from Brent & Parker PLLC, the law firm where she worked. Not only that, no other law firm would hire her, much to the chagrin of her sister. Rachelle was also granted an emergency order of protection. However, this did not stop Octavia from messaging her and Nick from burner accounts on social media. This resulted in Octavia being arrested yet again.

"Hey, Lexi, how's things with your dad?" Louise asked. Alexis sighed.

"Mom is still trying to fight the divorce," she said. "She keeps trying to get Dad into going to marriage counseling, but he's not budging. I honestly don't blame him. She lied to him for twenty-eight years." Louise nodded in understanding.

"I still don't get it, though," Sarai said. "Chelly got her powers from both her parents, and Mr. Ernie is her dad's twin. If he's not Lexi's father, and her mom doesn't have any powers that we know of, then where did Lexi's powers come from?"

"That's a good question," Kiana added.

"It's very possible that Alexis's powers came from her biological father," Kristy interjected.

"Damn," Sarai remarked.

"Well, as far as I'm concerned, Ernest Lawson is still my father," Alexis said. "I don't give a damn what that paternity test says."

"Exactly," Rachelle said. "We're family, no matter what." Smiling, Alexis embraced her cousin in a hug. Suddenly, the doorbell rang. "I'll get it!"

255

Nick announced as he went to the front door. A few moments later, Veronica entered the house with Trina in tow, both stylish in mink jackets.

"Happy Holidays, everybody!" Veronica exclaimed as she removed her jacket. Nick took the jackets from the women to the closet, while they made their rounds greeting everyone with a hug. "Something smells good in here."

"I just took the jerk chicken out of the air fryer," Rachelle said. "I also got gumbo simmering on the stove. Nick also made tamales."

"I see you two went all out," Veronica remarked as she sat the twins in her lap. Rachelle, Sarai, Kiana, Louise, Mariah, and Alexis stood around the tree, admiring their work.

"Mimi, would you like to put the star on the tree?" Louise asked, smiling down at her daughter. With an excited nod, Artemis waved her hand, and the star floated to the top of the tree, earning applause from the adults. Soon, the rest of the guests arrived, and the festivities truly began. When Tasha entered the house, she felt awkward. For years, there had been bad blood between her and Rachelle, due to her family's disrespect towards her. Yet, Rachelle and Nick greeted her warmly, feeling compassion for the sickly woman. Veronica and Sharon were also welcoming to Tasha, as difficult as it was, more so for Veronica. Rachelle had to convince her aunt to not go off on her.

"Your family is so beautiful, Rachelle," Tasha remarked, smiling as she watched the twins play. "I'm glad you were able to find happiness."

"Thank you, Ms. Tasha," Rachelle said. Tasha then cleared her throat.

"I know Sarai already told you, but I want to say this face to face," she began. "I just want to say, from the bottom of my heart, how sorry I am for how I treated you. You didn't deserve any of it. I also apologize for how my son treated you. I enabled him, and it only did him more harm than good."

"I accept your apology, Ms. Tasha, and I forgave you a long time ago," Rachelle said, and the two women hugged. Tasha then turned to Sharon.

"You raised a truly wonderful young lady," she said.

"Yes, I did," Sharon said with a warm smile.
"However, I can't take all the credit. Her father helped."

Tasha sighed. "What I said about your father at that dinner, Rachelle... it was disgusting. I don't blame you for wanting to fight me that night." Tasha was truly ashamed and disgusted at her ignorance back then.

"That's all in the past now," Rachelle said as she came into the dining room with a tall pitcher of a dark red beverage. "Now, who wants some Sorrel?"

"I'll have some," Sarai replied, and Rachelle poured her and the others a glass. "Damn, this is good!" Trina remarked. "Where did you learn to make this?"

"It was my Grandma Lula's recipe," Rachelle replied with a smile. "Sorrel is a very popular drink in Jamaica during the holidays. Daddy used to make it all the time at Christmas, but he died before he could give me Grandma's recipe. However, he had it written in an old journal that me and Mom found in the attic a couple of months ago."

"Well, it's delicious," Tasha said as she took a sip.
"How did you get it red like this?"

"Hibiscus," Rachelle said.
"It also has fresh ginger. That's why it tastes a bit spicy."

"Hmm," Tasha said as she took a bite from a tamale.
"Did you make these, too?"

"Nope, Nick did."

"You can thank my mom for the recipe," Nick said with a smile. Tasha then turned to Sarai.

"So, where's your daddy?" she inquired.

"Oh, he's volunteering at a soup kitchen," Sarai replied.
"He offered his catering services."

"That man sure could cook," Tasha said. "Now, Thelma may have been my sister, but she would burn water if given the chance. That's why Mama kept her out of the kitchen." Sarai burst out laughing, and the others followed suit. After everyone had eaten, they gathered in the living room to watch the children open their gifts, and watch Christmas movies on the large television. Artemis even played her new violin for them as they watched in awe. Louise and Wilfred watched their daughter proudly, knowing that she had a bright future in music ahead of her.

"That baby belongs in somebody's orchestra!" Simone said as she poured another glass of Sorrel.

"Trust me, we're already looking into that," Wilfred said as he kissed his daughter on the cheek. "She also does ballet and tap dance." Simone's eyes widened in astonishment.

"Sounds like you've got yourself a prodigy," Veronica remarked.

"We do, and we couldn't be more proud," Kristy said, gently pinching Artemis' cheek, making her laugh. Then, Sharon spoke up.

"Since the family is all here, my sister would like to make an announcement." She then turned to Veronica, who stood up with Trina.

"As a lot of you already know, I took Trina under my wing about three years ago, when she began her modeling career," she began. "Over the years, I have grown to love her as the daughter I never had. Now, we have made it official." Veronica then pulled out a manila envelope. She opened it to reveal a small stack of papers. Rachelle noticed, to her astonishment, that they were adoption papers. "Trina Michaels is now Trina Michaels-Miller. She is officially my daughter." The room erupted in applause, and Trina cried tears of joy as Veronica, Joanna, Sharon, Alexis, and Rachelle embraced her.

"Welcome to the family, cousin," Rachelle said. "Although, I already considered you family."

"Likewise," Trina replied, as the rest of the girls joined them in a group hug, making her cry more. Trina cried for the girl that was once alone in the world. She cried for the girl that grew up without a father. She cried for the girl who lost her grandmother, the only woman who had shown her any maternal love. Trina also cried for how far she had come. She was no longer the scared, insecure girl who craved acceptance. Now, she was fierce, powerful, and magical in every sense of the word, and she had friends and family that loved her. She had fans that adored her. She was accepted for who she truly was. While the child within her would always miss Esther Johnson, the woman who had given birth to her, Trina knew that Esther was a miserable woman who brought darkness to those around her. She would only bring her down with her toxicity. Esther would never accept Trina for who she truly was, nor support her in her aspirations. As painful as it was to admit to herself, Trina's life was far brighter and far happier without Esther in it.

"I think this calls for champagne!" Carmen exclaimed, and Rachelle went into the kitchen, returning with a bottle of champagne, and a bottle of sparkling grape juice for Louise and the children. Once everyone's glasses were poured, Louise stood up to make a toast.

"I'd like to toast to us. We have weathered many storms and have come through the other side stronger and more resilient than ever before. No matter how the world views us, we are powerful, divine, and magical because we have our ancestors' blood, power, and strength running through us." Louise then held her glass higher. "TO US!"

"To us!" the rest shouted in unison, as they touched their glasses together. The party continued well into the late hours, with the children passed out on the couch, tired out from playing. The friends bid each other farewell and went their separate ways. Rachelle and Nick took the twins to their room and tucked them in.

"Tonight was pretty eventful, wasn't it?" Rachelle asked as she and Nick stood in the doorway of the nursery.

"That's an understatement," Nick said, putting his arm around her. "I bet you didn't expect your ex's mother to apologize the way she did, after all these years."

"No, I didn't," Rachelle said. "However, I'm glad she did. It takes a lot of maturity to admit that you messed up and genuinely apologize. I guess it's true what they say: people can change." Nick smiled and kissed her on the cheek.

"It was also sweet of Ms. Ronnie to adopt Trina."

"I'm glad she did," Rachelle said. "Trina deserves it. She deserves a real mother, for once, after all she's been through."

"I agree," Nick said, and the two made their way to the master bedroom to finally lay down after a long night. However, they were far from tired.

Chapter 21

"**B**abe, can you get the door?" Louise called out from the bathroom.

Wilfred paused his game and headed to the door, with Comet meowing behind him. Opening the door, he was greeted by Sarai, Kiana, and Vernon. "What's up, fam?" Sarai said, hugging Wilfred as she entered the house with her wife and father. Wilfred took their coats and hung them in the front closet. Comet rubbed against Sarai's leg, purring. "Hey, cutie," she said, bending down to pet Comet, who purred even more. Artemis then rolled a ball of yarn toward Comet, who began to bat at it with her paws.

"Hey, y'all!" Louise said, emerging from the bathroom, her hand on her large belly. She was in her last month of pregnancy and due to give birth within two weeks. Both Wilfred and Sarai helped her to the couch.

"Damn, girl!" Kiana exclaimed.
"You look like you're about to pop!"

"I know, right?" Louise replied.
"I can't wait to pop this little one out."

"Are you sure you're up for a party?" Sarai asked, concerned. Louise waved her off.

"Girl, I'll be fine," she said. "I'm not due for another two weeks. Besides, it's not like we're doing anything too wild."

"True," Sarai said as she sat on the couch next to her cousin. Kiana sat next to Sarai, while Vernon sat across from them. "By the way, Rachelle and Nick said they'll be here in a few."

"Cool," Louise said.

"What about Trina?" Kiana asked.

"Ms. Ronnie took her and Ms. Joanna on a surprise trip to Barbados for the new year, and to celebrate the adoption," Louise answered.

"That's what's up," Kiana remarked. "I'm so happy for her. She's living her best life, and she's got a rich mama now?"

"I'm really happy Trina and Ms. Ronnie found each other," Sarai added. Suddenly, the doorbell rang again. Wilfred went to answer it, and a few moments later, Rachelle and Nick entered the living room.
"Hey, you two!" Louise said cheerfully as the three friends shared a hug. "Where are the girls?"

"His parents wanted to keep them so we can have some time to ourselves," Rachelle replied. "Lexi said she won't be able to make it. She and Bryce decided to have a family movie night with Bryson."

"Aww, that's so cute," Sarai said.
"So, what does your mom have planned?"

"She and her boyfriend are attending a party hosted by a city councilman," Rachelle said.

"Nice," Sarai remarked. Wilfred emerged from the kitchen with a large tray of pizza balls and set it on the dining room table, along with a tray of fudge brownies and chocolate chip cookies.

"These are still pretty hot, so be careful," he said. He then turned to Louise and said, "And don't eat them all." Louise playfully flipped her husband off, and the others laughed.

"Damn, these pizza balls are good!" Kiana remarked.
"Where did you learn to make these?"

"TikTok," Wilfred and Louise answered in unison.

"I helped!" Artemis chimed in.

"I'm gonna need y'all to send me that video," Kiana said as she took another bite. Rachelle, Nick, and Vernon also helped themselves to the pizza balls. About an hour later, Kristy and Xavier arrived with Mariah. Dannell arrived shortly after. About twenty minutes later, Simone arrived at the Eason home. Although the car accident she was in had left her with horrible injuries, she was able to make a full recovery and was back to her bubbly self. However, she was left with a deep scar across her left cheek.

"I brought cheesecake," Simone said, holding up the pie. "Hope you don't mind."

"Girl, please! Of course we don't mind," Louise said. "Just set it on the table."

"Awesome," Simone said as she put the cheesecake on the dining room table. "By the way, where's Trina? And Chris and Khalil?"

"Trina's in Barbados with her mom," Sarai replied. "Chris and Khalil are in New York."

"Her mom?" Simone repeated, her eyebrow raised. "I thought Trina cut her off."

"Oh, no, no, not her egg donor," Louise clarified. "Rachelle's aunt adopted her as her own. They announced it at the Christmas party."

"Wow," Simone stated. "I'm happy for her."

"Right? She's getting everything in life that she deserves," Rachelle said.

"By the way, how's the music coming along, Simone?" Kiana cut in. Simone beamed proudly.

"It's going great," she replied. She was so glad she was able to rekindle her love for music, in spite of all the trauma she had endured. "'Bad Witch Bitch' has reached over 20,000 streams."

"Oh my god! That's amazing!" Rachelle exclaimed.

263

"I'm so happy for you!"

"We all are," Kristy said with a smile, pouring herself a glass of plum wine.

"I'm happy, too," Simone said. "I can't believe that I allowed myself to turn my back on singing after what happened to me."

"Has anyone in your family heard the song?" Sarai asked. Simone sighed.

"My brother did, and he was not happy."

"Let me guess, was it because you were singing about casting spells?" Louise asked.

"Not just that," Simone replied. "He also didn't like how I called out Debra and the church for how they treated me."

"What did you say to him?" Rachelle asked.

"I told him that if Debra was actually a decent human being and mother, then she wouldn't have to worry about being called out."

"What did your brother say to that?" Nick asked.

"He basically went on a rant about how I need to stop holding grudges, and let go of the past, and to stop disrespecting our mother," Simone replied bitterly. "I'm not holding grudges. I've healed from what happened to me. However, that doesn't mean I'm obligated to keep Debra in my life or forgive her." Simone took a deep breath. The anger she felt during the conversation with her brother once again bubbled to the surface. "Anyway, once he started going off on me, I simply hung up the phone and blocked his number. I'm staying No Contact with him for a while." Sarai nodded in agreement.

"I don't blame you," she remarked. "No one has the right to police how you heal from your traumas. I have to deal with the same thing from my dad's side of the family."

"And I have no problem putting my family in their place if they come for you," Vernon interjected. Sarai smiled at him.

"It's nice that you got your dad to back you up, Sarai," Simone said, sighing sadly. "I don't have any family in my corner."

"Nonsense!" Louise exclaimed.
"You have us, remember?"
"Yeah, that's true," Simone said as she took a bite of a pizza ball. "Remember what you said in my shop to your mother?" Kristy said. "Love makes you family. Loyalty makes you family. We love you, Simone, and we will always be in your corner." Simone gave her a small smile.

"Thanks, you guys," she said as they all joined in a group hug. Simone's heart felt full from the love and support that surrounded her. With them in her corner, she didn't need Debra or Nathan Monroe. Misery loved company, and she wanted no parts.

"Alright, that's enough mushy stuff," Louise remarked as they broke the hug. "Y'all are gonna make me cry."

"Yeah, with your hormonal ass," Mariah teased.

"Oh, I know you ain't talking!" Louise said. "When you were pregnant with Dy'Anna, you were crying over Kay Jewelers commercials!" The room erupted in laughter as Mariah flipped off her older sister, jokingly, of course.

"Cut it out, you two," Kristy said musingly. The family and friends spent the next two hours playing board games and watching movies, enjoying each other's company. 2022 was finally approaching its end. To say it was an eventful year was putting it lightly. It was a year full of drama and loss, but it was also a year of triumph and celebration. Little did Louise know, however, that she was going to ring in the new year with a loud bang.

"Hey, babe, can you get another pop from the fridge?" Wilfred asked as he was helping Artemis set up her game.

"Yeah, I got it," Louise replied as she made her way to the kitchen. As she grabbed a red Faygo from the refrigerator, she felt a sharp pain in her abdomen, followed by a gush of fluid from between her legs. She looked down to see that her yoga pants were soaked and she was standing in a puddle. "WILL!"

"What's wrong?!" Wilfred cried as he jumped up and ran into the kitchen. His eyes widened as he saw the puddle. "Shit!"

"What's wrong?" Kiana asked.

"Lou's water just broke!" Wilfred answered as he led Louise to the couch. He then went to the front closet and grabbed their coats. After helping Louise into hers, he led her outside to their car, followed by Kristy.

"Is Mommy gonna be okay?" Artemis asked, panicked.

"Don't worry, sweetie," Rachelle said gently. "Your mom's going to be fine. It's just that your sister is ready to come out."

"Ohh," Artemis said, still a bit confused.

"We should follow them to the hospital," Kiana suggested. The others agreed, and they followed Louise and her family in their vehicles. When they arrived at Hutzel Women's Hospital, Louise was immediately taken to Labor and Delivery. Wilfred and Kristy went with her, while the others waited in the hospital lobby.

"I hope everything goes smoothly," Simone said.

"Trust me, with Ms. Kristy as her doula, she'll be fine," Rachelle said, although deep down, she was also worried about her friend. She would never forget the anguish she saw on Louise's face when Apollo had died and the deep despair that followed. To Rachelle, Louise was the strongest woman she knew, aside from Sarai, and it broke her heart to see her friend so shattered. "The Ancestors will watch over her," Sarai said, as if reading Rachelle's mind, and the others murmured in agreement. Hours passed as Louise waited to push. Her contractions were occurring more frequently, and she was growing increasingly anxious. While this was not her first time in the maternity ward, it didn't make the experience any less nerve-wracking.

"It'll be alright, babe," Wilfred said gently, taking Louise's hand in his.

"Easy for you to say," Louise said in a strained voice. A pained expression was painted on her face. She couldn't wait until this was over with. However, once she was administered the epidural, the pain became slightly more bearable. After forty-five minutes, the long-awaited moment finally arrived.

"Okay, Louise, you're now ten centimeters dilated," the doctor said. "I need you to start pushing." Taking a deep breath, Louise began to push, squeezing her husband's hand as he and her mother coached and encouraged her.

"That's it, babe. You got this," Wilfred said, giving Louise a soft kiss on the forehead. Pain shot through the lower half of her body as she continued to push, praying that she didn't tear. She felt heavy and dizzy, as if the room was spinning around her. The room was growing warmer, and her face was covered in a light sheen of sweat.

"I can see the head!" the doctor exclaimed as the baby started to crown. "You're doing great, honey. Just keep pushing." Louise gritted her teeth and pushed with everything she had. Wilfred was in awe of how stoic his wife was. There was no screaming or hysterics. While she was experiencing intense discomfort, she bore it with great strength. Kristy's heart swelled with pride for her eldest child. With a final push, Soleil Céleste Eason made her debut into the world. Louise's heart swelled, her eyes brimming with tears upon hearing her daughter's cries.

"Congratulations, Louise," the doctor said with a smile. "You now have a healthy baby girl." The nurse gave Wilfred a pair of scissors, and he cut the umbilical cord. The nurse then cleaned up the newborn, swaddling her in a clean, pink blanket. Louise broke down into tears as the nurse placed the baby in her arms. Soleil was beautiful, with soft, black curls, like her mother had before she dyed them. The baby slightly opened her eyes, and Louise could tell they were a bright, silvery gray. Looks like you reached several generations back for those eyes, she thought musingly. She looked up to see an apparition of Kamaria, smiling at her. The princess was also standing with Louise's grandmother, who held baby Apollo in her arms.

IT'S A GIRL!

SOLEIL CÉLESTE EASON
BORN JANUARY 1, 2023

"Welcome to the world, Baby Girl," Louise said, placing a gentle kiss on the newborn's head. Kristy left to go to the lobby, giving the couple some time alone with their bundle of joy.

"Damn, it's 4 am already?" Kiana remarked, looking at her phone. "It was only 10:45 when we left!"

"I know, right?" Sarai said. She looked up to see Kristy walking toward them.

"Is everything okay with Lou?" Kiana asked. Kristy beamed.

"Everything is just fine," she said.
"Soleil just made her debut."
"She had the baby?" Rachelle asked anxiously.

"Yep. A juicy nine pounds, six ounces."

"Damn!" Simone remarked. "That's a big baby." Kristy chuckled.

"Mimi, would you like to go up with Pop Pop to see your new sister?" she asked. Artemis nodded excitedly, getting up from her chair. She then took Xavier's hand as they went to the maternity ward. Louise smiled upon seeing her daughter and father.

"Hey, Daddy," she said in a tired voice. Xavier smiled, kissing his daughter on the forehead.

"How are you feeling, *cher*?" he asked.

"Ça va," Louise replied. "Just tired, and a little sore." Xavier nodded and sat in a chair next to Wilfred, who was holding Soleil. Louise then turned to Artemis. "Moonbeam, come say hello to your baby sister." Artemis walked over to her father, who showed the newborn to her. Soleil was sleeping soundly against his chest.

"Was I this small when I was a baby?" Artemis asked.

"A little smaller, but yes," Louise replied. "Do you want to hold her?" Artemis nodded, and Wilfred carefully placed the baby in her arms. Artemis smiled down at her sister, who grabbed her finger. "Aww, look, they're bonding already." Artemis giggled as she gently snuggled the baby. Xavier took out his phone and snapped a photo of the happy family.

"Wow," he said, warmly.
"Three granddaughters."

"And you're going to spoil this one rotten, too," Louise said jokingly. Xavier chuckled as he gently stroked Soleil's cheek with his finger.

"You should rest," Wilfred said as he handed Soleil to the nurse. "We'll be back tomorrow." Louise simply nodded, and she gave her husband, father, and daughter a goodbye kiss and hug. She turned to look at her daughter, who slept peacefully. With a contented sigh, she laid back in her bed.

"Happy New Year to me," she said softly, before drifting off to sleep.

Three Months Later

Chapter 22

"So, how's Uncle Ernie doing?" Rachelle asked as she and Alexis made their way through Dom & Mari's. Louise was hosting another Girls' Night gathering at her home, so Rachelle and her cousin were shopping for refreshments to bring.

"Things are a little better," Alexis replied. "Mom finally stopped fighting the divorce, so it should be finalized this month. I think she realizes that Dad is not budging, and that she messed up."

"How are things with you and Corrine?" Rachelle inquired, and Alexis let out a sigh.

"She thinks I need to stop 'holding a grudge' against her. Her words, not mine," she replied. "It's like she just wants to sweep this under the rug, instead of taking accountability. This woman lied to me my entire life! I'm not just going to 'get over it'. I love her and all, but I'm really not liking her right now."

"That's completely valid," Rachelle said.

"I still let her see Bryson, though," Alexis said. "Our issues have nothing to do with their relationship. Although, I did have to check her because she kept asking Bryson to get me to forgive her. I told her if she didn't stop doing that, Bryson wouldn't be seeing her anymore."

"She's actually doing that?"

"Yep, and it's pissing me off. You don't bring children into adult issues."

"Exactly," Rachelle said as she put a few two-liter bottles of Faygo in the shopping cart.

"Anyway, how's business going?" Alexis asked.

"Business is going great," Rachelle replied with a smile. "My cosmetics keep selling out, especially the lip glosses."

"That's awesome!" Alexis remarked. "I'm really happy for you. Pretty soon, Sephora will be selling your stuff."

"You really think so?"

"Girl, I know so," Alexis said as they put a few bags of candy in the cart and made their way to the checkout line. Before they reached their destination, they heard two women arguing loudly near the frozen food aisle. Feeling a bit nosy, the cousins made their way to the aisle. Rachelle, to her shock, saw her former friend, Nikki Jacobs, arguing with a woman who was two heads taller than her, with a curvy frame, dark skin, and a chic pixie cut. On one side of her stood a short, plump, light-skinned woman with red box braids. On the other side stood a slim woman of average height, with brown skin and a black bob with brown highlights. Rachelle recognized the tall woman instantly. She was Pamela Jacobs, Nikki's cousin. Rachelle assumed the women standing with her were her friends.

"Yeah, I fucked your man, bitch!" Nikki spat. "It was damn good, too. I can see why you had three babies by him. Jerome said this was the best pussy he's ever had." Nikki then licked her fingers sensually. Rachelle could only shake her head. Nikki Jacobs was up to her usual antics: sleeping with other people's men and talking shit, regardless of the consequences. Nikki was outnumbered, and Pamela could easily stomp her out. Any sensible person would disengage and walk away. However, Nikki was not a sensible person, and she always had to have the last word.

"Yo, Pam! You wanna mess this bitch up!?" the short, light-skinned woman asked, staring daggers at Nikki. "I know she's your family and all, but she's being mad disrespectful." Nikki sucked her teeth.

"Janisha, shut up! You ain't gonna do shit!" she said. She then turned to Pamela. "It's not my fault you can't please your man. He slid into my DMs. Maybe you should've fucked him better, you washed-up bitch!" Nikki was immediately met with a punch to the face, causing her head to snap back.

Before she could react, Pam and her homegirls immediately descended upon her like a pack of lionesses, punching and kicking her relentlessly. Nikki cried and pleaded for the women to stop, but to no avail.

"Don't cry now, bitch!" Pam barked as she continued her assault. "You was talking all that shit a second ago!" Nikki tried her hardest to fight off the brutal blows, but her cousin was stronger.

"Goddamn!" Alexis cried in a whisper, holding her fist over her mouth. Rachelle simply smirked, feeling a twisted sense of satisfaction. In her mind, Nikki was getting exactly what she deserved. She had screwed over and disrespected far too many people. Now, she had written a check that her ass couldn't cash.

"Hey!" Marisol shouted, running towards the small crowd that had gathered. She was checking inventory when an employee had alerted her to the commotion. "You break this up right now!" With a wave of her hand, the crowd immediately dispersed, some of them falling flat on their asses. Pamela and her friends stared at Marisol in shock as they stepped away from Nikki. Her face was black and blue, and her left eye was swollen shut. Blood was flowing from her nose and split lip. She lay in a fetal position, sobbing.

"Bet you won't fuck anyone else's man, bitch!" Pamela spat, delivering one last kick to Nikki's abdomen.

"You three get out of my store right now!" Marisol barked, her aura glowing a fierce red.

"Gladly," Pamela said coolly. She and her friends turned to leave, but not before spitting on Nikki's battered form. Marisol kneeled down next to her. "Milo, can you call an ambulance?" she asked one of her employees.

"I already did. They're on their way," Milo answered. Marisol simply nodded.

"Don't worry, honey," she said soothingly. "Help is on the way. Let's get you some ice." Nikki nodded, whimpering. Marisol got up and went to retrieve an ice pack. Shaking her head, Rachelle went to the checkout line, with Alexis following close behind.

Hmph. I knew it would only be a matter of time before you messed with the wrong person, she thought musingly. *I don't feel one bit sorry for you, Nikki. That ass-whooping was long overdue!* After paying for her items, Rachelle and her cousin left the store, making their way to Rachelle's car. However, before pulling off, she called her fiancé.

"Babe, you'll never believe what just happened in your folks' store!"

"Yo, are you serious?" Louise exclaimed as she set the pizza on the table. "Nikki got jumped for real?"

"Yep," Rachelle said. "Apparently, Nikki had been sleeping with her cousin's man, and as usual, Nikki was running her mouth." Louise shook her head in disgust. *That woman has no morals or boundaries,* she thought.

"Damn," Sarai remarked.
"I can't say she didn't deserve it, though. Damn, her own cousin?"

"It's dirty as hell," Rachelle said. "It's bad enough that she slept with Lamar while we were together, but she also hooked up with Jay while he was with Mike. She hit on Wilfred and Nick, so I'm not surprised that she would betray her own family. She deserved what she got."

"I 100% agree," Louise interjected as she went into the kitchen. "That beating was years overdue."

"Anyway, enough about that trifling bitch," Rachelle said, turning to Trina. "So, Trina, how are things with you and Monsieur Pierre?" Trina giggled, blushing.

"Things are great," she replied.
"We're living together now."

"That's awesome!" Sarai exclaimed.

"How does Auntie Ronnie like him?" Rachelle asked.

"Mom adores Pierre," Trina replied. "She's hoping that we get engaged, so she can spoil us with a big wedding." Rachelle giggled.

"Yeah, that sounds about right," she said. "But, I'm really happy for you. I'm so glad you found the Papi to your Angel."

"Aww, thanks, cousin," Trina said, and the two shared a hug. "I still can't believe we're family now."

"I know, right," Rachelle said.

"So, Sarai, do you have any plans for another book?" Louise asked.

"I'm still brainstorming ideas, but I'm thinking of doing a horror anthology series," Sarai replied. "I've been doing a lot of research on legends and lore in the South. Anansi has been helping me with this."

"Who's Anansi?" Simone asked.

"He's a spider god of knowledge, storytelling, and wisdom in Akan folklore," Sarai answered.

"Like in American Gods?" Khalil interjected.

"Yep."

"I hate how they fired Orlando Jones after that monologue, though. He told the truth," Louise said, and the others agreed.

"That idea sounds dope," Simone remarked. "I hope you write it, so I can read it."

"I second that," Rachelle added.

"So, I do have some news," Simone said.

"What is it?" Louise asked.

267

"Megan Thee Stallion's people reached out to me. Megan heard my song, and she wants to collaborate," Simone replied, and all the women squealed in excitement.

"Oh, my god!" Louise exclaimed.
"Please tell me you agreed!"

"Girl, of course I did!" Simone said.
"You really think I'm gonna pass up an opportunity like this?"

"I'm so proud of you!" Sarai squealed, embracing Simone in a bear hug.
"You have come such a long way," Simone said, smiling.
"So did you," Simone said.

"So did all of us," Trina interjected.
"I love you guys."

"We love you, too," Khalil said, and the friends joined in a group hug. However, the touching moment was interrupted by the sound of Soleil crying through the baby monitor.

"I'll be right back," Louise said as she broke the hug and went upstairs to the nursery. Upon seeing her mother, the infant immediately began to calm down. "Aww, what's the matter, Sunbeam? You can't be hungry. I just fed you." Then, the smell hit her. Aww, you just need to be changed, she thought as she proceeded to change her daughter's diaper. Once she was clean and dry, Soleil appeared to be much happier. Louise's heart melted at her daughter's smile. Soleil was truly a beautiful baby. She had Wilfred's skin tone, chubby cheeks, and nose, and Louise's thick, curly hair. However, she had inherited her silver eyes from Kamaria. Smiling, Louise then took the baby into her arms and brought her downstairs to the dining room.

"Aww, look who's up?" Rachelle cooed.

"I take it we're not smoking then?" Kiana asked.

"You can still smoke, but only in the den," Louise said as she put Soleil in her swing. Once the baby was situated, Louise turned on the television, launching the Crunchyroll app. "So, what do y'all want to watch?"

"How about *My Hero Academia*?" Khalil suggested.
"Are y'all caught up with the latest season?"

"I'm only a few episodes in," Sarai said.

"Same here," Rachelle added.

"Honestly, I'm feeling nostalgic," Kiana said. "Why don't we watch *Soul Eater*? Sure, the ending sucked, but it's still a good show." The others shouted in agreement, and Louise selected the anime. While Alexis and Simone weren't very versed in anime, they still found it entertaining.

"Mimi loves this anime, by the way," Louise said as she took a seat on the couch. "She thinks Death the Kid is hilarious." The friends spent the evening binge-watching anime, as well as the latest movies on Netflix. They always looked forward to these gatherings because they were an escape from the mundane and strengthened their bond. They were more than mere friends. They were sisters.

"Hey, Lou. I know that this is random, but can I ask you a question?" Khalil asked.

"Sure."

"Your dad's last name is Reynolds, right?"

"Um, yeah," Louise replied, raising an eyebrow.

"I remember you mentioned that your grandma on your mom's side also had the last name Reynolds." Khalil continued. "I was wondering—"

"You're wondering if they're related?"

"Uh, kinda?" Khalil replied. Louise let out a loud cackle. This was not the first time she got this question about her family's surname. However, she wondered why it took so long for one of her friends to ask. She probably thought she would offend me by asking, she reasoned to herself.

"No, no, they're not related," she answered. "My dad's birth mother died while giving birth to him, so he spent the first four years of his life in a parish orphanage. He doesn't know who his birth father is because his mother was assaulted when she was only twelve, and she got pregnant as a result. He was adopted, but his adoptive family was abusive. Once he was of age, he cut ties with them and joined the Navy. Two years after he enlisted, he met my mother. They got married a year later, and he decided to take her last name. He didn't want any ties to the family that raised him."

"Wow," Khalil said.
"That's heavy."

"Yeah," Alexis added. "But what about those family members that came to your baby shower?"

"They're not our family by blood or in the legal sense," Louise explained. "Aunt Louise was actually the neighbor of Dad's adoptive family. She would often cook meals for him and make his lunches for school because his family would neglect him. She and her family were the only ones to show him any kind of love. As far as we're concerned, they're our family."

"So, your dad named you after her," Khalil concluded.

"Yep," Louise said. "Dad named me after Aunt Louise. I was given the middle name Josephine after his birth mother."

"Wow," Simone said. "I have mad respect for Mr. Reynolds. Not that I didn't before, of course."

"Yeah," Khalil said. "Well, I'm glad you felt comfortable enough to tell us this." Louise gave her a warm smile.

"Of course," she said. "You're my sisters. I'd trust you guys with my life. We have to be there for each other."

"Amen!" Sarai interjected, making the others giggle. The soul sisters embraced each other as they continued to watch *Grey's Anatomy*. Rachelle was truly grateful for the friendships she had. Because of them, she gained the strength and courage to embrace her power, to embrace that she was a magical, divine being. Because of her soul sisters, she learned to love herself, finding true love in the process. Because of her soul sisters, she was able to repair the strained relationship between her and Alexis. Because of her soul sisters, she was whole.

Chapter 23

*O*ctavia lay in bed, staring up at the ceiling. It seemed to be all she did these days, when she wasn't reading a book for the millionth time or binge-watching YouTube. She was bored and miserable. Unemployed, friendless, and with a criminal record, she felt trapped. After pleading guilty to assault and battery, as well as violating a protection order, she was sentenced to ninety days in jail, a $1,000 fine, and a year of house arrest. Octavia, who had never even received a parking ticket, now wore an ankle monitor and adhered to a 9 PM curfew. She could no longer come and go as she pleased. To say she was unhappy would be an understatement.

In addition to her sentence, Octavia was ordered to attend regular therapy sessions. However, she refused to accept that there was anything wrong with her. She simply told her therapist what she thought he wanted to hear to look good in the eyes of the law. Octavia was at her wits' end. Nick wanted nothing to do with her, which devastated her, and the friends she had made through him had also turned their backs on her. Nick's family had cut contact with her out of respect for him. Her relationship with her sister, Kendra, was also strained. Due to Octavia losing her job at the firm and being blacklisted from nearly every law firm in the metro Detroit area, Kendra bore the sole responsibility of maintaining the household, as Octavia's legal fees had eaten into all her savings. Kendra was furious with her sister, feeling burdened by the added responsibility. If Octavia had been a friend or roommate, Kendra would have kicked her out. However, she didn't have the heart to toss her only family out onto the streets.

Octavia still lay in bed, staring across her bedroom at a small wooden chest in the corner. Suddenly, she had an idea. The chest had belonged to her late mother, and it was among the many possessions that the sisters had divided. However, Octavia had never gotten around to opening it, afraid that it would only add to her grief. *But if I open it, I might find some info on my birth parents*, she thought. She knew that she wouldn't find what she was looking for on her birth certificate. At her birth, an amended certificate was issued, containing only the name of her adoptive mother, with no father listed. She wouldn't be able to get the original birth certificate without a court order. However, she would be content with just having a photo of her biological parents.

"Here goes nothing," she said to herself as she got up and made her way to the chest. Her heart pounding, she opened it and began rummaging through its contents. Octavia soon came across a 5x7 photo of an interracial couple. They appeared to be in their early twenties and were dressed in winter attire. The man in the photo was tall, with a golden-brown complexion and deep, brown eyes. His hair was short, black, and wavy. His features were chiseled, and he looked like he belonged on the cover of GQ. The young woman next to him was of average height and slim, with golden blond hair that fell past her shoulders. However, what really caught Octavia's attention were the woman's eyes, which were ice blue. Octavia knew in her heart that these were her birth parents. She turned the photo over and saw that there was writing on the back:

Kevin + Jane
Campus Martius, Valentine's Day 1991

This was two years before I was born! Octavia concluded. She stared at the photo with a wistful expression. The couple looked happy together and very much in love, and that's what Octavia couldn't understand. If they loved each other, then why was she given up? So, I know Kevin's last name was Simmons, but what about Jane? Is she still alive, and if so, where is she? All I know is that Kevin died in 1998 when I was five... Octavia thought. She had learned of Kevin's death in a freak accident from an old news article she had found online while looking for information on him. However, she couldn't find anything on her biological mother, which frustrated her. Octavia continued looking through the chest, hoping to find some clue that could lead her in the right direction. She was so engrossed in her task that she did not hear her sister enter the bedroom.

"Hey, dinner's ready," Kendra said. She noticed that Octavia was oblivious to her presence. "Um, what are you doing?"

"I found this photo in Mom's chest," Octavia replied, showing Kendra the photo. "I think they're my birth parents." Kendra let out a deep sigh.

"Tay, again with this?" she asked, pinching her nose in exasperation. "Why can't you leave this alone? Weren't I and Mom enough for you?"

"Of course you were!" Octavia replied defensively. "But there's nothing wrong with wanting to know where I came from."

"I'm not saying there is," Kendra started. "I just don't want you to get your hopes up. These people haven't been in your life for twenty-nine years, nor have they reached out to you. Suppose you do find them. What makes you think they'd be interested in having a relationship with you now?" Octavia sighed. "I don't know," she said. "My birth dad is dead, so it's too late to find him. I also don't even know if my birth mother is even still alive. She might not want anything to do with me, and I can live with that. But I can't live without at least trying." Kendra understood where her sister was coming from. While she was blessed to have two parents in her life, although her father died when she was three, Octavia was given up without a second thought. However, Octavia was welcomed into the family with open arms and was always assured that she was loved and wanted. As if she were reading Kendra's mind, Octavia said, "I know you love me, and I know Mom loved me. But I always felt like a part of me was missing."

"Why didn't you say anything before?"

"I don't know," Octavia said with a shrug. "I guess I didn't want to sound ungrateful. I didn't think you would understand." Kendra's heart stung at that last statement. She always told Octavia that she could talk to her about anything. However, she understood why Octavia felt she wouldn't understand. When she had mentioned getting an ancestry DNA test, Kendra had gotten defensive. After all, she knew coworkers that had gotten those tests, only to have their entire lives turned upside down. They either learned that their children that they had raised weren't biologically theirs, or that their parents weren't biologically theirs. In Kendra's opinion, ancestry DNA tests left more questions than answers, especially for her sister. She saw firsthand how these tests could destroy families that were once happy, such as with the Lawsons. However, deep down, she understood why Octavia wanted to know. She would want to know if it was her. She also wondered if this was also fueled by a desire for a male role model. Kendra's father, Nathaniel, had died in a truck accident before Octavia was adopted into the Baker family, so she never had a father in her life. It was always just her, Donna, and eventually, Octavia. Kendra knew that most girls who grew up without a father grew attached to any male presence in their lives. Octavia also struggled with making friends and fitting in. When they moved into the Ramirezes' neighborhood, and Nick began to befriend Octavia, Donna was relieved and encouraged the friendship. She believed that Nick would be a positive influence on her.

"Tay, is this why you've been so obsessed with Nick?" Kendra asked. Octavia turned around and stared at her sister as if she had lost her mind.

"Where the hell did that come from, Kendra?" she demanded.

"I'm just asking a question," Kendra said defensively. "A valid question, at that. You've never had a male role model or father figure since Daddy died before Mom adopted you. Nick was the only man you really connected with."

"That doesn't make me obsessed!" Octavia argued.
"I'm not obsessed with him. I love him."

"No, you don't Tay," Kendra said. "You love the idea of him. The Nick you knew when you were kids doesn't exist anymore. He's matured, and he is building a whole life with someone else. The sooner you accept that, the better off you'll be." Octavia simply scoffed.

"I don't have to listen to this," she said as she got up, heading towards the door. "I'm going out for some air."

"No, the fuck you're not!" Kendra shouted, following behind her sister. "It's ten minutes until curfew. You know you're not supposed to leave the house after 9 PM. I'm not bailing you out of jail again, Octavia!"

"I'm a grown-ass woman, Kendra!" Octavia argued.

275

"You can't tell me what to do!"

"You're a grown-ass woman?" Kendra repeated. "I can't fucking tell! A grown-ass woman wouldn't do half the shit you did. A grown-ass woman would have accepted Nick not wanting to be with them, instead of buying a fucking spell online! A grown-ass woman would not have attacked Rachelle at the mall like you did! A grown woman would not have violated a restraining order!"

"Fuck that restraining order!" Octavia barked. "If that bitch Rachelle hadn't turned Nick against me, I wouldn't have needed to beat her ass!" Kendra stared at her sister, flabbergasted. *This girl has lost her fucking mind!* she thought. She no longer recognized the woman standing in front of her. What happened to her baby sister? "Do you hear yourself, Octavia? Like, do you seriously hear the things coming out of your mouth? Rachelle didn't turn Nick against you. You did! Nick doesn't want anything to do with you because your ass didn't like being told no."

"Whatever!" Octavia said as she made her way down the stairs.

"Octavia Noelle Baker, if you set foot outside that door, I'll call the police!" Kendra shouted. Octavia turned around and stared at her sister with a mixture of shock and hurt.

"You wouldn't."

"Try me," Kendra replied, folding her arms. She could see tears forming in her sister's eyes, and her heart sank. However, she knew she had to be firm. Octavia didn't need any more legal trouble. Her expression softened a bit. "Look, I know you hate being stuck in the house, but a year will go by in no time. But you need help, Tay. This isn't healthy, and this isn't you. Do you think Mom would want this for you?" Octavia looked down at the floor, convicted. "If you keep this up, you're going to destroy your life. Now, why don't we eat this food before it gets cold? I made your favorite, and I know you haven't eaten today. We can also watch a movie together, like we used to. Wouldn't you like that?" Kendra gave her sister a small smile. Octavia sighed.

"Sure, I guess," she replied, and the two women headed to the kitchen to make their plates. Octavia's nose was greeted by the delicious aroma of pork chops, collard greens, and garlic mashed potatoes. The smell was a welcomed comfort for her since it reminded her of her mother. Donna Baker definitely knew her way around the kitchen. Kendra went into the living to find a movie to put on. She was really looking forward to a movie night. It made her feel like she had her sister back. She missed spending time with her.

"What should we watch?" she asked.
"*Mean Girls* or *Friday*?"

"Um, I guess we can watch *Friday* first, then *Mean Girls*," Octavia replied. Kendra nodded and turned on the movie. As she ate, Octavia silently mulled over what Kendra had said to her. *"If you keep this up, you're going to destroy your life."* That statement played in her head over and over. She looked down at her feet, staring at the ankle monitor. Never in a million years did she think she would be in this situation. She never thought she would be arrested or serve time in jail. While her ego wanted to blame Rachelle for all her troubles, she knew it was no one's fault but her own. She continued to pursue Nick when he made it clear that he had no romantic interest in her. She chose to cast a spell to break up his relationship, and she chose to attempt a love binding. She chose to go to Oakland Mall and attack Rachelle. Everything that happened in the past few months was of her own making.

"Look, Tay, I know I was harsh earlier," Kendra said, snapping Octavia out of her daze. "I only want what's best for you. I love you, and I want to see you happy and thriving. I don't want you to let your life pass you by because of a man. You can understand that, can't you?"

"Yeah," Octavia replied.
"I know." Kendra took her hand in hers.

"You're young, you're beautiful, and you're smart. You have plenty of time to find happiness. It may not be with Nick, but your soulmate is out there. You just have to be patient." Octavia simply nodded and continued eating.

"Oh, what does she know?" a voice said. Octavia looked around, confused. *"What does she know about true love?"*

"Who are you?" Octavia asked in her head.

"That will be revealed in due time," the female voice said. *"However, we share the same blood."*

"We're related?"

"Precisely," the voice said.
"I am part of your mother's family."

"What is your name?" Octavia asked.

"That is not important right now. I will reveal myself to you in due time."

"So, what do you want with me?" Octavia demanded.

"I want to help you."

"Help me? Help me how?"

"Tay, is everything okay?" Kendra asked, concerned. "You're awfully quiet. You're usually cracking up at this scene." They were watching Red get uppercut by Deebo. "I'm fine," Octavia replied. "Just thinking." Kendra shrugged and continued watching the movie, laughing her ass off.

"I want to help you get what you want, Octavia," the voice spoke. *"You love Nick, don't you?"*

"More than anything," Octavia said.

"I can help you with that," the voice said. *"You come from a powerful line of witches. I can help you unlock your power."*

"My power? How can you help me unlock it?"

"By leading you to your mother, of course."

"My mother? You mean she's alive?"

"Yes," the voice spoke.
"Jane is alive and well."

"Then why hasn't she reached out to me?"

"That woman kept you from her," the voice replied.
"The woman you know as Mom."

"What?!"

"Yes, she wanted to see you, to watch you grow up, but that woman wouldn't allow it. She wanted you all for herself. Her daughter knows about your mother, too. That's why she didn't want you to learn about your heritage."

"Kendra knew, too?"

"Yes, and that is why you need to get rid of her. She's standing in the way of your happiness, dear."

*"You want me to **kill** her?!"* Octavia exclaimed.
"I can't do that! She's my sister! We grew up together!"

"She also lied to you. She's been against you finding your true family, and she's keeping you from the one you love. What kind of sister does that?" Octavia looked over at Kendra as the voice cackled in her head. She thought back to their argument and how Kendra threatened to call the cops if she left the house. All the times Kendra tried to talk her out of taking the ancestry test. Octavia's insides began to bubble with anger. Now, it all made sense. Kendra didn't want her to find her birth family because of her selfish reasons. Donna, too. *"That's it,"* the voice cooed. *"Allow that anger to course through you."*

"Even if I wanted to get rid of her, how would I? We don't have a gun in the house, and if I stabbed her, it would leave evidence. Plus, she's stronger than me, so I can't strangle her. She would definitely fight back."

279

"You just have to get creative..." the voice said slyly. *"Surely you have something in your kitchen cabinet that would do the trick."* Octavia looked towards the kitchen, the wheels in her head turning. Then, it hit her.

"Hey, I'm gonna go make some popcorn," she stated as she headed towards the kitchen. "Awesome," Kendra remarked. "Can you put some garlic seasoning on mine?"

"Sure thing," Octavia called from the kitchen, as she put a bag of popcorn in the microwave. She rummaged through the spice cabinet until she found the bottle of garlic seasoning. She also retrieved a bottle of boric acid from under the sink. While they never had pest problems, Kendra preferred to be safe than sorry. However, she didn't intend for the poison to be used in the way her sister had planned. Octavia opened the bottle of seasoning and saw that it was only half full. She opened the boric acid and added a few spoonfuls to the seasoning. She then closed the bottle of seasoning and shook it vigorously, ensuring that the contents were mixed together. Once the timer on the microwave went off, Octavia retrieved the hot popcorn bag, opening it, and emptying its contents into a bowl. She then put another bag in the microwave for herself. She sprinkled a generous amount of the deadly concoction onto her sister's popcorn. Once her popcorn was finished, she poured it into another bowl. She then brought the bowls into the living room, handing Kendra her bowl before returning to her seat.

"So, Nikita and I were thinking of having brunch next weekend," Kendra said as she ate a handful of popcorn. "I want you to join us. I know you can't leave the house, so I was thinking that we can have brunch here. I think it'll be fun. What do you think?"

"Sounds... cool," Octavia said with a wistful smile.

"This popcorn tastes kind of weird," Kendra said with her nose turned up.

"My popcorn tastes fine," Octavia said with a shrug. "Maybe the seasoning is old. I did find it in the back of the cabinet."

"Hm, maybe," Kendra said. "I guess I'll just have to buy some more. I'll just go get some lemon pepper." She then got up and went to the kitchen and returned with a bottle of lemon pepper seasoning. She sprinkled a generous amount onto her snack and continued eating as Octavia watched in anticipation. She hoped that the poison worked quickly, so that her sister wouldn't suffer. Once *Friday* had ended, Octavia put on *Mean Girls*. The two sisters continued to talk and gossip as they watched the film. Octavia felt a pang of guilt for what she had just done. After all, she and Kendra had grown up together and were incredibly close. However, Octavia felt that Kendra was a snake for keeping her away from her biological family and kicking her while she was down. Kendra had to go, and when she was done, she would get rid of Rachelle, too.

"I'm gonna go to bed," Kendra said as she rose from the couch while the film's ending credits rolled. Suddenly, she began to feel intense pain in her abdomen. She doubled over, holding her stomach.

"Are you okay?" Octavia asked, putting on a frantic voice. However, she knew that the poison was starting to take effect. Before Kendra could respond, she began to vomit profusely. The dinner she had eaten earlier spewed from her mouth, tinged with blue from the boric acid. Octavia stood frozen, as if her feet were glued to the hardwood floor. She knew the right thing to do would be to call an ambulance, but she couldn't bring herself to do it. Unable to bear watching her big sister suffer, she grabbed a pillow from the couch and proceeded to smother Kendra. Kendra tried her hardest to fend off her sister, but the poison had weakened her, and she was dehydrated from the severe vomiting. After a five-minute struggle, Kendra stopped breathing and went limp. It was not a quick death by any means.

"I'm sorry," Octavia whispered in a cracked voice. "Why did you make me do this? Why did you lie to me?" Tears streamed down her face. She was heartbroken for her sister. However, there was no going back now. She had committed murder. Now, she was left with a body to dispose of.

"I know this is hard for you, but it was for the best," a female voice said. Octavia looked up, startled by the presence of a tall, middle-aged woman. She had fair skin and was slender, with dark brown hair styled in a long plait. Octavia noticed that the woman had the same striking, ice blue eyes that Jane had. She was dressed in black, and around her neck was an ornate silver amulet with a ruby in the middle. So, she was the voice in my head! Octavia thought. When Octavia and the woman's eyes met, the woman's lips curled into a smile. "You must be wondering who I am." Octavia simply nodded, still awestruck. "I am Anne Neilson. I am your aunt." Octavia's eyes widened.

"M-My aunt?" she repeated. "Are you my mother's sister?" Anne nodded. "How did you get in here? All the doors are locked." Anne simply chuckled.

"Teleportation, dear," she said. She waved her hand, and a large portal appeared. "It's just one of our family's many gifts."

"So, that must mean that I have those gifts, too."

"Precisely," Anne replied. "However, your power is dormant because you were never given the chance to hone it." Octavia looked down at the floor, her resentment towards her adoptive family growing. While it was possible that Donna and Kendra knew nothing of her magical roots, they still hid her true family from her. Donna had a photo of her birth parents this entire time and never considered that maybe Octavia would want some kind of memento of them. What else was she hiding?

"So, what happens now?" she asked.

"Well, you will need to come with me. You can't stay here," Anne replied. "I will take you to your mother. You will also get to meet the rest of our coven." Octavia pondered for a moment, staring at Kendra's lifeless body on the couch. Vomit was caked around her mouth, and her eyes were wide open, staring straight at Octavia. As much as she hated to leave Kendra's body, she knew that if she stayed, she would be looking at life without parole. "How are you going to get me out of here without the police finding me?" Octavia asked, gesturing to her ankle monitor. Anne waved her hand again, and the monitor fell to the floor. Octavia looked at the woman, astonished, as Anne helped her to her feet. With another wave of her hand, flames began to rise from the ground, engulfing the house. Anne then took Octavia's hand, leading her towards the portal. Taking one last glance at her sister, Octavia stepped through into her new life.

Chapter 24

One Month Later

"**D**amn! This house is huge!" Kiana exclaimed as she and the others stepped inside the spacious, exquisite mansion. The luxurious home belonged to Rachelle's aunt Veronica, granted to her by her second husband in their divorce settlement. Veronica had allowed Rachelle and her bridal party use of the mansion for their bachelorette weekend.

"Your aunt has damn good taste," Daniela added.
"It was really nice of her to let us stay here."

"Of course. She wasn't about to let us waste money on a hotel," Rachelle said as she took her luggage upstairs. The other women followed behind her. "I bet you're glad to be in New Orleans again, Lou," Kiana said.

"Girl, you have no idea!" Louise remarked. "I haven't been back since my cousin Paul's wedding, and that was almost ten years ago."

"Well, since you're from here, I hope you don't mind showing us around," Carmen said. "

Girl, I got y'all," Louise said as she entered one of the guest rooms and began to unpack. "So, what do y'all wanna do first?"

"Well, for one, I want to take a nap. I'm exhausted," Sarai said, and Kiana agreed.

"Same," Louise said with a yawn. "I think we should all get some rest and relax. Afterwards, we can go out to eat. Aunt Louise actually owns a restaurant on Bourbon Street."

"If your aunt's cooking is as good as your daddy's, I'm definitely in," Kiana said, and the others agreed. After mapping out their plans for the evening, the women retreated to their rooms for much-needed rest. However, Rachelle did not go to sleep right away, her mind plagued with worry. She had heard about Kendra's death on the news a month prior, and she was deeply disturbed, especially when it was revealed that Octavia was nowhere to be found, leaving behind only her ankle monitor. The authorities knew she had not died in the fire, since only one body was found, but they had no leads as to her whereabouts. It was as if she had vanished into thin air. While Rachelle did not show it, she was terrified. What if Octavia decided to come after her or her family? If she was sick and twisted enough to murder her own sister, then there was no limit to what she was capable of. Octavia had reached the point of no return. Rachelle prayed that she was caught soon. She cursed the day that woman had come into their lives. To ease her anxiety, she grabbed her phone and dialed Nick's number. After the third ring, he answered.

"Hey, *muñeca*," he said in a husky voice.
"You got settled in okay?"

"Yeah. The house is gorgeous," Rachelle replied.
"We're gonna take a nap and then head out to eat later."

"Sounds fun," Nick said. Rachelle let out a sigh.
"What's wrong?"

"I'm just worried," Rachelle said.

"About Octavia?" Nick knew that Rachelle had been on edge ever since they learned about Kendra's murder and Octavia's disappearance. "I know, I'm worried too. I genuinely hope that nothing bad has happened to Octavia, but she needs to face the consequences of what she did."

"Me too," said Rachelle.
"I really hope she's found. Kendra didn't deserve that."

"Yeah," Nick said. "In the meantime, though, I want you to relax. This is your weekend to unwind, and I want you to enjoy yourself. But I also want you to be careful."

"I'll try," Rachelle said with a smile.
"I love you."

"I love you more, baby," Nick said.

"So, how are the girls?"

"They're with your mom, so I'm here by myself. I miss you, though."

"Aww, but I just left," Rachelle said.

"I know, but it always feels lonely when you're not here," Nick said, and Rachelle felt her heart swell.

"I miss you, too."

"How bad do you miss me?" Nick asked as he began palming himself through his sweatpants. "I miss you really bad," Rachelle said, her heart racing at his suggestive tone.

"Maybe you could send me some pics to hold me over until you get back." Rachelle felt her face flush.

"Well, I did pack that red lingerie set that you like," she said.

"You know how much I love seeing you in that," Nick said, his breathing slightly hitched.

"Nick...are you touching yourself right now?"

"Yeah," Nick replied.
"I'm hard as fuck right now."

"Maybe you can send me a video," Rachelle said suggestively. Nick smirked on the other end.

"I think I can do that for you," he said, slowly stroking his length, cursing under his breath.

"I'm about to send some pics now," Rachelle said before hanging up. She then got up from the bed and walked over to the beautifully engraved armoire. She pulled out the delicate lace bodysuit, which Nick had bought for her birthday two years ago. Whenever she wore it, Nick couldn't keep his hands off of her, and she felt like a goddess. After putting on the lingerie, she set her phone by the full-length mirror, setting the timer on her camera. She posed seductively as the timer counted down, her camera snapping the photo. She took a few more photos in different poses and angles. She even took a few of herself topless and fully nude. Satisfied with the images she had taken, she sent them to Nick. In response, Rachelle received a video of Nick pleasuring himself to her. Feeling flushed all over, her core throbbing, she reached into her duffle bag and pulled out a pink massager. Nothing like a good orgasm to help me fall asleep, she thought as she turned it on. She played the video, and the sweet, husky moans of her fiancé filled her with a pleasure that was indescribable. After reaching her climax, she drifted off to a peaceful sleep.

Later that Evening

It was around 5pm when the group stepped inside Lulu's Place. They were immediately greeted with the smell of fresh jambalaya, seafood gumbo, and red beans and rice. The delicious aroma brought back fond memories of Louise's early childhood. Lulu's had been around since before she was born, and her father would bring her to the restaurant every Sunday as a treat. The Crescent City always held a special place in Louise's heart. She planned to one day bring her children so that they stay connected to their Creole roots. "Damn, it smells good in here!" Trina remarked, and the others agreed. Suddenly, an elderly woman emerged from the kitchen. She was in her early seventies and short with a plump figure. Her skin was the color of toffee, and she had silver hair that she kept styled in a bun. Her eyes were a warm hazel, and she wore a sky blue dress with a white apron. The friends recognized her immediately, having met her at Louise's baby shower. She was Louise DuBois, Xavier's surrogate mother, and Louise's 'aunt,' whom the latter was named for.

"Is that my baby?" she said as she sauntered over to the group. She embraced Louise in a loving hug and gave her a kiss on the cheek. *"Koman sa va?"*

"Mo manje," Louise replied, and Aunt Louise cackled.

"I just bet you are. Well, you came to the right place. Come on," she said as she led them to a large table and gave each of the women a menu. "So, what are you all dressed up for?"

"We're here for Rachelle's bachelorette weekend," Louise answered. The ladies were definitely dressed for a night on the town. Rachelle wore a shimmering gold mini dress that clung to her figure, complemented by her sun brooch, with gold heels and hoop earrings. Her hair was loose and hung past her shoulders. Her makeup was stunning, with gold eyeshadow, black eyeliner, and cranberry lip gloss. Louise was dressed in a black, form-fitting jumpsuit with black heels, her moonstone necklace, and silver moon earrings. Her makeup was natural, with the exception of her silver eyeshadow. Her hair was styled in two buns on the top, with the rest of her hair hanging down. Sarai and Kiana were also dressed in black, with Sarai wearing a black corset and black lace bustle skirt, lace stockings, and black boots. In her ears, she wore a pair of skull earrings and her skull locket that was given to her by the coven. Her hair was in a poofy twist-out, accentuated by a cute skull hair clip. Kiana wore a black mini dress, black fishnet stockings, and black thigh-high boots. Her hair was styled in two ponytails. Both women wore smokey eye makeup, with Sarai wearing dark purple lipstick and Kiana opting for dark red. Trina looked exquisite in an orange, crocheted crop top and matching skirt made by Louise. Her outfit was complemented by gold heel sandals, gold chandelier earrings, and gold bangles. Her hair was styled in a curly ponytail, accentuated by her enchanted jeweled comb. Her makeup was natural, yet stunning. Khalil wore a purple skater dress with matching shoes and Sailor Moon-themed accessories. Her makeup included pastel eyeshadow and shimmery lip gloss. Mariah wore a Tiffany blue jumpsuit in a design similar to her sister's, with gold sandals, gold hoops, and bangles. She also wore her opal brooch. Her amber-colored hair was flat-ironed and hung to her shoulders. Her makeup was also natural, except for her false lashes and lip gloss. Carmen and Daniela wore matching mini dresses in different colors, with Carmen in dark blue and Daniela in plum.

They both wore heels that matched their dresses, along with chandelier earrings. Carmen had a seashell clip in her hair, while Daniela wore a silver deer pendant. Alexis was dressed to kill in a black bustier and red shorts, with red pumps. Her hair was styled in a chic bun, complemented by her amethyst hair pins. She wore a pair of large gold hoop earrings and a gold chain bracelet. For her makeup, she had a gold smokey eye and red lipstick.

"When's the wedding?" Aunt Louise asked.

"August 15," Rachelle replied.

"Well, I hope you all enjoy your weekend. Now, what can I get y'all to drink?"

"I would like some of your homemade sweet tea," Louise said. Aunt Louise smiled as she wrote down Louise's order.

"Can we all get sweet tea?" Sarai asked.

"You sure can," Aunt Louise said. "I'll be right out with a pitcher for you." She then made her way back to the kitchen as the friends chatted amongst themselves, soaking in the friendly atmosphere of the restaurant.

"So, are you guys going to that new con Terry and Angelo are running?" Khalil asked.

"Isshocon, right?" Rachelle asked, and Khalil nodded. "Oh, Nick and I are definitely going. We might even bring the girls."

"When is it again?" Kiana asked.

"It's in January," Khalil answered.
"I'm definitely applying to get an artist's table."

"Same," Louise added.

"Sarai, you should apply to be a guest!" Rachelle said.

"You really think folks would want to see me?" Sarai asked.

"Girl, bye!" Louise interjected. "You're a bestselling author with a massive fan base, especially in the nerd community. Of course people would want to see you. I really hate when you doubt yourself, Sarai."

"I know," Sarai said. "I'm still working on breaking out of that." Kiana kissed her on the cheek, making Sarai's face grow warm. Soon, Aunt Louise returned to the table with a large pitcher of sweet tea and ten glasses.
"Here you go, ladies," she said. "Have you decided what you want to eat?" Louise looked up happily.

"Yes, I would like to order the crawfish étouffée with red beans and rice," she said. "You want some Oysters Rockefeller, too? I remember how you used to tear them up when you were a little girl."

"Yes, please," Louise said with a smile. Aunt Louise then turned to Rachelle. "And what can I get for you, baby?" she asked.

"I'll have the jambalaya," Rachelle replied, and Trina, Carmen, and Khalil ordered the same.

"We'll have the gumbo," Sarai said, and Kiana nodded in agreement

. "Can I get the Shrimp Creole?" Alexis asked. Daniela and Mariah ordered the same dish.

"Alright, I'll get your orders to the kitchen. Y'all just sit tight," Aunt Louise said, and she retreated back to the kitchen.

"I can't wait to try her food," Kiana remarked.
"I know it's gonna slap."

"For real," Sarai added.

"So, Sarai, how's everything with Ms. Tasha?" Rachelle asked. After reconciling their differences at Christmas, Sarai and Kiana had been spending time with Tasha, and Sarai was kind enough to take her to her chemotherapy appointments and help her around the house. Sarai was even generous enough to contribute to Tasha's mounting medical bills.

"She's getting better," Sarai replied, taking a sip of her sweet tea. "Damn! You can taste the diabetes in this!" The others laughed, and she continued. "Anyway, she's still recovering from her hysterectomy, but she's gotten stronger. I honestly feel she's gonna be in remission. That healing ritual we did at our last coven meeting is really helping."

"I'm glad," Rachelle said.
"She has really changed for the better."

"Yeah, and I'm glad Shawna and Keisha are letting her build a bond with her grandkids," Sarai said.

"So, Carmen, how are things with you and Derrick? Nick told me y'all have been seeing each other for about six months now," Rachelle said, and Carmen blushed.

"We're doing good," she replied. "I'll be bringing him to the wedding as my plus one, so you guys can meet him."

"So, what does he look like?" Louise interjected. Carmen pulled out her phone, going into her photo gallery. She pulled up a photo of her beau, showing it to everyone at the table. Derrick was a handsome man, with mahogany skin, black cropped hair, and warm brown eyes. His lips were full and kissable, complemented by a piercing on his bottom lip.

"Damn, he's fine! Where did you find him at?"

"I met him at work," Carmen replied. "He's one of the few men at my job that isn't a misogynistic *pendejo*." While Carmen enjoyed a successful career as a software developer, she absolutely despised how women were treated in the tech field. She received the same education and possessed the same skills as the men at her job, yet she was treated like a bimbo because of her gender. Worse, if she wasn't being treated as less intelligent, she was often fetishized due to her mixed heritage. What attracted her to Derrick was not only the fact that they had similar interests, but he actually treated her like a human being and admired her drive and intellect.

"Well, I can't wait to meet him," Rachelle stated, pouring herself another glass of tea.

"By the way, did you see the poster of Simone outside when we came here?" Sarai asked. "She's performing tonight at Kat Daddy's across the street. We should go."

"I second that," Louise said. After forty-five minutes, Aunt Louise emerged from the kitchen with her daughter, Jacqueline, carrying everyone's orders. The group's stomachs grumbled in anticipation.

"Here you go, ladies," Aunt Louise said as Jacqueline set their dishes in front of them.

"Jackie!" Louise exclaimed. "Long time no see!"

"I know," Jacqueline said. "I'm really sorry I couldn't make it to your baby shower. I was really sick."

"Girl, it's fine. Soleil loves the toys you got her," Louise said.

"She's such a gorgeous baby," Jacqueline said, smiling.
"Both of your girls are." Louise beamed.

"Hey, it runs in the family," she said, and the two women gave each other a high five. "By the way, ladies, this is on the house," Aunt Louise said.

"Aww, Auntie, you don't have to do that."

"I want to."

"Well, at least let us tip you," Louise suggested. She knew it was pointless to argue with her Aunt Louise, but she still wanted to show her appreciation. Aunt Louise pretended to ponder for a moment, then smiled. "Deal," she said, gently pinching Louise's cheek. "Y'all enjoy your meal, ya hear?"

"Yes, ma'am," the others answered in unison. Aunt Louise smiled and made her way to the other tables, with Jacqueline following behind her. The moment the women took their first bite, they were in heaven. There was nothing like good, authentic Louisiana cuisine in Louisiana. As Louise savored her food, it reminded her of why she missed being in her hometown. While her father did his best to bring New Orleans into the home, it wasn't the same as actually being there. Louise even contemplated moving back home. The only thing that stopped her was the fact that she and Wilfred had businesses, and Artemis didn't want to leave behind her school and friends. Another thing was the constant storms that plagued the city. Not to mention, the cost of living was high as hell. So, she would just settle for visiting every once in a while.

"This food is good as fuck!" Kiana remarked, making everyone laugh as her mouth was full of rice. Sarai simply shook her head and continued to eat, although she shared her wife's sentiment.

"Hey!" Louise exclaimed in protest as Mariah took an oyster off her plate.

"Girl, bye! You ain't about to eat all this by yourself. Greedy ass," Mariah replied.

"Yeah, whatever," Louise said. "Anyway, besides watching Simone perform, y'all have any other places you wanna go see?"

"Well, I've always been curious about the occult shops here," Rachelle replied.

"Trust me, you ain't missing shit," Khalil stated. She and Chris had taken many trips to New Orleans. "Most of the shops here are novelty stores owned by white people. There's no real power in them."

"Damn, for real?" Rachelle said, slightly disappointed. "There's no Black-owned stores?"

"Now, I ain't say all that," Khalil replied. "There are Black-owned stores, but you got to weed out the bullshit to find them." Rachelle simply nodded in understanding. She knew that magic and spirituality had

293

become a trend when it was once demonized, especially African spirituality. Now, there were colonizers acting as if they were the supreme authority on Hoodoo, Voodoo, and the like. It was exhausting.

"There's Antoinette's House of Conjure," Louise interjected, scrolling through her phone, having searched for occult stores in the area. "It's a few blocks from here. Ms. Bernie owns it."

"Bernadette Devereaux? Didn't she come to one of our coven meetings?" Carmen asked.

"Yep. She opened this shop almost a year ago," Louise replied. "It closes at 9pm, though. It'll be closed by the time we leave the club."

"We can always go tomorrow," Rachelle suggested, and the others agreed. The friends finished their delicious meals, and before leaving, they left Aunt Louise a massive tip for her hospitality. They also promised to come back the next time before returning to Detroit. The group walked across the street, stepping into Kat Daddy's Music Club. A large crowd was gathered near the stage, where a blues band was finishing their set. The club reeked of booze, and drunk patrons could be heard either laughing obnoxiously or arguing. After the band had finished playing, they were met with applause and cheers. The club's manager then stepped onto the stage to announce the next performer.

"Alright, guys, our next performer comes all the way from Motown. She is a new artist, and her single, 'Bad Witch Bitch,' has been at number one for six months, with over five million streams!" The crowd erupted in cheers, with Rachelle, Sarai, Louise, and the others cheering the loudest. "Please give a warm welcome to our enchantress of the evening, Christina Simone!" The audience applauded as Simone stepped out onto the stage, looking absolutely radiant. She was dressed in a green bustier embellished with crystals, a black high-waisted skirt, and green platform heels. Her hair was styled in a fierce black bob with electric blue tips. Her makeup was dramatic, with green and blue eyeshadow, black eyeliner, and dark brown lip gloss. Her look was complete with peacock earrings, her mermaid pendant, which was gifted to her by Kristy and enchanted, and silver bangles on each wrist. The crowd was in awe of her beauty. After Simone gave the signal, the music began. As she began to sing, her pendant began to glow, emitting a subtle orange aura. It was obvious why Kristy opted to give Simone a mermaid necklace because her voice captivated her audience, like the mermaids of folklore that lured sailors to their deaths with their voices. The audience was glued to her. It was as if her voice had them in a trance. Her friends stared at her with awe and pride, especially Sarai. The two of them had come a long way from their traumatic upbringings. Now, they were successful, happy, and thriving, free of their religious trauma, and free of their abusers.

"Oh my god, she sounds amazing!" Louise gushed.

"She looks amazing, too," Trina added, and the others agreed. Rachelle observed the crowd, and was glad to see that Simone had so much support. However, she noticed that there was a woman standing by the wall, watching her and the rest of the group. She was fair-skinned, with dark brown hair and green eyes. She was also dressed in a black maxi dress and wore a ruby necklace around her neck. Their gazes met, and Rachelle was a bit weirded out. Although she had never met this woman a day in her life, there was something about the young woman's energy that gave Rachelle a sense of familiarity. However, she brushed it off.

"Is everything okay, Chelly?" Sarai asked.

"It's nothing," Rachelle said with a shrug.
"I just thought someone was watching us."

"I mean, we do look good, so I wouldn't be surprised if someone was staring at us," Khalil said, and they gave each other a high five. Simone finished her song and was met with thunderous applause, cheers, and whistles. Her heart was pounding as she blew a kiss to the audience. This was her first time since her choir days that she had performed in front of a crowd, and she felt a rush of adrenaline. She wanted to experience this feeling again and again. As she stepped off the stage, she was immediately surrounded by her friends.

"You were great up there!" Sarai exclaimed as she hugged her.

"You really think so?" Simone asked.

"I know so," Louise said as she hugged Simone. "I even got footage of it."

"Awesome," Simone said. Suddenly, the woman that Rachelle saw earlier approached them. "Excuse me, are you Duchess Holliday?" she asked.

"Um, who wants to know?" Rachelle replied, her guard up.

"I am a huge fan of your beauty line!" the woman said with a bright smile. Rachelle breathed a sigh of relief. *She's just a fan of my products*, she thought. "Yeah, my name is Duchess," she replied.

"I have something for you."

"That's sweet of you. What is it?" Rachelle inquired. The woman's smile faded, replaced by an evil grin.

"This!" she shouted, and before Rachelle or the others could respond, she was blown back against the wall by a powerful force, to the shock of the other patrons. Pain shot through her body as she attempted to get off the floor. Sarai and the others ran over to her.

"Chelly!" Sarai shouted. "Chelly, are you alright!?" She grabbed Rachelle's hand and pulled her to her feet.

"Yo, what the fuck is your problem?" Carmen demanded. The woman said nothing and calmly walked over, as everyone stared at her. With a smirk, she waved her hand, and her appearance began to change. Her hair went from brown and straight to red and curly, and her eyes changed from forest green to brown. Suddenly, tiny freckles began to appear all over her nose and cheeks. The women stared in utter shock.

"O-Octavia?" Rachelle said. Octavia stared coldly at her, her aura glowing a dark, menacing red. The ruby in her necklace also glowed.

"I bet you thought you'd never see me again... did you, bitch?"

Chapter 25

"**W**hat the fuck are you doing here?" Sarai demanded, standing protectively in front of Rachelle. "Nick ain't here, if that's who you were hoping to see. You know the police and the FBI are looking for your ass, right?"

"Which is why I've been hiding out here," Octavia replied. "New Orleans is such a wonderful city, don't you think? And with this glamour I cast on myself," she waved her hand, revealing the disguise she had earlier, "I've been able to enjoy myself here without being recognized."

"How did you even end up down here?" Daniela asked. Octavia giggled. Suddenly, a large portal appeared in the middle of the dance floor, to the astonishment of the patrons. A large group of women stepped through the portal, each clad in black, wearing *Valknut* necklaces. One of the women appeared next to Octavia, while the others stood behind them. She was middle-aged, with fair skin, a slender build, waist-length blond hair, and striking blue eyes. *She's the woman from my dream!* Louise thought. *She killed that informant!* The woman also wore a large ruby and onyx amulet around her slim neck.

"Ladies, allow me to introduce you to my mother, Jane Nielson... also known as Queen Nanna," Octavia said. Rachelle's jaw nearly hit the floor, as did her friends'.

"Queen Nanna?" Carmen repeated. "You're in charge of that Daughters of Odin coven!" Jane smirked.

"I'm pleased to see that you've heard of me," she said.

"This is your mother?" Louise asked, dumbfounded.

"My biological mother," Octavia replied, smiling at Jane. "I've finally managed to find her."

297

"I believe you also know my sister," Jane said. Louise stared at her, confused. "Your sister?" she said. "I don't know your sis-" Suddenly, a woman stepped through the portal. Like Jane, she was middle-aged and slender with ice blue eyes, but she had dark brown hair instead of blond. She stood on the other side of Octavia and gave Louise a wicked smirk. Her blood boiling, Louise immediately lunged at the woman, but Sarai and Kiana held her back.

"You fucking bitch!" she snarled as the woman cackled.

"You know this woman?" Simone asked.

"She's the bitch who killed my son!" Louise roared. Audible gasps could be heard from the crowd. "How the hell is Anne Nielson here?" Sarai asked. "She was given twenty years!"

"Did you honestly think I was going to let my only sister rot away in a cell?" Jane asked incredulously. "Of course not! I got her out. It's amazing what a bit of compelling magic can do. It also didn't hurt that one of our coven worked at the prison."

"I told you one of them was a fucking cop!" Trina whispered.

"You're really with these racist cunts, Octavia?" Sarai asked, appalled. "Do you have any idea what they've done? The people they've hurt?"

"I know all about those ludicrous accusations!" Octavia countered. "However, they have no proof that my mother is involved."

"How can you align yourself with someone like this so easily?" Carmen demanded. "This woman may have birthed you, but she gave you up without a second thought! Ms. Donna and Kendra were there for you! They welcomed you into the family with open arms, and this is how you repay them?! And Kendra... poor Kendra. How could you kill your own fucking sister?!" Tears were now streaming down Carmen's face. Before the Bakers left Michigan, she, Daniela, and Kendra were good friends. They would play together, have sleepovers, and spend their weekends at the mall or cinema. When the sisters learned of Kendra's death, they were gutted.

"She lied to me!" Octavia argued. "She and my so-called mother! Donna knew where my mom was the whole fucking time and never told me! She had a picture of my parents in her chest, and she never thought to ask if I would want it, to have any kind of memento of where I came from! Aunt Anne told me how Mom wanted to see me, but Donna kept me away from her! When I found Mom, she confirmed it."

"Maybe she did that for good reason," Sarai reasoned. "She probably just wanted to protect you. And look, she was right."

"Shut the fuck up!" Octavia shrieked, her aura glowing brighter. "I'm done talking!" She then turned to Jane and said, "Please let me end these bitches once and for fucking all!" Jane and Anne smirked, relishing Octavia's bloodlust.

"Have at it, darling," Jane said affectionately. "Show them no mercy." Octavia grinned evilly. The room suddenly grew colder, and everyone could see their breaths. Icicles began to emerge from Octavia's hand and from the floor. The club erupted in chaos as the patrons frantically ran to the exits, nearly trampling each other. Hearing the commotion from the back room, Riley Mereaux, the club's manager, hung up the phone and ran toward the dance floor. He had seen Octavia's face on the news, as there was a nationwide manhunt for her. She was reported as being wanted for murder and arson and was considered extremely dangerous. However, it was not the safety of civilians that motivated Riley to make the call to the FBI tip line. The FBI stated that anyone who could give valuable information leading to Octavia's arrest would receive a two-million-dollar reward. The money was too good to pass up and could pay off his debts twenty times over. He would be able to save his club!

"I've called the police," he said. "You're going to prison for a very long time. That is, if you don't end up with a needle in your ar-" Riley was abruptly cut off by an icicle impaling his heart, killing him instantly. Coughing up blood, he collapsed in a heap. Horrified, Rachelle grabbed her enchanted brooch and held it up in the air. The brooch began to grow warm, glowing a powerful pink light. Her friends followed suit, activating their magical accessories. Beams of pink, blue, purple, green, yellow, aqua, silver, peach, and lilac shot up into the sky. They began to create a large crescent moon, with roses intertwined, a symbol of their coven. Octavia's hand created a large ice spear and aimed it at Rachelle's chest. However, before Octavia hit her target, she was lifted into the air and thrown against a nearby wall. Pain shot throughout her body as she stumbled to her feet.

"You wanna play?" Rachelle taunted. "Let's play, bitch, because I'm tired of your shit!" Enraged, Octavia charged at Rachelle but was suddenly restrained by a large, thick vine, courtesy of Trina.

"Nice one, cuz." Trina smiled at her.

"Khalil, go down the street to Antoinette's." Louise instructed. "Find Ms. Bernie, and tell her we need backup."

"No need to come find me. I'm already here!" Bernadette called out from the doorway. She was dressed in white from head to toe, and her eyes seemed to glow in the darkness. "However, I need you to get everyone outside to a safe location. It might get ugly in here, and I don't want innocent people hurt."

"Right." Khalil replied with a nod and immediately did as she was told. Bernadette's aura glowed a bright cyan as she stared Jane down.

"*Laissez les bon temps rouler*, you raggedy bitch!" she exclaimed as she lifted Jane into the air and threw her over a table. Jane retaliated by hurling a fireballt in her direction. However, Bernadette snuffed it out with ease. "Come on, *cher*. You gots to do better than that!" Snarling, Jane's aura grew brighter and bigger, with glowing vines emerging from it. Before Bernadette could react, she was suddenly ensnared. She struggled against her restraints as she felt her energy draining from her.

"Ms. Bernie!" Louise and her friends cried in unison. With a wave of her hand, flames began to emerge from where Jane stood. Her long, black dress caught fire, and she frantically tried to stomp out the blaze. One of her coven members ran towards her with a glass of clear liquid and threw it onto the flames. However, what the poor woman didn't realize was that liquid was not water, but in fact, vodka, which only exacerbated the flames.

"Helga, you fucktwit!" Jane shrieked. "Don't you know that alcohol is flammable?!"

"F-Forgive me, My Lady!" the plump woman cried. Suddenly, another coven member threw a bucket of water onto Jane, extinguishing the blaze. Meanwhile, it was Octavia against Rachelle, Trina, and Sarai, with

301

Louise and Mariah against Anne, while Carmen, Daniela, and Simone took on the other coven members. No matter how hard she tried, Octavia was no match for the powerful trio. Rachelle flawlessly blocked Octavia's attacks, while objects within her reach were used as projectiles. Sarai was able to use her darkness manipulation to obstruct Octavia's vision, while Trina used plant manipulation to impede her efforts. Octavia was growing increasingly frustrated. It seemed that no matter what she did, Rachelle would always win. "Give it up, Octavia!" Sarai demanded, standing over her. "You're making things worse on yourself than they have to be. You used to be so sweet, and we genuinely wanted to be your friends. You've let your obsession over Nick corrupt you. For fuck's sake, you've murdered two innocent people!"

"IT'S NOT AN OBSESSION!" Octavia screamed, her voice rising a few octaves. Even Anne and Jane were caught off guard. "I'm sick of you bitches calling it that! I love Nick, and we would be together if that bitch hadn't gotten in the way!" She pointed at Rachelle. Her eyes held a viciousness they had never seen before. She glared at Rachelle as she continued. "Bitches like you make me sick! Spoiled, stuck-up princesses who have everything handed to them, while the rest of us have to work to get what we want. Vapid whores that have guys eating out of the palms of their hands by just looking at them. Is that how you seduced my Nicky away from me?"

This bitch is delusional, Rachelle thought to herself, aghast at the narrative Octavia had painted in her head.

"Listen to yourself!" she said. "When, in the time we had known each other, did I ever give you that impression? I welcomed you into our home because you were Nick's friend, and I wanted to be your friend as well. We let you around our girls. We had been nothing but kind to you! A spoiled, stuck-up princess? Really?" She shook her head in dismay and continued. "It's not my fault that my parents worked to provide me with the things they never had. Contrary to what you think, I was not born with a silver spoon in my mouth. My parents had me while they were still in college. They had to work and focus on their studies at the same time! I spent fourteen years of my life on the East Side! You don't know a damn thing about me, bitch! I don't know what kind of girls you had to deal with growing up, but that has jack shit to do with me! You need to unpack that shit, and quit blaming people for your own problems!"

"SHUT UP!" Octavia screeched, launching an icicle at Rachelle. Thankfully, it missed her head by an inch. "You don't deserve Nick! You're nothing but a cheap whore that was lucky enough to have his kids, if they're even his!"

"Octavia, that's enough!" Everyone turned around to see Nick standing in the doorway, his aura glowing a fiery red. His *elekes* and Lightning quartz necklace also glowed. Standing behind him were Marisol, Kristy, Violet, Danelle, and Anthony. However, standing with them was a man that Louise and her friends had never seen before. He was of average height and stocky, with light skin and shoulder-length black locs that had orange tips. He also wore glasses and a goatee. "Nicky…." Octavia breathed, her heart pounding against her chest. She felt herself getting hot all over. Although Nick looked angry, and even disgusted, she thought he was the sexiest man on Earth. "I-I didn't know you were here."

"I wasn't, but Ms. Kristy got the coven's distress signal and alerted us," Nick replied as he glared at his former childhood friend. He walked over to Rachelle and pulled her into his arms. "Baby, are you okay?" Rachelle nodded slightly. Although she was calm on the surface, she was shaken up. They were outnumbered, and Riley Mereaux's body lay less than two feet away from them. While she and her friends were giving it their all, she feared that they would not make it out of New Orleans alive.

"Octavia, the authorities have been called and are on their way," Kristy said in a calm, yet icy tone. "You would be wise to turn yourself in."

"My daughter isn't going anywhere!" Jane hissed. "Neither are we. If you value your lives, you'll leave right now." Kristy let out a thunderous cackle.

"You really think I'm afraid of the likes of you?" she retorted in an amused tone. "You honestly think I'm afraid of someone who has to *steal* magic from others?"

"Mama, what are you talking about?" Mariah asked.

"The reason why we have been targeted by these women is because they want to harness our power. Turns out, they've been doing it for nearly three decades."

"That's a lie!" Jane spat.

"Is it also a lie that you killed Kevin Simmons?" Jane's face turned white as a sheet. Octavia turned to look at Jane, whose glare was fixed on Kristy.

"I don't know what you're talking about," Jane said haughtily. Kristy chuckled as she circled around the blond woman. She then turned to Octavia.

"She told you that your mother kept you from her, right?" she asked, and Octavia nodded. "Well, she was telling the truth about that. Donna did keep you away. However, it was not for the reasons that Jane gave you."

"W-What are you talking about?" Octavia demanded.
"How do you even know all this?"

"I'll show you." Kristy replied. Her golden aura shined bright as she held her arms upward. She began to call upon the spirits of Donna Baker and Kevin Simmons, invoking them into herself. Jane stared at Kristy in astonishment. What incredible power! she thought. Perhaps if she got her hands on Kristy, she could harness this ability for herself.

"Hello, Jane," Donna's voice spoke coldly through Kristy.

"D-Donna?" Jane said in a voice barely above a whisper.

"Mommy?" Octavia said.

"Octavia, I'm so disappointed in you," Donna said, as Kristy shook her head. "I loved you, and gave you and Kendra the best life I could. How could you turn your back on us? How could you murder your own sister?"

"How could you lie to me all these years?" Octavia snapped. "Every time I asked you about my birth parents, you told me you didn't know, that it was a closed adoption, and that you weren't given any information. The whole time, you had a photo of them! Why?"

"There's a lot that you don't understand, Baby Girl," Kevin's voice spoke.

"Then help me understand!" Octavia shouted, tears threatening to fall from her eyes. "Why did you abandon me?!"

> *"I didn't abandon you, Baby Girl,"* Kevin said.
> *"I never even knew you existed."*

> "Liar!" Octavia cried.

"He's telling the truth, sweetheart," Donna said. *"There's a lot about my life that you and Kendra didn't know. Before you were born... Jane and I were lovers."*

"What?!" Octavia cried, her glances darting from Kristy to Jane. Rachelle, Nick, and the others were absolutely flabbergasted. *I definitely wasn't expecting that!* Rachelle thought, her mouth agape.

"It's true." Donna continued. *"Jane and I met in college, and we even shared a dorm. We grew closer and eventually fell in love. However, we had to keep our relationship a secret because our families were very conservative, especially Jane's family."* Octavia looked at Jane, expecting her to deny this revelation. However, Jane remained quiet. The members of her coven were aghast and appalled at the idea that their High Priestess had not only been in a romantic relationship with a woman but a Black woman to boot! "Even if what you say is true, what does this have to do with my father?" Octavia asked. Kristy shot Jane a glare and continued.

"Kevin was in our literature class. The three of us became friends, and we would hang out often. However, Jane and Kevin started hanging out without me when I was busy with my studies. One day, I had finished a term paper and went back to the dorm. I heard noises coming from behind the door. I walked in and saw Jane on top of Kevin." Octavia stared at Jane

in disgust. She was the product of her mother being a cheating whore! *"Of course, they pulled the cliché, 'It's not what it looks like!' line, but I wasn't buying the bullshit they were selling. I broke up with Jane, and I also spoke to Kevin. They started dating each other after that. It was hard, but I moved on. I started dating Nathaniel, I eventually had Kendra, and things were good. Then, Nathaniel got into his accident and died. A year after I lost Nathaniel, I ran into Jane in a supermarket and noticed that she was pregnant. She and Kevin had been seeing each other for almost four years by this point. She told me that her parents refused to accept the child, and she was giving it up for adoption. Despite her betrayal, I felt bad for her, and I didn't want an innocent baby tossed into the system, so I offered to adopt you as my own."*

"Where was Kevin in all of this?" Octavia asked.

"When Jane told me she was pregnant, I wanted to be a family with her," Kevin replied. *"However, she told me that her family would never accept us together, or accept our child, so she was going to get an abortion. I begged her to reconsider, but I understood that since it was her body, it was her choice. However, after she told me she had the procedure, I cut ties with her."*

"After Jane gave birth to you, she put the father down as 'Unknown' on the birth certificate, so that Kevin couldn't contest the adoption, and she made me promise not to say anything," Donna said. *"I realize that it was wrong for me to make that promise, but at the time, I was still angry at him, so I agreed. However, when you were around five years old, I couldn't live with the guilt anymore, so I found Kevin and told him. He had given me the photo of him and Jane to give to you."*

"So, what happened then?" Octavia asked.

"Kevin found out where she worked and confronted her as she was leaving her shift. She invited him to her place so they could talk. That's when she killed him! She slit his throat, and when she called the police, she told them Kevin tried to force himself on her! She even ripped her clothes and used makeup to give herself bruises to make it more believable."

"You fucking bitch!" Louise seethed, rounding on Jane. She hated people who accused innocent people of sexual assault since it had life-ruining consequences and even life-threatening consequences. This was doubly true for Black men, as with the murders of Emmitt Till, George Stinney Jr., and Willie McGee. *"Tell her what you did after, Jane!"* Kevin demanded. *"Tell her that after you killed me, you took some of my blood and used it in a ritual to gain my power for yourself! You also made it so you could siphon the magic of any descendant of the Zira tribe!"* The room erupted in utter chaos at this revelation. Louise felt pure rage coursing through her body. As her mother revealed earlier, this racist bitch had been targeting them for her magic because she had no power of her own.

"What about me?" Alexis interjected, her eyes brimming with tears. "Why weren't you there for me? Why did you use my mother and abandon her?"

"I didn't abandon her, and I certainly didn't use her," Kevin countered. *"She pursued me, and we fooled around. However, I wasn't looking for anything long-term, so I eventually stopped seeing her. She never told me she was pregnant with you. If I had known, I would have been there for you."* Alexis said nothing. She was stunned.

"Baby, I didn't keep you away from Jane because I wanted to keep you for myself," Donna said. *"I kept you away because of what Jane had become. I was afraid that she would hurt you, especially since there was a possibility that you inherited Kevin's power."*

"You knew he could do magic?" Octavia asked.

"Yes. I saw him moving objects without touching them. I was freaked out at first, but then he explained to me that he was descended from a magical bloodline, and that he was born with his abilities. I think Jane somehow found out later down the line and wanted his magic for herself. See, there are a lot of things that you learn on the other side, and I learned something very interesting about Jane."

"And what is that?"

"Jane's ancestors were plantation owners," Donna explained. *"That's not all, however. They were the enslavers of Princess Kamaria, who is also your ancestor."*

"WHAT?!" Louise and Octavia exclaimed, glancing at each other.

"It's true." Kamaria's voice spoke. *"Jane's ancestor, Frederick Nielson, was a Norwegian immigrant who had come to New Amsterdam, what you now know as New York. My sister, Nyota, and I were captured from our village. He had given me the name Freija, which I despised. Nyota was given the name Ingrid. That devil forced himself on my sister. The result was my nephew, Erik, who died a month after his birth. His true name, however, was Shujaa. Frederick had known about our powers, having witnessed us using them during our chores. He had come from a family of alchemists and used the baby's blood to create a potion to grant his family our powers. This outraged us, and we led a revolt on the plantation. Unfortunately, they had gotten the best of us. Nyota, in despair, sacrificed herself on a pyre that she had created. I, being pregnant at the time, was sold to a plantation in Virginia, where I gave birth to my daughter. She was named Nyota in honor of my sister, but our captors had given her the name, Pearl. Over time, the magic that Frederick had stolen from us eventually died out, due to them only marrying within their race. That is why Jane pursued Kevin. She knew of his power."* Everyone had turned towards Jane. Her coven members stared at her with a mixture of shock and revulsion. She had portrayed herself as an honorable and strong woman that was proud of her Norse heritage. Yet, she had betrayed her race by procreating with a man of a race that they had considered to be inferior, bringing a mixed-race bastard into the world. Jane looked around and saw the looks of contempt that her coven was giving her, and she lost it.

"Don't look at me like that!" she screeched. "You're honestly going to believe the word of a lying, black bitch like her over your queen?!" She gestured to Kristy. "This is a trick! She's lying to you in order to turn you against me! If you believe her lies, you have no right to call yourselves Odin's daughters!"

"None of you have the right to call yourselves that!" Anthony declared, stepping forward. "You are a disgrace to everything Odin stands for! He is the father of all, and you spread your white supremacist bullshit in his name!"

"SHUT THE FUCK UP!" Jane bellowed, and with a wave of her hand, Anthony was thrown against the wall. "How dare you allow our father's name to leave your filthy mouth!" She subtly touched her ruby amulet, which glowed dark red. Suddenly, the members of her coven all stood straight, including Octavia, with their eyes glowing red.

"What do you need us to do, Mother?" Octavia asked in a monotone voice.

"Kill them!" Jane ordered, and the women immediately charged at Louise and her friends. They attacked relentlessly, with the intent to obliterate them. However, they were no match for the Children of Moonlight coven. Nick shot bolts of lightning their way, his power amplified by the Quartz pendant he was wearing. The women convulsed as the powerful currents surged through their bodies, and they collapsed to the floor, unconscious. Enraged, Jane charged at Nick. She shot a fireball his way. However, Nick dodged it effortlessly. Jane attempted to restrain him, in order to drain his energy from him, but out of nowhere, Marisol appeared. Her long, thick curls began to glow a bright fuchsia, and grew several feet longer. Her tresses began to wrap around Jane's limbs and torso, lifting her into the air. Jane tried to free herself, but her efforts were fruitless.

"¡Aléjate de mi hijo, puta!" Marisol spat, her voice dripping with venom, her eyes glowing. She then threw Jane towards the stage. Jane slid across the large stage, slamming into the DJ booth. Rachelle stared at her future mother-in-law in awe. She had been told about Marisol's magical hair, but she had never seen it in action. She was shook! She wondered if her twins had inherited their grandmother's ability. Jane slowly got up, revealing a deep gash in her forehead. Warm blood ran down her face, and her body was bruised. She gave Marisol a wicked smile.

"That's an extraordinary power you have there," she stated, vines emerging from her aura. "Why don't you hand it over?"

"Not a chance, bitch!" Carmen spat, as she and Daniela stood protectively in front of their mother. "You and your magic-thieving days are over! You're going to have to kill us if you want our power."

"Oh, trust me... I intend to do just that." Jane said, turning to Octavia. "Eliminate this trash!"

"Don't do it, Octavia!" Nick shouted, lightning emitting from his hands. "I don't want to have to hurt you, but I will if you force my hand!" Octavia looked at him, and Nick could see that her eyes were empty and soulless. There was a hint of red in them, an indication of Jane's control over her. Still, he wanted to reach her, to bring her back to reality. "Tay, this isn't you. This isn't the Octavia I know. What happened to you?"

"You know what happened to me!" Octavia cried. "You turned your back on me! You rejected me for... her!" She glared at Rachelle, who stood behind Nick.

"I didn't reject you for her, Tay. I fell in love with her. You were gone for fifteen years! Did you honestly expect me to not date anybody for all that time? I didn't even know that you felt that way about me. If I had known before you left, *maybe* there could have been something between us. But that's not reality. I love Rachelle, and I'm marrying her. We have children together. You need to move on. Why are you willing to throw your life away for a woman who didn't give a damn about you?"

"Don't let him manipulate you, Octavia." Jane said. "He never cared about you. He threw you away the first chance he got. You gave him your heart, and he just stomped all over it."

"She's the one manipulating you, Octavia!" Nick countered. "She gave you up without a second thought, and only came around when she thought it could benefit her. She doesn't care about you. Ms. Donna cared about you. Kendra cared about you. We care about you!" Nick gestured to his mother, sisters, and friends. "Yes, I know Ms. Donna kept things from you, but she wasn't doing it to hurt you. She was trying to keep you safe. Do you honestly think Jane is going to stick around when you are no longer of any use to her? I saw how disgusted you were when you learned about what she did to Ms. Donna and your father. You can't trust her, Octavia. She's only going to hurt you in the end."

"Why would you listen to someone who broke your heart so brutally?" Jane said as she placed her hands on Octavia's shoulders. "Remember all the things he said to you when he cut ties with you? What did he say you were? Immature? That you had no integrity?" Octavia's mind went back to the moment when she went to Nick's studio to plead for his forgiveness. The harsh words he flung at her rang in her ears. *"You want to know what Rachelle has that you don't? Integrity. Maturity. Rachelle doesn't throw a tantrum like a damn child when she doesn't get her way."* Tears stung Octavia's eyes.

"...You don't care about me," she said, her voice cracking. "You only care about Rachelle. It's always Rachelle!" Large, sharp icicles began to form in her hands, and she aimed them at Rachelle. "This bitch always gets everything! Well, since you broke my heart, how about I break yours!" Octavia launched an icicle in Rachelle's direction, while Nick simultaneously shielded her.. Before the weapon could reach its target, Alexis shoved them out of the way. Unfortunately, the icicle struck Alexis square in the chest, impaling her heart. Louise, Sarai, Kiana, and the others stared in utter horror, unable to comprehend what had just happened. It was as if the scene were playing out in slow motion. Alexis stared at Octavia with a look that was a mixture of shock, betrayal, and sadness. Coughing up blood, she collapsed to the floor, as Jane howled with laughter.

"LEXI!!!" Rachelle screamed in anguish, a river of tears streaming down her face. She kneeled down and pulled Alexis into her arms. Her cousin's blood drenched the front of her dress, but she didn't care. She placed her hand over Alexis' wound, and her hand began to glow as she attempted to heal her. "Heal, damn it!" she cried as she held her hand over the wound. However, blood continued to flow, and Alexis' breathing was growing increasingly labored.

"Chelly, I don't think it's working..." Sarai said, choking back her own tears.

"No!" Rachelle shouted.

"I can heal her! I-I just need a minute!"

"Rachelle..." Alexis said weakly.

"Don't try to talk, Lexi," Rachelle said.
"You need to save your strength."

"I'm not gonna make it, Chell..." Tears were falling from Alexis' eyes as she stared up at her cousin. Rachelle opened her mouth to protest, but Alexis cut her off. "It's okay. I'm ready. I'm really sorry that I spent all those years resenting you..."

"Let's not think about that right now," Rachelle replied, smiling at Alexis softly. "That's all in the past."

"I will always be grateful to you, Chell," Alexis said. "All of you. You literally saved my life. I will always love y'all for that."

"We love you too, Lexi," Louise said, tears flowing down her face. "And we're so proud of you." Alexis smiled up at Louise. "I'm proud of myself,

too," she said. She was growing weaker, and her body was getting colder. She turned back to Rachelle. "I want you to promise me something..."

"*Anything.*"

"Promise that you'll look after Bryson for me," Alexis replied.

"You don't even have to ask," Rachelle said, choking back a sob. "I also want you to let Mama know that I forgive her..." Tears were flowing freely down Alexis' face now.

"I also want you to tell Daddy that I love him, and he was the best father anyone could have asked for. Also…" Alexis coughed up blood.

"Yes?" Rachelle said, squeezing her hand tighter.

"I want you to live your life to the fullest," Alexis said. "I want you to continue chasing your dreams. No matter how insecure and jealous I was of you, I always admired you for living your life on your own terms. Grab life by the balls, and never let go. You understand me?" Rachelle let out a chuckle at her cousin's crass manner of speaking.

"I promise," she said, smiling.

Alexis gave Rachelle a tremulous smile, squeezing her hand. She then took her last breath and closed her eyes. Realizing that her cousin was dead, Rachelle let out a high-pitched, earth-shattering scream before breaking down into sobs over Alexis' body.

Chapter 26

*R*achelle stared at Alexis's lifeless body. Her grief turned to anger, and her anger turned to pure rage. The moment she got her hands on Octavia, she would tear her to shreds. It was Octavia's fault that Alexis was dead. Octavia had intended to kill Rachelle, but Alexis had taken the fatal blow. Because of Octavia's deranged jealousy, selfishness, and entitlement, three innocent people were dead, including Rachelle's cousin.

Octavia stared at Alexis, horrified by what she had done. She wanted Rachelle dead, not her own sister!

"I-I'm sorry...." she began. "I didn't mean-"

"Cut the shit, Octavia!" Nick barked, cutting her off. "It doesn't matter if you meant to hit Alexis or not! You had the intent to kill."

"She was in the way!" Octavia cried, trying to defend herself. She began to hyperventilate. "If she hadn't jumped in front of Rache-" Octavia was cut off by a powerful force, and she was thrown through the window of the club, completely shattering it.

"Holy shit!" an onlooker shouted, running towards Octavia. "Miss, are you alright?" Octavia attempted to get up, the shards of glass cutting into her palms. Pieces of glass were also stuck in her hair, and her face was littered with cuts. She and the onlooker looked up to see Rachelle calmly walking towards them, stepping over the glass. Her expression was menacing, and her eyes flashed with fury. Khalil, horrified, ran into the club and found Alexis' body. Now she understood why Rachelle was so angry. In Rachelle's hand was a large knife she had summoned from the kitchen. She grabbed Octavia by her hair, pulling her to her feet.

"Give me one good reason why I shouldn't slit your fucking throat, you worthless bitch!" she seethed, her face inches from Octavia's, the tip of the knife poking into her flesh.

"Chelly, stop!" Sarai cried, but Rachelle ignored her.

"Yeah, what's your problem, lady?" the onlooker said.

"You can mind your own fucking business!" Rachelle barked, before turning her attention back to Octavia. "Alexis didn't do a goddamn thing to you! She was your sister! But you don't care about anyone but yourself, given what you did to Kendra!" Octavia tried to form ice with her hands, but her injuries prevented her. "You don't deserve to live!"

"Rachelle, stop!" Nick cried as he wrapped his arms around her. "She's not worth it! You have too much to lose. Let the authorities deal with her!"

"Where are the authorities, anyway?" Simone interjected. "I thought Riley called them!"

"He did, but they're not coming," a sly female voice spoke. Rachelle and Nick turned around to see a petite female police officer with bright green eyes and shoulder-length mousy brown hair. Around her neck was a *Valknut* pendant, glowing emerald green.

"You're one of them," Rachelle remarked.

"That's right," the officer said with a smirk. "If you thought the police were going to swoop in and save you, think again. My entire precinct is dead."

"What did you do to them?" Nick demanded, and the woman cackled.

"Let's just say there was a little fire at the department," the officer replied with an innocent smile, infuriating Rachelle. The officer removed her gun from its holster and aimed it at Rachelle. "Now, I'm going to need you to drop your weapon, or else I'll be forced to shoot." Rachelle immediately dropped the knife. "Good girl."

315

"Nice of you to join us, Ilse," Jane said as she stepped outside with Anne. "Sorry I'm late," Ilse said. "I got held up at the precinct. But don't worry, they won't be a problem anymore." Jane smirked.

"Perfect," she said. She turned to Octavia and barked, "What are you doing just standing there? Kill them!"

"I-I can't...." Octavia said in a low voice, holding up her bloodied hands.

"Completely fucking useless!" Jane spat as she grabbed Octavia's hands, examining her wounds. "I guess your father didn't inherit any healing abilities. No matter, though." She turned to Rachelle, smiling wickedly. "I'm sure this lovely young lady's power will suffice."

"You're not gonna lay a hand on her!" Nick snarled, standing in front of his fiancée. "You'll have to kill me first!" Rachelle felt her heart swell at how protective Nick was of her.

"And you'll have to kill us to get to them!" Carmen added as she and the others walked over to Nick, gathering around him protectively. Their auras glowed brightly, and glowing, upside-down crescent moons appeared on their foreheads, a symbol of their tribe. Although Jane did not show it, she was terrified. She knew the powers of the Children of Moonlight coven far superseded her own. However, she was not going to go down without a fight. She certainly wasn't going to be beaten by those she considered inferior.

"You might as well give up now," Louise said, as large flames materialized in her hands. "There's more of us than there are of you. Half your folks are knocked out."

"That's where you're wrong, girl," Jane said. "My coven has chapters all over the country. I have plenty of witches that will come to my aid. All I have to do is call them."

"That's supposed to scare us?" Sarai said. "We have multiple chapters, too." Her onyx locket started to glow again, and her body began to grow warm.

"Besides, no matter how many racist bitches you call for backup, we still have the upper hand," Louise added. "This is New Orleans. This place was built on the blood, sweat, and tears of our people, and it's inhabited by the spirits of our ancestors. You're outnumbered, *cher*."

"We'll see about that!" Jane spat as she tore her Ruby amulet from around her neck and held it up in the air. The sky turned dark red, and a giant orb formed in the middle of the street. Onlookers frantically ran from the scene, not wanting to be caught up in whatever was about to happen. Within the orb grew a wide-reaching portal. Louise, her family, and her friends held up their enchanted jewelry and accessories into the air. As their coven's symbol formed in the night sky, Kristy called out:

"Children of Moonlight, I call out to you!
Children of our warrior ancestors, healers, and diviners
I ask you to stand up!
I call you to stand and fight with us, and for us!
To fight for our future generations,
And against those that wish to oppress us
Children of Zira, stand up!
Children of Anga, stand up!
Children of Kamaria, stand UP!"

Suddenly, a large, bright beam extended from the moon to the ground, encasing the group in a glowing dome. A portal appeared behind them, allowing a horde of people to charge through, including Amir and Marcus, surrounding them. More members of Jane's coven also appeared, surrounding their leader. Jane and Kristy stared each other down, their auras glowing larger.

"This is going to be fun," Jane mused as she turned to her horde. "Eliminate every last one of them!" With evil glints in their eyes, the women charged at Kristy and her coven. Octavia stood around helplessly as Bourbon Street erupted into pure havoc. With her hands injured, she could not form ice efficiently, and attempts at doing so caused her intense pain. However, when she saw one of Jane's coven members advancing towards Nick, she picked up the knife that Rachelle had dropped and hurled it at the woman. The weapon hit her square in the back, and she howled in agony.

"What the HELL do you think you're doing?!" Jane roared. She advanced towards Octavia, slapping her to the ground.

"She was going to hurt Nick!" Octavia replied in a cracked voice, holding her stinging cheek.

"You useless, half-breed bastard!" Jane seethed. "You're really going to betray your mother for this immigrant?!"

"I love him!" Octavia exclaimed, her eyes burning with tears.

"You're pathetic!" Jane spat. "I should've aborted you!" She grabbed Octavia by the neck. Her aura enveloped the two of them, and Octavia felt herself weaken as Jane began to drain her life force. However, before Jane could complete her task, she was thrown back, slamming into a telephone pole, while Octavia collapsed to the ground, coughing. Octavia looked up to see that her savior was none other than Rachelle.

"You...you saved my life," she croaked out, still trying to catch her breath as she climbed to her feet. "Look, I'm sorry about everyth-" she was cut off by a vicious right hook to the jaw, followed by a kick to the abdomen. Before she could react, she was met by an uppercut to the chin, knocking her to the ground. Octavia curled into a fetal position as Rachelle stood over her, with a vicious look in her eyes.

"That's for Lexi, you trifling bitch!" Rachelle barked as she kicked Octavia in the abdomen. "And that's for fucking up my bachelorette weekend!" Octavia whimpered as Rachelle spat on her. Long, sturdy vines began to emerge from Trina's hand, wrapping around Octavia's limbs, tying her to a nearby car.

"Hopefully that holds her until we can get her to the authorities," Trina remarked as she and Rachelle rejoined the fight. Octavia sobbed as she tried to free herself. Rachelle had saved her from death not because she forgave her or cared about her, but because she felt that death was too good for her. She wanted Octavia to live so she could face the full consequences of her actions.

"Hey, I know this might not be the best time to ask, since we're kind of preoccupied right now, but who are you?" Sarai asked the man with the black and orange locs as they fought alongside each other.

"My name's Michael. Michael LaBorn," he replied as he picked up one of the women and threw her by her hair several feet down the street. "I'm Bernadette's nephew."

"I take it that superhuman strength is one of your abilities?" Sarai asked.

>"Yep," Michael said with a proud smirk.
>"Nice shadow manipulation quirk, by the way."

"Did you just make a *My Hero* reference?" Sarai asked, amused.

>"Sure did."

"You're alright, Michael," Sarai said, and Michael grinned. Meanwhile, it appeared that Olga had gotten the best of Mariah. The young woman had twisted her ankle in the melee, and Ilse stood over her, gloating.

"Aww, did you hurt yourself?" she cooed mockingly, as Mariah shot her a death glare.

"Fuck you!" she spat.

"That's really no way to speak to an officer of the law," Ilse replied with a sadistic grin as she pulled out her gun. She aimed it at Mariah's head and said, "Didn't your mother teach you to respect authority?" However, before the officer could pull the trigger, she was suddenly engulfed in flames. Ilse screeched like a banshee as she burned to death. Mariah looked up to see her siblings standing in front of her.

>"You okay?" Louise asked as she kneeled down.
>"Can you move?"

"I don't think so," Mariah answered in a pained voice. Trina rushed over and placed her hand over Mariah's ankle, healing it instantly. "Better?" she asked. Mariah nodded as Dannell helped her to her feet.

"Good thing we have a healer in this fight," Louise joked. Her siblings rolled their eyes, while Trina giggled.

"Can we go one day without one of your nerdy references?" Mariah remarked.

"Whatever," Louise quipped as she lifted a few women in the air telekinetically. Invoking Kamaria into herself, her aura glowed brighter as a white light formed in her hand. Ropes of white light emerged, wrapping themselves around their victims. The women fought against their restraints as their power was drained from them, rendering them helpless.

"NO!" Jane bellowed as she lunged at Louise, ropes of red light emerging from her aura, twisting around themselves. Before she could reach her target, however, she looked up to see a large, rainbow-colored ball of fire descending upon her. She jumped out of the way just in time, before she could be consumed by its flames.

"What the hell was that?" Louise asked as she looked up.

"Guys, look!" Dannell exclaimed, pointing towards Rachelle. They were astonished to see that her aura was no longer pink, but a bright, rainbow color. Her eyes glowed a bright white, and she was surrounded by a ring of rainbow fire. Her brooch was also glowing. "Holy shit!" Sarai exclaimed. Her best friend had never displayed this kind of power before, but she was definitely impressed. She watched in awe as Rachelle slowly raised her arms, striking a pose like she was in a magical girl anime. Inhaling deeply, the multicolor flames rose, swirling around her. The fire took the form of a giant swan, gracefully extending its fiery wings. It soared through the crowd of white supremacists, turning them into human torches. Those that weren't caught in the blaze fled in horror, not wanting to be subjected to the same fate as their compatriots. This was not what they signed up for.

"Where the hell do you think you're going?!" Jane demanded, as several of her subordinates zoomed past her, screaming.

"Get back here!"

"Yeah, I don't think so!" a plump, red-haired woman exclaimed. "Look, I admire what you were trying to do, but I'm not dying for your ass!"

"Traitors!" Anne screeched. "Cowards, all of you!"

"You're calling us traitors?" another coven member shot back. "Your sister is a race traitor and a liar! I bet you're not even descended from Vikings like you claim you are! You can deal with this shit! I'm out!" She then continued running away, followed by several others who shared her sentiment. Anne screamed in frustration. They were now outnumbered.

"What the hell do we do now?!" she cried.

"I don't know!" Jane replied.

"What the hell do you mean you don't know?!" Anne shouted. "They're running away, and we're outnumbered!"

"I KNOW!" Jane roared. "Will you just shut the fuck up and let me think?!" Jane knew all hope was lost. She founded Daughters of Odin with the purpose of not only re-establishing what she considered the natural order of things but also restoring what her family had lost generations ago, as her father had wanted. She promised him on his deathbed that the Nielson family would be restored to their former glory. Now, it seemed that she had failed at keeping that promise. Feeling hopeless, Jane broke down and wept. Octavia stared at her biological mother in disgust. She had put Jane on a pedestal, seeing her as some powerful, regal being. Now, she realized Jane was nothing more than a fraud at best, a monster at worst. She hated herself for turning her back on the only people who truly loved her, who never made her feel unwanted. She now had no one. This fact hit her like a ton of bricks, and she burst into tears.

"Is this bitch really crying?" Kiana remarked. Louise shook her head in dismay at the pitiful display. Jane Nielson, formerly known as 'Queen Nanna', was nothing more than a weak, pathetic coward who felt the need to steal from others in order to feel powerful. Louise almost pitied her. Almost. While she belonged in prison for the hate crimes she had committed, Louise felt that too many people had suffered and died at Jane's hands for her to be allowed to live. She felt that it would be better to just obliterate the Nielson bloodline, especially Anne, due to her being responsible for Apollo's death. As if reading her mind, Simone stepped forward.

"You all might wanna cover your ears," she warned. Her friends clamped their hands over their ears, and Simone, with a smirk, began to vocalize. Her mermaid pendant began to glow, and a bright orange orb formed in her throat. It reminded Louise of a scene from the film, *The Little Mermaid*, when Ariel had her voice taken from her. The pupils of her eyes also glowed orange. Upon seeing Simone, Anne covered her ears, but Jane was completely enthralled. Simone's voice was hypnotic, and suddenly, thoughts of death invaded Jane's mind. Under the influence of the siren song, Jane grabbed Ilse's gun from near her charred body and put the barrel to her temple.

"Jane, what are you doing?!" Anne shrieked, her hands still clamped over her ears. "Sis, don't do this! Don't-" *BANG!* Anne jumped from the sound of the gun. Covered in her sister's blood and brain matter, she wailed in anguish.

"Holy fucking shit!" Khalil shouted as she and her friends looked on in horror. Anne began to hyperventilate as Jane collapsed near her feet. She turned towards Simone, her anguish turning into fury.

"You black bitch!" she seethed as she charged towards her, her eyes blazing. However, before she could unleash her wrath on Simone, she was suddenly restrained by long, woody vines, which emerged from the ground. She cursed as she was thrown to the ground. Simone had stopped singing, and Louise stepped forward, smirking.

"Any last words, Anne?" she asked in an amused tone. Glaring at her, Anne spat near her feet. "Have it your way, then." Suddenly, the sky turned dark purple. Her friends looked up to see a large murder of crows descend upon Anne. The brunette cried out as the crows began to peck at her eyes and flesh. She let out an unearthly scream as her ice-blue eyes, the one feature that gave her the most pride, were gouged out. Louise waved her hand, and Anne suddenly became engulfed in flames. She screamed in agony as the fire crept closer. Rachelle and the others looked away, Anne's screams piercing their ears. Eventually, the flames completely consumed her body, and an eerie silence followed. Louise calmly walked over to Anne's charred remains, glaring down at her. "Say hello to your ancestors in Hell for me, you worthless bitch, because you damn sure ain't going to Valhalla!" She spat as she kicked Anne's head. A few of the crows flew to her, nuzzling against her face affectionately. Thanks again, Missy, she thought. She then turned to her friends and family, who were no doubt stunned.

"Damn, Lou!" Sarai exclaimed.
"That was fucking metal!" Their friends laughed.

"You need to teach me how to do that!" Michael added.
"Having crows do my bidding would be awesome!"

"Louise wins. Flawless Victory…" Kiana said in a deep, menacing voice.

"FATALITY!" their friends shouted in unison, laughing.

"Alright, now. Let's settle down," Kristy interjected, shaking her head in an attempt to erase Anne's last moments from her mind. "First things first, is everyone okay?" Everyone answered in the affirmative, and Kristy sighed. "Alright. We need to find a police station so we can tell them what happened here. We'll also hand Miss Thang over to them, so they can deal with her. They can also send a coroner to collect the bodies."

"Will we be arrested?" Trina asked. She was scared to death at the prospect of prison, and she didn't want to lose everything she had worked so hard to build.

"I don't think so," Daniela replied. "They attacked us first and were going to kill us. Everything we did in response was self-defense."

"She's right," Marcus added.
"That's why I have a hidden camera. I recorded everything."

"Good looking out, cuz!" Louise remarked, giving her cousin a fist bump.

"Shall we get going, then?" Kristy said, and she, Louise, Rachelle, and the rest of the group went to a nearby police station, while the other coven members went their separate ways. A statement was given to the authorities, along with the video evidence. Since the group had in fact acted in self-defense, they faced no charges. Octavia was handed over to the police and would be held in a cell until the FBI could collect her. The police also accompanied the local coroner to the scene to collect the bodies of the deceased.

"So, Delacroix, how the fuck do we write this up?" the lieutenant asked his partner as Rachelle and her friends left the station. "I have no fucking clue," replied Officer Delacroix. "Do we even have a protocol for supernatural incidents?"

"I don't think so, but honestly, we should. This is New Orleans, after all."

"You're definitely right about that!" Officer Delacroix said.

Chapter 27

*I*t was the day of Alexis' funeral service, and Rachelle was completely numb. For the past week, she had been in a near catatonic state, just going through the motions of her everyday life. The day after their encounter with the Daughters of Odin coven, the bachelorette trip was abruptly cut short, and they caught the first flight home. Telling her Uncle Ernie that Alexis was gone was the hardest thing she had ever done. Watching her usually stoic uncle fall to pieces after learning of the death of his only child nearly killed her. Seeing little Bryson in tears when he learned that his mommy wasn't coming home hurt her ten times worse. However, Corrine took the news the hardest. For the past two weeks, the woman wouldn't stop blaming herself. The grief took such a toll on her that she had to be held in a psychiatric hospital for almost a week, out of fear that she would hurt herself.

This isn't fucking fair! Rachelle thought as a tear fell from her eye. Lexi had everything going for her, only for it to be snatched away! Her insides burned with anger as her thoughts shifted to Octavia. It was because of that delusional, selfish bitch that her cousin was no longer here. It was because of her that Alexis would not get to watch her son grow up, go to prom, or get married. The only silver lining to this injustice was that Octavia would get exactly what she deserved. The arrest of Octavia Baker was nationwide news, as well as the gruesome deaths of Jane and Anne Nielson. Not only was Jane the leader of a white supremacist organization, but she was also heavily involved in acts of domestic terrorism across the country. Even more shocking, it was discovered that the home in which she held her coven meetings also housed a laboratory for manufacturing methamphetamines! The millions she raked in from her drug enterprise funded her coven's activities. Octavia, along with countless surviving members of the now-disbanded coven, were charged by the federal government with multiple counts of drug distribution, terrorism, arms smuggling, and money laundering. Octavia was also charged with the murders of Kendra Baker, Riley Mereaux, and Alexis Lawson, as well as arson. Because she was being tried under federal jurisdiction, and had committed three murders in two different states, she faced the death penalty since the state of Louisiana still practiced capital punishment. *I hope the bitch rots!* Rachelle thought angrily.

"Mommy?" Rachelle snapped out of her thoughts and peered down to see her daughter, Selena, gazing up at her, her green eyes wide and innocent. The toddler reached up and gently patted her mother's face. "Mommy, no cry." Rachelle's eyes softened as she took her baby girl into her arms.

"Mommy's okay, baby," she said as she straightened the dark blue bow in Selena's hair and kissed her on the cheek. Nick squeezed her hand gently. He knew Rachelle was putting on a brave front for their girls, but was a wreck on the inside. His heart broke for her and the rest of her family. While they had gotten off to a rough start when they first met, Nick had grown to respect and admire Alexis. She had overcome tremendous obstacles in her life and come out on top. He partly blamed himself for her death, because he had welcomed Octavia back into his life and let her into his inner circle. He didn't think he would be able to forgive himself.

"Nick, I know what you're thinking," Sharon spoke gently. "None of this is your fault. Octavia was an adult capable of making her own choices. She chose to go down that dark path. That's not on you." Nick let out a sigh.

"I know," he said. "But-"

"But nothing," Veronica interjected. "You didn't know that bitch was deranged!" Nick had to hold back a laugh at the older woman's absence of a filter. It was a good thing Rachelle had covered their daughters' ears. "You were being a good friend. That's nothing to be ashamed of."

"Auntie Ronnie's right, baby," Rachelle added, softly stroking his hand. "It's not your fault that Octavia did what she did. Don't you dare blame yourself. Not for one minute."

"I just hate seeing you in so much pain," Nick said. Rachelle softly kissed his cheek and leaned against him. Suddenly, the limousine stopped.

"Looks like we're here," Sharon said as the driver opened the door. They had arrived at Reynolds Funeral Home for family hour. Rachelle stared up at the bright, sunny sky, feeling that Mother Nature was mocking them. There was nothing bright about this day. As they stepped into the reception room, they were greeted by Xavier, who led them into the display room. Everyone was dressed in dark blue, which was Alexis' favorite color. Alexis had always mentioned if she died, she didn't want anyone wearing black at her funeral. She wanted people to celebrate her life, not mourn her death. Easier said than done.

"You okay?" Sharon asked in a whisper, stroking her daughter's hair. Rachelle nodded and stared straight ahead. Ernest and Corrine were the first ones to approach the casket, their hearts breaking further with each step. Ernest broke down into sobs upon the sight of his daughter laying in a dark blue, silk-lined casket. Her body was adorned with a beautiful, blue lace gown. Her curly, black hair laid against the soft pillow like she was Sleeping Beauty. Around her neck was a simple heart pendant with a sapphire stone, her birthstone. In her ears were simple sapphire studs. Her makeup was natural and made her look angelic. Alexis looked

Alexis Imani Lawson
July 20, 1994 – June 28, 2023
Beloved Mother, Daughter, and Friend

as if she were simply in a peaceful slumber.

*"MY **GOD**!"* Corrine wailed as her legs threatened to give out. She wept uncontrollably as she clutched her chest, tears flowing down her face. She had lost weight and appeared ten years older than she was. "I'm sorry, Lexi! I'm so sorry! God, why did you have to take my baby from me?!" Sharon and Veronica helped the heartbroken woman to her seat in the front row. Ernest held her, allowing her to cry on his shoulder, as his own tears flowed. Seeing her uncle's state shattered Rachelle. He was a shell of his former self. Sharon gave her longtime friend a cup of water, as Veronica fanned her. Rachelle's heart pounded against her chest as she approached her cousin. Nick held her close to him as they walked, fully prepared to catch her if she collapsed. She sobbed softly as she stared down at Alexis. She reached out to touch her hand and almost recoiled at the sudden coldness. Rachelle thought Alexis looked so beautiful, so peaceful when her demise was anything but. As much as she tried, Rachelle could not forget the look of betrayal in her cousin's eyes as Octavia's icicle struck her. She felt her rage bubbling to the surface again and took a deep breath. The last thing she wanted to do was make a scene and potentially frighten her babies.

"Don't be afraid to let it out," Nick whispered as he gently rubbed her back. Rachelle openly wept as she bent down to give Alexis a kiss on the forehead before Nick led her to their seats with their daughters in tow. Seeing their mother distraught, the twins also began to cry. Nick held them in her arms and whispered soothingly to comfort them. Soon, his own tears began to fall. The couple watched as Bryson was led into the display room by his father, Bryce. His face was wet with tears as he begged in vain for his mother to wake up. Bryce covered his face with his hand as he sobbed. Before her murder, Alexis and Bryce were growing closer and were even working towards getting back together. They wanted the three of them to be a family. Now, that was never going to happen, and Bryce was devastated. After saying goodbye to his mother, Bryson went to sit with his grandparents. More relatives entered to pay their respects. Rachelle could hear whispers of how it was such a waste that a beautiful Black woman had her life cut short so brutally. She could also hear some of the older women whisper about how Alexis allowed herself to fall victim to addiction and degraded herself by selling her body. These remarks made Rachelle's blood boil. *Who the hell are they to judge? They probably weren't angels themselves. Fuck them!* she thought. *They haven't achieved half the things Lexi had. They're nothing*

329

but a bunch of miserable, old, jealous-ass bitches! Once family hour was over, friends and colleagues of Alexis were allowed in. Louise, Sarai, Kiana, and Khalil each came to pay their respects, as well as Nick and Louise's families. Members of the Children of Moonlight coven also came, as did those that worked with Alexis at the magazine. Even Mia Hines, who once worked at Vincent's strip club, showed up. She had since stopped using drugs and selling her body and was now working at a dental office as a receptionist. Once everyone was seated, Xavier got up and led the opening prayer. Afterwards, Sharon got up to read Alexis' obituary, as well as cards that had been sent to the family. Friends, family, and colleagues alike got up one by one to say a few kind words about Alexis and the good times they shared with her. Soon, it was Rachelle's turn. Her stomach was in knots as she stepped up to the podium, her eyes scanning the crowd. Nick and their friends gave her an encouraging smile, which put her mind at ease.

Taking a deep breath to calm herself, she spoke:

"Good day, everyone. My name is Rachelle Lawson, and Alexis was my cousin. When Lexi and I were children, we were joined at the hip. You would never see one without the other." A few people chuckled, and Sharon and Ernest smiled at her through their tears. "I remember how we would always have sleepovers at each other's houses and had tea parties with our dolls. We would fight over dolls, too." More people laughed, and she continued. "She was more than a cousin. She was my sister. However, once we became teenagers, we started growing apart and had different interests. Eventually, we started to resent each other, and that resentment only festered as we got older." Rachelle's mind went back to her mother's Christmas dinner over five years ago. "However, a while back, Lexi had gotten into some trouble, and after helping her, we started to fix our relationship." She turned to Nick and her friends, who gave her a knowing look. "We were able to set aside our differences and become close again. We wasted so much time being mad at each other over things that didn't even matter, but I am thankful that we were able to be friends again before she left us." Rachelle wiped away a tear before continuing. "I am very grateful to have known Alexis Lawson, and I am proud to have called her my family." She then turned to Bryson and said, "Even though your mommy is no longer here physically, she'll always be watching over you. You meant the world to her, and I promised her that

I will always look out for you." The two of them shared a hug as she returned to her seat.

After a few more remarks, Simone sang an emotional rendition of "Amazing Grace," which left everyone in tears. Xavier then had everyone stand up for the closing prayer. After the service, the pallbearers, which included Nick, Dannell, Bryce, and Wilfred, carried Alexis' casket outside to the hearse. Ernest followed after them with Corrine, who was inconsolable. In addition to her grief, she felt unbearable shame. She had never fully appreciated her only child and constantly pointed out her faults. On top of that, she had lied to her for her entire life, as well as Ernest, and their family was forever fractured as a result. Although she had been repeatedly told that Alexis had forgiven her, Corrine couldn't forgive herself. Rachelle was genuinely scared for her aunt. She knew that losing a child caused unimaginable pain, as she witnessed with Louise, and she hoped that Corrine wouldn't go off the deep end.

"I still can't believe she's gone," Trina remarked, as the others murmured in agreement. What was supposed to be a weekend of fun ended in tragedy. Once the casket was loaded into the hearse, everyone returned to their vehicles and drove to the cemetery for the burial. Alexis was interred next to Dr. Robert Lawson, Rachelle's father. As her cousin was committed to the ground, Rachelle could see her standing with her father, smiling at her, as if to assure her that everything would be okay. This gave Rachelle a small comfort. While she could never forgive Octavia for what she had done, she knew that Alexis was now among the Ancestors and would always be there to watch over and protect her.

"Chelly?" Bryson piped up, gazing up at her.

"Yeah?"

"Is Mommy really watching over me?"

"Oh, honey, of course she is," Rachelle said, kneeling down to his level. "Your mommy is an Ancestor now, just like my daddy. Your mommy will be able to talk to you in your dreams and help you when you need it."

331

"I guess that's good," Bryson said as he looked down at his mother's casket being lowered into the ground. Rachelle gave him a comforting hug.

"Come on, let's go eat," she said, and the two of them walked back to the limousine to go to the repast. The banquet hall was beautifully decorated in dark blue and silver, with candles with Alexis' face on every table. As everyone enjoyed their delicious meal, all provided by Vernon's catering service, they reminisced over their memories of Alexis, sharing funny stories of their antics. Though she was heartbroken that her cousin was gone, it warmed Rachelle's heart to know how loved she was. She knew that no matter how many years passed, Alexis would never be forgotten. She would make sure of that.

Chapter 28

Two Months Later

*R*achelle paced back and forth in the spacious, opulent suite of the Hotel Saint Regis. Her stomach twisted in knots, and her heart pounded a mile a minute. The day she had been waiting for had finally arrived: her wedding day. Today, she and Nick would promise, in front of all their family and friends, to love and cherish each other until the day they died. They had even written their own vows for the ceremony. Despite her joy, Rachelle was experiencing wedding day jitters.

"Girl!" Sarai exclaimed as she stepped out of the bathroom, a gold satin bathrobe wrapped around her thick frame. "If you don't sit your ass down and relax! This is your day. Everything is going to be perfect."

"But what if everything isn't perfect?" Rachelle cried. "What if Nick changes his mind? What if Inez decides to crash the wedding? What if Octavia—" Rachelle was cut off by Sarai pinching her lips shut.

"I'm gonna need you to get it together," Sarai said, letting Rachelle's lips go. "Take a deep breath and let it out." Rachelle did as her best friend told her. "Feel better?"

"A little."

"Good." Sarai sat in a chair. "Now, do you honestly think Nick would leave you at the altar after everything the two of you have been through? You're tripping."

"I second that," Louise said, taking a sip of water while Soleil babbled on her hip. "You two have built a family together. He ain't going nowhere. As far as Miss Thang is concerned, you have nothing to worry about. She's going to be put away for a very long time. She'll never see the light of day again with all those charges she's facing."

"Sarai and Lou are right, Rachelle," Carmen added. "One thing I know about my brother is that when he loves, he loves hard. I see the way he looks at you and how his eyes light up when he talks about you. He never felt that way about anyone! He loves you and my nieces more than anything and would die for you." Rachelle felt a lump in her throat as she choked back tears. She loved Nick more than anything, and she knew his sister was right. He was in it for the long haul. Why would they come this far if he wasn't truly committed?

"Nuh-uh, we can't have you starting the waterworks, *chica*," Daniela warned as she handed Rachelle a Kleenex. "You don't want your eyes red and puffy for the wedding." Rachelle nodded as she wiped her eyes. Suddenly, there was a knock at the door.

"That must be Geneva and Bri," Trina said as she went to open the door. A few moments later, Geneva Watkins, the makeup artist Trina had recommended, and Bri Jordan, Rachelle's hairstylist, entered the room, carrying the tools of their trade. They were followed by Sharon, Veronica, Joanna, Marisol, and Magdalena.

"There's the blushing bride!" Bri exclaimed as she and Rachelle hugged, kissing each other on both cheeks. "How are you feeling?"

"Nervous as hell," Rachelle replied, and Bri chuckled.

"Don't worry, girl. I got you." After exchanging pleasantries with the rest of the bridal party, the seasoned stylist immediately went to work. Taking the bride's desire to keep her hair's natural texture into consideration, she styled Rachelle's long, thick curls into an elegant 1940s updo, using Rachelle's own haircare products. She also gave the bridesmaids exquisite updos and styled the flower girls' hair into adorable puff ponytails with pink bows. Once Bri was done working her magic, Geneva started on their makeup. Keith, a photographer with whom Rachelle had done many photoshoots, was also present, snapping photos as they got ready. He was honored that Rachelle wanted him to be a part of her special day.

"Girl, you look amazing!" Trina remarked as they stared at their reflections in the vanity mirror. Rachelle's makeup made her look radiant, with gold eyeshadow and dark pink lips. The beauty gods were certainly smiling upon her.

"Would I win a face category at one of your balls?" Rachelle asked.

"Tens across the board, honey," Trina replied with a snap of her beautifully manicured fingers. The cousins giggled and embraced.

"Speaking of ballroom, it's awesome that your house children are performing at the reception," Sarai remarked.

"Simone, too," Kiana added. "It sucks that her first big gig got ruined the way it did."

"True, but it was great how she finished Jane off," Khalil stated, admiring her makeup and hair. "Anyway, enough about that. This is supposed to be a happy occasion. Let's not bring up bad memories."

"I agree," Sharon said as she helped her daughter into her wedding gown with assistance from Sarai and Veronica. Renee Milano had truly outdone herself. The vintage gown fit Rachelle perfectly, like it was made solely for her, despite being an heirloom. The delicate pearl and crystal beading was immaculate, and the long train made her look and feel like a princess. After her mother placed the pearl diadem on her head and attached the delicate veil, Rachelle turned around to stare at her reflection in the floor-length mirror. She was awestruck at how regal she looked. She felt as if she were in a dream. If she were, she didn't want to wake up. Her eyes burned with tears as she thought of her father and cousin. She wished they could be here to see this day. She quickly blinked her tears back, not wanting to ruin her makeup. She looked up again to see Robert and Alexis smiling back at her.

> *"You look so beautiful, Chell,"* Alexis said.

> "It isn't fair," Rachelle said in her head.
> "You're supposed to be here with me."

> *"I am always with you,"* Alexis replied.

"Lexi, are you sure you're okay with Uncle Ernie walking me down the aisle?"

"Chell, we've been over this," Alexis said. *"I'm gone, and Daddy will never get a chance to do this again. Besides, he and Uncle Bobby are identical twins, so you'll basically have your dad there."* Rachelle let out a chuckle as she wiped away a tear. She thanked her ancestors for waterproof mascara.

> "I love you, Lexi."

> *"I love you, too, Chell."* Robert then spoke up.

"My little princess. I've waited so long for this day. I just want you to know that I am fiercely proud of you, and even though I am not there physically, I am always there with you in spirit."

> "I know, Daddy," Rachelle said through her tears.

"Sharon." Sharon turned around and teared up upon seeing her late husband.

"Bobby?" she breathed.

"I'm here, baby." Sharon put her forehead against the mirror. Her heart swelled with joy to see her beloved husband again, even just for a moment. The rest of the bridal party watched in stunned silence as they witnessed the emotional scene with tears in their eyes. *"We did good, didn't we?"*

"We did," Sharon said, smiling.

"Our baby girl is grown up," Robert said, his voice filled with emotion. *"And our grandbabies are so beautiful and smart. I'm confident they'll grow up to be fine young women."*

"I know they will because they have you watching over them," Rachelle said.

"Knock 'em dead, Princess," Robert said.

"That boy better take good care of my baby, or else he'll have to deal with me!" Lula interjected, making everyone laugh.

"I'll be sure to tell him that," Rachelle said. Robert blew his daughter and wife a kiss, and he, his mother, and niece soon vanished. Rachelle wiped her eyes and took a deep breath to calm herself.

"Ready?" Sharon asked. Rachelle nodded, and they all made their way outside, where a white limousine and a white horse-drawn carriage awaited them. Rachelle looked up at the sky and admired how clear and sunny it was. She looked at the carriage to see several Monarch butterflies fluttering around it. She was once told by her grandmother that butterflies were a sign that one's loved ones were always present. Rachelle felt herself getting emotional again. She knew that her ancestors, as well as Nick's, were smiling down on them. It was always a cause for celebration when descendants of their lost tribe found their way to each other.

"Damn, your auntie didn't pull any punches with this wedding, did she?" Khalil remarked.

"Sure didn't," Veronica said as she helped her niece into the carriage. She got in with Rachelle, along with Sharon, while the bridal party entered the limousine. Once everyone was settled, they left the Hotel Saint Regis, making their way to The Roostertail, where the ceremony and reception were being held. When they arrived, Amina, the wedding planner, was waiting for them. She looked especially radiant in her traditional Punjabi attire. She wore an orange Salwar Kameez suit in the Abaya style, complemented by ornate jewels. On her feet, she wore orange heels. Her long, dark hair was styled in an elegant updo, and on her forehead, she wore a bindi. Her makeup was also stunning.

"Rachelle, you look so beautiful!" Amina gushed as she circled around the bride. "Nick is definitely a lucky man." Rachelle blushed.

"Thank you, Amina, for everything," she said. Amina took her hand.

"You don't have to thank me," she said with a smile. "I just want you and Nick to enjoy your big day and live out your lives in happiness." The two women hugged.

"Amina, everyone is seated and ready," Melinda, Amina's assistant, said. "Perfect!" Amina said, clasping her hands together. "Okay, everyone! Time to get in your places!" The bridesmaids all lined up, holding their bouquets, while the groomsmen stood next to them. Artemis and the twins stood in front, each holding a basket of red rose petals. Amina kneeled in front of them, smiling. "Ready for your first big girl job?" The girls nodded excitedly, and Amina hugged them. Once everyone was ready, "At Last" by Etta James began to play. Selena and Solana walked down the aisle, tossing rose petals as they went. The crowd cooed over how adorable the girls looked, and Nick smiled proudly at his daughters.

"Daddy!" the girls shouted upon seeing their father, running towards him and dropping their baskets in the middle of the aisle. Everyone laughed as Nick scooped them up in his arms, kissing their cheeks. Even Amina, who went to pick up the baskets, was tickled. Artemis began to descend the aisle, accompanied by Bryson, who carried a large satin pink pillow with two gold rings in the middle. Corrine smiled at her grandson, pinching his cheek as he walked down. Now, it was the bridesmaids' turn. Sarai walked down the aisle with Wilfred, whom Nick appointed as his Best Man. Louise stood on the other side of him. They were followed by Kiana and his college friend and dorm mate, Mitch Roberts. Khalil walked down the aisle with her husband, Chris. Trina walked down with Mike, who had since reconciled with the friend group. Carmen walked down with her maternal cousin, Armando, while Daniela was accompanied by his younger brother, Carlos. The procession finished with Mariah and Dannell walking together. Soon, the music changed, and "Until" by Derric Gobourne, Jr. began to play. Kristy, who was officiating the ceremony, instructed everyone to stand in anticipation of the bride's appearance. The moment the song transitioned into the chorus, the doors opened, and everyone looked on in awe as Rachelle walked down the aisle, arm in arm with her uncle. When her eyes met Nick's, he suddenly began to cry tears of joy. He looked dapper in a black tux with a pink vest embroidered with gold and a pink tie. His dark hair was combed back and cut slightly shorter for the wedding. Rachelle's eyes also began to tear up, especially as she saw the spirits of her father, cousin, paternal grandmother, and maternal step-grandfather, along with the rest of her ancestors. She could also see the spirit of Nick's maternal grandparents. Her heart swelled with love and pure joy as she walked closer to the altar, the train of her exquisite gown trailing behind her. This was it. She was finally marrying the love of her life. As she got closer to Nick, the rose quartz on her engagement ring began to glow. She looks so beautiful, Nick thought to himself as he wiped a tear from his eye. Sharon, Marisol, Joanna, Magdalena, and Veronica were also crying, as well Sarai, Louise, Kiana, and Trina. They knew how far Rachelle had come to find true love, especially Sarai. Once Rachelle and Ernest reached the altar, Ernest gave her a kiss on the cheek and a loving hug. Rachelle then stepped up to the altar, and Nick took her hands in his.

"Dearly Beloved," Kristy began, smiling warmly at the couple. "We are gathered here to witness the sacred union of this couple in matrimony. We are here to witness them be united in the eyes of our Creator, as well as our great ancestors. If there is anyone who thinks that these two should not be wed, speak now, or forever hold your peace." Rachelle and Nick looked around to see if anyone would object, and Sarai stared the audience down, silently threatening to whoop the ass of anyone who dared say that Nick should not marry her best friend. Kiana had to stifle her laughter, as did the other bridesmaids. Thankfully, there were no objections. Kristy smiled as she continued. "The bride and groom have written their own vows and would like to recite them for you today. Rachelle, why don't you go first?" Blushing, Rachelle gazed up into Nick's eyes and saw the pure love and devotion they held. Clearing her throat, she spoke.

"Nick, when I first met you, I thought you were the most handsome man I had laid eyes on. The fact that you were cosplaying as one of my favorite male anime characters was a bonus." The audience laughed, including the wedding party. "However, what made me really fall for you was your mind and your heart. I love your strength, your intelligence, and how deeply you care for your family." A tear fell from Nick's eye, and Rachelle wiped it away. "This is another reason why I love you. You're not afraid to be vulnerable with me. You're not afraid to show how much you care. I thank God every day for you. You have been my rock and have been nothing but loving, nurturing, and supportive. You're a wonderful father to our girls, and I feel sorry for any boys or girls that try to date them when they get older." The crowd laughed again, including Kristy. "I promise, Nick, to love, honor, and cherish you until the day I take my last breath. I love you, Nicolas Ramirez, now and forever." Nick reached out to gently wipe away the tears that fell from her eyes, softly kissing her hand. Their mothers silently sobbed, and even Domingo and Ernest had shed a few tears. Now, it was Nick's turn to say his vows.

"Rachelle, you are the most beautiful woman I have ever met, inside and out," he began. "I love your compassion, your ambition, and your strong mind. Sometimes, I wonder if I even deserve you. The day I first met you, when I saw how you were willing to fight for your friend," Rachelle chuckled at the memory. She was fully prepared to stomp Ashley's ass that day. "I knew right then, that you were someone I wanted to get to know. I admire your loyalty to those you love and how you are willing to fight to protect them. You are one of the strongest women I have ever known, and I am honored to call you my wife. Rachelle Dominique Lawson, I promise that you will have my heart, my loyalty, and my protection as long as we both live, and even beyond that." Kristy was in tears now.

"Way to show me up," Rachelle joked in a whisper, and Nick smirked.

"May I have the rings?" Kristy asked softly.

Bryson shyly stepped forward, holding up the pillow. As they exchanged rings, strings of bright red and pink light encircled their hands, intertwining. Some of the crowd gasped at the sight, but those who were part of the coven simply beamed. They knew that when this happened, it meant that two soulmates had found each other and were bonded forever. The couple gazed into each other's eyes, tears flowing from them. Smiling ear to ear, Kristy said,

"By the power vested in me, by the State of Michigan, I now pronounce you husband and wife." She then turned to Nick. "You can kiss your bride."

"*Te amo*," he said softly as he pulled Rachelle close to him.

Their hearts pounded against their chests as Nick dipped her, kissing her passionately. The room erupted in applause, cheers, and whistles, with their friends cheering the loudest of all. Amina then laid a beautifully embellished broom at the couple's feet. Holding hands, they jumped over the broom, eliciting more cheers and applause from their guests.

"I now present to you, Mr. and Mrs. Nicolás Ramirez!" Kristy announced. Rachelle and Nick beamed at each other as Stevie Wonder's "Signed, Sealed, Delivered (I'm Yours)" played from the speakers. They walked up the aisle hand in hand as their loved ones congratulated them. Their mothers, grandmothers, and Nick's sisters were a sobbing mess. After signing their marriage license, the newlyweds joined their wedding party and families for photos. Rachelle and Nick were on cloud nine. They were finally married and surrounded by the love and support of their family and friends. If their ordeal with Octavia had taught them anything, it was that their love would withstand any obstacle.

"So, how do you feel?" Nick asked as they posed for photos with their daughters.

"I feel amazing," Rachelle said, smiling at him. "And to think I was worried that you would change your mind. Sarai was right. I was definitely tripping."

"Yeah, you definitely were," Nick said as he gave his bride a peck on the cheek. "You're stuck with me, babe." Rachelle giggled.

"Ditto," she replied. After their photo session, it was time for the reception. Veronica spared no expense for her niece's special day, and it was obvious why Amina Aggerwal-Russell was one of the most sought-after wedding planners in Detroit. The reception hall was beautifully decorated with dozens of red roses, and candles adorned every table.

Vernon provided the catering, and as usual, the food was incredible. He even took the time to learn recipes from Nick's family, as well as Jamaican recipes. The guests' mouths watered at the sight of the trays of jerk chicken, pernil, *arroz con pollo*, fried plantains, *baliche*, and good old-fashioned soul food.

"Girl, that ceremony was beautiful!" Mika remarked as she approached the couple. "Those vows had me bawling." Rachelle giggled.

"I'm glad you liked it, and thank you for coming," she said.

"I'm really sorry about your cousin, though," Mika said. "It's fucked up what that chick did to her."

"It was but she's getting what she deserves," Rachelle replied, and Mika nodded. "Anyway, I'm really happy for you two. Also, I'm gonna need your designer's number because you are slaying in that dress." Giggling, Rachelle gave Mika Renée's business card before making her rounds to the other guests. Rachelle was stunning in a pink satin, beaded gown with a plunging neckline. She wore gold heels and had pink and gold flowers in her hair, along with the pearl necklace and earrings she wore for the ceremony. As she watched her guests enjoying themselves, Nick embraced her from behind, his lips inches from her ear.

"She's right," he said in a low, seductive voice. "You're looking good in that dress. I can't wait to see you out of it." Rachelle playfully hit his arm, yet her core was throbbing.

"Nasty ass," she said.

"You love it, though," Nick retorted as he kissed her lovingly. After a wonderful dinner, the bride and groom shared their first dance to "I Only Have Eyes For You" by The Flamingos. They gazed into each other's eyes, and it was as if there was no one else but them.

"I love you," Rachelle said, and Nick smiled.

"I love you more," he replied as they kissed again, with Nick dipping her. After their dance as husband and wife, they cut the cake, feeding a slice to each other. However, Nick did not smash the cake in Rachelle's face, which was traditional for most weddings. One, he would never humiliate the woman he loved that way. Two, he knew that Rachelle would cut his ass if he did. The rest of the evening was filled with revelry as the guests danced the night away to The Jacksons, Celia Cruz, Elephant Man, Daddy Yankee, Megan Thee Stallion, and Selena. They could feel their ancestors' presence in the room with them as they danced. They even enjoyed a performance from the House of Nyx, Trina's ballroom house, as well as a rendition of "Loving You" by Simone. Rachelle was on top of the world. She felt that nothing could top this day.

She was married to her soulmate, and no one could take that from her. She laughed internally that Octavia really thought she stood a chance against her. The better woman won, and Octavia had learned the hard way that it didn't pay to be a pick-me. She was languishing in a jail cell, awaiting her fate, while Rachelle was having the time of her life.

"They're so perfect together," Sarai said as she danced with Kiana.

"I agree," Kiana said. "How much do you wanna bet she's gonna be pregnant after the honeymoon?" Sarai playfully hit her arm, and the two of them laughed.

"They probably have their hands full with the twins, so I doubt they'll be having another baby anytime soon," Louise interjected as she wiped frosting from Soleil's face.

"Would you ever have another one?" Simone asked. She was dancing with Bryce.

"Shiid, fuck no," Louise exclaimed, covering Soleil's ears. "I'm definitely done having babies. I'm content with my girls."

"I feel you," Sarai said, nodding. "I don't think I will ever have any. I'm content being the rich, fun auntie." The others laughed as they continued dancing. After the festivities, Rachelle and Nick left for their honeymoon in Havana, Cuba, all paid for by her aunt. The couple was excited, as they had never been to Cuba, and Nick was excited to see his mother's ancestral home. Another reason they were excited was the thought of the passionate sex they'd be having for those two weeks. As she relaxed in the first-class cabin, she admired her wedding band. Rachelle Lawson-Ramirez, she thought as she stared out of the window, the gleam of the moon shining upon her. She could imagine Kamaria smiling at them. I'm going to have to get used to being called that. With a contented sigh, she leaned against Nick, and the two of them dozed off for a much-needed nap because one thing was certain: when they arrived at the resort, they definitely would not be sleeping...

Epilogue

Halloween 2024, One Year Later

Alexis Imani Lawson
July 20, 1994 - June 28, 2023
Beloved Mother, Daughter, and Friend

Rachelle laid a bouquet of daisies near the foot of the headstone, blinking back her tears. It had only been a year since her cousin's tragic murder, and the grief was still fresh in her heart. Rachelle would visit Alexis once a month, often leaving flowers and offerings such as liquor, coins, and cigars. Nick and their twins would sometimes accompany her, with the five-year-olds leaving candy. They would also leave treats for their grandfather, sharing with him stories of their adventures, as children often did.

"It's amazing how a lot can happen in a year, Lexi." Rachelle began. "Nick and I have been married for a whole year, and I love that man more every day." Nick smiled down at her. "We've been talking about having another baby. The girls really want a little brother. I can't believe they're in kindergarten already! Where does all the time go?"

"*I know, right?*" Rachelle looked up to see her cousin smiling at her. Alexis looked radiant in a flowing blue dress, with daisies in her hair. "*I can't believe how big Bryson is getting. He's so smart and sweet, and gets all A's in his classes. Did you know he talks to me every day?*"

"He told me." Rachelle replied. "He misses you a lot." She felt her heart burn with anger towards Octavia, but she pushed it down. Alexis let out a sigh.
"I know her trial was about a month ago." she said.

"Yep, Guilty on all counts. Now she's sitting on Federal death row. You should have seen her reaction when they handed down the sentence. Crying like a big ass, pathetic baby."

"Damn." Alexis said, shaking her head. *"Can't say she doesn't deserve it, though. You know, I wouldn't have minded having her as a sister, if she wasn't so screwed up."*

"She actually called herself sending us a letter, asking us to forgive her." Rachelle said, rolling her eyes. "Girl, bye! Anyway, you know Eloise Beauty reached out to me last week. They want to do a collab with me."

"That's what I'm talking about!" Alexis exclaimed, grinning. *"Girl, I told you that was gonna happen! You're about to take over the beauty game. I'm so proud of you."*

"We all are." Nick said, putting his arm around his wife.

"I'm proud of myself, too." Rachelle said, smiling.

"So....about Daddy and your ex's mom..." Alexis said. *"I definitely didn't see that one coming!"* Ernest and Tasha had met at Rachelle's wedding, and immediately hit it off. They had made their relationship official over six months ago. Tasha's cancer was also in full remission.

"Girl, me neither." Rachelle replied. "I guess the pain of losing an only child brought them together. He's happy, though, and that's all that matters."

"Yeah." Alexis said. *"I know Mom was hoping she and Dad would get back together, but she's finally accepted that she messed up. Counseling really helped her get her shit together. I'm also glad that Bryce found someone, too. Simone is a good woman."*

"It's funny how my wedding brought two couples together." Rachelle said, and the two women giggled.

"How's Sarai and Kiana doing?"

"They're still going strong." Rachelle replied. "Sarai's books got picked up for a TV series."

"Are you serious?!" Alexis exclaimed. *"That's awesome! I'm so happy for her!"*

"Me, too. She definitely deserves it." Rachelle said, thinking back on everything her best friend had gone through. Thelma must be rolling in her grave!

"By the way, where are my little cousins?"

"Mom took them to Cedar Point for Halloweekend." Rachelle answered. "I know they're going to talk our ears off about it when they get back."

"Kind of how you used to do when your folks took you somewhere fun." Alexis teased.

"Yeah, yeah." Rachelle said. "Anyway, we should get going, or else we're gonna be late."

"Yeah, isn't Louise's crowning today?"

"Yep."

"Well, you better get going, then."

"Love you, Lexi."

"Love you, too, Chell." Rachelle left offerings for her cousin and father, and then made her way across the cemetery, stopping at Kendra's memorial. Since she and Octavia had no other family, Rachelle had paid for Kendra's headstone. While she hated Octavia for everything she had

done, Kendra did nothing to her, and didn't deserve the horrible fate that befell her.

"Hey, Kendra." she said, leaving a small bouquet at the foot of the stone. "I don't know why I always feel so awkward when I visit you, but I do."

"Trust me, I understand." Kendra spoke. *"I'd feel the same way if I were you."* Rachelle looked up to see Kendra standing in front of her, wearing a flowing white dress.

"I take it you already know about your sister's conviction." Rachelle said. Kendra let out a deep sigh.

"Yeah." she said. *"I'm not happy about her getting the death penalty, but these are the consequences of her actions. I still can't help but feel responsible, though."*

"What happened wasn't your fault!" Rachelle countered. "Octavia is an adult. She chose to do the things she did."

"Still, I feel guilty." Kendra replied. *"Mom does, too. Even though she was trying to protect Tay, maybe if she knew what that woman was really like, then she wouldn't have been so quick to align herself with her. I should have been more understanding of her wanting to know where she came from."* Rachelle's heart went out to Kendra. She even felt a tiny bit of compassion for Octavia. While she was lucky enough to be raised by her biological parents, who doted on her, Octavia was given the misfortune of being born to a racist, and given up without a second thought. The same woman also tried to kill her, before Rachelle intervened. However, there was still no excuse for Octavia's actions.

"It's a tragedy all around." she said. "You and Alexis are both gone, Jane and her sister are dead, and Octavia is probably going to wait ten or twenty years to die. Shakespeare has nothing on this." Kendra chuckled slightly at Rachelle's joke, giving her a pained smile.
"Yeah." she said. *"Anyway, I appreciate you coming to talk to me."*

"Of course." Rachelle said, getting up. "I need to be going, though. But I'll definitely be back."

"I look forward to it." Kendra said, giving Rachelle a genuine smile. Then, she vanished. Rachelle then returned to the car with Nick. The couple drove home to shower, and change into their ritual clothing. Afterwards, they drove to Belle Isle Beach, where the ceremony was being held. When they arrived, their friends, as well as Nick's mother and sisters, were waiting for them. They also noticed members from the coven's other chapters were present, including Bernadette, and her nephew, Michael. Everyone was dressed in white from head to toe.

"Ayy, look who's here!" Sarai exclaimed as she hugged Rachelle and Nick. "Damn. I can't believe Lou's gonna be running the coven now."

"I can." Rachelle said. "She's definitely more than capable. We're in good hands." She then turned to Trina. "So, what is this surprise you were talking about in the group chat?" Smiling from ear to ear, Trina held up her left hand, flashing a gorgeous, Topaz engagement ring. "Oh my god! You got engaged?! When did this happen?!"

"A few weeks ago, Pierre surprised me with a trip to Venice." Trina replied. "He took me on a romantic evening on a *gondola*, and he popped the question under the moonlight. It was perfect!" Rachelle embraced her cousin, squealing.

"Girl, I'm so happy for you! You know Auntie Ronnie's going all out for the wedding, right?"
"Yep, and you know you're gonna be my Matron of Honor, right?"

"Girl, of course!" Rachelle said. Soon, Kristy stepped into the circle with her daughter. The older woman was dressed in black from head to toe, to represent the strength and power of their people. Louise was dressed in red, a symbol of the blood that their people had shed.

"Looks like we're starting." Sarai whispered. Kristy, smiling, instructed everyone to join hands. Then she spoke.

"I'd like to thank you all for joining us on this full moon. This coven was founded over two hundred years ago, by my great-great-great-great grandmother, and it has grown tremendously since then. I only hope it continues to grow as more witches find their way to us. Tonight, I pass the torch to my eldest daughter, who has shown incredible strength in the face of adversity, and who has shown a great fortitude for leadership. I have no doubt that she will continue to lead us to greatness."

"Amen!" Sarai shouted from the crowd, and the others laughed. Kristy then took Louise's hands in hers. Their auras began to glow, and crescent moons appeared on their foreheads. Kristy began to call the names of their ancestors into the circle. One by one, the spirits of those that walked the earth before them began to appear, surrounding them. Kamaria, along with Diana, Natalie, Ivy, and Faith stood among them, smiling. Louise's eyes began to tear up when she saw that Missy was also standing among them.

"Ancestors,
We ask that you surround Louise Josephine Eason,
Child of Kristy Henrietta Reynolds,
With strength, love, and protection.
We ask that you light her way,
So that she leads this coven with compassion, wisdom, and love.
We also ask that you light the way of those that are lost,
That share our spiritual gifts, but suppress them out of fear and shame.
Help them find their way to us,
So that we can guide them to embrace and stand in their true power.
Asè!

"Asè!" the rest of the coven shouted in unison. Kristy then opened a small wooden chest, revealing moonstone, obsidian, and amethyst waist beads. She then took the beads and fastened them around her daughter's waist. The waist beads began to glow brightly, and Louise's aura transitioned from purple to gold. The coven looked on in awe as Louise slowly floated into the air, surrounded by the moon's bright light, her curls swirling around her. Louise felt a warm sensation on the back of her neck, and to everyone's astonishment, her coven tattoo began to glow, turning from black to gold. This was symbolic of a High Priestess' ascension. Louise then slowly floated back to the ground, her aura still glowing.

"Holy shit!" Kiana exclaimed in a whisper. While she had been a part of the coven for over a year, seeing magic in its raw form never ceased to leave her in awe. Kristy embraced her daughter, and kissed her on both cheeks. Smiling, she turned to the crowd.

"I am pleased to present to you, on this Halloween night, our new High Priestess!" she announced, and the crowd erupted in cheers and applause. Louise's siblings, cousins, and aunts embraced her, as did her friends. Artemis ran to her mother, and Louise littered her face with kisses.

"So, how do you feel now that you're basically the Queen of Black Witches now?" Simone asked.

"I feel pretty good." Louise replied with a smile. "I definitely feel more powerful."

"I feel that. I felt pretty powerful after I got initiated." Khalil said, her aura glowing a powdery blue. "So, what will be our first order of business?" A smirk crept onto Louise's face.

"Well, on the next Dark Moon, we will definitely be visiting some spiritual justice on those genocidal pieces of shit." she said, referring to the Zionist regime. "For now, however, a bonfire dance is in order!" She waved her hand, and to her and everyone's astonishment, her flames were now white. Louise lit the bonfire, and she and her friends gathered around it. As they danced the night away, Rachelle, Sarai, Simone, and Trina couldn't help but think about how grateful they were for Louise's friendship. Through her, they learned who they truly were. Through her, they had learned to unapologetically stand in their power, and their lives were much better for it. Rachelle was happily married to the love of her life, created a beautiful family, and was on her way to starting a beauty empire. Sarai had broken free of her abusers, was a successful author, and surrounded by people that loved, supported, and encouraged her. Trina, after being tossed away by the woman that birthed her, had found her true family, and achieved her lifelong aspiration of being a model. Simone had overcome her trauma to rediscover her love for music, and was now a successful recording artist. They had achieved success beyond their wildest imaginations, and they hadn't even reached the age of thirty five! And all it took was a little bit of magic.

About the Author

Photography Credit: Steven Jon Horner

Jade Aurora is a Detroit-based model, cosplayer, artist, and dancer. Coming from a family of creatives, she began drawing at the age of 8. What started out as a fun hobby turned into a lifelong passion. A self-proclaimed "blerd", Jade passes her time watching anime, and cosplaying at conventions. She began her modeling career in 2012, and has been featured in publications such as Black Pinups Magazine. She resides in Detroit with her husband, Matthew.

Jade's artwork can be found on Facebook
www.Facebook.com/JadeAurora